I forced my eyes open and stared up at the shiny bars above me. *Bars?* Turning my head sent spikes of agony into my skull. The pain blotted out my tumbling confusion.

Where was I? I caught a whiff of a burlap pallet beneath me, lumpy as an overused futon. Old animal odors drifted up from it. I looked down. The last thing I remembered couldn't have happened. A surge of relief ran through me as I saw that my hands were my hands. My arms were long, thin, and pale. Human arms.

The floor beneath the pallet was as shiny as the bars. A strange, high-pitched hum buzzed up from it. I focused on staying calm. *Go slow. First things first. Where am I?*

A polished cage squatted around me like a silver spider, less than five feet high and not much longer than my body. Every inch of my skin recoiled from it as if from a hot stove. All my life I'd had a rare allergy to silver. Now I was trapped in a pen made of it.

"You weren't out long." A male voice, young, came at me from beyond my cage. . . .

"My name's Caleb," he said. I was struck by the harmony woven into his voice. "What's yours?"

Otherkin

NINA BERRY

KENSINGTON PUBLISHING CORP.
www.kensingtonbooks.com

K TEEN BOOKS are published by

Kensington Publishing Corp.
119 West 40th Street
New York, NY 10018

All Kensington titles, imprints, and distributed lines are available at special quantity discounts for bulk purchases for sales promotion, premiums, fund-raising, and educational or institutional use.

Special book excerpts or customized printings can also be created to fit specific needs. For details, write or phone the office of the Kensington Special Sales Manager: Kensington Publishing Corp., 119 West 40th Street, New York, NY 10018. Attn. Special Sales Department. Phone: 1-800-221-2647.

Kensington and KTeen Reg. U.S. Pat. & TM Off.

ISBN-13: 978-0-7582-7691-9
ISBN-10: 0-7582-7691-5

First Kensington Trade Paperback Printing: August 2012
10 9 8 7 6 5 4 3 2 1

Printed in the United States of America

For my parents

ACKNOWLEDGMENTS

In the beginning there was my critique partner and friend, Elisa Nader, whose brilliant ideas helped me land my fabulous agent, Tamar Rydzinski, whose intelligent notes and professional savvy helped me find my beloved editor, Alicia Condon, who understood my book in the way I'd been longing for.

The support, love, and respect of my father and mother paved the way for any success I can claim. I also got big help from professionals Jill Santopolo, Kristen Kemp, Chuck Sambuchino, and the members of SCBWI SoCal.

Then there are my friends, who provide inspiration, encouragement, and sanity-saving laughter. They are too many to name, but special thanks to John Mark Godocik, Brian Pope, Wendy Viellenave, Ruth Atkinson, Valerie Ahern, Natalie Downing, Shelley Zimmerman, and my gaming pals, whose imaginations helped me play out one of the ideas that lead to *Otherkin*.

I also must acknowledge the ineffable contributions of the mini-tigers I have known, particularly Max and Lucy.

If you're interested in helping save tigers and other big cats in the wild, check out Panthera, an organization I support with all my heart, and occasionally some cash. Go to www.panthera.org for information and easy ways to make a difference.

What are you when the moon shall rise?

—Sir Henry Wotton, 1620

CHAPTER 1

"Freak." I tore off the back brace and threw it on the floor. "Why'd you let him touch you?"

I stared at the brace, anger curling in my gut. It sat tilted on the floor like an ancient broken statue with no head, no arms, no legs.

Oh God, it had happened. A cute boy had asked me out. And not just any cute boy, but Jake fricking Peters, hottest senior in school, who could have any girl he wanted. He'd not only invited me to the lame-ass dance this weekend, he'd put his hands on my waist as he did it. Only to feel my rock-hard robot contours. I pressed my hands to my heated cheeks. Shame had seared the scene into my memory.

"What's that?" Jake had asked as his fingers grazed my hip. His eyes lit with surprise.

"Nothing." I backed away from him, avoiding his gaze. I'd known this would happen. I knew getting close to anyone was a mistake. "I . . . I've got to get home. See you later." The words rattled out of me, and I had scuttled away.

Now I breathed deep, trying to squash my rising frustration. At least I was home where nothing could touch me. Safe in my own room. With Mom and Richard out at work, I was alone, where no one would laugh at me, or pity me, or call me a mutant.

I peeled off the sweaty undershirt I had to wear under the thing and hurled it into the laundry. *God, I hate those stupid shirts.* I slid my hand around my own waist, the waist no boy could ever put his arm around.

I wasn't that goddamn brace, not anymore. *To hell with the brace!* I looked around for something to hit it with, something to break it, so I'd never have to wear it again.

But there was nothing. Nothing but my bare hands.

Even as I yanked it off the floor, a small part of my brain knew this wasn't like me. I never flew into rages or whined about the brace. I was a good girl, a nice girl, and tantrums were for people with no self-control.

But I'd worn the damned thing twenty-three hours a day for two years to prevent my spine from curving further, donning baggy clothes to hide it, unable to bend, enduring the agony as it fought against my body, unable to swim or climb trees, avoiding any proximity to boys.

Something had snapped. I pulled and scraped at it with my bare hands, trying to tear it apart, fingernails splintering. But the plastic wouldn't give. The surface didn't even scratch.

Rage blazed through me, so hot I thought I'd explode. I screamed. A convulsive thrust of power shot from the center of my chest along my spine, down my limbs, and out of every pore. The scream became a full-throated roar. I dropped my hands to the ground. Only they weren't hands anymore, but huge paws, orange on top, white around the claws, striped brownish black. I whipped around, trying to see myself.

What? A long, thickly furred tail knocked the lamp off my nightstand. *This can't be happening.*

The crash of the lamp sounded like an explosion. I crouched, tail tucked between my back legs, and looked up to see my reflection in the mirror on my closet door. Had I gone insane? Great golden eyes blinked back at me. I flinched. The tiger in the mirror winced too, ears back, white whiskers bristling.

I barely had time to take in my orange coat, white underbelly, and wide pattern of dark stripes when a loud thwack sounded from my bedroom window. Something stabbed into my side. A growl of pain and surprise escaped me. A dart lodged in the pale fur beneath my right front leg. Pain ran up my body, too real to be a dream.

I looked up to see a young man, almost angelically blond, dressed all in white, standing outside my window with a rifle. The screen was torn. He'd broken a couple of stakes Mom and I used to get the tomatoes to climb. We stared at each other. His face was alive and hot with anticipation. Burning pain spread through my veins from the dart. Instinctively, I gathered my new body to leap at him. He fired again. Another barb speared my shoulder, and I reeled back.

I snarled at him and tried to stand. But a painful lethargy took over. I shook my head, trying to clear it. Air whipped across my whiskers, a strange sensation.

An older man, also in white, joined the first to observe me through the window. He clapped a hand on the younger man's shoulder. "Good job, son," he said.

"It's taking two," his son said. "She's strong for one so young."

The older man had a head of thick silver hair. His even teeth flashed almost blue white as he smiled. "We'll see about that," he said.

And everything went black.

CHAPTER 2

I forced my eyes open and stared up at the shiny bars above me. *Bars?* Turning my head sent spikes of agony into my skull. The pain blotted out my tumbling confusion.

Where was I? I caught a whiff of a burlap pallet beneath me, lumpy as an overused futon. Old animal odors drifted up from it. I looked down. The last thing I remembered couldn't have happened. A surge of relief ran through me as I saw that my hands were my hands. My arms were long, thin, and pale. Human arms.

The floor beneath the pallet was as shiny as the bars. A strange, high-pitched hum buzzed up from it. I focused on staying calm. *Go slow. First things first. Where am I?*

A polished cage squatted around me like a silver spider, less than five feet high and not much longer than my body. Every inch of my skin recoiled from it as if from a hot stove.

All my life I'd had a rare allergy to silver. Now I was trapped in a pen made of it.

"You weren't out long." A male voice, young, came at me from beyond my cage.

My heart pounded against my ribs as I pushed myself up to sit. "I..." Speaking set off a bout of coughing. My body throbbed with pain. I curled into a seated fetal position, careful to stay on the straw pallet and not touch the silver floor. Something about the position felt wrong.

The brace! I wasn't wearing it. Someone had put me in a thin cotton hospital gown that barely covered my bruised knees. Without that shield of plastic and metal around me I felt utterly vulnerable. A deep trembling began in my shoulders and hips and spread out to shake my fingers and toes.

"Take it easy," said the voice. Something in its tone smoothed out the jagged edges of my fear. "Breathe. You'll be okay."

"Oh, sure, I'm great," I said hoarsely.

The half gloom of the world around me was completely unfamiliar. A single floodlight set into a wall beyond my cage cut a white swath of light across my prison and sent the long shadows of the bars stabbing into the space beyond. My eyes adjusted, and the gaps of darkness opened to me.

About thirty feet from me lay another cage, also shiny, equipped with a cot, and inhabited by a tall boy about my own age in a long black coat, dark pants, and a white shirt smeared with grime. He stood almost touching the bars, staring out at me, hands plunged into his pockets. Eyes black as onyx considered me. His dark hair curled back from his tan forehead in short unruly waves, framing the bold line of his nose, his strong jaw, and a full but severe mouth. He stood with a dangerous sort of grace, as if a coiled strength waited beneath the surface, ready to cause havoc. Even in the shadows I could see an indigo bruise forming around his right eye. His intense stare plus no brace or normal clothes made me feel naked. I looked away from him. *If only I could disappear.*

"My name's Caleb," he said. I was struck by the harmony woven into his voice. "What's yours?"

"Desdemona," I said. "Dez. Where are we?" Trying to remain calm, I looked around and spotted a pile of something in the darkest corner of my cage. "My clothes. Thank God."

"It's a shame to cover up those legs of yours," he said with a small smile.

I startled, flushing.

"But you are looking kind of blue, literally," he went on. "And you'll feel better facing them if you've got something on."

I jerked my gaze up from my legs, which were indeed splotched blue and purple from the cold. "Them—who?"

"The ones your parents warned you about," he said. "Lazar's their best shot. Was he the one who got you? Tall guy, around my age, blond hair?"

The guy in white with the rifle.

None of it made sense—the striped paws, the crash of the lamp, the tiger in the mirror. I rubbed the spot on my shoulder where the first dart had hit. "He did. But nobody ever warned me. He shot me right after . . ." I couldn't say it. The cute boy in the neighboring cage would think I was crazy. *Neighboring cage?* How was this now my life?

"After you shifted?" He looked me up and down. "You've got the grace of one of the big cats. Let me guess. Mountain lion?"

"Tiger," I said faintly.

"Really?" His black eyes sparked. "What are you doing here? Your English is very good."

"Thanks, I've been speaking it my whole life," I said. It came out angrier than I thought it would. Nothing he said made sense, and that didn't help the rising tide of panic in my chest. "I grew up in fricking Burbank, California. Is this some weird cult or something? God, they must've shot me up with hallucinogens." I pulled the pile of clothes toward me. It contained my undershirt, my billowy dress, and sandals, all lying on top of the back brace. Its familiar boxy shape gave me a weird rush of relief.

"More likely a fast-acting tranquilizer spiked with silver nitrate," he said. "Are you saying you don't know what you are?"

"I'm not a *what*," I said, willing myself to believe it. "I'm a who, and I want to be left alone."

"Too late for that," he said.

My imagination was on serious overdrive. I could've sworn the silver in the cage wanted to bite me. Caleb was circling the edges of his cage, staring at the bars with a hatred that made me almost feel sorry for them. I said, "So what are you, Captain Blackcoat? A panther?"

He brushed his long black coat with the back of his hand to acknowledge my reference to it. "No, I'm something else."

"You're something else, all right. Would you mind . . ." I twirled my finger, asking him to turn around while I dressed.

"Of course." He smirked, but bowed at the waist, like one of those elegant men in a Jane Austen movie, then turned away.

I pulled open my hospital gown, relieved to find myself wearing my ordinary white bra and underwear. Deep purple bruises grooved along my waist and down in front of my hip bones, but those were normal. Years of wearing the brace had left me with these imprints. The encircling plastic also acted like a corset, squishing my waistline and hips so relentlessly that they'd permanently shrunk by a couple of inches.

I hated the damned thing with every cell in my body. But I had to wear it. Just before I turned fourteen I'd been diagnosed with idiopathic scoliosis, fancy talk for curvature of the spine with an unknown cause. Every three months I went in for X-rays and got a big fat reminder from Dr. Mwesi.

He'd lean back in his chair, peering over his glasses at me, and tell horrible stories of girls who'd had iron rods placed in their spines because they hadn't worn their brace.

I slipped on the undershirt, then opened the back of the brace. I sat up on my knees to clamp it around my torso. Thick plastic pads inside corresponded with the bruising at my waist. One rigid arch of plastic came up high under my left arm, then dipped under my breasts, cut low at the waist on my right side, and circled around me to come up high again at my spine. Industrial strength Styrofoam pads pressed up against my vertebrae, shoving them into place. I reached behind and tugged on the first strap, shoving it into the buckle as I did so.

The solid plastic tightened around me, and I felt like an ancient knight, donning his armor before a fight. In the brace I was back to normal, barricaded. But as I tightened the other strap, contrary wings of wrath fanned against my ribs. I tugged at the bottom edge of the brace, trying to find a more comfortable fit. Stubborn body. Stupid spine.

I took a deep breath to squash the anger. If I let it escape it might never stop. My torso expanded as I inhaled. I imagined it swelling until it burst the straps and tore off the buckles.

"I sense shadow," said Caleb, beginning to turn toward me. "Shouldn't be possible with all this silver . . ."

"Don't look at me!" I barked at him, shoving my arms into my dress and pulling it over my head. I couldn't stand it if he saw me in that thing. Better to be invisible.

"Sorry," he said, turning away again. "I wish I could help you. It's just very odd. The silver should keep it from manifesting."

"Keep what from manifesting?" I awkwardly stretched my arms out and shoved my feet into my sandals. Being unable to bend at the waist made shoes a challenge. "What is it about the silver?" I said. "It's like . . ." I was ashamed to say it. "Like I can hear it singing. And it makes my head hurt."

He turned back around, his dark eyes intent. "It does sing, but usually only to a caller like me. I've never heard a shifter say they heard it too."

"What the hell . . ." I tried to stand and slammed my head into the top of the cage. I sat down hard. Part of the brace cut up into the soft flesh of my underarm. "What are you talking about?" I rubbed the crown of my head.

"You really don't know, do you?" He crossed his arms and looked down at me. "It doesn't make any sense. No shifter would ever let their child grow up without knowing their heritage."

I took a deep breath. *Stay calm.* "What the hell are you talking about? What is this place? And why is my goddamn cage so much smaller than yours?"

Caleb resumed pacing. "The Tribunal is more afraid of you than they are of me," he said. "Your cage is smaller because they need to get the silver as close to you as possible, to keep you from shifting."

"What's the Tribunal?"

"The ones who captured us. They hate people like you and me, and they'll do whatever they can to strip away everything we are." He looked more like a wild animal than I did, pacing like that. "You and I are otherkin," he said. "We're human, yes, but we are also other. The silver suppresses your shifting abilities and prevents me from seeing your shadow self. I felt shadow vibrating from you a moment ago. But that shouldn't be possible. All the silver around us should keep me from sensing anything, and render you barely conscious, let alone able to shift."

"Shift," I said. "You mean, into . . ."

"Abomination." A different voice echoed off the bare walls. "Demon."

"Fiend," said another, female. "Filth. Perhaps we can wash you clean."

The young man who'd shot me walked toward my cage,

his gold hair catching the light. He had perfect cheekbones, thick brows, and deep-set brown eyes straight out of a Romantic painting of some implacable archangel. A large gold cross over a snowy white shirt completed the picture of vengeful purity. He didn't look older than eighteen, but he carried an authority that seemed more man than boy. Something jingled slightly as he walked. Then I saw a ring of keys, half tucked into his right pants pocket.

Behind him a girl about my age glided in a long white gown that covered her modestly from neck to toes. But it couldn't hide the luscious curves beneath it. I felt a stab of envy. I could never wear a dress like that. It would show every contour of the brace. Her hair lay stick straight and pale over her shoulders. She had the same deep-set, brown eyes as the boy with her. They had to be brother and sister, bright as morning in a meadow, or the harsh glare of a flashlight in the face.

"Desdemona," said Caleb. "Meet our hosts, Lazar and Amaris, acolytes of the Tribunal."

The girl, Amaris, glanced over at him, her face shuttered. He gazed back at her, blank. "Does he have to be here?" she asked. "Couldn't we . . ."

"When Father gets back he'll decide what to do with him," said Lazar. He also had a musical voice, but harsher than Caleb's. "Until then, he stays in the cage."

I saw a flash of defiance as Amaris opened her mouth to argue. But in a heartbeat she crushed it down. I felt an instant of kinship; I knew how it felt to squash down your feelings.

She came close to my cage, hunkering down gracefully. Her gaze traveled over me as if I were a curious specimen. "The demon is remarkably awake," she said of me. "Are you sure she can't shift?"

So much for kinship. "I'm right here," I said. "And I can talk."

They looked at me as if the couch had spoken. "The silver

makes it impossible for her to shift now, just as it keeps Caleb from calling to shadow." Lazar squatted down next to her, scrutinizing me. "We may have to drug her again before we remove her though. Her system purified itself more quickly than we anticipated."

"When I get out of here," I said, "you'd better run. Fast."

Had I really said that? Lazar and Amaris drew back an inch.

"You heard the girl," said Caleb. "You don't know what you've gotten yourself into, Lazar. Without Daddy around, you're not up to the job."

"Shut up, Caleb," Lazar said, his voice deepening into a grand chord of command.

Caleb's eyes narrowed derisively. "Doesn't work on me, remember?"

"Are you sure Father would want him in the cage?" Amaris asked.

Lazar's pure face clouded with anger. "I'm in charge while Father's away. He trusts me."

"You don't sound like you mean that," Caleb said. "You sure you're worthy?"

"Be silent, or I'll have you gagged." Lazar's face when he looked at Caleb was pure fury.

Caleb bowed, the corners of his mouth deepening in a mocking smile.

Amaris moved her face close to the bars of my cage, staring at me. *How easy it would be to tear her throat out.* I blinked. Had that thought come from me?

"Don't be afraid," she said, in a voice people reserved for infants and the deranged. "We just want to help. We'll make you all better."

Something I didn't understand growled inside me. "Get me out of this cage right now or I'll rip your lungs out."

Amaris gasped and scrambled back from me, repulsed. Her fear gave me a strange jolt of satisfaction.

Lazar leaned in close. "You're helpless," he said. Something quavered in his voice, and a wave of despair overtook me. "You're alone. No one knows where you are. No one cares."

The gloomy pitch of his words enveloped me like a smothering blanket. Loneliness welled up from a bottomless pit inside me. I had a vivid flash of waking from a nightmare as a child, a nightmare where a horrific weight pressed down on me as I ran in circles in the snow, crying for my family. My birth parents had abandoned me, and sure, Mom had adopted me. But maybe I'd been dumped because I hadn't been good enough. Maybe they were glad I was gone. If they could dump me, Mom could too. *I'm lost. And she'll never come looking for me.*

In the periphery of my sight, I saw Caleb yelling at me. But all I could hear was Lazar. His every syllable dripped truth, and I was bereft.

I took a deep, sobbing breath and tried to curl into a ball. But as always when I tried to bend, the brace jabbed deep into my ribs and hip. The jolt of pain sliced through the weight of Lazar's words, and I uncurled to see him frowning at me. Caleb's words filtered through; somehow Lazar was hypnotizing me.

Black rage shredded my despair. This jackass had shot me, put me in a cage, and now he was trying to take my mind from me. *How dare he?* Without thinking I lashed forward between the bars to grab his wrist. As I brushed against the silver it stung my skin, but I didn't care. I dug my nails into Lazar's arm and felt them cut deep, drawing blood.

Lazar gasped in pain. Amaris screamed on a twin note a half second later. I jerked Lazar toward me with all my strength. Off balance, he slammed into the cage bars. His forehead knocked against them with a clang. His eyes rolled slightly, concussed.

Amaris shrieked again and grabbed her brother around

the shoulders, trying to drag him away from me. I tore at her with my other hand. The skin of her neck scraped beneath my nails, leaving four red stripes.

"Dez, you don't need to hurt her!" Caleb yelled. "Just get his keys!"

Crying with pain now, Amaris shoved herself back, the neck of her white gown stained crimson. "Help!" she shouted, getting to her feet and running toward the door to the outside. "Help, she's got Lazar!"

She threw the door open and dashed out. Cool night air poured in. Lazar struggled to loosen my grip. He took a breath to speak, but I heaved again, smashing him against the bars. Blood gushed from his forehead. He moaned and lay still.

The skin on my arms blazing from the silver, I pulled Lazar's hips closer to the cage to bring his pocket within reach.

"That's it, Dez!" Caleb shouted from his cage. "Hurry. There'll be more of them here any second!"

The silver burned my knees through the thin cloth of my dress. Straining against the brace to bend forward, I fished into Lazar's pocket and pulled out the keys. I felt a surge of triumph, then a plunge of horror. My fingers, holding those keys, brandished three-inch claws, dripping with blood.

I dropped the keys.

"Hurry! Unlock your cage. Get out while you can!" Caleb shook the bars of his own cage, trying to get me to focus.

"My hands," I said, turning away from him so he couldn't see the claws. "There's something wrong with me. I'm . . ."

"A tiger-shifter," he said. "That's a good thing. It's what's going to get you out of here."

"Tiger-shifter." I said the words, but they made no sense. Neither did my razor-sharp claws.

"Listen to me," said Caleb, and something in the lush intonation of his voice pulled me to take note. I focused on him. His eyes glowed, like obsidian set in gold. I could look at nothing else. "You are strong. You can do this. I call upon you to pick up those keys. Pick them up."

My inner turmoil receded, and all I wanted to do was obey that voice. I took hold of the keys. "Put the silver key in the lock," he said in the same luxuriant tone. "That's right, reach around outside the bars and unlock the cage with the key."

The power in that voice could not be denied. The biggest key on the ring, shiny with silver, scorched my hands as I singled it out. But the pain didn't matter. It slipped into the lock and turned with a loud click. The door of the cage snapped open. I was free.

Startled out of my concentration, I looked over at Caleb. The glow faded from his eyes, and they took on an odd, distracted look. His tan face paled to gray as he leaned heavily against the cage bars. "It worked," he said, his voice thin. "Shouldn't have, with all the silver. But it did. Something's different..." He shook his head as if to clear it. "Now get out of here. Hurry."

He slumped to his knees. I pushed open my cage door and crawled out, skin stinging. Somewhere nearby a high-pitched alarm sounded. Beyond it I heard the pounding of running feet.

I ran to the door of Caleb's cage and fumbled with the keys. "What are you doing?" he said, looking as if he were about to pass out. "There's no time. Get out of here now!"

"Shut up. I'll be damned if I leave anyone in a cage." I tried first one key, then another, my hands shaking. Shouting voices neared.

"You're sweet. I bet you save puppies on death row, but just get out." Caleb rubbed his face and stared past me, as if seeing a ghost.

"Yeah, puppies," I muttered, ignoring the jolt his words gave me. He must be out of his head a little. That thing he'd done with his voice to help me had somehow drained him. I skipped what looked like a car key to try the only remaining possibility. That key slipped into the lock and turned.

I opened his cage and was next to Caleb in a heartbeat. The running feet would be here any second. How were we going to get past them?

"Maybe it was the moon," he said vacantly. "The moon's almost full."

I grabbed him under the arm and hauled up with a strength that surprised me. "Babble all you want, but you're coming with me." He stumbled to his feet, and we made it out of the cage to hide behind the half-open door to the outside.

A sliver of moonlight fell across the planes of his face. He took a deep breath and straightened to his full height, even taller than I was. His color returned as he gave me an appreciative half smile. "Thanks."

Lazar moaned, pulling himself up to sit against the bars of my cage, wiping the blood from his eyes. His white outfit was splotched with scarlet. *I did that.* My hands shook, and I saw that the claws were gone. My hands, still covered with blood, were my hands again.

Footsteps neared. I held up three fingers to show Caleb that I heard three coming our way. He nodded, saw my fingers trembling, and put his hand over mine. The warmth from his skin brought a rush of heat to my cheeks. His black eyes smiled into mine, and hope surged through me. We might make it. Our fingers laced together as we shrank back against the wall and the first armed guard cautiously entered. I barely had time to register that I was holding hands with a boy, an intense, gorgeous boy. I'd never done that before.

Lazar moaned again, his eyelids fluttering.

"Reverend!" exclaimed a guard, running through the door to Lazar. "He's hurt!" he shouted over his shoulder. The second guard rushed in after him as the third approached more slowly. We'd been lucky. Lazar's distress had caused two out of three to pass by without spotting us. Now we just had to dart past the third, and we'd be outside.

I glanced up at Caleb. He laid one hand on the door, stared at it as if looking through it, and hummed, almost imperceptibly. Something sparked in his black eyes, and he grinned. As the third guard edged into the warehouse, just two feet from us, Caleb held up one finger, telling me to wait. His other hand gripped mine hard, and we got ready to run.

As the guard cleared the edge of the door, we hauled it back and jetted past him. Caleb pushed me before him, and I darted into a blast of cool, dry air to see a large full moon vibrating with light on the horizon. Caleb stepped into a glowing pool of moonlight and spun, his long black coat fanning out behind him.

The guard had his rifle at his shoulder, aimed at us, about to shoot.

His shadow long and black before him, Caleb stretched out his hand and said, in a voice sonorous as a symphony, "I call on you, come out of shadow!"

The man aimed right at him, just ten feet away, and pulled the trigger. Or he tried. A swirl of darkness roiled out from Caleb's hand and enveloped the gun. The guard stood aghast, now holding a long, smooth staff of wood. The rifle was gone.

The guard stood there, stupefied.

The warmth of Caleb's fingers tangled with mine again, and we ran.

CHAPTER 3

We dashed across a small parking lot carved out of the desert landscape. Behind us lay the warehouse and other buildings. Before us sat four cars and a large white van. The guard at the warehouse door threw down Caleb's stick and yelled, "They're over here! The parking lot!"

Caleb headed straight for a large white BMW. "Give me the keys."

I was still clutching Lazar's keychain, its edges digging into my sweaty palms. "Here!" I handed it over.

He released my hand so he could riffle through the keys as we ran behind the BMW, putting its steel bulk between us and the guards in the warehouse.

"How do you know it's this car?" I said through uneven breaths.

"I'm a knowledgeable person." He pressed a button on the

fob attached to the key ring, and the lights of the Beemer flashed. The locks ka-chunked open.

There was a loud sound by the warehouse. I caught a whiff of sulfur and warm iron. Caleb grabbed my arm and jerked me down behind the BMW as something whizzed over my head. "Silver bullets, probably," he said, then held out the keys. "Can you drive?"

They were actually shooting at us. The sound had been a gun going off. "Kind of, why?" A bullet pinged into the side of the car. It rocked slightly.

"Just do it. We're running out of time!"

"Fine!" I grabbed the keys.

Caleb opened the passenger side door. "Get in!"

I crawled awkwardly into the car. The brace bit into my right breast and upper thighs. I clambered over the passenger seat to the driver's side. Caleb followed, keeping low.

I jammed the key in the ignition. The car roared to life. Three more shots rang out, and bullets thumped into the side of the car.

He slammed the door. I shoved the car into gear and stomped on the gas. We took off toward the dirt road at the end of the parking lot. I peered into the rearview mirror as another bullet hit the rear bumper. One guard had his gun trained on us. Another was running toward the other cars. The third had an arm around Lazar, who stumbled to the doorway just in time to see us take off in his car. Then we curved away. They shrank into a distant pool of light. The night swallowed us.

"Holy crap," I said. My ears still rang from the gunshots. A slick sheen of sweat coated my skin.

Caleb let out a free, ringing laugh. "We're out! I can't believe it. You got us out." He grabbed my right hand off the steering wheel and gave it a loud kiss. I blushed all the way down my neck and forced myself to keep my eyes on the road. "Did you know that once you save somebody's life, they're yours forever?"

"Well, you saved mine too, so I guess we belong to each other," I said, then realized how that sounded and pulled my hand out of his. "You can thank me by telling me what the hell just happened."

"Deal," he said, twisting to look behind us. "Damn."

I checked the mirror. Two faint lights moved down the road behind us. Headlights. "They're coming after us."

"Figures," he said. "We have to get off this road right now."

I looked out at the tumbleweeds, cacti, and rocks as they slid past us. "You want to drive over that? We'll get a flat or something. Besides, he'll see the headlights."

"First thing we do, we turn off the headlights." He reached across me and clicked the lights off. I gripped the wheel tightly as we barreled down the road. For a moment, the world around us went black, then the desert floor opened up to me again, almost as clear under the moon as during the day.

"Go faster," he said.

I accelerated, squinting out at the faint track of road. "The moonlight's too strong. He'll spot us whether we're on the road or not."

"The moonlight works for us," he said. "And he doesn't have your eyesight in the dark. No one does." He glanced over at me, a smirk around his mouth. It took me a moment to realize what he was saying. "That's why I wanted you to drive."

"And that means what exactly?"

"You're a cat-shifter. That means that all your life your eyesight at night has been ten times better than a human's. Your hearing's even better, and your reflexes are ridiculous. You've never known anything else, so you think it's normal, that everyone sees and hears and moves like you do. Believe me, they don't. And when you shift, your senses will be even better. You can see the road just fine without the headlights, right?"

I nodded.

"Well I can't," he said. "Time to get off the road. Don't step on the brakes or they'll see the brake lights."

"I don't know. It's not safe off the road. We'll crash into a cactus or . . ."

"Too late!"

He grabbed the wheel and turned it to the left. I almost hit the brakes, but remembered in time. I took my foot off the gas and shouted, "Okay, okay, give me the wheel!"

He let go. The car bounced into the untrammeled desert.

We careened over small tufted plants and hillocks where unsuspecting snakes and lizards probably slept in their burrows. *Sorry to disturb you like this, guys.* I kept my foot off the gas, and we slowed down, silent now except for the bumping and creaking of the BMW.

He pressed a button to roll down his window. "I need to open yours too," he said, leaning over me to press another button. My window buzzed down.

"Why?" The cool air rushed over me, smelling of dust and cactus sap. Moonlight spilled through the open window, falling across my left arm. Gooseflesh crawled up my skin.

"Shhh," he said, then hummed a deep, thrumming note.

"What are you doing?" I asked.

"Calling out to shadow, looking for something out there that can help us. Don't stop, keep going slowly."

I hit the gas gently to keep us moving forward as he hummed once more. The hair on the back of my neck stood up as the sound moved over me. I wanted to ask more, but I could tell from the set of his brows that he was concentrating hard.

"There." He turned his head to the right, peering into the dark. "What's over there?"

I glanced in that direction. "There's a pile of rocks that looks like a tired whale," I said. "It's pretty big."

"I see it," he said. "A bushed beluga. Get us behind it."

"Okay." I looked in the rearview mirror and zeroed in on the headlights of the pursuing car, far away but still behind us. I steered behind the rocks. They hid us completely from the other car.

"Perfect." He flashed a grin and squeezed my arm approvingly. "Now try to stop without hitting the brakes."

The black bulk of the rocks loomed to our right. I downshifted. We rolled to a stop, and the airy silence of the night floated in the open windows.

I caught the faint rumble of the other car's engine in the distance. "They're coming closer," I said. "If they see where we left the road they might find us. Can you hear them?"

"No, but I trust your ears." He opened the car door to get out. I followed suit.

Caleb walked past the long shadow of the rocks to stand in the moonlight and stare at them. The whole pile stood only a few inches taller than he, dominated by the huge whale boulder on top of a series of smaller rocks. It didn't look very stable. "Showtime," he said, then sang out an intense note that rumbled deep in his chest. It grew in volume and force, dominating the air around us, for about a minute.

No way he can keep this up much longer. But Caleb continued the note, then stretched out his arm, pointing at the small hill of stone. His black eyes glinted with gold, and all the power of the night seemed to fold itself around him like a cloak. Speak-singing on that same note, he intoned, "I call you forth from shadow."

A dark, churning fog shot from his hand toward the pile, where it encircled a small rock at the base. The rock seemed to shake itself, like a dog waking up from a nap. For a moment it looked like it overlapped the other rocks, as if the world had been double exposed. Then it rooted itself into the earth and shot up toward the stars.

I stumbled back, tripped over a tuft of desert grass, and fell flat on my butt onto something prickly. Above me now loomed a rocky mountain ridge over ten stories high, stretching left and right in a jagged line of unbroken stone for what had to be miles. It shone pure white and shiny as marble, alien, cold, and beautiful in the flat, red-brown landscape. My mind was blank, my mouth dry. I shut it and tried to swallow.

I heard a thud and looked to find Caleb lying on the ground on his back. I got to my feet and ran as he struggled to sit up, his face deathly pale and drawn. He startled as I leaned over him, his eyes wild.

"Tell Her Majesty I'm sorry," he said. "But it won't be gone for long."

"You're babbling," I said. "Is that what you do after you do this—whatever it is you do?"

"They quarried the stone for the Queen's summer palace here, you know," he said. "That's what it told me."

I glanced up at the smooth white stone, suitable for palace building. Maybe it wasn't babble. "The stone told you that?"

He nodded.

I hunkered down to look him in the eye because I couldn't bend at the waist. "Let me know if it tells you this week's lottery numbers."

He chortled, shut his eyes, and leaned his head back, as if basking in the moonlight. The silvery radiance bathed his long black eyelashes and ran down his strong neck. "Thank the moon," he said. "It saved our lives."

I couldn't stop staring down at him. In the clean white light he looked like a statue by Michelangelo, all smooth skin over lean muscles and wild hair. Then he opened his eyes. They were pure black and clear of distraction. He sat up. "All right, my canny co-conspirator. Let's get out of here."

"Excellent plan, my able accomplice," I said, standing up and taking his hand so I could pull him to his feet. "Let's find a gas station. I'm starving."

Caleb was too out of it to talk for about an hour. After the GPS led us to another dirt road and pointed the way, he ripped out the system's wires, saying the Tribunal also used it as a tracking device for the car. Then he fell into a deep sleep, head thrown back against the headrest.

We were out in the Mojave Desert of Southern California, not far from the 15 freeway. As Caleb slept I turned west toward Barstow, back in the direction of Burbank.

"You startled me back there, you know," he said after a while, lifting his head and rubbing his eyes. "You move so quietly."

"My friend Iris hates it when I come up behind her in the halls at school," I said. "She never hears me, and then she jumps ten feet in the air when I say hi."

He let out a weary laugh. "Just don't tell her you're a highly evolved predator. It might make her nervous."

"Yeah, about that," I said. "Start with this Tribunal. They kidnapped us. They're chasing us. Why?"

He glanced over at me, his black eyes serious. "Their order was created nearly two thousand years ago to wipe people like you and me from the face of the earth. They call us witches, demonspawn, creatures of the devil. They exist to sever all connection between this world and the shadow world. If things keep going the way they are, they'll probably succeed."

"So Lazar shot me because I . . . shifted." I still had a hard time with that word, that concept.

He nodded, brow furrowed. "The question is, how did he know who you were? How did he know where to find you and when you'd shift? That was the first time for you, right?"

I ignored the sudden pounding of my heart and pushed away the heated image Caleb's words conjured. Something about him made my mind go to all the wrong places. "Um, yeah. And an older man with white hair was there with him when he did it. He called him son."

"That's Ximon, Lazar and Amaris's father." His voice held a note of steely anger. "Ximon with an X. He's the lead asshole for the Tribunal in this part of the world."

"How do you know so much about them?" I said. "You know all their names, what they do. You knew this was Lazar's car and exactly how to disable the tracking device on it."

"Know thy enemy," he said. "Your kind and mine have not always been friendly, but we've shared the same adversary for the last two thousand years. If you'd been raised like other shifters, you'd know all of this. And I've been keeping an eye on Ximon's group for a while now."

"So you're not a shifter." I said. "You make other things shift."

He gave me an appreciative glance and nodded. "Exactly, smart girl."

"Okay," I said, settling into my seat. The white line down the center of the 15 freeway ran for what seemed forever before me, and stretched out into the darkness behind. "Tell me everything. From the beginning."

CHAPTER 4

"The many worlds lie alongside each other like spoons in a drawer," said Caleb. His voice took on a singsong intonation, as if he'd been told this story himself many times. "Although some would say they lie heaped in a messy pile, like kittens in a basket. One world lies closest to our own, and through the years it has been known by many names—the Dreamtime, Valhalla, the Underworld, or as we call it, Othersphere. From the earliest days it cast its shadow into our world. Not a shadow of darkness, but a power shadow, a vibration.

"The first people to recognize this were called by different names too—shaman, wizard, medicine man, seer, druid, witch. They found and called forth the shadow in certain people, and the animal forms of the first shifters came forth. They sought the shadows of plants, of animals, of stone and earth. Today we are referred to as callers of shadow. And for a long time, we were the only source of what might be called magic, but which we call shadow."

"It all comes from this Othersphere?" I said.

"Yes. No one has ever traveled between worlds, except perhaps in dreams, but the worlds affect each other. We can't know what our world does to Othersphere, but a caller can sense Othersphere's potential effect on this world."

"Then why did you say thanks to the moon?" I glanced over at him. The lights from the dash caught the dark glint of his irises and outlined the bruise around his eye.

"Certain circumstances make it easier to call the shadow forth." He frowned, thinking. "When the moon is full, the conditions are optimal for a caller to bring forth shadow, and for a shifter to change to their animal form. There are other things that make it easier too—certain locations are more closely connected to Othersphere. The ancients called them faery mounds or built henges and temples to mark a place of power. My mother also said that places where huge bursts of energy took place, like Hiroshima and Mount St. Helens, lie very close to Othersphere. She thought events like that tear at the veil between this world and the other."

"Is your mother a caller too?"

He hesitated. Pain flickered across his face. "She was," he said. "She's dead."

"I'm sorry," I said.

"It was a while ago." He turned his head to look out his window, so I could only see the strong line of his jaw. "I learned everything worth knowing from her."

"And your father?" I asked.

"Don't know him." He kept staring out at the sky.

The road rumbled beneath us as we sat in silence. The moon had risen, shrinking to a dime-sized pool of pulsating light, shining down through the BMW's moonroof. It cast Caleb's eyes into shadow.

"What about the Tribunal?" I asked after a few minutes.

"What about it?" His velvet voice sounded distracted.

"Well, you said that in the beginning were the callers, and they called forth the shifters. Where do the members of the Tribunal come from? Lazar did something with his voice. . . . It made me feel awful. That's kind of like what you do, right?" He didn't reply, so I pushed on. "I mean, you did the opposite. You helped me, but you did it with your voice too. Same with that ridge of rock you conjured out there."

"Vibration." He relaxed into his seat. "Callers use the vibration in their voices to bring out the shadow form of an object. The Tribunal refers to its callers as objurers now, but they were callers once."

"So they think using shadow to get rid of shadow is okay, but not for anything else."

"Exactly. Hey!" He pointed to a green sign that read GAS, FOOD, LODGING by the side of the road. "You still hungry?"

"Ravenous." The lift in his voice picked up my spirits.

"Two more miles and then it's lukewarm hot dogs and Pop-Tarts for everyone. After that I know a safe place we can go, north of here."

"Now?" I said. "I'm going home."

"The Tribunal knows where you live," he said.

I'd forgotten that. Remembering how Lazar stomped through the vegetable garden outside my bedroom made me queasy. "I could tell my mom what happened," I said. "She's pretty cool and believes some stuff that's kind of out there. She's a Wiccan, in touch with nature, believes in astrology, stuff like that. She could call the cops, tell them I was kidnapped by these weirdos. Get them on the case."

"No cop's going to believe you," he said, his tone dismissive. "I've had my run-ins with them, so trust me. If anything, they'll send you off to a therapist, and no head shrinker's going to protect you from the Tribunal."

"Well, I *am* going home," I said. He shook his head at me, but I ignored him and pressed on, still wanting more information. "So tell me, Lazar and his dad. They do what you do?"

"With a few differences." He ran a hand through his hair and seemed to relax. "Over the years, the Tribunal has trained its members to focus on certain areas of expertise. Mostly they excel at forcing shadow back to Othersphere."

I frowned, trying to work this out. "So instead of calling things out, they push them back in."

He let out a half laugh. "That's basically it, yeah. They're also good with technology and chemistry, guns with silver bullets, silver-based tranquilizers, stuff like that. They experiment with their drugs and machines to see if they can permanently erase the shadow from otherkin and from the places connected to Othersphere."

Experiment. I didn't like the sound of that. "Is that what they were going to do with me?"

Sympathy glinted in his eyes. "Probably."

"And if their experiments didn't work?" I almost didn't want to hear the answer.

He shrugged and remained silent. That was answer enough. I took a deep breath. "And you?"

"Same thing," he said.

"So they could push back that ridge of stone you called out of the desert," I said.

His dark brows drew together. "Lazar might manage it," he said. "His father's an expert. If Lazar can't figure it out, Ximon could objure what I called forth without breaking a sweat."

"Let's say Ximon never came and Lazar couldn't do it. Would that ridge of stone just stay there forever?"

He shook his head. "No. Objects called forth like that shrink back to their normal form within a few hours, depending on the conditions. With the moon full, it may last until moonset, assuming they don't get rid of it first."

"What about, you know, shifters?" The word still felt strange in my mouth.

"You mean people like you?" His eyes raked over me. "Five types have survived—cats, wolves, bears, birds of prey, and rats."

"Rats?" I said, staring at him. "Bears?"

"There used to be thousands of different kinds of shifters," he said. "Back before the Tribunal, the sea lion–shifters and dolphin-shifters were mistaken for mermaids, the swans and bulls helped create the legends of the god Zeus, and the spider-shifters . . . well, I've heard they were as big as dogs. The five remaining tribes don't get along, but each has a seat on the council for their area."

"Wow." The world was getting stranger by the minute. "The Tribunal killed all the rest of them off?"

He nodded sadly. "Those that survived were mostly the top predators—wolves, large cats, bears, and birds of prey."

"And the rats?" I said.

"Guess they can survive anything. If there had been cockroach-shifters, they probably would've made it too."

"That is amazing!" I tried to picture a full-grown person shifting into a rat. "Do they all have trouble shifting when they're young, like me?"

He nodded. "You learn control as you get older. Shifters first start changing form when they hit puberty. Their families help them learn to control it, or there are callers who help train the ones who have difficulty with it. Here's the off-ramp."

He pointed to the exit, and I curved right. Ahead, a brightly lit sign announced the price of gas and pointed the way to a small Eat and Go mart. Its umbrella of light enveloped it like a shield against the endless dark of the surrounding desert.

I pulled into a parking space next to the only other car in

the lot and realized what was missing. "Do you have any money?"

"Shit!" He patted his pockets. "Nothing. Bastards took everything, which wasn't much." He leaned over to stare at the gas gauge. His nearness made my stomach jump. "How much gas do we have left?"

"Less than a quarter tank," I said. "We'll never get out of the desert."

"Okay, new mission. Search the car." He reached down under my seat, head nearly in my lap. "There's got to be some money in it somewhere, even if it's just some change."

"Good idea." I tried to control my breath. "I'll check the trunk."

I got out of the car fast and popped the trunk. The dry, cool air of the desert night felt welcome on my hot skin. His proximity rattled me.

I lifted up the trunk lid. The harsh fluorescent lights of the convenience store shone down on a couple of manila folders, a flat shiny box, a Christian rock CD, two tennis racquets, and three loose, bright green balls. "Lazar plays tennis," I said loud enough for Caleb to hear.

"Why does that make perfect sense?" said Caleb. "Bet you five bucks I find something in the glove compartment."

"And how will you pay me if you don't find it?" I asked, reaching for the shiny box. I pulled it toward me, then snapped my hand away as it burned like a hot stove. I shook my fingers. "And there's a very pretty silver box back here that I can't open."

"Be right there." Fumbling noises came from the front of the car. "Score!" He jumped out of the car, brandishing a couple of bills. "Forty bucks! Right where I said it would be. Wanna bet me now?"

"That'll get us enough gas to get me home, plus some snacks."

He nodded. "Okay. If we're lucky, they'll have one of

those hot dog merry-go-rounds." He stuffed the money in his pocket and came to stand next to me facing the trunk. "Interesting box."

"You can touch silver, right?" I said.

"Most of the time. It only affects me when I'm actively calling something out of shadow." He leaned over and tugged the box toward him. "It's locked."

"Here." I handed him the ring of Lazar's keys. "Bound to be on here somewhere."

"Thanks." He shuffled through the keys and found a small shiny one. "This looks right."

The key slid into the lock on the box. As he turned it, the lid clicked open. I inhaled sharply. Caleb became very still.

A large pistol nestled in black velvet gleamed inside the box. Two burnished magazines of bullets sat in their own form-fitting slots.

"The gun isn't silver too, is it?" I didn't want to touch it and find out. I'd never touched a gun, let alone fired one. My stomach fluttered just looking at it.

"They make them out of an alloy that includes silver. Typical Tribunal weapon." He touched the gun, then tugged one of the magazines out of its niche. "But the bullets are silver. Through and through."

"Close it up." I scanned the front of the Eat and Go and found a security camera under the eaves.

He slid the magazine back into place and snapped the box closed. "Good thinking. If we end up needing more money, we can pawn it."

I made a face at him. "Before we end up in jail, why don't you go pay for the gas. I'll check around the trunk for change."

He grinned. "I'll get food too." He waved the money at me. "Hot dog or ancient burrito?"

"Dog, please. And chips. And soda. And candy, chocolate." I waved him toward the store.

"Yes, ma'am." He touched his forehead in a mock salute. I couldn't help watching him saunter away, trying to ignore the fluttering in my stomach. The door chimed as he entered the store.

I felt for the edge of the rug covering the bottom of the trunk and lifted it slightly to reveal the spare tire underneath. The manila folders slid back. I saw them and froze. The tab on one folder was marked in thick black ink, "Grey, Desdemona."

CHAPTER 5

My hands trembled as I reached for the folder with my name on it. The glare from the lights of the gas station easily illuminated the pages as I turned back the cover. Several pages of jagged handwriting stared up at me. I read the first words: "Notes taken from the central file on Desdemona Grey, suspected Shifter. Subtype: Feline. Species: Tiger, Siberian aka Amur." In the same hand, written at an angle across this was jotted: "Shifter confirmed Nov. 11, 16:05 hours."

Through the store window I could see Caleb paying for the gas and pointing at the rotating rack of hot dogs behind the clerk. Hastily, I scanned the other pages, turning my back to the store so he wouldn't see what I was doing.

It became clear that the writer, probably Lazar, had tracked me closely in those final hours before the shift. He noted everything, from my estimated height ("Approx. 6'0", normal for larger feline shifters") to my interaction with Jake Peters

("Flirtatious male teenager put hands around subject, came into contact with back brace. Subject fled.").

They must have been following me for a long time if they knew I had the brace. God, possibly years. Only the last half a day before my capture was recorded here, but this was a temporary file, used while Lazar was on the move. He'd probably planned on later copying the information into a central file.

The clerk handed Caleb his change, so I stuffed the pages back into the folder. I didn't want him to see the file. It was too private, too weird to have my own fanatical stalkers. I needed time to digest it all. I could read it closely later.

Caleb was coming through the door of the Eat and Go, his arms piled high with food. I slammed the folder shut, got in the car, and threw it in the backseat.

He tapped on the glass with his elbow, hands too full to open the door. I leaned across and pulled the handle. He slid into his seat, bringing a warm smell of cooked meat with him.

"I left yours plain in case you have a phobia of ten-year-old condiments, but here's some mustard and ketchup packets." He brandished the food.

"Mustard's great," I said a bit too shortly, and relieved him of a hot dog, condiments, soda, bag of chips, and two chocolate bars, glad to busy myself with something normal.

"We're poor again." He ripped open his own bag of potato chips. "I put twenty down for gas, and all this added up fast. Did you find anything else in the trunk?"

I took a huge bite of hot dog to give myself a moment. "No," I said, chewing. Warm, salty meat taste coated my tongue, offset by gooey, bland bun. "God, this horrible food tastes amazing."

"Ambrosia." He crunched into his chips. "So I was thinking about what you said earlier, about going home." He glanced at me, sounding too casual.

"What about it?" I gulped down a fizzy mouthful of soda. It followed the hot dog down to my stomach to form a hard, buzzing lump.

"I still don't think you should go," he said. He held up a hand as my eyes widened in alarm. "No, hear me out. I know it's an impossible choice for you, but I know a safe place not far away. You could meet other shifters there and learn a lot about how it all works."

I stared at him. "Not everyone leads a lawless, under-the-radar kind of life, you know. I can't just abandon my family without a word. They'd think I was kidnapped by some perv and start dragging the river. If your mom were still around, would you do that to her?"

He looked down, thoughtful. "Touché. So you're going to tell your mother and the cops that you changed into a tiger and someone stuck you in a cage?"

I realized he was right, about this at least. If I told them the truth, my parents would think I was crazy. "I could, you know, shift for them. Show them that I'm sane."

"And how would you do that?" He raised his eyebrows and sucked on his soda straw.

"I'd just, you know . . ." I made a swiping motion with my hand, as if it were a claw.

"And if you could shift at will into a tiger, how would you go about shifting back?" He crumpled up the foil from his hot dog, aimed out the car window, and threw it right into the garbage can outside.

I looked at him, exasperated. "I changed back just fine before."

"You were unconscious the first time," he said. "And the second time you had no idea how you got those claws or why they went away."

"You think I'd get stuck?" I said.

He shrugged, rattling his bag of chips to get the last bits at the bottom. "It happens all the time to shifters when they're young. That's why their families keep close tabs on them or send them to experts. I've never heard of a shifter like you, growing up without knowing their heritage, having no one to teach them the basics."

"I'm an orphan," I said, thinking of the passage in Lazar's notes. "My biological parents are dead," I said. "My mom adopted me when I was eighteen months old from an orphanage in Russia."

"That starts to explain it," he said. "I was wondering what you were doing living in Burbank."

"Yeah, you said that thing about me speaking good English . . ."

"Because tiger-shifters live only two places on earth—northern India and eastern Siberia. I've never met one until you. My mom traveled all over the world and met every other kind of shifter, but even she never met a tiger. They went to ground decades ago. Some people think they're myths. But Mom said that's probably what they want us to think."

I took the keys, started the car, and drove us a few feet to the gas pump. As he stood at the gas tank, I tried to lean out the window. The brace pinched my thigh. I had to open the car door to get comfortable. Caleb didn't notice, but stood staring at the ground, frowning.

"So this place you're going—you'll be safe there, right?" I asked.

He nodded, but didn't look completely certain. "My mom told me to go there in case of emergency. No money, on the run from armed Tribunal members . . . I guess this qualifies."

"Won't the Tribunal tell the police someone stole this car?" I asked.

He shook his head. "The Tribunal is obsessed with secrecy. They never rely on what they call 'heretic' agencies to do their work for them. If they called the car in as stolen, they'd have to make a report, give a name, an address, make up a story. And then there would be a record of their existence somewhere. Questions might be asked. No. They'll deal with us in their own way."

"Once we get to my place, I can sneak you some money to pay for more gas," I said. "Make sure you get where you need to go."

He raised his dark brows at me. "I can always find money. Don't worry about me," he said. "Worry about yourself."

The hair on the back of my neck prickled. I couldn't tell if it was the look on his face or the implication of his words that made me shiver. I forced myself to harrumph derisively. "Find money? You mean steal it. Better if you take my cash," I said.

He shrugged. "Let's see how it goes. You might change your mind about staying home."

"Stubborn," I said.

He replaced the pump and closed up the gas tank. "Move over," he said. "I'll drive the rest of the way. You can take a cat nap."

I groaned as he shot me a mischievous smile. "Thanks. I think." I started to get out of the car, but with him standing over me I couldn't. He didn't realize how hard it would be for me to haul my unbending torso over to the passenger seat. "Um, I need to get out and go around. Sorry."

"Oh, sure." He stepped back. I sidled past him. Comprehension dawned on his face. "It's that brace, right? Must be hard to move in that thing. I should've realized."

"It's okay." Talking straight out about it like this made me nervous. I glanced up at his face, dreading the inevitable look of disdain and pity.

Instead, he looked mildly interested. "How long have you had it?"

"Two years." I swallowed hard, trying to act like this was

normal. Today had hit a new high in abnormal. "My spine is curving wrong, and this is supposed to stop it before it gets too bad."

"Can't you just take it off?"

I wish. "I have to wear it twenty-three hours a day until they're certain I've stopped growing," I said. "If I don't, it could really mess me up."

"If I hadn't seen it, I never would've guessed you wore one," he said, walking around the car to open the door for me. "You carry it off like it's nothing."

"Really?" My nervousness drained away in surprise. "I feel so stiff."

"You move like a cat," he said. "All grace and power. I guess nothing can change that."

"Thanks." I ducked into the car so he wouldn't see the deep flush that traveled from my heart to heat my neck and face.

I didn't think I'd be able to sleep after all that had happened, but I must've nodded off after we hit the road. I woke to see that we were on the 5 freeway, just a few miles from Burbank.

"Hey, sleepy," Caleb said. "Did you know you snore?"

I straightened and stretched. "Are you sure I wasn't purring?" I brought the seatback up to its fully locked and upright position. Caleb must've reclined it during the drive so I could sleep more comfortably. The clock read 5:46 a.m.

He threw a manila folder onto my lap. The label read: "Grey, Desdemona."

My stomach plunged. Of course worldly thief-boy had found it.

"You found it in the trunk?" he asked.

"Yeah," I said, very quietly.

"You could've shown it to me, you know."

"But it's a file on me!" I sputtered. "I thought my life was mine, private. But they've been following me, making notes, planning to take me down like I'm some rare animal for their zoo. It's just such a ... a ..."

"Violation," he said. "I get it."

"Yeah, that's it." The buzzy lump in my stomach settled a bit at his words.

"I'm sorry." He kept his eyes on the road, but he reached over and took my hand. "It's a lot to take in."

"No shit," I said. I wasn't big on swearing, but right now it felt necessary. And he was flustering me. Should I interlace my fingers with his or move my hand away? "That's my exit coming up—Olive Avenue." I moved my hand to point at the big green sign. "Get off there and turn left."

"Got it." He cast a sideways glance at me. "Who's this guy in the file they talk about, the one who walked you through the park? Your boyfriend?"

"It's not safe to read while driving."

"Just answer the question."

I laughed. "Jake Peters my boyfriend? No way."

"I don't know. He sounds interested in you, even in Lazar's bad handwriting." He moved us into the right lane. "It says you ran away from him. Did you guys have an argument or something?"

"Not exactly." I didn't want to revisit those moments with Jake.

"But he put his arms around you, right? Something like that?" He looked at me again, then focused on the road as we took the off-ramp.

"It's no big deal," I said. "He just, yeah. He grabbed my waist. Not a good idea with me, you know, because of ..."

"The brace." His voice hardened, almost angry, protective. "What did he say to you?"

"Nothing. I just left." My insides felt dry as dust. Empty.

"Oh." He relaxed, easing his hands on the wheel. "You assumed he'd reject you, so you pulled away first."

"What else would he do? I mean, look!" I made a fist and

knocked on my stomach the way you rap on a door. "Boys don't want to literally knock first before you let them in."

"How do you know?" he said.

I hadn't thought of it that way. He cleared his throat. "I mean, this guy's obviously not that smart or he would've come after you. But don't just run away out of reflex. Someone might surprise you someday."

Silence fell. As we headed into the Burbank Hills, a peach-gray hint of dawn smudged the sky. I was just a few minutes from home, but for a moment I didn't want to go. I wanted to keep on driving and see what happened.

CHAPTER 6

My house lay sleeping in a patch of fog on the corner of Delaware and Kenneth. Caleb parked the BMW across the street. "You sure about this?" he said. "You can still come with me."

"You won't even tell me where it is you want me to go!" We'd been arguing about this for the past three minutes.

He shook his head. "No offense, but I can't tell you unless you promise to come with me. If I tell you and you don't come, the Tribunal might get the information out of you."

I thumped my head against the headrest and stared up through the moonroof in exasperation. "And I can't promise to come with you without knowing where I'm going!"

"Impasse central. Here." He leaned across me to open the glove compartment and took out a pen. He didn't touch me, but I could feel the warmth from his arm like a low-banked fire. "The Tribunal took my phone along with my wallet.

Give me your phone number. I'll call you as soon as I get a phone, make sure you're okay."

He wanted my number. What did that mean? Were we going to stay in touch? I didn't want to think that this might be the last time I'd see him. He looked up at me expectantly. "Okay." I grabbed the pen, scribbled my cell phone number on a corner of the folder, then tore off the corner and handed it to him. "Did you try to take them on all by yourself? That seems like something you'd do."

"Noticed that, hunh?" He inhaled deeply. "I got my butt handed to me." He leaned into me, very serious. "Look, I just wanted to say thanks. You risked your life to free me. If it wasn't for you, I'd still be in that cage."

"And without you I never would've gotten past the parking lot," I said. Our faces were very close. The dark womb of the car enfolded us. Deep in his black irises I saw a glint of gold. Faint stubble roughened the tan skin of his cheeks and neck. Under his shirt, his broad chest rose and fell.

"You'd be safe with me." His warm voice was soft, as if he'd reached out to caress my cheek. "Come with me."

For the briefest moment everything stopped. My breath, my heart, the turning of the earth, everything paused, awaited my reply. I saw myself falling into him, pressing my mouth to his, his hands on my skin.

But as I leaned farther, the edge of the brace cut up under my breast. I blinked, jolted back into the real world.

I looked away, adopting a light tone. "I bet you say that to all the girls you meet in cages. I need to hurry up and get money out of my dresser for you before Mom and Richard wake up and start yelling at me."

He didn't say anything for a moment, running a hand through his wild hair. Then he got out of the car. "What are you going to tell them?"

I got out too. "No idea."

He walked to my side of the car, staring at my house, a

typical low-slung, California ranch–style three-bedroom. I could just see the tops of the tomato stakes in the side yard where Lazar had stood. Mom and I had started planting there when I was six. The plants liked me. They grew at a wild pace, clustering close to my bedroom window. "What was it like, growing up in a place like that?" Caleb asked.

"You know, normal, boring," I said. "Or maybe you don't know."

"I think I saw it in an old TV movie in a hotel room in Singapore once," he said. "Let's go."

"Wait here. I'll be right out." I started across the street.

But he followed, his long coat flapping behind him. I stopped at the curb, whispering, "What are you doing? What if they see you?"

"I'm walking you to your door," he said. Unlike most people, when he lowered his voice, it just got quieter, not whispery. The effect was strangely intimate.

I struggled to keep my own voice down. "Now is not the time to be a gentleman."

"I can't help it. My mother used to smack me on the arm if I didn't stand up whenever a woman did, open doors for her, all that stuff." He shrugged.

"Then she must've taught you it's not polite to make so much noise that a girl's parents wake up and ground her," I said.

"Maybe you deserve to be grounded." He smiled. "You *were* out all night with a strange boy."

I gasped a quick laugh and smacked him on the bicep.

He gave an exaggerated wince and rubbed his arm. "Ow. Okay! I'll stay here."

"Good. Thanks." He stepped back into the long shadows of the cypress trees along the driveway. With his black coat, dirty face, and dark hair, he blended almost seamlessly into the darkness. Throwing a "not bad" look at him, I tiptoed up the walkway to the fat pottery Buddha my mom kept by the front door. It lounged next to statues of the white rabbit in a waistcoat and a pot of overflowing azaleas. I tilted Buddha and slid the hidden front door key out from under him. Looking over at the cypress trees, I put a finger to my lips. I thought I saw Caleb nod, but it might have been the wind in the branches.

I unlocked the front door, then put the key back under Buddha. With one last glance in Caleb's direction, I silently entered and shut the door behind me.

My heart thumped hard. Mom and Richard would go ballistic as soon as they knew I was home. I'd never stayed out all night before without them knowing where I was. Had they called the cops?

I glided into the living room, past the ceiling-high shelves stuffed with books, sidestepped Richard's rowing machine, and headed toward the hall to my bedroom. I kept about a hundred dollars stashed in my dresser. With that maybe Caleb could make it to his mysterious destination.

"Desdemona, is that you?" My mother's voice swooped up out of sleep to a hysterically high pitch. A light clicked on. I turned to see Mom and Richard, uncurling from the couch in the living room, shell-shocked and furious.

"Are you all right? Where have you been?" Mom was on me in a flash, grabbing my shoulders, scanning my face, checking me for injuries. Richard walked up slowly behind her, rubbing his bearded cheeks with one hand as he shook his head at me. I hastily rolled the folder I was carrying into a tube and held it down at my side within the folds of my dress.

"I'm fine, Mom, really. I'm sorry. I didn't mean to . . ." Had Caleb seen the light go on?

"We called the police!" Mom looked more upset than I'd ever seen her.

"Your mother was very worried," said Richard in that soft

voice of his that cut through any argument. "Why didn't you call?"

"I know. Did I mention that I'm sorry?" Neither of them was softening.

"You are going to sit down and tell us exactly where you were and what you were doing!" Mom pointed at our threadbare wingback chair. "This is so unlike you, I thought . . . I thought something had happened to you." She fiddled with the Triple Goddess symbol she always wore around her neck. Tears sprang to her eyes. Richard put his arm around her shoulders and led her to the couch.

My heart gained about eight hundred pounds. I sank into the wingback chair. "I am so sorry, Mom, really. I forgot my phone, and I met this boy after school . . ."

"A boy?" Mom's eyebrows almost popped off the top of her forehead. "You were out with a *boy?*"

"Yeah. I met him after school and he invited me to a party." My brain was working overtime. How to make this plausible and yet not give anything important away?

"You've been at a party this whole time?" She exchanged a look of disbelief with Richard. "The only party on the planet without a single phone in it?"

"It was out in the desert," I said. That was true. "And I didn't realize how far out it was till we got there, and by then nobody could get reception."

"Okay, okay." Mom's hands were shaking. Richard stroked her back, but she started to pace. "So I'm expected to believe that you were at a party in the desert with a boy you've never mentioned before, for fifteen hours?" She paused to give me her "I know better than that" look. "Honey, you've never even been out on a date."

"Guess I have now," I said, making sure to look her right in the eye. "He didn't tell me how far it was—somewhere out past Barstow along the 15, like, halfway to Vegas. They had a bonfire next to this big rock formation, and I think I sat in a cactus." I stood up and tugged the back of my dress around, searching for the holes.

Mom studied me, as if I were some new life-form she'd just found under a rock. "So you went to a party with a boy. Did you drink any alcohol?" She walked right up and sniffed at me, scrutinizing my face.

"No!" My voice had the ring of truth in it now. "I swear to you, Mom, I did not have a drink. I just had a soda and a hot dog, and so did Caleb."

"Caleb?" Mom's eyes bored up into mine. I'd towered over both her and Richard since puberty. "So his name is Caleb?"

Damn. I'd meant to use Jake Peters's name, but Caleb had slipped out. No going back now. "He's just this guy."

"How crazy was this party?" She took my chin and tilted my head down to look her in the eye again.

"Marijuana? Ex? Meth?" asked Richard.

Mom was pacing again. "We've been to a few parties in our lives too, you know."

"Mom, you know I'm not into that stuff. I don't like the thought of being so out of control."

"Okay." Mom stopped pacing and gave me a determined look. "It's nearly six a.m. You and I are going to have a talk. Then I want you to take a shower and get ready for school."

School? After the insanity of the past hours, I couldn't imagine dragging myself to classes. And how was I supposed to get the money to Caleb? "Mom, I'm really not feeling all that hot . . ."

"That's what happens when you stay out all night partying," she said crisply. "Maybe next time you won't go so far, remember your phone, and come home at a decent hour. Now, excuse us, Richard." She took me by the arm and led me toward my bedroom. "It's time for a mother-daughter chat."

"I'll call the police, tell them to stop looking." Richard walked to the phone.

I cast a final glance out the front window but saw no sign of Caleb in the gloom outside. Richard mouthed "Good luck" at me as we headed down the hallway.

"I know you know the facts of life," Mom said, shutting my bedroom door. "But we need to talk about this boy you're seeing and why it's not okay for him to take you out to all-night parties."

"He's not really like that, Mom." I knew how that sounded as I pulled my dress over my head and slipped off my sandals. I slid the folder onto my desk out of sight. "He got dragged into it too. And before we knew it, we were hours away."

"But what does that say about his judgment? And yours?"

She talked on as I eased out of the brace and stepped into the shower. I'd heard a lot of this before; Mom often babbled her free-living beliefs to me. Only this time she sprinkled in more warnings. I made the appropriate responses from behind the shower curtain as she paced my tiny bathroom.

She finished up by saying that if I ever needed to talk to her about anything, she'd be there for me. And I was grounded for a month.

I didn't protest. Any chance of sneaking money to Caleb was gone now. Would I ever see him again? I couldn't imagine never looking into his dark eyes again.

I got out of the shower, and wrapped a towel around myself; then my mom gave me a tight hug. "You know I love you, Desdemona," she said.

I hugged her back. "Me too, Mom. And I really am sorry."

Her hazel eyes shifted back and forth between mine. "Anything else you want to tell me about this Caleb guy?"

Did she sense I was lying? "Like what?"

"Is he cute?"

Holy crap, she was smiling.

I shrugged. "Um, yeah. He is." *He's ridiculously hot, Mom. In fact, if you knew how hot he was, you wouldn't want me near him.*

Her smile widened. "Okay, you get dressed and I'll make you some eggs." She started to leave.

"Mom, can I ask you something?" I said.

"Of course, honey." She turned in the doorway.

"What exactly did they tell you about me in that orphanage in Russia?" I tried to make it sound casual, grabbing a comb and looking into the bathroom mirror. "Did they say anything about my biological parents?"

She took a moment, standing there, then cleared her throat. We didn't talk about the adoption much. I avoided it so she wouldn't feel like she wasn't enough of a parent. Maybe she avoided it for the same reason. "No, unfortunately. I asked them, but they had very little information. I found you in an orphanage in Moscow, but you'd been transferred from out in the boondocks and the records on you were minimal."

I turned to face her, running the comb through my hair. "Did you notice anything, like, weird about me?"

"Don't be ridiculous," she said automatically, then froze, her eyes flickering with thought.

"What?" I said. "You thought of something."

"They were afraid of you," she said. "The people at the orphanage. I never told you before because I didn't want to disturb you. But they didn't tell me about you at first, and when I saw you and wanted you, they tried to persuade me not to take you. That just made me want you all the more."

"Afraid of me?" I realized I was combing the same section of hair over and over and stopped. "Why?"

"Well." She furrowed her brow. "You were only eighteen months old, but you'd already had more adventures than most folks have in a lifetime, or that's how I saw it. The orphanage had a thin file on you, but I can still remember it—gray and creased and stained. It was written in Russian and some tribal tongue from the place they found you. I hired a lawyer to help me with the red tape, and she got a translator to help with the tribal language. Isn't it funny? I haven't thought about this in years."

I stopped pretending to comb my hair and turned to stare at my reflection in the mirror, trying to see past the green eyes and the freckles to a large feline underneath. As far back as I could remember, I'd known I was adopted. I often wondered what my biological parents looked like, moved like, sounded like. I hadn't let myself wonder too much, since I figured I'd never find out, and poking at the tiny empty space inside me was painful.

I didn't look like a cat. Had my father's nose been a bit too long, my mother's eyes large and green? I held up my hands and scrutinized them. One of my parents had given me slender fingers and nails that always easily grew long and strong. Was that typical for a tiger-shifter?

"Where did they find me?"

"You'd been transferred to Moscow from some tiny town in Siberia," said Mom. At the word "Siberia," a strange chill ran through my bones. "The section of your file in that tribal tongue was a transcription of what the person who first found you said to the officials. He was a reindeer herder."

"I was found by a *reindeer herder?*" This was getting stranger and stranger. "Was he my father?"

"Oh, no." She shook her head. "He's just the one who found you, out in the woods. That's what he said anyway. And they had a photo of him. He looked like he was Chinese or some sort of native Mongolian tribesman. Nothing like you."

"I was found in the Siberian woods by a Mongolian reindeer herder," I repeated. "That is the weirdest thing ever."

"He spoke rather poetically," said Mom. "He was out in

the snow with his deer, and the sound of angels and your cries led him to you. You were the only thing alive in a great circle of dead trees. I think he said you were wrapped in furs, or maybe he wrapped you in furs."

"A circle of dead trees..." I said. "Is that what scared the orphanage people?"

She shrugged. "They didn't say much. I almost didn't even get to see you. I was waiting alone in the reception area of the orphanage in Moscow for a while, and this skinny old man I'd never seen before came out and motioned for me to follow him. I couldn't understand a word he said, but he pointed at a door. When I went inside I found you, smiling right at me. Vines had sneaked through the window and wound themselves around the slats of your crib, as if Nature herself was tending to you. You had your green thumb even then. And I never saw that old man again. I'm certain now he was an angel."

Mom really believed in angels too. It always sounded like wish fulfillment to me. "So I wasn't scary to you?"

"Scary, Desdemona? Not at all! You held your arms out to me right away, and that was it. I was yours forever." She smiled, her eyes misting with remembrance. Tears formed in my own eyes. I was used to hearing her say how much she loved me; Mom was touchy-feely like that. But that was the moment when we'd become a family.

"At first they told me you weren't available for adoption," she continued. "But when my lawyer checked, she found out that wasn't true. They called you Varvara, which means 'stranger.' You were my little fairy child from the start. Well, now you're my tall fairy child." She smiled.

My heart jolted in my chest. Stranger? Had they known what I was?

Mom didn't notice my disquiet. "They said you made flowers bloom and clocks stop. Stray cats would sneak in and snuggle up to you. I just hoped it was all true."

"You don't still have this file, do you?" I tried not to let the deep urgency I felt creep into my voice. "I'd love to read it."

"No, sorry." She shook her head. "They wouldn't let me take the original, and they took the transcription from the lawyer. I got a whole set of new files once the adoption went through, of course. All cleaned up and sanitized so that it didn't look like they ran a country where babies were found abandoned out in the woods."

"Stranger." I stared at my racks of brace-mandated waist-less dresses, elastic-waist pants, and long tunic T-shirts, pretending to select an outfit. But in my mind's eye, I saw a man in fur from head to toe, walking toward one of his reindeer as it nuzzled a squirming, squalling bundle in a ring of dead trees. Who had left me there, and why?

"You were three months old when he found you, and someone had cared for you very well. They must have loved you, Desdemona."

"And you think they're probably dead?"

"Who knows?" She shrugged. "Maybe the herder lied and killed your parents, but couldn't bring himself to hurt you. Maybe your family ran out of food and knew he'd be coming by. We'll probably never know."

"Yeah." I tugged a new dress out of the closet. "Can't see me rushing off to Siberia anytime soon."

"Maybe after you graduate we can take a trip to Russia so that you can get a sense of where you came from. Would you like that?"

"Yeah," I said, warmth spreading through me. "That'd be great."

"It's a deal." She opened the bedroom door and headed down the hall, shouting. "Who wants eggs?"

I threw on my clothes and grabbed the cash from my dresser. Caleb might still be waiting for me. Mom was humming to herself in the kitchen. Avoiding the creaky board in the middle of the floor, I crept down the hall, out of sight of the kitchen, and ran to the front door. Chilly early morning air embraced me as I stepped outside. The cypresses murmured in the breeze, and a few birds sang toward the rising sun.

But no tall boy in a long black cloak stepped out of the shadows. The curb across the street sat empty. Caleb was gone.

CHAPTER 7

School had been mild torture for years, but that day it was a blur of torment. I literally ran into Iris after history, my head down, trying to move through the halls unnoticed.

"Whoa, there," she said, stepping back hard. "You don't know your own strength."

"Sorry," I muttered. The tide of students eddied around us, two small stones in the stream. Iris had her long dreadlocks piled up to show off eight different earrings, four in each ear, every one a different color. Around her neck hung several chains featuring a silver unicorn, a gold Cheshire cat, and a tarnished Eiffel Tower. Her "friends," as she called them, were nearly popping out of the top of her sleek white blouse. She'd painted purple flowers on her Doc Marten boots.

She fell into step beside me. We had art class next. "You okay?" she asked. "No offense, but you look like shit."

"Thanks," I said. "I like the flowers."

"Aren't they cool? Inspired by your azaleas." She kicked up one of her feet to get a better view of the blossoms on her boots. "This hippie phase I'm going through has totally fueled my creativity."

"Iris, you've been in a hippie phase for two years," I said, weaving my way through the throng. "If you got any more creative you'd be growing flowers out of your ears."

"Hey, great idea!" She laughed her infectious, deep-throated chortle, and I couldn't help smiling. "That's better," she said. "Now quick tell me what's wrong before I kick your butt in pottery class."

"Competitive art, the way it should be," I said. "I just didn't sleep last night, that's all." Did that spiky head of hair up the hallway belong to Jake? I slowed down. No way I wanted to run into him today. I leaned down and spoke low. "Jake Peters asked me to the dance."

Iris's perfect eyebrows shot up. "Holy shit. What did you say?"

"I said I don't dance." I tried to adjust the brace without being seen. It was extra uncomfortable today, as if my body was rebelling. "And then he put his hands on my waist and, well, that was it, right?"

She frowned. "Why? Did you knee him in the balls or something?"

I threw her an exasperated look. "No. He touched the brace. He looked all crazy, and I got the hell out of there."

"Oh, right. I forget you have that thing."

She forgot? How was that possible? Was I really that good at pretending it wasn't there?

Iris's big brown eyes shifted back and forth in thought. "So you didn't talk about it with Jake, give him a chance?"

"No!" I started down the hallway, my stomach twisting. "Why does everyone say that? Like Jake Peters or anyone else is going to date a girl encased in rigid nonbiodegradable materials."

"Anyone else?" She craned her neck to get a look at my face as I sped up. "Who else you been talking to about this?"

"It's not important." This was too hard. The lies were piling up. First Mom, now Iris. If I couldn't tell them the truth, it was better to be left alone. "I'll see in you class, okay? I'm going to hit the bathroom."

"Okay, but I need more details!" she yelled after me.

I headed for the bathroom. Maybe a few moments of quiet in a graffiti-covered stall would clear my head. I slipped past a few guys outside the boys' bathroom, almost there, when one of them turned in my direction.

Damn. The spiky hair did belong to Jake Peters. He looked at me, then turned away. I ran the rest of the way to the bathroom,

A toiled flushed, and a girl in a yellow sweater emerged from a stall and headed to the sink. I kept my eyes down, moving toward the other faucet, hoping she'd leave me there alone. But the door from the hallway swooshed open behind me.

"You okay?"

I whirled. Caleb stood there, looking somehow more solid, more real, than anything else in school. The girl in the yellow sweater saw him in the mirror and squealed.

"I could ask you the same thing," I said. "What are you doing here?"

Yellow sweater girl didn't wait to dry her hands, but ran past Caleb, glaring at us both. The door thumped closed behind her. We were alone.

"Where have you been?" I asked. "I came outside this morning as soon as I could, but I didn't see you anywhere nearby."

"I saw your lights go on and thought I'd better get out of

the area in case the police had been called or your parents came out looking for the scalawag who hijacked you."

The door from the hallway opened, and a girl walked in. She stopped dead at the sight of Caleb, then swiveled on her heel and walked right back out again. He turned back to me, his mouth twisting in a smirk.

"Scalawag indeed," I said.

But he was staring at me now from under his black eyebrows, like I was a puzzle with some pieces missing. "Where's the shadow?" he said.

"What?"

He moved up to me and took my right hand in both of his, never taking his eyes from mine. I stared back, confused. He hands were slightly rough, but strong and warm. His touch sent a flutter through me. "Last night the shadow was coming off of you in streams. Now, I can't see it at all."

My heart leapt. "Does that mean I'm normal again?"

He shook his head and hummed low in his throat, pressing my hand between his. The vibration moved through me, as if I were the body of the guitar and he were strumming the strings. At first that was all. Then something deep inside me stirred.

I heard myself gasp. My hand curled inside his. The thrumming continued, pushing at me, relentless. The core of me trembled, began to awaken. Something dark in my heart reached out, filled my veins, extended its claws . . .

"There it is," he said, his voice uneven. He cleared his throat. "I found it, but it's buried deeper than any shadow I've ever known."

Our faces were inches apart, his breath hot on my skin. The purring inside me took on a different tone as I fell into his night-black eyes. I felt paralyzed, yet so alive, electric. His gaze fell to my lips as he dipped his head toward mine.

"No!" I pulled away and turned to lean my hands on the

sink to steady myself. God, he'd almost pressed up against me, against the brace. "That's enough. I can't . . ."

He didn't say anything for a moment. I looked up to see him in the mirror, standing behind me. He looked unnerved and slightly flushed.

"I'm sorry," he said, pushing his hands into his pockets. "Something about you . . ." He shook his head and turned away so I couldn't see his face. "I lost track of what was going on there."

My own reflection looked wrong somehow. I leaned in to look at myself and inhaled sharply. My eyes were even rounder and now startlingly gold instead of the usual green.

"My eyes. They're . . . tiger eyes." I brought my hands up to touch my eyelids. The lashes looked longer, thicker, blacker. Caleb's warm scent lingered on my palms. I turned, breathing in, and a hundred different smells passed into me. Acrid cleaning agents mixed with old makeup, mold, and urine. And then there was Caleb. Even more than before, I caught his scent, like the woods just before a thunderstorm. I could have been placed on the other side of the room, blindfolded, and known for certain that he stood there.

I heard Caleb's shirt slide across his skin as he turned to look at me. Water dripped behind the second toilet, and out in the hall, footsteps hurried and disappeared as another door squeaked open and bumped shut. Classes must have started. I'd be late to competitive art.

And I'd nearly been kissed.

"That explains why I couldn't see the shadow in you. And why you didn't shift before yesterday. Somehow, the shadow in you has been suppressed." Caleb lifted one dark eyebrow sardonically, and my heart did a little flip. "I seem to have brought it out."

"How could it be suppressed?" The new smells and sounds retreated as this sank in. My eyes were shifting in the mirror, getting greener, smaller, more human. My thoughts remained a crazy jumble: Caleb's lips moving toward mine, the purring in my chest. My skin was about to jump off my body—or was that normally how shifters felt?

"I don't know." His eyes ran up and down me as if they couldn't help themselves. "You're full of surprises."

My whole face flushed. I'd worked so hard at being invisible for so long, I wasn't used to being looked at that way. "Maybe I'm doing it myself," I said. "Pushing it back subconsciously."

"You're pushing something back." He seemed to tear his gaze away from me, looking a little lost.

The late bell blared.

Oh, thank God. An excuse to bolt. "I'm late," I said.

"Late for what?"

"Uh, my next class?"

"Oh, right. Humdrum education. Just meet me after school," he said, his voice catching.

I moved to the bathroom door, head down. "I've got a doctor's appointment at four thirty," I said. "But I can still get you the money."

"Doctor's appointment?" Alarm took over his voice. "What's wrong?"

"Nothing," I said. "Just a checkup on my progress with the brace. I'll get a spine X-ray, hear the same old lectures, no big deal."

"Okay." He put a hand on the door to the hall, took a breath, and gathered his thoughts. "Look, I don't care about the money," he said. "I just need to see you again. Make sure you're okay."

"I'm fine," I said, willing it to be true and looking up into his eyes firmly.

He opened the door to the hall for me. "Meet you outside after school?"

I nodded and darted past him, careful not to touch. The halls were empty. "Meet me at the oak tree in the park next door," I said. "You can't miss it."

His smile flickered with relief. Then he bowed at the waist, like a courtier. I shook my head, laughed, and ran to class. I'd never been late before. But a lot had changed since yesterday.

CHAPTER 8

Iris nabbed me at the end of the day to get the dirt on what had happened with Jake and who the guy in the bathroom was. I tried to slip away, but she tracked me down and followed me out into the park, lobbing questions.

As we walked, I fudged the truth and said I'd met Caleb, a boy from another school, by the old oak tree and gone out with him to a party. He had cut school today to see me.

"What is it with you and tall, pretty boys all of a sudden?" Iris had a thing for short, fireplug types who excelled in shop. "Overnight you're this femme fatale."

"You'd like Caleb," I said. "He's handy with tools, fixes cars, stuff like that."

"He is cute," she said, staring ahead at the old oak tree. A lean figure in a long black coat stood looking up into its canopy of crooked branches.

He waited as we approached. I hadn't meant for them to

meet, but Iris could be hard to shake off when she had an agenda.

"He-ey." Iris gave a little wave.

Caleb lifted his hand slowly to wave back. I said, "This is my friend Iris. Iris, this is Caleb."

"Nice to meet you, Iris." Caleb gave her one of his quick bows.

Iris looked him up and down, then blurted out, "So are you dating Dez now or what?"

I felt my eyes get huge. Caleb choked a little. "Well, uh . . ."

"And that's your cue to go, Miss I," I said, putting my hands on Iris's shoulders and gently pushing her back toward school. "You'll miss the bus."

"Nobody likes to get right to the heart of things." Iris moved out of my reach. "But I can take a hint. Call me."

"If I can," I said. "Later!"

"She's . . . forthright," said Caleb as Iris headed back toward school.

"You think?" I shook my head and walked over to the tree. Under its limbs, speckles of sunlight ran over the patches of grass at its roots and decorated the gray bark with bright spots of brown. I ran my hand over the trunk, bumpy as a dragon's scales.

"You hang out at this tree a lot, don't you?" Caleb said.

"How'd you know?" I leaned against the tree. It didn't mind the hardness of my brace. "I used to climb it every day when I was a kid."

"Because this is a lightning tree." He bent down to pick up a fallen leaf. "I've never seen one before, but my mother told me stories."

"A what?" I looked up at the tree.

"A lightning tree. There are only a few of them in the world." He held the leaf up before his eyes, gazing on it almost reverently. "Its shadow form is lightning."

I moved away from the tree, uneasy. "The tree is made of lightning?"

"Not in this world. Callers think lightning trees are portals to violent thunderstorms in Othersphere. So their leaves, branches, and roots all have shadows made of lightning. It's there just beyond the veil, crackling and humming." He looked around. "Watch this." He broke off a small piece of the fallen leaf, hummed low, then flicked it away. As it fell to the ground, the fragment flared bright as a small sun. The air crackled. My skin prickled as heat from it passed over me. Then it vanished.

Caleb smiled at my astonishment. "In the hands of a caller, it's a tiny lightning bolt."

"Wow," I said, taking in the tree. Its branches zigzagged up toward the sky, waving their leaves in the wind. "This is the coolest tree in the world."

Caleb squatted down and picked up a few more fallen twigs and dried leaves. "It makes sense that you'd be drawn here. As otherkin, you picked up on it at some level. This is the closest thing to a faery mound you'll find for hundreds of miles. Oh, of course!" He turned to me, calculations flashing behind his eyes.

"Of course what?"

"This is how the Tribunal found you. The lightning tree." At my confused look, he stuffed the tree-bits in his pocket and walked over to me. "The Tribunal and the more experienced callers try to keep track of all the places with connections to Othersphere—a sort of map of shadow. The Tribunal spotted the lightning tree and kept a watch on it. They knew otherkin in the area would be drawn to it, and they were hoping to capture someone. That must be how they found you."

So that's how Lazar tracked me, how he knew to watch for me in the park the day before. "I've lived in this neighborhood all my life," I said. "Do you think they've been keeping an eye on me all that time?"

"Depends on when they found the tree," he said. "But it's possible. They're very patient. Given how deeply the shadow was buried in you, they wouldn't have been able to know for sure. So they waited to see if anything would ever manifest. And it did."

I got a chill, thinking about the terrible patience required to wait and observe for so long. "They might still be watching."

Caleb got very still, then tilted his head up to look into the branches of the tree. "You're right. I see it." He grabbed the tree's trunk and hoisted himself up into the branches.

"What ... ?" I craned my neck, watching him climb up and around with grace. He paused in front of a knothole, then stuck his hand into it and pulled out a small device.

"Catch."

I stuck my hands out and caught it. In my palms lay a small box with what looked like a round piece of glass on one side and an antenna.

"It's a camera," Caleb said, climbing back down to land next to me. He took it from my hand and flicked open its back panel with a fingernail. "Motion sensitive, with a wireless feed. There must be a hard drive nearby that stores the footage until they're ready to download it."

He fiddled with something inside the camera while I looked around. "So they know we're here."

"Maybe." He took out a small pocketknife and used it to twist something inside the camera.

He hadn't had a knife last night. The Tribunal would have taken it. "Where'd you get the knife?" I asked.

"Found it," he said, not looking up. "They'll need to check in from their remote location. So if they're busy right now, they might not have viewed us yet. If we can find the hard drive now, there's a chance we can keep them from seeing it."

It was 3:48 p.m. "Okay. But I have to be home in twelve minutes or my mom will call the cops. I'm not even joking."

"It's okay, go now." He leaned against the tree, focused on fiddling with the camera. "I might be able to use this to pinpoint the location of the hard drive. It can't be far away."

"Okay." When would I see him again? "But what about the money I was going to give you?"

He looked up, distracted. His fingers were dirty from the climbing and tinkering with his tools. "Oh, yeah. I'll call your cell tonight. We'll figure it out then."

"Do you have a phone?" I said.

"I'll find one," he said, still avoiding my gaze.

I was starting to get the picture. "The same way you found that pocketknife?"

He raised his head and grinned, a spark of mischief lighting his face. "Living on my own has led me to develop a few skills society doesn't approve of."

"Okay." My watch now said 3:52, and home was at least six minutes away. I backed off as he watched, still giving me his smart-ass grin. "So you'll call me later, right?"

"Stop worrying," he said, walking toward me till our faces were close. "I'll find a phone that won't be missed too much. And I promise I'll call you. I don't make promises lightly." He stepped back from me, and I blinked, as if coming out of a trance. "Now get out of here before your mom throws a fit."

"Good luck," I said, then turned and ran for home.

CHAPTER 9

At the hospital, the X-ray technician was grumpy and took three sets of shots before muttering that I could go. I scurried back to the examination room, holding together my too-short backless gown, where Mom and my clothes were waiting.

"Everything go okay?" Mom said, not looking up from her phone.

"She took three sets of X-rays." I sat on the examining table, leaving the other empty chair for Dr. Mwesi. I hated this bright, shiny little room. The gray examining table was padded, then covered with a strip of paper, freshened for each new victim to climb up on and sit, half naked and cold, until the doctor came to stare at her spine.

Mom looked up. "Do you know why?"

I shrugged, settling in for the usual long wait. But the door burst open a second later, and Dr. Mwesi strode in, gripping my file in one of his large, perfectly manicured hands.

"Hello, Desdemona, Ms. Grey," he said in his deep, charcoal voice. He didn't give us a chance to say hello back. "Dez, how has your back been feeling?"

"Well," I said, taken aback at his abruptness. Usually he shook Mom's hand and smiled at me. "Today the brace was super uncomfortable, but I'm used to that."

"More uncomfortable than usual?" At my nod he pursed his lips, then put my file down and beckoned. "Come down off there and let me look at you."

I hopped down and turned so he could look at my back. Mom had her brows knitted together in concern. She knew something was up too.

"I'm just going to open the back of your gown," he said, and did so. Mom got up and came around to look too as he grunted in what sounded like surprise.

"What is it?" Mom said. "What's wrong?"

"Just one moment, Ms. Grey," Dr. Mwesi said. "Dez, can you bend over and touch your toes for me?"

"Sure." I reached down for my toes, knowing I'd never actually be able to touch them. The years of wearing the brace had cut down drastically on my flexibility. But as I bent, I kept going down farther and farther. Not only did my fingers touch my toes, but my palms hit the floor.

Dr. Mwesi kept hold of my gown as I bent, making sure it didn't gap embarrassingly. He ran one hand down my spine briskly, muttering something under his breath.

Mom said, "Her back looks different somehow."

"Different!" Dr. Mwesi said, his voice booming with atypical emotion. "That is putting it very mildly. Desdemona, please sit down again."

"Different how?" I straightened and jumped back up on the examining table, chilled now down to my bones. Dr.

Mwesi strode over to the computer and typed in a few commands. An X-ray appeared on the oversized monitor. I could see my name in the upper right corner and a date from three months back.

"This is an X-ray of Desdemona's spine three months ago," said Dr. Mwesi. He pointed at the twisted arc of my spine. "As you can see, here is the familiar curve we have seen the past two years. Note this bend here and these here. The angles of the curvature have remained constant since she began wearing the brace. So far, the brace has been a success, a success we had every hope of continuing until her growth period ended and we could take her out of the brace for good."

I stared at the X-ray. I'd been looking at versions of it since I was fourteen, dreading the news that one of the curves had gotten worse, terrified to hear that I'd have to have surgery to place an iron rod in my spine. That fear had kept me faithfully wearing the brace twenty-three hours a day for two years.

Dr. Mwesi hit a key, and the X-ray changed. Again my name appeared in the upper right, with today's date underneath. "This is the X-ray of Desdemona's spine today. I didn't believe it myself until I examined her just now."

I stared at the image. The vertebrae there lay straight as the spine of a book. The curvature we'd been tracking for years had vanished.

"I have never seen a spine this straight in my twenty years of practice," Dr. Mwesi said. "We all have some curvature. Most of the time it isn't dangerous. When it is, like Dez's, we do our best to catch it while the individual is still growing to prevent it from getting worse. But no one has a spine this straight. No one but Desdemona, apparently."

"That's me?" I said.

"I cannot believe I'm saying this," Dr. Mwesi said, blinking at me. "But this is you. I never would have believed it if I hadn't examined you myself. But the scoliosis is completely gone."

Astonishment filled me. *It's got to be a trick, or a mistake.* I felt for the edge of the examining table for support.

Mom sat down hard in her chair. "But that just doesn't happen."

"No, it doesn't," he said. "At least, not until now. I'd like to take some photographs of Desdemona's back and have my colleague Dr. Jessup come in and examine her as well, if that's all right with you both. We need a second and perhaps a third opinion on this situation, and it needs to be monitored very closely."

"That's why the brace felt so awful today," I said faintly. "Since last night it felt wrong."

Dr. Mwesi nodded. "It doesn't fit you anymore. We'll need to make a thorough list of all your recent activities and probably do some more tests. This is—this is most unexpected."

For the next hour a parade of doctors came in and looked at my spine. They poked at my muscles, prodded my vertebrae, took blood, urine, and several more X-rays. Dr. Mwesi finally sent us home with the brace in hand, telling me I wouldn't need it for now. He worried that my muscles would be too weak from years in the brace to support my newly straight spine and arranged for a generic elastic support for me to wear whenever I wasn't sleeping. The nurse would be calling to set up physical therapy sessions to build up the strength in my back to prevent a possible relapse.

But my back didn't feel feeble. Without the brace I felt light as a feather. In the car on the way home, Mom and I sat in silence as her favorite opera played on the radio.

I twisted to look at the backseat. There sat the brace, leaning to one side, lonely as a skeleton. And here I sat, wearing only a soft elastic band around my waist, able to twist. I ran one hand down my side and rested it on my stomach, something I hadn't done in two years. My big dress draped over my flat belly and the points of my hip bones. They looked unfamiliar, as if my body belonged to someone else. This body had no sharp edges, strange bumps, or squared-off shapes. I was soft, slender, strong.

"How do you feel?" Mom said.

"Weird," I said.

"It is pretty strange." We headed down Kenneth Street toward home. She looked in the rearview mirror at the brace. "I'm afraid to get rid of it."

"I know. What if I relapse or something?" I said. "It happened so fast. Let's wait a little while. Do you think it would burn?"

"Probably melt, if we could make a fire big enough." She smiled. "How about next month we have a big, poisonous plastic bonfire at the beach?"

I laughed. "We could roast marshmallows over it and die."

"Best Christmas plans ever," she said.

"Mom?"

"Yes, honey." We turned into the driveway.

I plucked at the fabric over my torso. "Do you think maybe I could get some dresses that have waists?"

"Of course!" She turned the key, then patted my knee. "We'll go shopping this weekend. You'll need new jeans, new skirts. I think I've got a dress that's too long for me that would look good on you. Come on, let's go see."

The afternoon passed with no thought of homework as we raided Mom's closet and dug deep into mine, looking for clothes that would flatter my waist, tiny thanks to years of being squeezed by the brace. When Richard came home, I greeted him wearing Mom's green wrap dress. At the good news, he danced me around the living room, his hand lightly on my waist. I couldn't remember the last time I'd felt anything other than plastic there.

It wasn't until after dinner that I remembered that Caleb was supposed to call me. I double-checked my cell phone and tried to pay attention to my biology homework. But the words swam before my eyes. My mind kept zooming back to how I'd left him by the tree to hunt down the Tribunal's hard drive all by himself. Had they caught up with him? Maybe he'd tried to steal a phone and been caught by the police.

I volunteered to take the trash out. I rolled the bins out to the curb, then walked a block up and down Kenneth Street, looking for the white BMW.

The stars looked cold and lost in the vast sky above me. I stared up at them and tried to summon the feeling I'd had in the school bathroom that afternoon, to tap into the creature that lay hidden inside me. I imagined my senses coming alive again, my hearing sharpening, my nose able to distinguish the smallest odor.

I inhaled deeply and caught the scent of warm pavement cooling in the night air, the sharper tang of the cypresses, the exhaust of a car as it rolled by. But it was nothing like I'd sensed earlier that day. My ears caught the rustle of the wind in the trees, the bark of a dog down the street, my own heartbeat. But they didn't sound any different from any other night of my life.

I scanned up and down the street again, saw a skunk walk unhurriedly across the road, watched a neighbor draw his curtains, and the faint light of the not-yet-risen moon rim the edge of the hills. The night was beautiful. A longing to venture out into it, to make it my own, stole over me.

By eleven o'clock I wished Mom and Richard a good night and forced myself to lie down in my bed. After a minute I got up and stared out the window. It was my first night in two years sleeping without the brace, now shoved into the back of my closet. I should be rolling around in the blankets, enjoying the feel of the soft mattress beneath me, able now to lie on my stomach and not just my back. But I couldn't enjoy it.

I picked up a book. Enough streetlight spilled through my window to allow me to read *No Exit* for English class without turning my lamp on. I'd often read late into the night this way, so that my mother didn't see the light under my door. Did other kids read like this? Or had it been my tiger night vision at work all those years?

I must have dozed off at some point, because I woke up and looked at the clock. 3:18 a.m. I stretched and noticed the window screen fluttering.

Then I saw the figure at the foot of my bed pointing a rifle at my heart.

I gasped, electrified by fear. Then I rolled. Something whooshed past my shoulder and thunked into the mattress. I fell to the floor on my back. The figure, all in gray with a ski mask over his face, aimed at me again. I spun to my feet, faster than I thought possible. Another missile punched into the floor. It was a dart, just like the one they'd used to kidnap me the first time.

"Demonspawn," said the intruder.

My mother's scream echoed down the hall. My whole body vibrated as something thumped hard against the floor next door. My parents' room. Behind the tiny mouth hole of the ski mask, the man was smiling.

He pumped the long gun to prime another dart. I dove at him low, catching him at the knees. He stumbled back, arms flailing, and crashed into my dresser. I grabbed the butt of the gun and wrenched it from him. He scrambled away from me as I aimed it at his chest.

"You can't escape," he said.

"*I* was just about to say that," I said, and pulled the trigger.

He grunted as the barb stabbed into his stomach. So much for my aim. He pulled it out, but his eyes were already closing, and he slumped to the floor. I eyeballed the gun. No more darts. I flung it at the man's head and missed.

My mother shrieked again from the other room. I leapt

over to my nightstand and grabbed my phone, dialing 911. The phone beeped. The display read "Call Failed." My phones were always mysteriously breaking, so I redialed frantically, but got the same message. Had they knocked out the cell tower?

I threw down the phone and hurtled out of my room. Over my rapid breathing I heard a struggle in my parents' bedroom, my mother's third cry suddenly cut off.

I crouched at the closed door to their room. A man whispered, "Hold her still, you fool!"

I pushed the door open. In a second I took it in: Richard lay unmoving on the floor, the sharp smell from the tranquilizer darts coming from his neck; a blur of two men fought with my mother, her head covered in a black hood. Her arms flailed at them, her legs kicking wildly. One man turned his head as I entered. Behind the gray ski mask I recognized his brown eyes—Lazar.

White heat poured down my spine, fueled by a furnace in my heart. Something ripped across my shoulders and down my arms. I fell onto all fours and shook off the shreds of my pajamas. Power coursed through me, flexing the great muscles in my hind legs, forepaws, and jaw. My claws dug into the carpet as my whiskers fanned out, assessing the currents of the air in the room. What had been blurry and dark before now came into crystal-sharp focus. I could smell the hot blood near the skin at their necks. Nothing would stop me from sinking my teeth into them.

I leapt as Lazar's eyes widened. He shouted "Shifter!" He let go of my mother to spin out of my way.

The other man holding her was not as fast. I landed almost on top of him, grabbing his shoulders with both front paws. He screamed as I dug my claws in. The screaming stopped as I sank my teeth into his throat. The blood ran hot and sharp over my tongue. I let him go and he flopped to the ground like a rag doll. A syringe rolled out of his lifeless hand. It smelled like Richard's neck.

My mother scrambled away from me, ripping the hood from her head. Her eyes bulged in terror. But I couldn't worry about that now.

I turned to Lazar. Something thudded into my side. Searing pain slashed down my body. A guttural yowl escaped me. I smelled more blood, my own.

Lazar held a shiny pistol, exactly like the one we'd found in the BMW. Smoke rose from its barrel. He'd shot me with a silver bullet. As he raised the gun to fire again, I saw that he was fast.

But he was human. I was not. Silver or no silver, I was faster.

I lashed out, claws extended. He yelled in pain, and the gun flew out of his hand. Dark blood ran down his fingers.

He stared at me, backing up toward the window. "You will go back," he said, and I felt the deep harmonic thrum in his voice. "Go back to the demonlands . . ." He raised his arm to point at me, and I realized he was going to send my tiger-self back into shadow.

Pushing back the agony of the bullet the way I had shoved back the pain of the brace for two years, I dug my back legs deep into the carpet and launched myself at him. My head and left shoulder slammed into his torso, and we both flew backward. We crashed through the window behind him, smashing it to pieces. The ground came at me fast. Instinctively I spread my legs out, bending ankle, knee, and shoulder joints as we landed.

Lazar lay beneath me, eyes closed. I smelled more blood oozing from new cuts on his back and legs from the broken window. I butted my nose against him, sniffing. His breath came shallow and fast. He didn't flinch as I rolled him. He was out cold. I bit gently into his backpack and lifted him as a cat lifts a kitten. He was heavy, but nothing I couldn't manage.

I paused to look around, ears cocked. A light went on in the neighbor's bedroom. Better for them to see just a broken window than a tiger with a man in her mouth. I put my forepaws on the windowsill and dragged Lazar back inside. Maybe if we kept the lights off, no one would notice the broken glass. Some of the shards sliced through my fur. None of it hurt like the silver bullet. Fiery bursts of pain spread outward from where it lay in my side, sickening me.

I dropped Lazar onto my mother's rug and bounded over to Richard's prone body. When I looked up, she was standing in the doorway. She stared at me with a mixture of fear and wonder.

"What have you done with Desdemona?" she asked, but not as if she expected an answer. She lifted her arm and pointed the shiny gun at me. Her hand shook, and the muzzle of the gun wavered. She must've checked my room, seen that I was gone, and grabbed Lazar's gun.

I needed to tell her who I was, but all I could do was utter a sort of growling whine. She swallowed, and I wondered why she didn't just shoot. Her eyes flickered down to Richard's body, lying beneath me. She didn't want to miss or wound the tiger further, in case that tiger took it out on her husband.

I leaned my head down to Richard and licked his face. Mom inhaled with fear as my tongue rasped over his cheek. Richard's breath warmed my whiskers. I could hear the blood still pumping through him. He was only unconscious. As I lifted my head, I saw her eyebrows come together in a question. Then I backed away from Richard. She kept the shaky gun trained on me.

I stopped to paw the backpack off of Lazar, not worried if he took a few more scratches. I picked the pack up in my mouth and tossed it toward Mom. She stepped back in shock as it landed at her feet. I turned my back to her, walked to the far corner of the room, and lay down. The bullet in my side throbbed with every breath. Blood oozed down my leg.

Mom stood there for another long moment, the pack at her feet, the gun trained on me. "Goddess help me," she said, her voice wobbling more than the gun. "There's a tiger in my house."

The pain in her eyes made me desperate to speak to her. But I couldn't. I shut my eyes and thought about my human arms and legs, my long red hair, my green eyes, hoping my coiled tiger form would shed itself to reveal me beneath. But nothing happened. I had no idea how to change back.

Mom was looking down at Richard, tears in her eyes. Then she glared at me. "I need to call for help, but I can't leave him here with you."

I nodded my head. It felt unnatural in this body, but I did it.

Mom's eyes widened. "Did you just nod at me?"

I bobbed my head up and down.

"This is insane," said Mom. I couldn't shrug my tiger shoulders, but it was so true. "You attacked those men, but not me, not Richard. And you threw this pack at me. Do... do you want me to look inside?"

I nodded again vigorously. "Okay." Mom wiped her free hand across her eyes and crouched down by the pack. "I've gone totally crazy and I'm taking orders from a tiger."

I dipped my head again. She shook her head in disbelief as she unzipped the backpack and reached in. "Drugs." She pulled out a bottle and peered at the label. "Some kind of tranquilizer, and syringes!" She pulled out a syringe in a tube. "Is this what they put in Richard? What they wanted to do to me?"

I nodded, very low and emphatically.

"But why?" she said. "And where did you come from? Where's my daughter?"

Bam, bam, bam! A fierce pounding on our front door

echoed through the house. Mom startled to her feet, forgetting to point the gun at me.

"Dez!" It was Caleb's voice, shouting at the front door. My heart jumped; my ears pricked. He was all right. And he had come back to me. "Desdemona, it's Caleb, let me in!"

"Caleb?" said Mom. "Desdemona's Caleb? What is he doing here?" She raised her voice. "Call the cops! Get an ambulance! We've been attacked, and there's a dangerous animal in here with wounded men!"

"Mrs. Grey?" Caleb's voice came down in volume, but was no less urgent. "Mrs. Grey, let me in. I can help you. I can explain everything. Don't worry about the tiger, she won't hurt you."

"How did he know . . ." She looked at me in astonishment, then yelled louder. "How did you know about the tiger?"

"I told you, I can explain everything." Something moved in the lock on the front door. Caleb's voice became smooth and soothing as a velvet blanket. "Dez showed me where you hide the front door key, so I'm going to let myself in. I'm a friend, don't worry."

Mom took a deep, calming breath. "Okay, but move slowly. I've got a gun on the tiger, but it's already wounded and I don't know what it'll do."

"Wounded?" The front door burst open, and I heard feet moving swiftly toward us. Before I could see him, I heard the unique beat of Caleb's heart, the determined pattern of his footfalls. Maybe I would live through this night after all.

CHAPTER 10

Caleb stood in the doorway of my parents' wrecked bedroom. I'd never seen anything more wonderful. His black eyes took me in. I got to all fours slowly, torrents of agony rippling down my side from the silver bullet still lodged there.

As I moved, my mother aimed the gun at me again, glancing back at Caleb a few feet behind her. "Be careful. It's wounded, and it killed one of those men."

But Caleb's eyes didn't waver from me. An awestruck smile lit his face. "Magnificent," he said, walking toward me. "My God, Dez, I should have known you'd be this glorious."

His voice warmed me. But my mother shot him a look you'd give a crazy man. "Don't get any closer! I might have to shoot it."

"It's all right," he said, eyes fixed on me. "She saved you, didn't you, Dez?"

"Stop calling it that!" Mom's voice hit an edge of hysteria. I couldn't blame her.

"No," Caleb said, in the most reasonable voice in the world. "No, because you see, this is your daughter. This tiger is Desdemona."

Mom frowned, incredulous, as Caleb edged toward me, reaching out his hand. I walked to him, my head as high as his chest. He flinched backward involuntarily, eyes wide, as I got close. I knew then how terrifying I must look if even he could not contain his fear.

I sat and bowed my head, to show him he had no cause for alarm.

"I'm sorry, it's just . . . instinct," he said, and knelt in front of me.

I let out something like a meow. Caleb leaned in and rested his forehead against mine. We breathed each other's breath. Calm flooded over me. We would get through this together.

My mother cleared her throat. "Is this *your* tiger?"

Caleb laughed, tracing one of the stripes on my left front paw with his finger. "Tigers don't belong to anyone," he said. "But this is your daughter. She has a special gift, and we need to get her back to her human form so we can help her." To me, he added, "You're wounded. Let me see."

As my mother shook her head and mouthed "No," I lowered myself with a groan to lie down on my unwounded side. Caleb examined the oozing hole in my flank.

"Looks like the bullet is still inside her," he said, looking up at my mom. "Is that the gun that shot her?"

She looked blankly at the gun in her hand. "Yes. But I didn't do it. He did." She pointed at Lazar, still lying unconscious on the floor. "And they shot some kind of tranquilizer into my husband. There's another man in gray in Desdemona's room, but he's out cold."

Caleb smirked at me appreciatively. "Took care of him too, didn't you?" To my mother, he said, "They wanted to kidnap all of you. They'd keep you and your husband as hostages to make sure Dez would cooperate with them and not try to escape again."

"Again?" My mother's voice shook, and she hunkered down suddenly, head drooping, as if overtaken by emotion. "I don't understand."

"Okay." Caleb's voice smoothed out. "It's time to show, not tell. Your daughter here is wounded and unable to change back into her human form because she hasn't learned how. So I'm going to help her. Then we'll figure out how to get her and your husband some medical assistance."

"I'm going crazy." Mom's voice cracked. I stretched one paw toward her, my heart aching. But she just drew back in fear.

"No, you're not," said Caleb. "Watch."

He shrugged out of his coat and draped it over me, covering me from shoulders to the base of my tail. He grabbed a handful of fur on either side of my head and looked into my eyes. "I'm going to help you push your shadow form back into Othersphere. I don't know how it'll feel on your end, but it'll probably help if you concentrate on making that happen."

I nodded, wondering how he was going to do it. Wasn't pushing back shadow something that the Tribunal specialized in? Did callers do that too?

He moved back to stand next to my mother. "Keep your eye on the tiger," he said. Then he hummed lightly, up and down the scale, as if searching for the right note. His black eyes fixed on me like laser sights. I stared up into them, hoping to hear something that would make me remember my weak human arms, my thumbs, my tiny jaw, my feeble ears, my fur-free skin. They all seemed now as distant as the stars in the sky.

As Caleb hit a midlevel note, his eyes flared gold. My hackles rose. I shuddered, flexing my paws. No fingers there yet, but for a moment I had a visceral memory of what it felt like to make a fist. Mom looked back and forth between us and took a step away.

Caleb slid back to that note, narrowing his eyes in concentration. I shut my eyes, leaning into the sound. I imagined myself human again, fragile, tool-using, able to laugh and speak.

"Return," said Caleb in that same tone, pointing at me. "Return to Othersphere."

My fur rippled, as if in a strong wind. I pinned my ears back, willing my tiger self to waft away. The tremor inside me grew, and something reached out from within. A strange pain, like scratching an itch, tore the skin from my bones. I roared. The roar swept upward and became a scream. The pain vanished. And I was a naked human teenager, huddled beneath Caleb's long black coat.

My mother's eyes were as round as quarters, her mouth fallen open.

"Mom—" I sat up and gathered the coat around me.

Caleb staggered sideways, shoulders slumping. He put his hand to the wall to steady himself. I stood up, tying the belt of the coat around me, and moved to him. His eyes were blank gold, staring through me. "It's okay," I said. "Come sit. Mom, help me get him over to sit on the bed."

"Desdemona," Mom said flatly.

"It's really me, Mom." I slid Caleb's unresisting arm around my shoulder and guided him over to the bed.

"Little cub," said Caleb absently, sitting heavily onto the rumpled sheets. "She is too strong for him to eat her now."

Goose bumps prickled up my arms at his words. Caleb had babbled like that right after working his magic two other times that I'd seen, and it was all probably nonsense. But then why did it give me the chills?

"I think he gets this way if he overexerts himself doing his . . . thing," I said to Mom.

Mom dropped the gun and hurtled into me. Her arms wrapped around my waist, squeezing till it hurt. "I'm okay," I said into the top of her head. "I'm sorry."

"They shot you!" She turned my back to Caleb and opened the coat to see my wound. Even as she poked at my side, I realized that the pain from the bullet was gone. The skin where the injury should've been was smooth and unscarred. All the other cuts and scrapes I'd gotten moving through the broken window were gone as well.

Mom looked as if her head was about to explode. "What happened? Was it all just some horrible hallucination?"

"No," I said. Caleb held his head in both hands, elbows leaning on his knees. My glance fell on a small piece of shiny metal lying on the floor in the middle of a red stain, where I had shifted back into human form. I picked it up, and it stung my fingers, a heavy piece of silver that looked like a squished gray raisin. "Look."

Mom grabbed my hand to get a closer view. "That's what they shot you with?"

Caleb looked up. The gold was fading from his eyes. "You ejected the bullet when you shifted."

"Shifted." My mother sank down next to him, as if her legs couldn't support her.

"We need to get you out of here," said Caleb.

"Stop!" Mom held up both hands, her voice quavering and shrill. "Nobody's going anywhere. What about Richard? What about these men? *What the hell is going on?*"

Caleb and I exchanged glances. "How about I tell her while you go through the backpack?" he asked. "Maybe there's something in there that can help Richard."

"Should we call the cops?" I asked him.

"And explain the marks on these Tribunal guys as what, a grizzly bear attack?"

I nodded and went over and kissed Mom on the cheek.

"Listen to Caleb, Mom. He's going to tell you what's going on."

Her lips got very thin, but she nodded. Caleb launched into a down and dirty explanation of Othersphere, shifters, and the Tribunal as I emptied the remaining contents of Lazar's backpack onto the floor. As Mom hovered over Richard, checking his pulse and asking terse questions, I lined up all the syringes and drugs. Nothing was labeled, and it all looked the same. I also found another magazine of bullets, which didn't look silver, and one that did, rope, duct tape, and lock picks.

"Nothing here to help," I said, as Mom pillowed Richard's head on her lap and clucked her tongue over the story of the Tribunal's crusade against the otherkin.

"I knew that the world was more fantastic and complicated than it seemed," she said. "But the Wiccan traditions don't cover this!"

"Don't forget to search the other guy," Caleb said to me, pointing at the other man, lying on the far side of the bed.

He went back to his explanation. I stood and walked closer, steeling myself. The man lay on his stomach, face to the floor, or what was left of his face. A large pool of blood had collected beneath him. The top half of his head still wore the gray ski mask. But most of his throat and lower jaw were gone, bitten off. I glimpsed a broken upper tooth and the white gleam of a neck bone amidst the raw red flesh before I turned away, stomach churning.

I had done this. I had killed a man.

Someone took my hand. I turned to find Mom, her eyes welling. I hadn't heard her conversation with Caleb stop.

"I always knew you were special," she said. "My faery child."

I laughed shakily. "So, you believe us?"

"What else can I believe?" She threw her hands up. "The Goddess knows the world is full of wonderful things. And you are one of them. Now, with my own eyes, I've seen past the veil. Short of waking up to find this is all a dream, there's no other explanation."

I nodded, but couldn't help looking again at the body of the man I'd killed.

Mom took my hand again. "You had to," she said. "You saved us."

"I'm sorry, Mom," I said. "I'm the thing that brought this down on us."

She squeezed my hand hard. "Don't you ever apologize for who you are," she said. "I'm very proud of you."

"Thanks," I managed to say. "How's Richard?"

"Sleeping hard, but otherwise okay, I think." She wiped at the blood on my cheek with her thumb. "Even if we can't wake him, Caleb says he'll come out of it eventually. You should get dressed. Caleb and I will search the other men for the antidote. Then we need to figure out what to do."

"Okay." I looked over at Caleb. He stood, hands thrust into his pants pockets, black hair falling over his eyes. "You'll look after her?" I said.

"I'll look after her," he said. It sounded like a vow.

I headed for the shower. I turned the water to scalding and scrubbed at the blood caked all over me till my skin turned bright pink.

All the cuts and bruises on my body were gone. I stopped scrubbing as a thought hit. The shift had healed me completely. If the shift could heal cuts and bullet wounds, maybe it could heal bones as well. Maybe the shift that happened yesterday, my first, had healed my scoliosis and straightened my back. The doctors had said it was a miracle. Maybe it was actually shadow.

I finished, got dressed, and hurried down the hall to tell them my theory. Caleb looked up from a pile of equipment and listened intently. "That makes sense," he said. "I'm no expert on scoliosis, but shifters don't get cancer, and if they get a cold or an infection, all they have to do is shift, and they're fine. So when you shifted, you healed your back."

"But then," I said, thinking hard, "shifters must live for a long time, like, over a hundred years or something."

"They can live for hundreds of years, actually, unless they're killed outright," he said.

"Hundreds of years?" It was my turn to sit down on the bed, my knees weak. My mother got up and sat next to me, putting a comforting hand on my knee.

"Every mother wants her child to live a long life free of sickness and pain," said Mom. "Another dream of mine you can make come true."

Tears stood in my eyes. It was all too much. "But what are we going to do? They'll keep coming after us."

Caleb sat back and looked at us both very sternly. "Dez must come with me to a school for otherkin up in the Sierra Nevada Mountains. It's small and very secret, and we'll be safe there."

"A school?" I turned to Mom.

"Your parents will be safer with you gone," said Caleb.

"No," said my mother. "I can't let her go, not now. Not when she needs me most."

My chest felt tight. It had all been my fault. If I hadn't been here, Mom and Richard would never have had to go through this. If I'd stayed in that orphanage in Russia, everyone would be a lot safer.

"You can't go with us to the school, Mrs. Grey," Caleb said. "If they sense anyone who isn't otherkin approaching, they'll vanish. You and your husband will need to go somewhere for a while. Otherwise the Tribunal will try to kidnap you again so they'll have a hold over Dez."

Mom exhaled forcefully. I was staring again at the man I'd killed. "Okay, now listen to me, Desdemona. I know you. You're blaming yourself for all this, but it's not your fault.

Blame the people who attacked us—the Tribunal—and then move on. Do you hear me?"

"Yes, Mom," I said. Her strength and support only made me want to cry more, but I swallowed my tears. There wasn't time for me to be self-indulgent now. Caleb was right. I was the source of danger. The only way Mom would ever let me go was if she thought it was best for me.

"You have to let me go, Mom," I said. "I need to learn about myself, how it all works, and more about these men, and about others in the world like me. And it sounds like this school Caleb heard about might be able to give me the tools I need."

"The leader of the school is Morfael," Caleb said. "He's a very old, very powerful caller of shadow. My mother spoke of him with respect. She told me that if anything happened to her, I should seek him out. Dez and I should be safe with him, and we could both learn a lot."

Mom looked back and forth between us. "You're very clever, appealing to my maternal instincts." She got up and paced, then clapped her hands together. "Sounds like Richard and I will be going on a long, much deserved vacation."

"When will I see you again?" I said, hating how wet and sticky my voice sounded.

"It won't be long. I'll create a new e-mail address before you leave and give it to you. Once you get to Marfy . . . Morfael's school"—she stumbled over the odd name—"you can e-mail me the phone number there, or give me a new e-mail address that you've created. And Caleb will tell me all about the location of this place. If we can't get in touch somehow, in a month, Richard and I will come and find you."

"Do you think we'll ever be able to come back here?" I asked. The house was old and a bit of a mess, but it was home.

Mom shook her head. "I'll have to talk to Richard about it, but we'll figure out a way to be together."

This was the right thing, but I hated it.

"Okay," I said. "What do we do now?"

"We clean up, pack, and leave. Then your mom wakes up Richard." Caleb held up a vial of yellow liquid, very different from the clear doses of the tranquilizer we'd found along with the syringes. "We found this in the other guy's backpack. It's labeled as an antidote to the sedative Richard's been given. They must've brought it along in case one of them accidentally got shot with tranquilizer."

"Oh, thank goodness." I hugged Mom. "But what about them?" I pointed to Lazar and the body of the other man. "And the one in my bedroom?"

"We leave them," said Caleb. "Ximon will send a clean-up party, probably very soon. He'll take them away, leaving as little trace as he can."

"I guess it's best if my daughter goes with you," Mom said, her voice firm. "But don't you get her into any more trouble than she's already in, young man."

He gave her a regretful smile. "I don't make promises I can't keep, Mrs. Grey."

"Call me Caroline," she said, then leaned in to me and added, so that only I could hear, "I know you'll be strong and smart about what you do and who you do it with. I'm trusting you."

"I hear you, Mom," I said.

"Okay." She patted me and stood up. "Time to get going."

It didn't take long to pack with Mom helping and Caleb chiming in. Before I knew it, Caleb was carrying my suitcase out to the BMW while Mom brought my back brace and a credit card. I had already stuffed my own stash of a hundred and twenty dollars in my backpack.

"Cash advance just down the street at that ATM," she said, as I put the credit card away. "That way if they're tracking my finances, they won't know where you're going from there."

I nodded, then watched as she put the brace in the BMW's trunk and slammed it shut. "You think I might need that?"

She shook her head. "I don't know why, but I feel like you should have it with you." She tried to smile. "Maybe it's the Goddess whispering in my ear. Maybe it's your crazy mother's whim."

"That's good enough for me," I said. "And you've got the antidote for Richard."

Her mouth widened into a genuinely rueful smile. "How the hell I'm going to explain all this to him, I have no idea. But we'll be checking into a hotel as soon as he wakes up. You've got my new e-mail address, now, right?"

"Yes, Mom." I couldn't stand looking at her, stalling, longing to stay with her, to help her. Better to get it over with and leave now, before I broke down and never left at all.

"I love you, Desdemona." Her eyes were wet.

I hugged her so tight she had to ask me to ease up. "Love you too, Mom," I said, and strode off to where Caleb and Lazar's BMW waited.

Mom watched us drive off, not waving, just looking. I turned to look back at her just before we turned the corner. She was still standing there.

CHAPTER 11

The night loomed black, thick, and full of weird portent as we drove. To distract me while I sniffed quietly and tried not to think how I was leaving everything I knew behind, Caleb told me where he'd been and the way he'd tracked down the hard drive holding the Tribunal's camera feed.

They'd lodged it in a fake utility box, and Caleb had disabled it while a crazy lady in the apartment next door yelled what sounded like Klingon at him out her window. He'd continued to lurk nearby until a white van and two Tribunal guys showed up. Then he'd snuck into the van and watched as they attended to two cameras trained on my house and three on my school. Problem was, Caleb couldn't get out of the van before they hit the freeway north. He'd been stuck there till they stopped in Valencia for gas. From there he'd hitchhiked back. That's why he'd been so late. I didn't ask where he'd acquired his new, fancy-looking cell phone.

As we got onto a smaller road and wound our way up the Sierra Nevada Mountains, he asked, "Can you dig out that map your mom gave you? Look for Coyote Peaks."

I pulled the Thomas Guide for California out of the side pocket and found our location. "We've got to tell the people at this school where the Tribunal's compound is."

"Good idea," he said. "They need to avoid it."

"Or fight them," I said.

He cast me a surprised look. "Fight them?"

"Don't you think the shifters should, you know—clean them out? I mean, that's what the Tribunal's doing to us, right? They kill us off or capture us for experiments as soon as they find us. We'd all be better off if they were driven away or . . ."

"You really want to kill them all off?"

I swallowed. There'd been enough killing for me tonight. "Or we could, like, just destroy the buildings, force them to relocate, shut them down somehow. We can't let them stay there. Even if you and I manage to avoid them, they'll just find some other shifter to capture and do Lord knows what to."

"I see what you mean, but I wouldn't hold my breath expecting Morfael or the shifters to do much," he said. "The different shifter tribes don't like each other. They've never banded together to do anything except argue in Council. And the individual tribes are all scattered, hiding from the rest of the world. None of them is strong enough to go against the Tribunal alone."

"But the Tribunal's everyone's enemy, right? Think how much safer we all would be if everyone banded together and got rid of them."

"You're talking about going against thousands of years of traditional hatred," said Caleb.

"But I can't go home as long as Lazar and all of them are

there," I said. "Me and Mom and Richard, we'll be on the run for the rest of our lives!"

"Welcome to being otherkin," he said, shaking his head. "Did you find where we are on the map?"

I was frowning in frustration. I didn't want to live always having to look over my shoulder. More importantly, I didn't want the fact that I was a shifter to ruin the lives of my family. I forced myself to look at the map and found Coyote Peaks. "We just keep going on this road," I said. "Do you know where to go after Coyote Peaks?"

"I think so. Mom made me recite it, like, a hundred times."

He had mentioned his mother a number of times, but all I knew so far was that she had been a caller, and now she was dead. "How long is it since she . . . since you last saw her?" I asked.

"You mean since she was killed?"

"Killed?"

"The Tribunal murdered her." The muscle in his jaw tightened.

"I'm so sorry." I touched his arm briefly.

"Feels like a lifetime ago, and it feels like yesterday."

"So you have no other family? No brothers or sisters?"

He didn't say anything for a long moment. His eyes flicked back and forth on the road ahead, his brows drawn together, as if he was trying to keep some dangerous emotion from erupting. "No," he said at last. His voice was tight. "No one."

"Sorry," I said again. "I didn't mean to pry."

Caleb just stared down the dark road ahead of us. In that silence I thought how I might never see my house in Burbank ever again, that Mom's and Richard's lives were in complete upheaval. I was headed into a forest filled with people who could change into hungry animals, taught by a powerful wizard type who could manipulate the very shape and matter of things.

And I had killed a man. I'd crunched his bones and swallowed his blood, and I hadn't even blinked when I did it. That was the heritage my mysterious biological parents had given me. Maybe it was better to never know them. It might've been better if I'd just put up with the damned brace for a bit longer and never shifted into a tiger. But then I'd never have met Caleb.

Caleb craned his neck, staring down the road ahead. "Okay, we're getting close. Expect a lot of suspicion. It's how they are with everyone, let alone an abandoned tiger. They won't like me much either."

That surprised me. "Why?"

"Callers don't like to hang out with other callers," he said. "It gets competitive. So I hope Morfael remembers my mother fondly. The shifters won't like me either because they hate anyone who might be able to control their shifting ability. Morfael's school is the only one of its kind I've ever heard of."

"But you said we'd be safe there." Trepidation jittered up and down my spine.

"Safe from the Tribunal," he said.

That didn't comfort me much.

We wound up a two-lane road into the mountains. Trees encroached, blacker than the night, and a thousand stars pocked the sky above. We passed a sign that said COYOTE PEAKS.

Then Caleb drove past a smaller dirt road, barely as wide as the Beemer. "That was it, I think," he said, and turned the car around. We hadn't seen another vehicle in half an hour.

The tires crunched over a large tree branch. Leaves scraped against the windows as foliage focused the headlights down to a narrow beam. A faint glow above us signaled that dawn was not far off.

"We have a habit of driving together at sunrise," I said.

"I can think of lots of better ways for a boy and a girl to

spend the night together." He glanced at me from under his brows. Then he looked back at the road, leaving me breathless.

Shoving down the riot of feelings inside me, I squinted into the darkness. A wall of trees put a stop to the road, with no sign of a cabin or path. "It's like the road just . . . ends."

Caleb put the car in park and turned off the ignition. We peered at the silent woods around us. "What now?"

"I don't know." He put the keys in his pocket. "Mom said to just follow the road and find the camp there. But I don't see any camp."

"It's probably not far . . ." I began to open my door, but he put a hand on arm, pulling me back inside.

"Wait. If the camp's nearby, they'll know we're here."

"Oh." Approaching the secret camp of a hunted group could be dangerous. Out in the dark, bears and wolves probably lurked, waiting to tear us to pieces. "I wonder if this car smells like silver or the Tribunal or anything."

"It'd be better if you shifted," he said. "If a tiger got out of this car, they'd know we're otherkin."

"Shift here, now?" I pulled as far away from him as I could to my side of the car. "I'd fill up the whole car, break the windows or something."

"Not if you got in the backseat," he said, sounding very reasonable. "I could help you out of your clothes first so you don't tear anything."

I swiveled my gaze to him, raising my eyebrows. His face was carefully blank. "Oh, you'll help me get naked, will you? How thoughtful. And then what? I don't know how to shift, remember? Or will you find some way to piss me off and push me to change . . . some very teenage boy in a backseat with a naked girl kind of way?"

He laughed. "It was just a thought."

"Scalawag," I said. "How about we roll down the windows and shout for Morfael, saying that your mother sent us? He knew her, right?"

"I think so," he said, leaning toward me. "But can we take that chance?" I could smell his scent, like an oncoming storm, and feel the heat emanating from his skin. Up close his eyes were pools blacker than the fir trees against the night sky.

I wanted him to put his strong hands on my shoulders and pull me into him, even though there might be wild animals outside waiting to kill us. Or maybe that thought made me want him even more. I'd killed a man that night, and barely escaped capture myself. Life could vanish in an instant. I moved toward him the barest distance. Our lips almost touched.

Bending at the waist was alien after two years in the brace, and suddenly I felt vulnerable, unarmored, without it. And I remembered my mother, telling me how much she trusted me. How she knew I wouldn't lose my head during these difficult times.

"Yes," I said, and pulled away, my head spinning. "We'll take that chance."

He breathed deep, looking as if he wasn't sure where our conversation had been going. "All right," he said. "But my way's better."

"Ready?" I said, not looking at him.

"Here goes." He turned the car key to give the windows power, and then inched the driver's window down.

I reached across him to turn out the headlights. My arm grazed his chest, and tension strained between us. I clicked and pulled back. The forest was plunged into darkness. "A shifter wouldn't need light," I said.

He nodded, then yelled out the window. "Morfael!" His voice echoed between the trees. "We were sent by Elisa Elazar, caller of shadow."

Outside, nothing stirred. My eyes adjusted to the dark, and I saw nothing but trees and the lightening sky. "Maybe waiting in the car isn't the right thing to do, etiquette-wise," I said. "It makes it look like we don't trust them."

"We don't." Caleb rolled the window down further. "Morfael, we are friends! Elisa Elazar sent us to learn from you."

Again, only silence came back to us. "Oh, the hell with this," I said, and got out of the car.

"Dez, wait!" Caleb grabbed for me, missed, then scrambled out of his side.

I slammed my car door, filled with a sudden desire to get this over with, one way or another. The night had been too long and full of uncertainty. For a moment, I listened. The forest was too quiet.

"I know you're there," I said in a normal tone of voice. "We really need your help."

I walked to the front of the car. Caleb joined me, turning his back to mine, so that we faced in opposite directions out into the forest, ready.

Silent as nightfall, a man moved out of the trees only twenty feet away. Gaunt as a starving man, he stood well over six feet, clad all in black, his bony hand resting on the head of a long wooden staff. I couldn't see the shapes carved on it, but they seemed to writhe beneath his grip. His long hair lay limp and white against his skull, his eyes, so light a blue as to be almost translucent, took us in. Goose bumps prickled my skin from head to toe. Here was power. It swirled out of him, coiled and unpredictable as a tornado.

A huge winged form arced down from the sky to land on a tree branch above the man's head. A bald eagle over four feet tall gripped the limb with talons as long as my hand, its yellow eyes focused on me.

Then I saw the others. A wolf the size of a Great Dane, eyes glowing in the dawn light, hackles raised, crouched on the other side of the car. On the other side of Caleb, a mountain of a bear stood on his hind legs, then shook the ground as he thudded his forepaws to the earth. His thick brown fur glistened with dew.

"You are not welcome, caller of shadow," said the gaunt man. His voice reverberated within the walls of my chest. He turned his strange light eyes to me. "You are not welcome, Amba."

I didn't know that word, but I felt as if I should. He aimed it at me like an arrow.

"We mean you no harm," I said. "And we have nowhere else to go."

He didn't answer. Somewhere high in the trees, a lark began to sing a song to the rising sun. The bear shifted his weight, scraping his huge black claws against the dirt, as if eager to use them on us. No one else moved.

Caleb cleared his throat. "My mother, Elisa Elazar, told me I could find shelter with you here. Dez did not know until yesterday that she's a shifter. We ask your help."

"I know who you are," said the man, who had to be Morfael. "Your mother was almost as reckless. Danger follows you. You come here only to escape. You may not stay."

"Please." My voice broke as a terrible desperation filled me. "It's true we're running away, but we're trying to run to the right place. And I've got information that'll help you fight the Tribunal."

The bear snorted. Every muscle in me tensed. If he lunged at us, we'd never get into the car in time. Morfael's pale eyes assessed me without expression. His thin frame, white hair, and pointed cheekbones gave him an unearthly appearance, like something out of a twisted fairy tale.

"Your heart is not here," he said. "You will learn nothing."

He was right. All my life I'd wanted to know more about my heritage, but now that I was here, I longed to be with my mother and Richard, back in the days before any of this had happened. I didn't want to camp out in some dark woods with people who turned into carnivorous animals and a guy who spoke and looked like someone out of *The Lord of the*

Rings. When I'd wondered about my biological parents, I never thought they'd be shifters or Ambas, or whatever the hell he'd said.

"That's true," I said. "I don't want to be here. But I came anyway, partly because I need somewhere safe, but also because I need to find people like me. I have to accept what's happening or I'll go crazy. And we share a common enemy. If we don't help each other out, they'll kill us all, one by one."

Something sparked in Morfael's pale gaze that reminded me of the gold glow Caleb's eyes took on when he used his power. "You shall be tried." He tapped his staff on the ground and something shuddered through the earth, like a noise too low to hear. The ground beside him yawned, making a black hole in the soil, ringed with rocks like jagged teeth.

"Come," said Morfael, jabbing his staff toward the maw in the dirt. It was less than three feet high, descending sharply into darkness. Behind us, the wolf and bear closed in. To get back to the car we'd have to move past them.

Caleb let go of my hand, moved to the hole, and got onto all fours. "I'll go in front," he said. "Follow me." He crawled headfirst into the cave.

"Good thing I'm not claustrophobic," I said, getting down on my hands and knees. I looked at Morfael. His thin lips twitched in the specter of a smile. But was he happy in a "you go, girl" way or in an "oh, good, my earth monster will have a nice breakfast" way?

Darkness swallowed me. The dirt was cold and moist beneath my hands. I could still feel and hear Caleb shuffling along in front of me. The rich, loamy smell of earth enveloped us. After moving in a few feet I risked a glance back. There was no break in the blackness, no slice of starry sky or last sight of the Beemer. We were trapped.

CHAPTER 12

The dark pressed against my eyes, as oppressive as a bright light. I usually liked small spaces, but anxiety washed over me when I wondered what weird things Morfael had planted ahead.

"The cave closed up behind us." My voice sounded oddly muffled.

"Surprise," said Caleb. His voice also seemed distant, but his sarcastic tone comforted me.

"It's opening up ahead," he said, and I felt his movement change. His hand took my elbow and pulled me up as the space around me expanded. I stood, pressing against his lean, warm frame. His arm slid around my waist. I started to pull away, a reflex. But then as his fingers moved over my hip I remembered that I no longer wore the brace. Instead of being hard and unyielding, my body felt smooth, pliant.

"Hey," he said softly, his breath tickling my ear. "It's pretty cozy in here. You think Morfael did this so we could make out?"

I laughed, stomach fluttering. "So that's his nefarious plan."

His arms tightened around me. His lips pressed against my temple, sliding down to my cheek. A furnace ignited inside me, every inch of me aflame and aware of his skin, his hands, his mouth. So this was what it was like, to have someone desire you, to want nothing more than to keep touching forever.

Something flickered in the corner of my eye, like a reflection on water.

"What's that?" he said, straightening. His voice sounded thick, reluctant. "Maybe I'm just seeing things."

"No," I said, also unwilling but remembering where we were. "I saw it too."

Something flickered again, and this time I saw a form silhouetted against the light. Then it vanished.

"We'd better take a look," he said, cupping his hand around my cheek before loosening his hold on me.

"Yeah." I moved around him to see better, straining against the dark. "How freaky is this?"

"At least we're together," he said.

I tried to reach for his hand but couldn't find it in the darkness.

The faint whoosh of running water hit my ears. "I hear a stream or something," I said, walking a couple of steps closer to the sound.

"No, it's wind." His voice was distant again. "Over here."

"I swear it's water," I said. The sound deepened. "Over here."

He didn't reply. I turned around but found only blackness. "Caleb?"

No response. My heart skipped several beats. I swatted the air where he had just stood. "Caleb? Where are you?"

I called out his name as my outstretched fingers hit a wall of dirt. I kept my hand there as I walked around, only to come back to the flickering of light on water and splashing in the distance. Caleb was gone.

"Morfael, you bastard." The sound of my own voice heartened me. "I was just about to get my first kiss covered in dirt in a mystical cavern."

No one answered. Nothing to do then but move toward the sound of water and see what came next. Rounding a corner, I squinted into a splash of light and found myself alongside a river, green with white firs and walnut trees. Red beams of dawn arrowed between the trunks. Behind me lay a sheer rock wall, and no sign of where I'd come from. Nice trick. I would have loved this place, so peaceful, so untouched by man and machine, if it hadn't felt like a trap.

"Caleb?" I moved closer to the water. A sheer drop plummeted down to a rushing stream at least thirty feet across. It curved sharply to either side, pinning me up against the wall of rock. To get anywhere, I would have to cross the stream.

I paced down the riverbank. The water looked swift, cold, and deep. I was a strong swimmer, but no way could I safely get across. A fallen tree lay across the stream close to where it ran into and under the wall of stone. The trunk spanned the river, resting on opposite banks like a weathered footbridge.

Would it hold my weight? Rubbing my chilled hands together, I bent over and leaned onto it. It didn't bend or sway.

I stepped cautiously up onto the tree and inched out. The ground dropped beneath me, replaced by gray water. I tried not to look down. One foot stepped slowly in front of the other, my sneaker treads gripping the wood. I was almost halfway across when I forgot and looked down. I laughed and swore. The plunge down into the water looked ridiculously high from here.

"Desdemona!"

I turned my head and nearly fell. Bending my knees, I grabbed the log, regaining my balance. Behind me, her short dark hair tousled by the morning breeze, stood my mother.

"Sorry, honey," she said, her eyes widening with fear. "Please be careful!"

"Mom? How did you get here?" She looked as solid as the log I stood on.

"Richard and I followed you." She beckoned. "Come back this way. I'm here to take you with us."

I looked around the forest, waiting for the punch line. "That doesn't make any sense."

"Desdemona." Her voice cut at me with a mother's concern. "It's far too dangerous for me to explain while you balance like that. Come here, and I'll tell you everything on the way back."

"But there's no way out back there..." I trailed off as I saw a jagged opening in the rock wall behind her. It hadn't been there before, had it? "I can't turn around, Mom."

"Of course you can. I'll help. See?" She moved over to her end of the log and stepped on top of it, reaching her hand out. "Just take my hand."

She smiled, and warming reassurance rushed over me. Everything was going to be all right now. I didn't have to leave my home and my family and go off to live in the woods with crazy people who thought they were animals. I was just a normal girl, heading back home to live a normal life.

I inched back toward her. She edged out a little, and the log rolled slightly. I bent over to clutch it, struggling for balance. "No! Don't! You're going to knock me off."

Bending felt wrong. *Oh, right, no back brace.* Feeling normal whirled away like dandelion fluff on a day when the Santa Ana winds blew.

"You won't fall if you come back," Mom said, leaning out to me. Her hand was pretty close. If I took a step toward her, I'd probably be able to grab it. "You'll be safe, I promise."

I wanted to believe her. But she'd said exactly the wrong thing. "You can't promise me that," I said. "No one can." I stood up slowly and began walking very carefully toward the other bank.

"You'll never make it that way!" She jumped off the log onto her side of the bank. Her leap rocked the tree trunk violently back and forth. I spread my arms wide, trying to sway with it.

I risked a glance at her. Her eyebrows were drawn in a terrible frown. "You're going to fall," she said.

"Then I fall," I said.

And I did.

The splash into the freezing water took my breath away. If this was all some kind of dream or hallucination, it sure didn't feel like it. I kept my mouth and eyes shut and kicked off my shoes. Water roiled around me. I reached up and tried to find air.

My face broke the surface and I sucked in a huge grateful breath. The current was bearing me rapidly downstream. The banks of the river whipped past. I thudded into something hard, a submerged rock. Pain stabbed through my thigh, but the water swept me on. It hurt to kick now, and the cold invaded my skin, penetrating to the muscles. Moving my arms took effort. I tried to push myself across the current to the bank, but the relentless flow beat me back to the center.

I gasped, and water trickled into my lungs. *Oh, God, I'm going to drown.* My arms and legs felt like lead.

I have to shift. As a tiger I would have the power to get to the riverbank. The process of shifting should heal my injured leg and keep the hypothermia at bay.

But I'd never shifted of my own accord, and I'd been unable to shift back to human form, even when my mother, my real mother, had a gun on me. Despair leeched more vigor from my muscles. *What a stupid way to die.*

The banks of the stream raced past me, blurring into a streak of brown and green. Anger pulsed through me at the injustice and waste of it all. That pulse felt like the fury that had pushed me to save my mother a few hours ago.

I put my head down into the water and curled into a ball, nurturing that determination and rage. It connected to something that burned at my core, black and infinite. I imagined breathing on the flames there, pouring all my thoughts, all my energy into that center. Like a stab of lightning, that nucleus flared outward, radiating out of every limb, out of my eyes, ears, and mouth. I flung out my arms and legs. Wet cloth shredded around me, then washed away. I flexed my powerful back legs and felt the rocky river bottom beneath my paws. With a mighty push, I moved like a striped submarine through the current toward the shore, paddling with my forepaws.

Water weighed down my whiskers and my tail, but where its cold had nearly frozen me stiff before, I now only felt a slight chill. I gulped down some water and tasted the cool moss and wet stone it had rolled over. The riverbank no longer looked so steep. My paws hit bottom without reaching. I leapt, feeling the power in my muscles, and landed on dry grass.

I shook myself. The twisting began at my head and traveled all the way down to the tip of my tail. Water drops flew from my fur, thudding into the bushes and leaves around me. It felt so good to stretch and shake and move. I was alive and whole, strong and lithe.

I looked up to see Morfael not ten feet away in his long

black robes, clutching his pale staff with its twisting figures. I held still, waiting.

"You are welcome, Amba," he said, his voice as clear and cold as the river water. "Come."

He turned and moved deeper into the woods. Even with my ears cocked, I could barely hear his footfalls. Then I followed him into the trees, more silent than he.

CHAPTER 13

I awoke sometime later on a narrow bed. Someone had covered me with a rough blanket. I could feel that I was human again and fully dressed except for my coat. My hair was dry and not as ratty as it should have been. Looking around, I saw that I lay on the bottom of one of two bunk beds in a snug wooden cabin. The room was large enough for the beds and a small kitchen against one wall, with a mini fridge, sink, and some counter space. A jute rug covered most of the floor. I spotted two doors and decided the bigger one led outside while the other led to another room.

The sound of running water behind the narrower door confirmed this. It opened to reveal a petite girl about my age wearing scuffed brown cords, boots, and a long sleeve T-shirt in pink with the words "Anderson's Pawn and Loan" printed across it. She hummed under her breath, then looked up, as if she'd felt my gaze. Her small eyes were dark brown, the same color as her short hair, which stuck out at odd angles. Her alert face was pointed, sharp.

"Awake, I see," she said. She smiled, revealing her upper and lower teeth. "About time. You cats sleep the day away given the chance."

So she knew I was a tiger-shifter. That disoriented me, but it didn't seem to faze her. "How long have I been asleep?" I asked.

"Twelve hours or so, since Morfael carried you in just after dawn. I'm November, by the way." She smiled again but didn't come forward to shake hands. "What's your name?"

"Desdemona," I said, sitting up. "Dez for short. I've heard of girls named April, May, and June, but never November."

"Eleventh month," she said. "I'm the eleventh child." As my eyes widened, she nodded. "And the other ten are all brothers. Can you imagine?" She moved toward the mini fridge. "You don't look Chinese. Or Indian."

"I was born in Russia," I said. "Raised here." She was getting a lot of information out of me fast. I decided to turn the tables. "Where are you from?"

She pulled a sandwich out of the fridge and unwrapped it. "My dad has a business in Oakland."

"Anderson's Pawn and Loan?"

"Exactly." She took a couple of small bites from the sandwich. Something about the way she held it in both hands made me realize what she was.

"You're a rat," I said. It sounded weird or even insulting to my ears, but she nodded and kept eating.

"Pretty sharp for a cat," she said. "But your kind used to hunt our kind, didn't they?"

"They did?" She had been keeping herself as far from me as possible. She didn't appear afraid, but she also wasn't coming closer.

"Siku heard you grew up not knowing you were otherkin," she said. "Is that true?"

"Yeah," I said. "Who's Siku? That's an interesting name too."

"He's the bear-shifter in the boy's cabin, from Alaska," she said. "Bears, cats, and raptors are usually indigenous. So Arnaldo lives in Arizona, but he's descended from the Aztecs or something. Siku's Inuit, I think. Grizzly bears are native to America and so is Siku, if you see what I'm saying."

"I think so," I said, working it out. "Tigers live in India and Siberia, so tiger-shifters are all Indian or Russian or Chinese in their human form. Lions are African, like that."

"You learn fast." She had finished her sandwich and began licking her fingers. "You're kind of an anomaly, you know. Shifters keep close track of their kids as a rule. There are so few of us, each one is precious, blah blah blah. We try not to kill shifters from other tribes now, much as everybody hates each other. The Tribunal's picking us off quickly enough as it is."

I was still working out what I'd just learned. "But your last name is Anderson," I said. "That doesn't sound very Native American."

"Oh, rats and wolves get around," she said. "Particularly the rats. The European division of the Tribunal had a bug up their butts about wolves for a few hundred years, calling them werewolves and so on. A few wolf-shifters are still there, but a lot of them ran off to America, Asia, Australia. So here in America you've got both Native American wolf-shifters and European types."

"What about the rats?"

She ran her hands under the faucet, then dipped her head to catch the water stream in her mouth for a quick drink. "Washing cups is a pain," she said, drying her hands and face. "We rats are not as territorial as the predators, and we pump out the kids faster." She waggled her eyebrows. "So we keep spreading out, finding new spots to live. My family's originally from Sweden, but we came over a hundred and fifty

years ago, been in Oakland for a few decades. We don't mind
cities the way you fangy types do."

It made a kind of sense. Rats flourished on every continent, in all sorts of environments. "Why don't the different
tribes get along?" I said. "Bears don't eat eagles. Cats don't
eat wolves, generally."

"You're all predators, competing for the same resources,"
she said. "Out in nature you don't see panthers and bears
being buddies, helping each other out. The Shifter Councils
formed only because the Tribunal presented a common
threat, and they only convene if they have to."

"The Shifter Council?" So much to learn.

She cocked her head. "You really were raised by humdrums, weren't you? Siku thinks Morfael should kick you
out, even argued with him." She shook her head. "Bears
aren't very brainy either. He should've known the old man
would give him the smackdown."

"Let me guess," I said. "Rats are the brainy ones."

"Yep, and the friendliest." She hoisted herself up to sit on
the counter. "Everyone else is muscle."

"I get it," I said. "You don't want to get eaten, so you need
to be smart, friendly, and manipulative."

Her lips twisted in an appreciative smirk. "Like I said,
pretty smart for a cat."

My stomach rumbled with hunger. "Any idea where my
stuff is?"

"Under the bed," she said. "Siku refused to carry your
bags in, so Arnaldo had to shift into human form and do it.
He's not crazy about you either."

"Well, I'm crazy about him," I said. She barked a short
laugh. I reached under the bed and pulled out my suitcase.
My coat lay on top. "And Arnaldo is . . . ?"

"Eagle-shifter and resident geek." November opened a
cupboard, took a lollipop out of a bag of sweets, and unwrapped it. "This is his second time at Fur and Feather

School, and everybody knows it's a disgrace not to graduate in one year. But he sucks at shifting back to human, and if you get less than a gibbous moon grade average, you have to come back and get labeled a complete loser."

It took me a second to figure out what she was saying. "You get graded in phases of the moon?"

She frowned at me, like I'd asked the dumbest question yet, then smiled. "Oh, right, you humdrums get letter grades or something stupid like that, don't you? Yeah, we get graded so that our parents can see if we're progressing. I don't know if Arnaldo'll graduate this year, again. Can you imagine failing out twice? He'll never be leader of his tribe and might never find a mate. London's doing pretty badly too. She's a wolf-shifter. Her real name's Laurentia, but we all call her London. She hates it."

"Why London?" I shook off the blankets and swung my legs over the edge of the bed.

"You don't know that song? 'Werewolves of London'?" She hopped down and did a couple of improvised dance steps, humming.

I blinked at her. She rolled her eyes. "Wolf-shifters hate being called werewolves."

"And here I thought I was escaping the politics of high school." I stood up and rolled onto my tiptoes, stretching my hands toward the rough ceiling. It felt so good to let my rib cage expand and to arch my back. How had I put up with the brace for two whole years?

She stuck the lollipop in her mouth and smiled around it. "Otherkin politics are worse."

"So the school has a bear, a wolf, a bird, and a rat," I said. "No cat?"

She shook her head. "No cat-shifters old enough to attend this year. Not till you came along. Morfael only takes one shifter from each North American tribe per year, so each

tribe sends whichever kid is doing the worst, figuring they
need his help the most."

"Help with shifting?"

"Shifting, otherkin history, all the basics of how to get by
in this crazy world. You'll see. It's not exactly an honor to attend this school, but it's better than never learning how to
shift properly."

"Did you see when Morfael brought me in?" I asked.

"Yeah," she said, muffled around her sucker.

"Was I in human form?"

"Morfael's strong for a skinny-ass caller, but I don't think
he could've carried a tiger," she said. "You're big enough as
it is."

"Was I, like, wet? And undressed?"

She raised her eyebrows. "Nope."

That was weird. Had Morfael dried me off and dressed me
in the woods? Or maybe . . . a light went on. Maybe the
events at the river hadn't happened, except in my head. "I
guess I passed the test," I said.

"You're still here, aren't you?" She spread her arms wide.

"Did you see the guy who came with me, Caleb?"

"The evil eye-candy? Yeah. He's in the boy's cabin. You
can imagine how excited Siku is about that."

"Caleb's only semi-evil," I said.

"But one hundred percent candy?" Her lips curved around
the lollipop stick.

"What's Siku got against him?"

She shrugged. "Everybody hates callers. Morfael's tolera-
ble because he helps us, but most callers are manipulative
bastards who get off on forcing us to shift. They lie at the
drop of a hat."

"So do you," said another voice. A lanky girl with a stony
face stood framed in the front doorway. Her long hair was
dyed black, showing light blond at the roots. It lay flat and

stark against her lightly tan skin. Two silver nose rings curled around her nostrils. Her sky-blue eyes slid like laser beams over me and took in November sucking her lolly. She didn't look impressed. "Dinner in five." She turned around and left. The door thumped closed behind her.

"And now you've met London. Isn't she charming?" November pulled a sweatshirt off the counter and slipped it over her head.

"Is that attitude a wolf thing?" I said, grabbing my coat.

"Nah, just a London thing. Can you believe the fake nose rings? Such a poser."

"How do you know they are fake?"

"Because I see her shift three times a day." When I looked blank, she rolled her eyes. "Shifting heals everything—tattoos, piercing holes, scars where losers like London like to cut themselves just to feel alive. Only thing you can change is your hair, since it's not living tissue. She'd be covered with tats of skulls and other clichés and punctured like a pincushion if she could. But she has to settle for a bad dye job and fake piercings."

"Must be frustrating, not to be able to express herself the way she wants." I put on my coat.

November smirked. "Self-hatred's a bitch, and so is she. Nice coat. But better not wear it during exercises or it'll rip when you shift."

"I hadn't thought of that," I said. "Do we have classes at night or something?"

"We have them whenever Morfael feels like it." Her eyes flicked to the door, then back to me. I stood between her and the exit. *Am I really that scary?* I felt about as frightening as a sleepy toddler. How long would she stand there if I didn't move?

"After you." I gestured toward the door.

She narrowed her eyes and smiled, as if in on some secret joke. "Don't play with your food."

I stared at her. Wow. These people really thought I might eat them. "I couldn't even cut up a frog in biology," I said. "Don't worry about me."

"Uh-huh." She didn't relax, but waved her hand at the door. "Just go already."

I suppressed an urge to lunge at her just to see what she would do. Instead I walked to the door and opened it.

Fresh forest air filled my lungs. The sky had darkened to indigo, although streaks of reddish purple still painted the fat clouds above me. The cabin stood in a cleared area surrounded by trees. An identical cabin faced the one I was in, about thirty yards away. Both cabins looked rough but sturdy, built to last, not to impress.

To the left lay a larger, weirder wooden structure built against the face of a sheer granite cliff. It looked like something out of a bedtime story. The curved roof met the walls at a precarious angle and had mistletoe and mock orange growing out of it. The door was more of a trapezoid than a square. The heavy logs around it looked more like living trunks of black oaks than lumber, sprouting out of the roof with a vigorous burst of leaves. I half expected a cloud of fairies the size of dragonflies to flutter out of the triangular windows. *It's been grown, not built.*

A hulking boy with straight dark hair loose down to his waist lumbered up to its door, then turned to stare at me. His thick brows lowered over deep-set eyes. His cheekbones were high and sharp. Given his huge size, he had to be the bear-shifter, Siku.

Not sure what else to do, I raised my hand. His expression didn't change. Then he opened the crooked door and went inside.

November slipped past me in a skinny blur, trotting toward the funky house. "Hurry up," she said over her shoulder.

I followed her slowly, buttoning up my coat against the

chill. Where was Caleb? I walked faster. Maybe he was in there with the other kids. I got warm all over just thinking about seeing him.

Up close, the building looked surreal, like I was viewing it in fantasyland hi-def. Climbing fig vines shiny and green as jade twisted up between sugar pines with bark like scraped chocolate and knotholes so much like eyes that I expected them to blink at me as I opened the warped door.

Inside lay a large, dark room with uneven wooden walls and a small hawthorn tree growing in the middle of it. November slipped through a door to the left, but I stopped to take in everything around me. To one side flames crackled in a huge fireplace next to a rickety, spiral staircase made of living branches covered with tiny leaves like green fur. I walked over to its base and looked up, but caught only a glimpse of a room opening up to the second story. A deep red leather sofa squatted nearby with a boulder serving as a coffee table.

I opened the door November had gone through and found a smaller room filled with a huge stone dining table. Chairs of different woods surrounded it. The surface teemed with steaming ceramic cups and platters filled with roasted meats, broccoli, corn on the cob, and bread. My mouth started watering, until I saw every face turned to me, and the fairy tale feeling fled. If Morfael's earth maw had been available, I would've gladly crawled inside.

Morfael sat at the head of the table, his narrow face as pale as ever despite the heat rising off the food. His moonstone eyes sent a chill through me. Siku towered to his right, plate in hand as if about to serve himself. His fist tightened around his fork as he glared at me.

Next to him sat another boy, maybe a year or two older than I but skinny as a pencil with an unbecoming line of black bangs falling into his coffee-colored eyes. His smooth skin was almost the same warm brown color, but he didn't look comfortable in it. His bony shoulders stooped forward, as if trying to hide his thin chest. Gawky elbows jutted into Siku's space. His head looked too big for his long neck, and his Adam's apple bobbed as he swallowed a bite of fish and stared at me. This had to be Arnaldo, the eagle-shifter.

London sat on Morfael's other side, shrunk down in her oversized black clothes, eyeing me, her plate empty. Next to her, November was smirking and looking around to see what everyone thought of me. The verdict did not look positive.

Caleb walked in from what had to be the kitchen, holding a big wooden bowl full of salad, and his eyes went straight to me. He didn't say anything, just set the bowl on the table and sat, ankle crossed over his knee. I sat next to him, wanting to take his hand, to talk to him alone and to find out what he'd seen after we'd parted under the earth. But this was not the time.

"If you pray before meals, do so now," said Morfael, his voice clear and cold. "There is much to do tonight."

"I'm good, thanks," I said. "This looks delicious."

As if freed from a spell, everyone unfroze and turned to the food, passing dishes back and forth in silence. Despite her heavy snacking in our cabin just minutes ago, November had her plate piled high and was tucking in with verve. Caleb uncrossed his legs and leaned forward, reaching for the platter of roast turkey. He was tense, angled away from me.

I grabbed a hunk of soft brown bread, sliced off a creamy slab of butter. "You okay?"

"Basically." His eyes slid over to me, eyes burning in a way I'd never seen before.

"What . . . ?" I began.

But Caleb interrupted, saying to Morfael, "What plans do you have for us tonight?"

I buttered my bread until I poked holes in it, trying to distract myself from my tumbling thoughts.

Morfael considered Caleb. "You and Desdemona will attend a meeting of the local Council within the hour."

Caleb stiffened as Morfael continued. "The rest of you will go to your cabins and shift to animal form and back again once more. Your cabin mate must witness this shift and report your success to me. If you're unable to complete the change back, I will tend to you when my meeting is done."

London frowned and grabbed a pork chop as Siku groaned and kept eating the pile of strawberries dipped in honey he'd accumulated on his plate.

"What about November?" Arnaldo said.

November made a tsk noise. "Big mouth."

Arnaldo pulled out a phone and pressed a button. "According to my log, November only shifted once today."

"You keep a *log?*" London asked, then looked surprised she'd said it.

"Geek!" November sang out.

Arnaldo ignored them. "The rest of us shifted twice; the first time when we went to greet *them* at five forty-seven a.m." He jerked his head toward me and Caleb. "So this will be our third shift, but only November's second for the day. It's not fair."

Morfael's pale eyes rested on Arnaldo, and Arnaldo got very still. "And what makes you think," Morfael said, his voice soft with a hiss of menace, "that I am concerned with being fair?"

Arnaldo shrank back in his chair. "I . . . I just . . ."

"Do not question my lessons again," Morfael said. Arnaldo flushed and said nothing more. Morfael resumed cutting up his steak with short, precise strokes of his knife.

It was quiet except for the various sounds of everyone slurping, chewing, and clanging their silverware.

"Why," I said into the quiet, "are we meeting with the local Council?"

November's eyes got very round, and London darted a nervous look at Morfael.

Morfael finished chewing. Apparently he liked to take his time between pronouncements. "Your arrival here is unprecedented," he said. "The parents of my current students would rightfully be displeased if I took in two strangers, one with no lineage, the other not a shifter, without clearing it with the Council."

"I can't pay tuition, if that's what you're worried about," Caleb said, shoving himself away from the table. "Dez's family might manage it."

Something sparked in Morfael's pale eyes, but I couldn't tell if it was amusement or anger. "If the Council votes in favor, you may stay until the end of the term, on scholarship. At that point I shall review your prospects."

"Who exactly sits on this Council?" I asked. "I like to know who's judging me."

"Every region on every continent has a local Council with five members," said Caleb, when Morfael did not respond. "One from each tribe. I bet all Morfael had to do was say 'tiger' and they all came running."

"Why are you consulting them?" I said to Morfael. "Do shifters rule over callers or something?"

As soon as it came out of my mouth I knew it was the wrong thing to say. Morfael's head reared back, his eyes alight, and everyone else at the table tensed. Caleb's mouth twisted, as if holding back an incredulous smile as he looked at me. "I mean," I said, stumbling onward. "I don't understand how this world is organized. That's all. "

The corners of Morfael's mouth curled upward. For a moment I didn't recognize the expression; then I realized he was smiling. The other kids didn't get it either, exchanging surreptitious glances with each other.

"Come, eat," said Morfael, stabbing a piece of meat with his fork. "We have little time."

The tension eased enough so that everyone began eating

again. Under the table, Caleb's hand touched mine. My heart lifted, and I curled my fingers around his. "Nice move," he said under his breath.

"You'd better explain this to me later," I said. "Or the next thing I say is going to get me killed."

CHAPTER 14

We helped the other kids clean up as Morfael vanished behind another door, telling us he would come for us soon.

When Caleb and I had a moment alone gathering empty dishes on the table, I lowered my voice and asked, "What happened to you? Where did you go when we got separated?"

He gave me one quick glance, then looked away. "Nowhere."

I stopped, holding a bowl full of salad dregs. Caleb's tone was light, but something in it rang false. "You must've seen something. I had this whole weird thing with my mom trying to stop me from crossing a river, and I fell in the river and had to shift to save myself. But when I woke up in the cabin, I was dressed and dry, so maybe it all just happened in my head."

"It was probably a dream if your mother was in it," Caleb

said. "I didn't have anything like that. Just wandered out of the tunnel and found the school. I was worried when we got separated, but then Arnaldo told me Morfael had walked back with you."

He kept gathering the plates, and I now felt sure he was lying. I put my hand on his arm. "Why don't you want to tell me?"

"There's nothing to tell, okay?" he said, and walked through the swinging door into the kitchen.

Morfael broke through my jumbled thoughts when he appeared and beckoned. Caleb and I followed him back out into the first living room area, expecting to go outside and maybe head deeper into the woods to find the Council's meeting place.

Instead, we went farther into the strangely angled house, through a wide door into a room lined with heavy shelves and row upon row of books. I barely had time to register the overstuffed chairs, low lamps, and dusty rolls of what looked like parchment before we went through another door.

Space gaped around us. We were in a cave. The house must have been built across the mouth of a deep opening into the cliff. Now we were inside the mountain, complete with a dirt floor, stalactites jutting down from the ceiling, and a yawning darkness ahead.

To the left someone had laid down rubber flooring and placed various pieces of gym equipment. I spotted a battered heavy bag, a gymnast's vault, parallel bars, and rows of free weights. Backed up against the wooden wall of the house was a jarringly modern computer area.

Morfael grabbed a black ring set in the wall, then pulled down a white vinyl screen, like the kind my teachers used for PowerPoint presentations. As Caleb and I stood there, he tilted a tiny camera at us, then clicked his mouse.

"The Council's deciding our fate via video conference call?" I asked.

"What were you expecting?" Caleb said. "Some kind of tribal circle with war paint, drums, and talking sticks?"

I almost said yes, but Morfael gave us a flinty look. "I will speak first," he said. "Do not speak unless a member of the Council addresses you directly."

"But we need to tell them about the Tribunal facility where we were kept in the desert," I said. "They need to know where it is, what they do there..."

"Speak only when spoken to." Morfael's voice cut through mine.

I shut up and nodded. Caleb raised his brows in acquiescence. Morfael clicked his mouse, and five windows appeared on the screen, each featuring an unsmiling adult face. I spotted a woman with tufts of gray hair; a man with wild reddish eyebrows; a sleek, brown-skinned man with hooded eyes; and a woman younger than the rest, her black hair in a messy bun. In the fifth window a heavyset woman with white skunk streaks in her black hair was just sitting down. Morfael gave us one more diamond-hard look, then raised his staff and knocked five times on the wooden floor.

He closed his eyes and lowered his chin to his chest. The five faces on the screen did the same in what looked like a ritual. Caleb pointed at the woman with the tufted gray hair and mouthed the word "cat."

I nodded, fascinated. So she was the cat-shifter in the group. Caleb pointed around the ring of faces rapidly as I memorized what he told me.

Man with bushy, red-gray eyebrows: wolf.

Man with hooded eyelids: hawk.

Woman with her hair in a messy bun: rat.

Woman with the skunk streaks: bear.

He was still pointing at the bear-shifter when they all lifted their chins. Caleb casually moved his pointing finger to scratch his nose. All eyes, flat, hooded, baleful, or indifferent, stared at us from the screen.

"It's late, so let's get down to the business at hand," said the cat-shifter. "Morfael you all know. Some of you have relatives who have attended or are attending his school. Welcome, Morfael."

Morfael bowed his head an inch to her. "Greetings, Chief of the Council, Lady Lynx."

So the cat-shifter was a lynx. Her ruddy brown skin, round dark eyes, and mussed gray hair looked more like a lady lumberjack than a wild predator.

"Moon above, are we going to do the formal set of greetings and all that bull?" The wolf-shifter leaned forward, elbows on his knees. "Can we stipulate that Morfael greeted us all with respect and we did so to him in return?"

"Seconded," said the lady rat-shifter.

"I agree, which carries the motion," said the lynx. "And we all know the basic facts. A young caller of shadow and a girl claiming to be a tiger-shifter wish to join Morfael's school until the end of the term."

At the word "tiger," all eyes slid over to me.

"Very well, then, girl," the lynx said to me. "What is your name? And what are you doing in this hemisphere?"

"My name's Desdemona Grey. I'm here because my mom adopted me from Russia. She brought me to California when I was eighteen months old."

"Adopted!" The wolf-shifter's voice boomed in consternation. "A shifter adopted by a family of humdrums? Never heard such a thing."

"What happened to your birth parents?" said the lynx, leaning forward until her nose almost touched the wide angle lens of her camera. "Tell us how you came to be adopted."

So I cleared my throat and gave them a halting account of what my mother had told me: how the reindeer herder had found me in the ring of dead trees in the forests of Siberia; how my mother had then found me in the orphanage. Caleb looked at me. The details of the story were new to him.

"Extraordinary," said the hawk, his tone skeptical.

"No tribe would allow it," said the bear.

"Who knows what the tigers would do?" said the rat. "No one's had contact with them in decades."

The lynx bit her lower lip. "Perhaps danger threatened, so her parents placed her where they thought she would be safe and left to draw the danger away from her."

I hadn't thought of that before. It made a weird kind of sense. But maybe I'd rather believe that than that I'd been left to die.

"Then why haven't they come looking for her?" said the wolf with disdain. "Our kind would move the earth to find one of our cubs and bring them back safe."

"You're assuming her parents survived," said the rat-shifter.

My throat got tight. There was a chance I'd been wanted. But that meant my biological parents were dead.

The rat-shifter continued, "If they both died, the rest of the tribe might assume their child had died as well, and not search for her."

"Both parents dead?" The hawk shook his head. "What could have killed off two tigers?"

"The Tribunal," said Caleb. All eyes moved to stare at him. "I'm sorry. But we all know how powerful the great cat-shifters are. It would take a force armed to the teeth with silver to take out one, let alone two, of them."

"He's right," said the rat-shifter, adjusting her knot of dark hair as it began to tumble down. She stuck a bobby pin in her mouth and spoke around it. "When he requested this meeting, Morfael said that the Tribunal knew of this girl's existence. How did they find her when none of us knew?"

"How they first became aware of her remains unclear," Morfael began.

"They were keeping watch on a lightning tree in my neighborhood," I said quickly, before Morfael could stop me.

Morfael did not turn his head, but his eyes narrowed. On the screen, the wolf frowned while the others looked thoughtful.

"Go on," said the rat. "What happened?"

"I've been climbing that tree since I was a kid," I said, and spilled out the story of my capture, including the location of the Tribunal base.

"That area must be placed under quarantine," said the lynx. "Be sure to alert all family representatives in your tribe so they know to give Barstow and that part of the desert a wide berth. I'll let the Continental Council know."

"What will they do?" I asked, earning another piercing look from Morfael.

All five of the Council stared out at me.

"That is none of your concern, cub," said the hawk.

I took a deep breath to quell the anger rising in me. Didn't they see? "These Tribunal people kidnapped me, then tried to take my family," I said. "If you don't stop them, they'll do it again to someone else."

"Wolves can take care of our own," said the wolf.

"But my family is on the run!"

"That is not our concern," said the hawk.

"How can you not care what happens to other people, people like you?" I said. "We have a common enemy. Why can't we . . ."

"We are not like you," said the bear. "We are bears, ursine, honey seekers. You are a tiger, feline, night prowler."

"But . . ."

Morfael grabbed my upper arm in a viselike grip. "None of this is relevant." His voice cut through my protest and closed up my throat. I couldn't have continued speaking if I'd tried. "I wish to take these two into my school until the end of the term. That is the only matter now before the Council."

"If she doesn't stay within the shelter of Morfael's school, the Tribunal will probably find her and kill her," said the rat.

"That's why we have to keep her away from the school," said the wolf, narrowing his eyes. "If the Tribunal hunts her down there, they find the other children. She's not worth the risk."

"Exactly," said the hawk. "What have the tigers ever done for us?"

The rat-shifter frowned, her straight black brows crowding her dark eyes. "A better question might be: If the situation were reversed, what would we like the tigers to do?"

"Wolf-shifters would never let this happen," huffed the wolf.

"We must try to contact her tribe," said the lynx. My breath stopped at her words. "The tigers must be told she is here."

"Unless the Tribunal has wiped them out," said the bear.

Grave silence greeted this remark. Blood pounded in my ears as I tried to process what they were saying.

The bear fidgeted in her seat. "Murderers. It would explain why no one's had any contact with the tigers for so long."

The lynx shook her head at me. "You, girl, may be the last of your kind."

"But we don't know for sure!" I said, surprised as the words tumbled out of me. "It's just one theory. Is there any way to find out the truth?"

"Let's send a message to the Asian Council," said the lynx. "They may have gained information on the tigers since the last Great Council meeting, or have reports of Tribunal activity that would shed some light on this."

"A lot of fuss for a girl we didn't even know existed until a few hours ago," said the wolf. "Danger follows her, but you want us to agree to shelter her?"

"What if the Tribunal tracks her down to your school, Morfael?" asked the hawk. "You and all your students would be dead."

Morfael's expression did not change, but his eyes held a dangerous spark.

"It's not a risk we can afford to take!" The wolf's voice rose, his face reddening. "Schools should be a safe haven for our kids, but you want to bring this threat inside. The only way to protect our cubs is to keep them hidden. We should kill the tiger-shifter now and tell no one, before her presence destroys us all."

I felt as if I'd been struck. Caleb put his hand on the small of my back as I swayed in shock. "Are you out of your minds?" he said.

Morfael shot Caleb a dark look. Caleb said nothing more.

"Quiet, boy," said the bear. "My wolf-shifter colleague has a point."

I waited for one of the others to tell her not to be ridiculous, but no one did. Nausea curdled my stomach. I'd fled from one murderous group into the arms of another. Maybe these weren't the good guys, after all.

"Think about it," said the hawk. "It solves all of our problems in one fell swoop."

The wolf nodded. "Our children will be safe from the tiger herself and those who hunt her."

Safe from me?

"If we let her go, she might provide a good distraction," said the bear. "She'd pull the attention of the Tribunal away from the school and the rest of us."

"But if they caught her, she'd tell them everything," said the hawk.

"Exactly," said the wolf. "And she might decide to hunt us down in revenge. She must be eliminated."

"So," said Morfael. "Are you asking me to kill her for you?"

All the blood seemed to drain from my body. Growing horror dawned over Caleb's face.

"We haven't cast the vote officially yet," said the lynx. "Let's not jump the gun."

"The Moon knows I'm not comfortable around the big cats," said the rat, "but this one is innocent of any crime. Killing her for convenience is a bit extreme."

"It's not for convenience!" snapped the wolf.

"You'd jump at any chance to kill a cat-shifter!" The lynx spat out the words. "Some things never change."

"As if you don't dream of ripping one of us apart," said the hawk. "You're a hypocrite."

"Hypocrite?!" exclaimed the rat. "Raptors kill my kind too, don't forget."

"We all kill each other, it's the way of things!" shouted the wolf. "Why should we hesitate to kill one who threatens us all?"

They hated each other. I saw that now. And they hated me, feared me, and wanted me dead. Here were people with abilities and insights normal humans would love to have, and all they did was fight amongst themselves, hide, and kill each other.

"What a stupid waste," I said.

The shifters stared at me again.

"Shut up, girl," said the wolf.

"Yes," said the bear. "You've caused enough trouble."

"I think the three of us agree, she must be . . . dealt with," said the hawk. "A three-to-two vote carries the motion."

"Go ahead," I said. "Go ahead and try." Caleb was holding my arm very tightly as I leaned forward, my fingers curling like claws. "You'll be doing the Tribunal's work for them, and I'm sure they'll thank you for it!"

The wolf made a scoffing noise, but the bear cocked her head at me.

"We each look after our own tribe," said the wolf. "As it has always been."

"Good idea," I said, matching his tone. "Because it's worked out beautifully so far."

The rat let out a short laugh, and the lynx half smiled. Emboldened, I went on. "You've been fighting each other for a few thousand years, and in the meantime the Tribunal's destroyed every tribe on earth except five. That's five left out of, what—hundreds? If I'm the last tiger and you succeed in killing me, that's one more snuffed out. *Moon forbid* we help each other and protect each other. It's far more important to maintain a tradition of isolation and murder."

The wolf's brows were ominous, and the hawk looked irritated.

But the bear was nodding. "She's got a point," she said. "It's not as if she's gone rogue. And if she is the last tiger, well, the humdrums call it genocide."

"But you just said . . ." began the wolf.

"I'm entitled to change my mind before the official vote." The bear's lip curled in a snarl. "Back off."

"Shall we bring it to a vote?" said the lynx quickly. "Cats vote to allow Desdemona to stay safely at Morfael's school for the rest of the term."

"Rats agree," said the rat.

"Bears agree," said the bear.

"Wolves vote no!" said the wolf.

"Raptors vote no," said the hawk, "for all the good it does." He leaned forward, did something out of sight of the camera, and his window disappeared from the screen.

"Desdemona Grey, you may stay there until the end of term," said the lynx to me, staring out from the screen with a faint smile. "Hopefully the next vote won't be quite so . . . dramatic."

"Thanks," I said.

"I'll have to consult with Laurentia's family," said the wolf, still glowering. "You can bet, Morfael, they won't be paying your tuition much longer."

His window disappeared as well, and with his lethal glare gone, I relaxed. Caleb's warm hand slid around mine, and our fingers intertwined behind his back, out of sight of the camera. Whatever coldness had been between us had vanished for the moment.

"Remember who stood up for you," said the rat, and clicked herself away.

"Prove yourself worthy of all this bother, please," said the bear.

"I'll e-mail the cat-shifter in the Asian Council," said the lynx. "Maybe he's heard something about the tigers or the Tribunal over there that will help us learn more about what happened to your family. Meanwhile, be good."

She and the bear disappeared from the screen.

I looked up at Morfael's pale, drawn face, feeling a weird mixture of relief and anger. "If they'd decided to kill me, you were going to help them."

Something like amusement flickered behind his opal eyes. "Was I?"

"You asked them whether they wanted you to kill her," Caleb said through his teeth. His lean body was tensed. "I guess my mother was wrong about you."

But Morfael raised his brows, as if asking me an unspoken question.

"You asked them if they wanted you to kill me," I said slowly, remembering his exact words, "but you never said you'd actually *do* it."

A full-fledged smile broke across Morfael's face, crinkling up his crow's feet and baring his narrow white teeth. At first he looked like an alien trying to mimic a human expression. But then I saw real warmth behind his strange-colored eyes, and he looked like a real person for the first time.

"How am I ever going to be able to go home?" I said. "Those people will never stand up to the Tribunal."

"You and your family may go home again," said Morfael. "But it is up to you to find the way."

"Up to me?" I stared at his sunken cheeks and bizarre eyes. "You're the one with the knowledge and experience and the cool magic staff."

Out of the corner of my eye I saw Caleb's eyes widen in alarm. Maybe folks didn't usually talk to Morfael that way.

Morfael considered me, taking his time. He didn't seem offended. But he didn't seem pleased either. "Watch, listen, and learn," he said. "Time to return to your cabins," he said.

"But . . ."

"Tomorrow your education begins."

Moments later, Caleb and I stood outside Morfael's crooked dwelling in the dark. The biting wind whirled around us before it rose to shake the tops of the trees and shove the clouds along.

"That was intense," Caleb said, staring down at me. His wavy hair was the same color as the star-scattered sky above him, his eyes glistened in the light of the waning moon like pools of black water.

"To put it mildly." I hugged my arms around myself, cold in spite of my layers. "And Morfael . . . it's like he knows something, something really important that'll help me go home, but he won't tell me what it is."

"I can't believe you challenged him like that." His half smile faded as he took me in. "You okay?"

A deep trembling had overtaken me. "Why does everyone want me dead?"

He slid his coat off and wrapped it around me over my own coat, his lips almost touching my forehead as his arms briefly encircled me. I wanted to bury my face in his neck and feel those arms hold me tight, so tight I'd stop thinking about the hatred on the wolf-shifter's face. For a moment I thought it might happen, we stood so close. But then he pulled away, rolling his shirtsleeves down against the chill.

"You're not like anyone else," he said. "You're something new. And people fear what they don't understand. Then they want to get rid of it, so they don't have to be afraid anymore."

"You're not afraid of me," I said.

He smiled. "You sure about that?"

I nodded. "Even when I was in tiger form, you treated me like a human being, or whatever the heck I am."

"Such language," he said, smile widening to a grin. "I'm a caller of shadow. When you're a girl, I see the tiger lurking inside you. And when you're a tiger, I still see the girl."

"I'd never hurt you." The wind blew a lock of long red hair across my face. "I want to say I'd never hurt anybody, but I did. I killed that man at my house."

He reached over and brushed the hair out of my eyes. "You were defending your family from a very real threat."

His fingers grazed my cheek, and my trembling increased. I cleared my throat. "But I was so angry, I couldn't even stop to think. As soon as I shifted, it just . . . it happened. I don't want it to happen again without thinking like that."

"That's one reason why you're here," he said. "It's very common for young shifters to lose control while in their animal form. Morfael will help you learn to keep hold of your human side after you shift."

"He's kind of creepy, isn't he?" I said, lowering my voice.

"He's weird, all right," said Caleb, shoving his hands into his pockets. "There's a strange vibration around him I've never sensed before."

I wished the wind would blow my hair across my face again, so that he would touch me. "It's like he's from another planet, or he's studying all of us the way scientists study insects."

"Well, when you think about it," he said, "we're not exactly normal ourselves."

I laughed. "Totally! 'He's creepy,' said the girl who could change into a tiger."

He chuckled. " 'He's weird,' said the guy who can turn rocks into mountains."

The shivering had stopped. It felt so good to laugh. "And I thought it was bad with the brace," I said. "I thought no one would like me because I was this freak, this untouchable monster. Turns out I'm an even bigger monster..." I stopped. I'd just said out loud something I'd never told anyone, even if it came out jokingly.

The smile slid from his face, his dark brows drawing together over his eyes. But the last thing I wanted was for him to feel sorry for me. "Sorry, never mind. Stupid," I said, shaking my head.

He looked at me another second, his face unreadable, then reached up to close the collar of his coat more tightly around my throat. I pulled back out of reflex, but stopped myself. I felt very small, very vulnerable with him so close. He said, "Anybody ever tell you that you look beautiful in black?"

My whole body grew warm and the back of my neck prickled with goose bumps. I stuttered, "It—it goes with my stripes."

Did that even make any sense? "You know, like, when I'm a tiger," I sounded horribly lame to my own ears, but somehow I didn't care.

He smiled in a way that twisted my heart. Keeping his hands on the coat collar, he stepped closer. I tilted my head to look up at him. "Don't ever let anyone make you think you're untouchable," he said, sliding one hand around my neck and up into my hair. "Sometimes touching you is all I think about."

I put my hand to his cheek and felt a deep tremor within. "Are you cold?" I asked.

"No." His gaze slid down to my mouth.

His lips met mine. I kissed him back without thinking,

sliding my hands around him, his heat enveloping me. His arms tightened around me, pressing our bodies together. All my senses expanded. His hands gripped me as if he'd never let go. A small involuntary moan escaped me as I arched into him. His mouth traveled down to my neck, his breath coming fast.

Something in my pocket buzzed. At first I barely noticed it, wanting only to kiss Caleb forever. But then it buzzed again.

He must have felt it too, because he broke away, frowning, and reached into the pocket of his coat, which I was still wearing. He pulled out his vibrating phone.

I swallowed, finding it difficult to wrap my mind around ordinary things like phones. Already I missed the pressure of his arms. But something about his posture struck me as odd as he looked down to see the number of the caller.

"Who could be calling you?" I said. "How do you even have reception out here?"

He shrugged a bit too nonchalantly. "Satellite phone. But wrong number." He pressed the ignore key and slid the phone quickly into the pocket of his jeans. "It's just as well."

"What? Why?" I reached out to him, but he took another step back from me, pulling his coat off my shoulders.

"We should probably get back to our cabins before anyone misses us," he said.

"They're not going to care," I said. "What's going on?"

He put his coat on and turned away from me, walking toward the boys' cabin. I followed him a few steps, then stopped. I didn't want to chase him like a child.

"I can't do this," he said, not looking back at me. "I'm too screwed up for you, Dez. Get some rest."

Then he vanished inside the boys' cabin. I stood there, freezing again, and replayed the last few seconds in my mind. The way he'd grabbed the phone, scanned the number, and hidden it from me so quickly . . . he was hiding something. He'd lied about what had happened to him in the cave, and he was lying now. He'd kissed me, and I could've sworn he wanted to go on kissing me, but something was holding him back. Something to do with that call.

The wind dove down from the treetops and shoved me, so I made my way back into the girls' cabin. I put my hand to my lips; the memory of that kiss still burned there. My first kiss. And it might be the last if Caleb kept acting this way.

Not only did both otherkin and Tribunal want me dead, but a wonderful boy had kissed me and thrown me aside. My biological parents were probably dead, along with the rest of my tribe. The only family I'd ever known was on the run. I didn't know when I'd see them again.

To hell with that. And to hell with this place and the quibbling factions who'd rather kill than compromise. And while I was at it, to hell with Caleb. I needed this school, for now. I would learn how to control my shifting ability. I would find out what Morfael was hiding from me that would help me go home. Then I'd leave this place to be with my real family, my only family.

Inside the cabin it was warm and dark. The top bunks held the motionless, deep-breathing forms of November and London. I undressed and slipped between the cold sheets of my bottom bunk as silently as I could, staring up at the planks of wood over my head until sleep took me.

CHAPTER 15

A slim form with lank hair was poking at my shoulder. "Hey, wake up."

It was London, dressed in slouchy black. I pushed back the strange deadly forms of the dream I'd been having and made my fuzzy tongue say, "What's up?"

"Morning workout in five minutes," she said, and slipped out the front door of the cabin.

I sat up. The place was empty. November must've already left. I hauled myself up, splashed water on my face, threw on some sweats, and stumbled out of the cabin into a lavender fog creased with predawn glow. *God, it must be early.* I hated morning.

Thank goodness I'd seen the workout area in the cave behind Morfael's house last night, or I wouldn't have known where to go. His front door creaked open, and I zoomed through the living room and the library, making note again of the stairs to the second story and the many old books in the library. I needed to explore every corner of the building to find out more about Morfael and what he knew about the Tribunal. The library might have old texts that were relevant, forgotten lore or something else useful. But I was betting Morfael kept his best stuff somewhere secret.

The left side of the cave was lit by harsh fluorescent bulbs. Their greenish luminescence revealed walled-off areas beyond what I'd seen before. All of the kids in the school, including Caleb, looking lean and sunbrowned in black track pants and a T-shirt that strained against his shoulders, were standing on the blue mat in front of Morfael.

As I entered, Morfael didn't bother to turn around, but everyone else's eyes slid to me. I forced myself not to smooth my rumpled hair or rub my bleary eyes. November was smirking, as usual, but all the others looked carefully blank. I tore my eyes from Caleb and marched over to stand next to London on the mat.

Morfael was saying something about focus, but all I could think about was Caleb standing behind me. *Stop it! Think about how you're going to get home, not some annoying, gorgeous boy who can't decide if he likes you or not.*

I was last in line for a trip through a makeshift obstacle course. It included things like high parallel bars, a twelve-foot-high wall, a low table to crawl under, and tires to run through. Morfael did not speak, just tapped his staff to indicate the next person should race as fast as possible through the course.

"Why are we doing this?" I said under my breath to London as Arnaldo leapt surprisingly high over the wall, all gawky arms and legs.

"Some bullshit about how exercise integrates mind and body," she whispered.

Morfael glanced at us sharply, and London shut down.

For an hour Morfael forced us through the course over

and over again. Something squeezed the air out of my lungs whenever it was Caleb's turn. He would hoist himself over the wall in one move, muscles flexing. Once, as he crawled under the table, his pants raked down to expose a lean hip bone, the skin there paler than his tanned face and arms. It was really annoying how that made me go all gooey inside.

Morfael made us do one more humiliating slog through the course, then said to our sweating faces. "Now you will effect your first shift of the day in the locker rooms with your cabin partners."

"Shift?" I heard myself say. "Just like that?"

Morfael's eyes bored into me. "After every one of you succeeds, you may have breakfast. Caleb, come with me."

Caleb and I caught each other's eye as he moved toward Morfael. "Good luck," he mouthed.

I opened my mouth to say thanks, but he had turned away to follow Morfael back into the main part of the house. Did that mean we were still friends? Right now the only thing I understood was my wet noodle muscles complaining. My emotions were knotted up into a big, crazy ball, and I couldn't tell one from the other.

The other kids were moving toward the back of the cave. Arnaldo and Siku pushed open a metal door that said MEN on it. November and London headed for the second door, marked WOMEN, and then we were in a locker room. The floor was the stone of the cave. The cheap wooden walls and lockers looked like they'd been purchased at Home Depot and erected by drunks.

November was already completely naked and heading toward the showers. I hastily looked away, but my eyes fell on London shedding her clothing with equal lack of concern. Her sweats fell off in seconds, and she padded after November, all lean arms and legs.

"I didn't bring a change of clothes, or soap, or anything," I said, averting my eyes.

"There are extra sets of clothes in each locker," said November. Pipes squealed, and water splattered. "Raynard does the laundry on Saturday. Soap and towels in there."

"Raynard?" I opened a locker and found a pile of gray sweats and socks, all neatly folded and smelling of lavender.

"Morfael's tubby boyfriend," November said. "He's, like, a hundred years old and comes in every day to cook, clean, fix stuff."

"Morfael has a boyfriend?" I couldn't picture Morfael snuggling up to anyone.

"A hottie stick insect like him? How could he not?" November smirked.

I hauled off my drenched sweatshirt, shoes, and socks, then dithered at the thought of removing more.

"Remember how we had to practice taking our clothes off fast when we first got here?" November said, turning to London. "Easier for me since I get so much smaller and the clothes just fall off. Harder for shifters who get bigger like Siku. Word to the wise: Stock up on cheap undies."

"You're even faster when it's cold outside." London squeezed out the ends of her hair. November splashed water at her. London pretended not to notice.

I remembered how Caleb had draped his coat over me before helping me shift to human. He was a gentleman, I'd say that for him. "Do we ... do we all shift in front of each other?"

"Well, it shouldn't be that big a deal if we do," said November. "You get used to nudity if you grow up around shifters."

"You obviously don't go to a humdrum high school," I said. "All the girls hate changing in front of other people. Only the cheerleader types, you know, the ones with the boobs and no cellulite, like to walk around naked and show off."

"Neurotic city," said November, and I couldn't disagree. "Not that shifters are so incredibly sane or anything."

London snorted. "We're all homeschooled," she said. "No

clubs to join, no dances, no new kids to meet. Just the same group you grew up with, every day, year after year."

Maybe high school wasn't so bad, after all.

November was smirking. "Looks like you bring out the chatterbox in London, Tigger."

I forced myself to take off my bra and panties, blushing like an idiot. Neither of them noticed. I stepped into the shower and blasted a stream of hot water. It pounded into my overworked muscles, and I stopped shivering.

"So obviously the Council is letting you stay," said November. "And we know the Tribunal is after you. Gory details are required."

London looked interested too. "You actually fought the objurers?"

"Sort of," I said. I had every ounce of their attention as I gave them an edited version of that long, horrible night. I finished by telling them what the Council had said when I tried to find out what would happen to the Tribunal's enclave. "They told me it was none of my business!" I was getting angry again. "But it's everybody's business!"

London shook her long blackened hair under the water. "What do you expect them to do?"

"The tribes should join forces and go after the Tribunal," I said. "Otherwise they'll wipe out everyone."

London frowned like I was talking crazy, while November rolled her eyes. "Oh, please, it's every tribe for itself in shifter-land," she said. "No matter how nice we rats try to be to other shifters, they just see us as prey. You can't go against nature."

"We're not just animals," I said. "We're people too. And people can unite to fight a common enemy."

November shrugged, as if it wasn't worth discussing. She pointed at my waist. "You get those this morning?"

Feeling exposed, I looked down and saw the purple bruises arcing over my hip bones just as they had for two years, since

I'd started wearing the brace. I forced myself not to rush over and grab a towel to cover them up. *Just pretend it's no big deal.* "No, I've had those forever. I used to wear a back brace. The plastic is really stiff, and I had to wear it all day and night. It squeezed me so hard that these are pretty much permanent."

November frowned. "But you've shifted since then, right?"

"Well—" I had to think about that, and decided not to count the shift in the river during what was probably a Morfael-induced hallucination. "Yeah, I shifted night before last, after the doctor said I didn't need to wear the brace anymore. The first shift I ever did cured my spinal curvature."

"It should've healed the bruises too." London squeezed water out of her hair. "Shifting heals everything."

"And she would know," said November.

London glared at her. I looked down at the bruises, which looked exactly as permanent as they always had. "I don't know. This is all so new to me."

"You should ask Morfael. That's just weird." November turned her shower off with a squeak. "Okay, here we go. I'll shift first."

Great. Now I was weird to the weirdos in this school. "So, we shift now? Like, right here?"

"Yeah," said November, padding over to the supply closet for a towel. "Morfael tries to get us to shift three times a day."

"Why three times a day exactly?" I asked.

November, now dry, stood unself-consciously naked in front of a full-length mirror, running her fingers through her short brown hair. I couldn't help staring, she was so confident. She had to be less than five feet tall, short-waisted and creamy-skinned with a flat chest, slender legs, and a surprisingly round, firm butt. "Most shifters under twenty can only manage to shift to and from their animal form every eight hours or so."

"But if you skip the morning shift, you can do it twice in a row later," London added. "Or three times in a row at the end of the day. Morfael wants us to be able to do it at the drop of a hat."

My stomach sank.

"And at least one of those times, he makes us hunt in animal form or find a hidden object in the back caves, stuff like that." November smiled at my discomfort in the mirror. "Once you're in action, it's harder to keep hold of your human side, so we work on that. And believe me, we rats want you guys to keep hold of it."

"You'll get the hang of it," said London. "Don't let Ratty scare you."

"I've only ever shifted voluntarily once," I said. "And that was a dream."

"Once?" November's mouth turned down for the first time since I'd met her. "You better not keep everyone waiting while you fumble around. We won't get breakfast till everyone's done it, and I'm hungry."

"Thanks," I said. "No pressure."

She studied me; then a smile broke over her face, showing all her sharp, tiny teeth. "Look, I'll show you, okay?"

"Okay," I said, not sure what she meant.

"Nobody stands between November and a meal," said London. She lowered her voice to a stage whisper. "She gets cranky when she's hungry."

"At least I've got a reason," said November. "Now, look. I'll talk you through it until I can't talk anymore. And I'm good at talking, as everybody knows. So . . ." She stood in a wide stance, hands on her hips, her hair dripping onto her bare shoulders. "Some part of us is connected to Othersphere, right?"

News to me, but it made sense. I nodded.

"For me, it feels like a window, like inside me there's a faint breeze blowing in from somewhere"—she waved her hand in the air—"out there. We rats, we're good with our noses, you know? We can identify the tiniest molecules, and to me, this breeze in my soul smells delicious. It smells like candy."

Her eyes sparkled. "Candy's my favorite thing ever. So if I want to shift, I feel the breeze." She closed her eyes and inhaled through her nose. "And I imagine the smell of gummi bears and lollipops. There it is." She inhaled again. "Now I'm going to follow that scent, right through the window, and you see me—"

Her voice cut off as the air around her vibrated. Her nose got pointier, and she shrank into something about a foot long and furry. A large, glossy brown rat stared up at me with dark, beady eyes. A thick pink tail added another eight inches to its length.

Goose bumps covered my skin in spite of all the hot water streaming over me. "Wow." Was that what it looked like when I shifted? There had been no cracking of bones or rending of flesh, the way werewolves changed in the movies. A wiggle in the air, a brief glimpse of her body morphing, and November had become a rat as big as a house cat.

She scuttled over to one of the benches in front of the lockers and leapt up onto it, chirping loudly. Her little pink paws pulled on her whiskers, then stroked her ears. Chattering away as if we could still understand her, she turned 360 degrees. Her skinny little rat arms caressed the fur on her sides, as if showing off her sleek, dark brown, pod-shaped body. For a moment it was like I'd stepped into an animated movie for kids, where animals talked, sang, and made you dresses for the ball.

She closed her beady eyes, still cheeping, and the air around her warped again. Her tail vanished, and she grew taller. A naked human girl stood before us, her hair still wet.

"... just follow the smell of this world back through the window. It smells like a damp basement with a touch of bacon. And here I am." She'd finished in English what she must have started saying as a rat. She grinned, putting her hands on her hips. "See? Not so hard. I'd ask London to talk you through her shift now, but she's about as helpful as a silver bullet."

London grabbed a towel, her hair hanging down around her face. "Go to hell."

"At least she's got a vast vocabulary," said November.

London's mouth became a hard line, her eyes averted. I knew how she felt: like she'd been shoved to the margins and marked "loser." November was too sexy, too gregarious to understand. And I needed to hear what London had to say if I was going to start getting a handle on shifting.

"You've done this way more than I have," I said to London. "And if you have a hard time with it, I'll probably learn even more from you than from November. You know, if you don't mind. I'd really appreciate it."

"Fine. Fuck it." London finished drying off and threw her towel in the hamper. "I have to shift anyway."

"Holy crap," said November. "One kind word and London crumbles like a cookie."

"Shut up, varmint," London said, padding to her locker.

I turned off my own shower and grabbed a towel, glad to be covered up once again. As I sat on the bench and November put on her clothes, London stood stiffly and closed her eyes. "So," she said, "it's like there's a wolf off in the distance, running away from me. I don't want to follow her, but I know that's the way I have to go." Under her eyelids, I could see her irises shifting, as if she was searching in the darkness.

"She's huge, all silvery gray, with eyes like big blue lamps. Sometimes I think it's my mother, but when I get close, I can see it's not." She inhaled sharply. "She's so fast. She's getting farther away. I wish she'd just disappear, but I want to graduate from this goddamned school before I die, so I have to run and run . . ."

She lifted her head as if looking at the ceiling through her closed eyes, the long column of her throat exposed. Her fists clenched, and the atmosphere trembled. Then her fists weren't fists, but huge gray paws. A wolf with silver-gray fur and penetrating sky-blue eyes dropped to all fours where London had been, not three feet away from me.

She took a step forward on her long, rangy legs, her wet, black nose sniffing. She stood nearly three feet high at the shoulder, larger than any normal wolf, her ropy muscles bunching effortlessly beneath her thick coat. I drew back without thinking, my heart thudding.

November laughed. "Now you know how we rats feel. Don't bite her too hard, London."

The wolf turned her glowing gaze and growled at November, the fur along her spine ruffling upward.

"Laurentia, I mean, Laurentia," said November, throwing a nervous smile at me. "When she's in wolf form, it's better to humor her."

London snarled, baring long, sharp teeth.

"Yes, I know you have bigger teeth than I do." November backed up a couple of steps. "But remember, now, you're not a wolf made hungry by a morning workout and shifting. You're Laurentia, a wolf-shifter who will now turn back into a girl so we can hurry up and have a normal breakfast."

"She wouldn't . . . eat you," I said, staring at the huge animal in front of me. "Would she?"

"Of course she wouldn't," said November. But she swallowed hard.

I took a step toward the wolf. London. She fixed her gaze on me. There was an alien wildness in those intense blue eyes that made the hair on the back of my neck stand up. "That's not why she won't do it," I said. "You won't do it because it's wrong. Right, Laurentia? You knew that before you shifted, and you know that now."

The wolf considered me for a long moment; then she sat down. November took a deep breath in relief.

"Are all wolf-shifters this big and gorgeous in their animal form?" I asked.

November raised her voice to an annoying whine. "Wolves are so magnificent, so elegant, so mysterious. Ugh." Her voice slid down to normal tones. "Bunch of romantic bull leftover from fairy tales and nature documentaries. All of our animal forms are bigger and more impressive than regular animals, including the rats."

I looked over at London. "Think we touched a nerve there. Do rats have an inferiority complex?"

London slid her laserlike gaze to November, her eyebrows twitching slightly.

"You try being hunted for generations and told you're filthy and slimy all the time and see how you feel!" November slammed her locker shut. "Hurry up, London. My stomach's growling."

The wolf's mouth opened in what looked like a panting sort of laugh; then she nodded and shut her eyes. I watched carefully for a long minute as nothing happened. London opened up her eyes and yipped in what sounded like frustration.

November gave an exaggerated sigh. "Now who's got the inferiority complex?"

"Wait, let's think about this," I said. "What does she have to do to get back her human form?" I thought about how London chased down her wolf form in order to shift to it, how she'd described that wolf in beautiful terms and didn't seem to think of it as being herself. Now that she actually embodied that magnificent animal, maybe she didn't want to give it up. "You have to let her go," I said to London. "At least for now. She'll still be there, waiting, the next time you look for her. Let her go. You'll find her again."

London let out a small whine and closed her eyes again. November frowned at me, as if trying to figure out what I meant by all that. The air around the wolf altered, and London stood there once more in her human form. Her brows were furrowed, as if she was thinking hard. She didn't look at me as she started to get dressed.

"Okay, Stripes," said November. "Your turn."

CHAPTER 16

I should've been eager to jump into shifting, to learn all about becoming a tiger. But now that the time had come, my heart was pounding unevenly, and my mouth went dry.

"You're stalling," said November. "Come on. Let's see the big bad kitty."

You can't go home until you get good at this. No more endangering myself or my family. I had to start somewhere. Seeing these two girls do it meant it had to be less impossible for me. "Okay. I'll try."

I closed my eyes. After falling into the stream I'd found a dark, burning place inside me that led me to shift. Maybe that was the link to Othersphere November talked about. Could I find it now, awake and with no danger looming?

I heard November sigh and shift her weight. So I took a deep breath and tried to remember how it had felt when I'd shifted in that stream. I'd been worried, panicked, desperate.

Shifting had been my only way out. Before that, anger had triggered it—frustration with the brace, then fury at Lazar and his thugs.

So maybe dark emotions were the key, all the ones I didn't like. *But I don't have any dark emotions.* I was a good girl who didn't worry her mom. I was so strong that the pain of the brace never bothered me. I was tough enough to take the isolation it kept me in. Everything was fine. Just fine.

But it's not. Just take a look at your life. Being afraid is getting you nowhere. And it was exhausting. I'd never get home at this rate. I knew what I had to do.

I found that uneasiness again inside me and pushed my mind toward it. It lay first within my heart. Then it went deeper. The churning darkness lay there still, bringing the weight of dread with it.

I couldn't breathe. I wanted to run. But instead of pulling back, I forced myself to move closer. The amorphous mass rolled toward me like an immense boulder. But rather than trying and failing to climb over it, I plunged in.

Hot shadows vibrated up my back and down my limbs. I would have called out, but my throat was gone, reformed into something mightier. I roared as I shook my head and the skin and fur around it realigned. My paws hit the ground.

All dread, all fear had fled. The world reoriented itself, and I wanted to smell, to taste, to listen to all of it. I opened my eyes to see November and London with their backs pressed against the lockers, mouths open in shock. A moment ago, that look would have made me cringe. But I was a tiger now, and it was right.

They looked not only sharper and more detailed to my tiger eyes, but they'd become a part of a larger whole. My whiskers detected the currents of air that swirled around them; my eyes analyzed the bounce of light off their skin and hair; I could hear their unique heartbeats. The smell of the room filtered through me, sweat and soap and a pile of candy

November must have hidden in her locker. Faint noises came from beyond the room, a locker door slammed, and heavy footsteps exited the boys' room next door. Arnaldo and Siku were done shifting.

"Holy shit!" said November, her voice scratchy. "You're huge!"

I lashed my tail, thumping it against the bench. I'd eaten nothing since dinner last night, and inside me lay a deep hollow place that needed to be filled. An artery under the skin of November's neck pulsed, and I flexed my claws, thinking how it would feel to sink my teeth into that tender flesh.

"Okay, you are looking at me, but not *at* me, and that's not good," said November. "Up here, Stripes. Look me in the eye."

I heard her but couldn't focus on her voice. One pounce and my hunger would be satisfied. I tensed the muscles in my legs, growing very still.

"*Desdemona.*" London said my name very clearly and deliberately. I looked at her. "Remember who you are, who we are. You're Dez." She turned to November. "What's her last name?"

"Hell if I know," said November. "But you better listen to London, Dez. Morfael will be royally ticked off if you eat me."

London swallowed hard and took a tiny step toward me. "You have a family somewhere, don't you? Do you remember them?"

My mother. I had a sudden vision of her, pointing the Tribunal's gun at me, her hands shaking with terror. And here was November, with the same expression on her face. God, I'd really been thinking about eating her. Poor girl. First London, now me. I couldn't say I was sorry, so I sat down and waved my tail around airily, twitching my ears to show I was no longer interested in anything involving blood and guts.

Both girls recognized my body language and relaxed. "Okay,

so deciding not to eat your cabinmates is the first step to shifting back to your human form," said November. "Which you will do chop-chop, right?"

I nodded. What I really wanted to do was wolf down some raw meat, go outside, smell the grass, hear the wind in the leaves, and stretch my legs while lying in a pool of sun. But I was a girl as well as a tiger, and the girl had breakfast waiting, if only she could find herself.

"Okay, so close your eyes," said London, her voice sounding unusually firm.

I shut my eyes and pictured my human body. I imagined the brace and how it had caged me. I had long red hair that frizzed in the rain, green eyes, freckles, and fingers with nails that grew fast.

I opened my eyes and twitched my whiskers at November and London. It wasn't working.

November sighed. "Cats are so lazy."

"And rats are so helpful," said London. "Dez, what are you picturing?"

I tried to frown, but the muscles in my tiger face curled my lip up into a snarl instead. London was squinting at me. "You're imagining what you look like as a human, aren't you?"

"I used to do that," said November. "But it never worked."

London said, "Don't think about the outside of your body. Think about the inside. How does it feel? Try that."

I didn't quite get what she meant, but it couldn't hurt to try. I shut my eyes again, trying to find that hot, black nucleus inside me. I found it faster this time. Maybe it was easier to locate in tiger form. It burned inside me, churning and pulling. I flashed on the heat that rose inside me when Caleb looked at me, how my skin thrilled to his touch, how it felt to press against him and have his mouth on mine.

Blackness flashed through me, and there I was, sitting on

the floor of the girls' locker room, naked and human once more.

I scrambled for my towel as November pretended to dust off her hands in satisfaction.

"That was good," said London. "What did you think about?"

I felt myself blush and got busy putting on my clothes. "Um, just stuff that you can only do in human form. Tigers can't do everything."

November let out a laugh and ran a hand down her hip. "Girl bodies are great for lots of things. My former fiancé can attest to that."

"You were engaged?" I found a pair of socks that were gray from many washings but smelled clean. The odors and sounds around me felt unusually magnified. As before, coming out of animal form changed my human senses for a while. "How old are you?"

"She's seventeen. Shifters tend to get married young," said London. She didn't sound as if she approved.

November nodded. "The tribes want us to start having kids ASAP. Lord knows Roger tried hard to get me there." She popped her eyebrows up and down.

"Plus, there's nothing else to do." London pulled her hair back so only her blond roots showed around her face. She looked young and pretty without the unnatural color spoiling things. "No going to college, no travel abroad, no jobs that take you away from the tribe."

"That sucks," I said. "I mean, sorry. It just sounds so limiting."

"Don't be sorry," said London, shutting her locker hard. "It does suck."

Arnaldo and Siku were waiting for us in the gym area, lounging silently on the equipment. November grabbed Siku's beefy arm and pulled him toward the door into the main house. "Breakfast, breakfast!" she said, grinning.

He trotted to keep up with her, a slow smile breaking across his face. He looked almost cute when he wasn't glowering.

A huge meal lay on the table. No sign of Morfael or the mysterious Raynard, but Caleb was there, pouring syrup on a stack of pancakes. He smelled clean, his black hair wet and curling a bit as it dried. He watched me, chewing, as I sat between London and November. No one said anything as huge platters of scrambled eggs, sausages, bacon, toast, and fruit made the rounds. I piled eggs onto my toast, topped it with bacon and took a bite, closing my eyes in ecstasy.

"So, Caleb, what did you do while we were busy shifting?" November asked, looking a little too interested in his answer.

"Turned a teapot into a volcano," said Caleb. I choked a little on my toast, and he smiled. "Well, not exactly, but I did get it to pour out lava instead of hot water."

"What good is that?" said Arnaldo.

Caleb shrugged. "Could be handy if you wanted to burn something. But I think Morfael just wanted me to practice. It's easy to find big shadows, like the ones in you guys. But small ones, like that teapot, are tough."

"Does every person have a shadow?" I asked.

"No, only shifters," he said. "And not every object has one either. That's part of the challenge: to find things with shadows and then figure out a way to use that shadow to your advantage."

"Are the shadows of people always animals?" I asked.

Morfael spoke as he entered from the kitchen. "In this world, yes."

"But in Othersphere, maybe there are people with shadows of trees or teacups?" I said.

"Perhaps." His eyelids half veiled his eyes. "Or perhaps in one of the many other worlds we cannot see."

"Hey, Siku, what do you think about in order to shift into

a bear?" I asked him. "November and London told me what they did, and it really helped."

The good humor vanished from Siku's face. "That's a personal question."

"Oh, I'm sorry." His shuttered expression made me draw back. "I figured you guys had all talked about this already."

"Nobody ever asked before," said November, sucking on a slice of pineapple. "Come on, Sik. I want to know too. What goes through your mind?"

Muffled through a bite of apple, Siku said, "Okay. Bees."

"Bees?" said Arnaldo.

He nodded, wiping his mouth. "I hear bees buzzing, and I follow the buzzing because bees mean honey."

November laughed. "Oh, my God, you're Winnie the Pooh!"

"Could be worse," said Caleb. "Could be picnic baskets."

Laughter broke out as Siku shrugged and spooned more honey onto a pancake. Even Morfael had a thin smile on his face as he sat down at the head of the table and helped himself to a piece of toast.

"Your turn, Arnaldo," I said.

Arnaldo was frowning. "Is that how it is for all of you?" he said. "You think of something you like and you follow it?"

November, London, and Siku nodded. I didn't do anything since that's not how it was for me. But I sure didn't want to discuss what I went through to shift, especially what it took to get me back to human.

"But there's no way to turn that info into an equation," Arnaldo said.

Everyone but Arnaldo and Morfael laughed. After a second the shifter kids stopped, eyeing each other self-consciously. *They're not used to laughing together.*

"Maybe it's more like a sequence," I said. "Like the countdown before you launch a spaceship."

Arnaldo blinked at me as something lit up behind his eyes.

"Goody," said November. "Someone else who speaks geek. Oh, hey." She leaned over to catch Morfael's eye. "Why does Dez still have bruises on her waist? Even after she shifted, they didn't heal up."

"November!" My face was turning red.

"Oh, please, we'll all be seeing each other naked at some point," she said. "Well—" She gave Caleb a sidelong glance. "Most of us anyway. And maybe there's something wrong with you that Morfael can fix."

"They're just old bruises from my back brace," I said as Morfael gazed at me, expressionless. "It's no big deal."

Siku shook his head. "Bruises should heal when you shift. Mine do."

"The mind is powerful," said Morfael. "It can cause wounds deeper than the shift can cure."

"So . . ." November's brows drew together. "She's still got the bruises because she *thinks* she's got them?"

Morfael just kept eating.

CHAPTER 17

After breakfast we got a break to check e-mail or make calls. Morfael had a landline in the library that Siku made a call on. The rest of us went to the computer corner in the cave.

I looked for Caleb, but Morfael drew him aside to speak in low tones. I logged onto my e-mail account and found six from Iris and one from a strange account I recognized as the new one my mother had set up just before Caleb and I fled my house. Tears sprang to my eyes as I clicked on it.

"My darling Desdemona," it began. "Richard and I are safe. I'm not going to write you where we are, just to be cautious."

I wiped my eyes a bit and looked around to make sure no one saw me crying. But the others stared at their monitors, engrossed. Morfael was pulling a cloth from what looked like an ancient motorcycle as Caleb crouched down to look at it.

Mom's e-mail continued, "Richard woke up about two minutes after you left the house. The bodies of those men in gray helped me convince him that we had to get out of there fast and tell no one where we went.

"Richard was pretty angry about it all, understandably. He insisted on parking a few blocks away and sneaking back to watch our house. We saw a white van pull up to the house.

"More people in gray got out of it. One was a girl about your age with blond hair. The tallest of them, a man with white hair, seemed to be in charge. They brought out the bodies very quickly, and the girl started crying when she saw the one you called Lazar. Then something amazing happened. The girl knelt beside Lazar and put her hands on his face. I tell you, the Healing Mother must be strong in her, because a moment later that young man sat up, demanding to know what had happened.

"I dragged Richard away after that. It looked as if they were searching the house, probably for clues as to where you and Caleb had gone.

"I've had a lot of time to think about you these past couple of days. Now that I clearly see your special gift, I understand some things that happened when you were younger.

"I thank the Goddess that old man in the Moscow orphanage pointed me toward your room. It was destined, and more strange and wonderful adventures are fated to befall you. When I'm tired and worried, I wish you could lead a quiet, ordinary life. But that would mean wishing you were other than you are, and nothing could ever make me want that. I love you more than I can ever express in words, sweetie. Be good to yourself; trust yourself; don't be afraid of yourself."

I paused there a moment. What did she mean, *afraid of myself?*

"Richard sends his love," she continued, "and says not to let that young man Caleb lead you around too much, no matter how nice he is. Richard was a young man once himself, so he knows what he's talking about. Love and what the Goddess wills to you, Mom."

Her words, so familiar, so very *Mom*, fell over me like a warm blanket on a cold night. I stifled my sniffles as I typed out a long reply.

Iris's e-mails were a study in worry and dramatic speculation. They went from ramblings about the cute guy in English to hurt to stark worry when she stopped by and found no one home. If I didn't get in touch soon she would call the police.

Feeling horrible for having worried her, I clicked reply and hesitated. The real story was impossible to tell. So, I guiltily typed that we'd had to leave town on a family emergency. I couldn't be in touch much because we were out of the country.

Feeling better than I had since leaving home, I logged off. Mom and Richard were safe. That was the important thing. Somehow I was going to find a way to keep them that way.

I got up to join the others sitting on the floor in front of the motorcycle. Caleb was lining up a bunch of different tools on a piece of fabric on the floor.

Morfael tapped the rock floor with his staff. The creatures on it now looked only like clever carvings. Had I imagined them writhing before?

"Although he is not a shifter, Caleb will attend classes that are relevant to him. Occasionally, I will take him aside to teach things pertinent only to callers of shadow. In return for this short-term apprenticeship with me, he has agreed to teach you some things never taught here before. The Tribunal utilizes mechanical objects in the war against us. Most otherkin don't have this knowledge, trusting only to their animal nature.

That is about to change. Caleb has facility with these objects and will begin our lesson today."

Caleb rubbed his hands, already spotted with motor oil, and grinned at us. "So, the internal combustion engine, hallmark of civilization and perhaps its downfall. Learn how it works and you're halfway to understanding many mechanical devices. I'm going to take apart this old motorcycle engine and you're going to help me put it back together. Get closer."

Two hours later, the engine was still a mess, but we washed our hands and followed Morfael in some yogalike moves that ended in silent meditation. We were supposed to make our thoughts follow our breathing. But that lasted about three breaths for me. Images of Caleb with tousled hair and a smudge of dirt across his cheekbone as he bent over the motorcycle's carburetor kept intruding.

On the way outside for a nature walk with Morfael, I made sure to be the last one out. As the door to the living room closed behind London, I darted over to the spiral staircase. I ascended a few steps and craned my neck, catching sight of a hallway and a thick wooden door. Morfael's quarters, probably, and a spot where he might hide books or info containing the secrets I suspected he was keeping from me about how I could go home again.

I padded silently up the rest of the leaf-covered spiral staircase in the living room. A narrow hall led to a carved wooden door, which loomed taller than any normal door and was at least eight feet wide. A flash of light from the living room zipped across its surface, and the carved shapes on it moved.

Like Morfael's staff. I leaned closer to the door, trying to distinguish the figures on it. Even with my excellent vision in the dark, I could barely make out what the shapes represented. At first they seemed to be animals; then I thought I saw a tree, and a cup, and a waterfall. Only one shape kept recurring, a black circle surrounded by wavering flame shapes, like a dark sun.

No matter how hard I looked, I couldn't find a doorknob or handle. Maybe the door didn't open at all. Or maybe whatever lay behind it was dangerous. As the shapes writhed before my eyes, the door seemed to grow taller and more shadowy, vibrating with dark. Cold panic took hold of me. I breathed deep, forced myself to memorize that recurring dark sun symbol, then bolted down the stairs.

On the nature walk, I kept thinking about the shifting dark sun rune. Morfael recited the names of local plants I already knew as we walked. But I had no idea St. John's wort could deter the ability to shift or that hawthorn trees grew near places of power. After an hour, we made our way back to the school and I headed for the kitchen, starving.

"We've got to shift before lunch," said November. "Come on."

Again? I followed her into the girls' locker room and shifted into a tiger for the second time that day. It was still terrifying, though now at least I knew I probably wouldn't stay a tiger forever. Probably.

This time we didn't shift right back to human, but emerged in animal form, and Morfael led us outside. I had trouble tearing my eyes from Siku, nearly as big as a minivan in grizzly form. His brown fur was tipped with blond, his massive legs slightly bowed as he walked, the big black nails of his claws digging furrows in the earth. He looked awkward until Morfael ordered him to climb a huge tree. Siku's massive form broke into an easy gallop, fast as a horse, and he sprang with surprising grace as high as he could up the sturdy trunk of the tree. The climbing wasn't easy for him, though, and he scrabbled and grunted, biting onto limbs and sending a shower of shredded bark onto the ground below.

Morfael ordered me to do the same up a different tree. I spiraled up the trunk, amazed at how all four of my legs worked independently to find a hold, smoothly pushing me upward as my tail swayed, providing balance. I'd felt like this as a kid, scrambling fearlessly up the old oak tree, never thinking I'd fall. It was still marvelous, my muscles working in concert, my fur shrugging off the scratches of random limbs and rough bark.

Then Morfael shouted for me to stop. I stood aloft, fifty feet above the mottled tapestry of the school compound. A clot of earth coming from a burrow showed where November was completing her assignment to dig herself a hiding place. Arnaldo's brown wings dipped and rose as he slanted and sliced between trees, where his ten-foot wingspan could get him in trouble. London's silver wolf was running back and forth across the top of a fallen log, like a rough balance beam. Every now and then her paws slipped and she'd scramble to keep herself from falling as Morfael urged her faster.

Not far off, I glimpsed a hunk of white metal that had to be Lazar's stolen BMW. A tall form in a long dark coat stood by it, holding something to his ear: Caleb, and he was on his phone. I could just see his head nod and perhaps his lips move, but at this distance I couldn't hear what he was saying. *Who could he possibly be talking to?* A spark of anger and confusion ignited in me, and I dug my claws deeper into the wood, whiskers bristling.

"Very good, Desdemona and Siku," Morfael was saying. Siku's bulky form swayed the strong branches of the tree near me, about twenty feet off the ground. "Now come down."

This was the real challenge for me. Siku hadn't climbed far, so all he had to do was hang from a limb and drop. His huge form rolled with the fall, and he got up uninjured, shaking the dirt off his fur.

I was too high for that, and my claws curved the wrong way for me to go down head first. So I went down butt first.

The cat in me didn't like it at all. I stalled, eyeing the branches. But the girl in me had climbed a million trees before she got the brace. If I could do it without claws and a tail, then I sure as heck could do it now with them.

Gripping a branch with my front claws, I let my back legs dangle until they found a grip on a lower branch. Front paws then let go and grabbed the lower branch. Repeat. It went fine for about twenty-five feet. Then my back legs missed their branch. My tail end swung out into the air as my front paws scrabbled at the tree limb. They slipped, and I fell.

Even as panic flooded me, my head twisted until my eyes found the ground. My body followed my head, turning in midair, paws splayed wide, legs bent as I hit the earth right side up. The impact sent a shock along my legs and spine, but it dissipated in a heartbeat, leaving me shaken but unhurt.

"Your first fall as a cat," said Morfael, walking up to me. "Well done."

Praise from Morfael! I should have felt exhilarated. But the thought of Caleb on the phone kept intruding. Back in human form, I joined the others in the library for a history lesson. Caleb was there, his face shuttered. I sat as far from him as I could. He was keeping something from me, something big. The thought made my throat ache.

Morfael began talking about something he called the Schism, when the Tribunal had split from the Catholic Church in the sixteen hundreds and went completely underground. At first my mind wandered, distracted by worries about my mother and Richard and how we could ever lead a normal life again.

Then I realized what Morfael was saying. Witch hunts in America and Europe took on a whole new meaning when you realized that the women accused of being able to turn into cats and birds were shifters. Even Dracula had a basis in truth, since the original Vlad Tepes had actually been a batshifter.

Our homework was to pick a famous person and prove whether they were a shifter or not. I was so intrigued I almost didn't mind the work.

The afternoon passed in a haze of martial arts exercises and drills on getting dressed and undressed fast in groups segregated by gender and with Caleb excused. We had lessons on how to start a fire without a lighter and how to keep warm in the woods if you were stuck in human form, and pointers on recognizing locations of power.

Another shift was required before dinner. I whipped off my clothes as fast as I could for practice, then hunkered down and closed my eyes. Might as well try to find my connection to Othersphere while I was here. I directed my thoughts to that dark place and found it. It felt exactly as full of dread and anxiety as it had before.

As I plunged through that frightening black window, a by-now familiar surge of power raced through me, and in seconds I stood once again in tiger form. I looked down at my paws and flexed the claws to make sure I wasn't dreaming.

"You're getting good," said November. "Stop it, or I'll lose my crown as best shifter at school."

I butted my head against her shoulder. She shoved me away with a nervous giggle. I shifted back to human a moment later and got dressed for dinner.

Caleb looked at me a couple of times as we ate. We hadn't talked all day, which felt wrong after all we'd been through. Our legs were really close under the table. I could've rubbed my foot against his calf. But I didn't. I wasn't going to give him the chance to push me away again.

During cleanup, I could feel how near he was in the tight space of the kitchen. As we finished and began filing out, he put a gentle hand on my elbow and tugged me back.

"Hey," he said in that intimate nonwhisper tone that made my stomach flutter. "Tell me about your mom."

"She's fine," I said, not quite looking him in the eye, and told him what Mom had written about the Tribunal.

"Leave no trace for the unbelievers to find, that's Ximon's way," Caleb said, leaning against the counter. "Where did your mom and Richard go?"

"She didn't tell me where, in case the e-mail account gets hacked." I leaned against the opposite counter. Avoiding his gaze meant my eyes had to trace the small veins in his biceps, his smooth brown skin, how his jeans hugged his hips.

"Your mom's tough," he said. "I see where you get it."

"I'm adopted," I said. "I didn't inherit..."

"You think genes are the only things you can inherit?"

I accidentally looked up and met his smiling gaze. Warmth stole over me. "I guess not," I said. "She wasn't tough enough to stop Richard from hiding out and waiting for the Tribunal though."

"He what?" He leaned forward in surprise. "But they're okay?"

"Yeah, Ximon and his group didn't see them, but Mom and Richard watched him arrive with some other guys in a white van. Lazar's sister Amaris was there too."

He straightened. "Oh?"

"Mom said she was upset at Lazar's injuries, but then she laid her hands on him, and seconds later, he sat up, looking fine."

He leaned back again. "She healed him."

"She can do that?" I said. "I don't get it. How does that fit into being an objurer? Can all of them do that?"

"She's not an objurer or otherkin," he said. "Once in a generation, a healer is born. Amaris is the youngest in the world. She's still learning how to harness her ability."

"Does she acquire the healing from Othersphere? Or is it something else?"

"Healing is much harder than shifting or calling something forth from shadow," he said. "I'm not sure exactly how it works, but she pulls energy from Othersphere that makes the body whole. My mom had a theory. She said everyone in this world has a shadow double in Othersphere, a doppelganger. Somehow the healer finds the vibration of the healthy body of the double and uses it to create health in someone here."

I frowned, trying to work that out. "So, she sucks the life out of someone in Othersphere and transfers it to that person's double in our world."

"We don't know what it does to the shadow double," he said. "We can't cross over into Othersphere to find out. The Tribunal thinks it's a blessing from God if one of theirs is born with the ability, and a curse from the devil if it's one of ours."

"At least they're consistent in their inconsistency," I said.

"Healers are rare, and very valuable. It's a huge advantage to the Tribunal to have one working for them."

"Because they can't heal like shifters can." An idea struck me. "Is that why we heal when we shift? Are we drawing health or whatever from our shadow double?"

"That's the theory." He cracked a half smile. "Smart girl strikes again."

I didn't respond, torn between feeling good at his compliment and wanting to know the truth. Truth won. "Who were you talking to on the phone this afternoon?"

"What?" His eyebrows arched. "I wasn't talking to anyone."

"I saw you on the phone while you were standing over by Lazar's Beemer." I mimicked his earlier stance, hand to ear.

"Oh, then." He looked away. "It's not important."

"You had the phone to your ear," I said. "That's not how you play games or access the web."

"Or listen to messages." His expression turned stony. "I

keep old messages and sometimes I replay them so I can hear my mother's voice. I told you it's not important." He headed for the kitchen door.

The pain in his voice drained all the anger out of me. "I'm sorry," I said. He kept walking, and I grabbed onto the back of his sweatshirt, making him turn around. "I'm really sorry, Caleb. It's just..." I broke off, unable to figure out how the next part went.

He studied me for a long moment. "Last night," he said. "You don't trust me now because of last night."

"I know you're lying to me," I said. "Not necessarily about the phone call today, but about the earlier one, and other times too."

His hand moved like he was reaching for mine, then pulled back. "I should've never let it go so far, but you're a magnet."

I cleared my throat. My voice came out very small. "Why can't we be...?"

"We just can't," he said.

"Is there someone else?" I said. The last thing I wanted to hear was "yes," but at least then I'd know what was going on.

"I told you, it's complicated," he said, his voice taking on a firm "no more questions" tone. "Maybe..." He stopped himself, then shook his head. "The important thing is that you're safe here. And maybe they'll find out something about your birth parents. You need to forget about me. I won't be here much longer."

I felt as if I'd been punched in the gut. I tried to imagine being here without him, my one friend in this mysterious, lonely new world.

Damn it, I wasn't going to cry. Not in front of him. I clamped down on the hollow feeling and kept my voice cool. "Where are you going?"

"I don't know yet," he said. "I'll stay for a little while

longer, but this isn't a school for callers. Morfael's been more than kind, but I have to earn my own way through the world."

"He seems to think you're an asset here, teaching us about technology."

"It's charity, and I appreciate it, but I'm not earning my keep," he said. "And I have things to do."

"I get it," I said. Anger circled around the edges of the pain inside me. "You've finished leading me on, so it's time to go."

His face tightened as I walked past him, out of Morfael's house and into the dark of the early evening. The other kids were back in the library, researching their papers, but I felt the urge to run, to scream. The cold autumn wind cut through my sweatshirt as I paced past the tree I had climbed earlier, a rising tide of emotion flooding through me. Fur would be warmer. And cat's eyes would be better for a walk through the woods at night.

I walked to the oak I'd climbed earlier and leaned against it, missing my own tree, the lightning tree, back in Burbank.

Why was shifting so scary? So far it had been safe, and I'd proven I could shift back to human.

Don't be afraid of yourself.

Maybe I was starting to understand what Mom meant by that. It was easier to pretend I was fine, that I was strong, that nothing hurt me. Facing up to the reality of who I might be was much scarier.

A longing to run through the grass and feel the night air started up like a purr inside me. I wanted to leave the pain of everything behind, even for just a few moments. I pushed through the fear and shifted in a heartbeat, and all the cool scents of the forest washed through me. A breeze ruffled my fur, and I cocked my ears to catch the skittering insects among the leaves.

A small voice in my head worried. *You shouldn't be able to shift four times in one day.*

But I didn't want to think about that now. Digging my claws into its bark, I climbed up into the rough arms of the oak, just as I had when I was a kid. Cradled there, I felt homesickness and fear of the future overwhelm me. Some of the oak's dying leaves brushed my whiskers, and I let myself believe I wasn't alone.

CHAPTER 18

A week passed in a blur of shifting, classes, workouts, meals, and avoiding Caleb. I met Raynard, the burly fifty-ish caretaker who came every other day to do the laundry, mend things, and grumble under his breath. We weren't exactly introduced. He grunted at me when I said hello as we filed past him hosing down the cave floor one morning. It was hard to picture that schlubby figure getting romantic with anyone, let alone the elegant, alien Morfael.

Morfael's decision to teach us to use the weapons the Tribunal used against us lead to lessons in gunfire. It made sense to teach the shifters modern warfare, but I had to watch and listen to Caleb when he made us put on gloves and shoot the silver gun we found in Lazar's BMW. Having him so close made me ache all over. Maybe that's why I fared the worst on the shooting range, although I also hated the noise and smell of the gun. Even with the gloves on, the silver burned my hands. I couldn't wait to shift after that to heal my itchy red skin.

The others didn't have the same level of sensitivity. After some initial fumbling, Arnaldo turned out to be a deadeye and got a little obsessed. During free time he got the key to the gun locker from Morfael and coaxed Siku to throw rocks and bottles so he could shatter them like a skeet shooter. Raynard groused but replenished our supply of bullets two days later with dozens of boxes.

Every morning I woke expecting to find Caleb gone. But he was still there at the end of the week, participating in all the physical exercises, making us rebuild the motorcycle, then teaching us how to drive it. Part of me wished he'd just go away already. I'd never get over him practically living with him like this. In spite of everything, I still couldn't take my eyes off him whenever he was around. A couple of times as I sat on the bike, his hand brushed mine, showing me how to brake or accelerate. I concentrated so much on keeping my face blank that I kept stalling out the motor. But he persisted until I could at least get the bike going and stop it without falling off.

I found several books on runes in the library, but none of them had a symbol in them like the dark sun on Morfael's door. I tried to get a good look at his staff, to see if the same rune was carved there. But it never seemed to leave Morfael's hand. His bony fingers covered up too much to see anything in detail.

November paid special attention to the lesson in which Caleb showed us how locks worked. She became the first to pick a padlock. She did it so well that Caleb challenged her in rapid succession to open the lock on the front door, a briefcase, and the BMW's trunk. After some initial fumbling, she managed all three. Later she batted her eyelashes at him and asked him to make her some lockpicks of her own. I fought off nauseating pangs of jealousy when he gave them to her the next day.

London kept as quiet as I did during these lessons. But then, she was always quiet. During Morfael's lectures on plants, animal species, and anatomy, she took detailed notes, and she always got full moons on those quizzes. But she never raised her hand when Morfael asked us a question. Sometimes he'd let the silence hang for minutes, scanning our faces. He seemed to scrutinize her the longest, but she kept her eyes down, pen moving. Once I caught a glimpse of a sketch she left out on her bunk. She had drawn a perfectly proportioned schematic of the musculature of a wolf.

The only classes I did well in were history, botany, and shifting. As quick as November was to shift, she had a hard time resisting when Morfael forced us to change form. I did better.

Caleb tried to talk to me exactly once. He found me alone in the library, researching my history paper. He sat down in the chair across from me, cleared his throat, and said, "Hey."

I didn't respond. The yellowing book page in front of me suddenly made no sense, but I kept running my eyes over it.

"I was hoping we wouldn't leave it like this," he said, his hands clasped tensely together. "I consider you a friend."

"Friends are honest with each other," I said. "I've never lied to you. Can you say the same thing?"

He looked down. I pretended to keep reading.

"I would tell you if I could," he said, his voice very quiet. "You should know that."

"Why should I believe anything you say?" I asked. It felt horribly good to see the hurt my words brought to his eyes. "Now, this paper about the Javanese chieftain tiger-shifter isn't going to write itself."

His jaw clenched. He nodded and got up. My pleasure

in hurting him drained away, and the room felt cold without him.

Things got awkward when Morfael told us that Caleb was going to try to force us to shift the other way—from animal into human form.

"That's what the Tribunal does, not callers of shadow," said Arnaldo.

"If you can learn to resist the powers of the objurers, you may be able to save yourselves and your families if they come under attack," said Morfael.

"You've brought an objurer into this school," said Siku, his deep voice rising. "He is one of them!"

"Callers and objurers are two sides of the same coin," Morfael said, his own powerful voice cutting through Siku's emotion. "Caleb has training in both calling forth the shadow and in pushing it back to Othersphere. Most callers do not have that opportunity, and you are very fortunate to have him here right now to help you prepare against the Tribunal."

Siku didn't dare speak out after that, but he silently refused to participate in the exercise. I wondered if Morfael would force him to shift, but he only ordered him to stay in his cabin for the rest of the day.

The rest of us took our turns, one by one, moving behind the bushes, piling up our clothes, and shifting to animal form. I watched as Caleb concentrated, pointed his hand at London, and hummed, deep and low. I thought of the night I'd been stuck in tiger form, my mother standing over me with a gun. He'd saved me that night, helping me become human. Now I couldn't even bear to speak to him.

Black vapor shot from Caleb's fingers and enveloped London's silver wolf form, barely visible through the greenery. She whined sharply, and the bushes shook. Caleb dropped his hand, looking a bit pale.

"London?" said November. "You okay?"

"Yeah," came London's human voice.

As she got dressed, I studied Caleb out of the corner of my eye. After he'd helped me out, he'd suffered a few moments of disorientation. Now Morfael expected him to do it four times in a row. Did Morfael also weaken when he used his powers? Maybe as callers gained experience, they became more immune to the bad effects.

Caleb stood very still, his eyes shut. He didn't sway or say strange things as he had before, but I could hear a faint hum emanating from him like an appliance on standby. Morfael must've given him pointers on how to maintain focus.

November went next and suffered the same fate as London, just as quickly. "This blows," she said from the bushes. "How are we supposed to fight it?"

I was racking my brain, trying to come up with a plan to do exactly that. Callers and objurers used vibration to manipulate shadow. There had to be something shifters could do to stop them.

My turn. I stripped down where no one could see me and shifted into tiger form. I felt the fear, but I did it anyway. I concentrated on my inner tiger, lashing my tail against the attack about to come.

Caleb's drone rose into a call, and my body shuddered with it. The pool of darkness within me shrank from the sound, and at the last minute I tried to roar. If Caleb could use vibration to his advantage, maybe so could I. But it was too late. Seconds later I lay on the grass, human, naked, and grateful for the screening shrubbery. I dressed fast, fingers trembling. Being naked in the open like this was mortifying. I wondered about my attempt to roar. Would it have made any difference?

As I passed Arnaldo on his way to take my place, I said, "Try making your own sound."

He stopped. "What?"

"He's using sound to make us shift," I said, keeping my voice down. "If you make your own sound, your own vibration, maybe it'll mess with his."

He frowned and kept walking. I sat down on the cold ground next to London, glancing at Caleb's face. Strain showed between his dark brows, and I could tell how hard he was focusing to keep his breathing even.

With a flapping of long brown wings, Arnaldo the eagle leapt up from behind the hedge and came to rest on the strong branch of a neighboring tree. It sagged and bounced under his weight as he fixed us all with a piercing gaze out of one eye.

"He's getting cocky," said November. "He'll fall for sure. Hey, bird boy!" She cupped her hands around her mouth. "Can't wait to see how your package likes it when you shift and end up sitting naked on that branch!"

Arnaldo tilted his white feathered head and croaked as Caleb's humming grew louder. His voice seemed to gather up all the sounds in the world to aid it. Even though the hum wasn't aimed at me, my body thrummed with it, wanting to follow but not knowing how. As the intensity grew, nearing its peak, Arnaldo opened his cruel beak and screeched out a high, penetrating note, neck thrust forward.

Caleb winced, and the pitch of his call wavered. The eagle cried out again, a blood-freezing scream so strong I could almost see it slicing into Caleb's resonance, like a knife through a smothering blanket.

The hum ceased. Caleb staggered back, his skin ashen. His eyes widened, glowing with gold shot through the black irises. His face went blank as he stared right at me with a look I didn't recognize. His legs buckled beneath him.

I was on my feet, moving toward him. As if in slow motion, he fell. All my anger at him fled as I got my arms around him in time to keep the back of his head from striking a rock.

His black eyes were spiraled with gold. It almost made me dizzy to look into them.

"The lost one," he said, staring at me in awed horror.

"Is he okay?" November was at my side. London approached hesitantly, and Arnaldo flew in to land heavily beside her.

Caleb stared around at all of us, as if he'd never seen us before. "Vermin. Lupine. Raptor," he said, his voice raw. "Beware. She is not one of you."

"What the hell?" said November.

"You mean Dez?" said London. Everyone was staring at me.

"Move aside," said Morfael, his staff jabbing into the hard ground as he approached. "Desdemona, let him go."

I'd forgotten that my arms were still around Caleb. He felt cold, unfamiliar, and I wanted to press him close until he was warm again. But I lowered his head to the ground and took my arms away. The others moved back, but I stayed there, inches away, in case he needed me.

Caleb gazed up at Morfael, eyes narrowing as if in recognition. "Shadow walker," he said. "You are the guiltiest of all."

"Shhh." Morfael made a hushing noise. I could feel the soothing vibration of it. Caleb's eyes closed, but his face and body remained tense.

Morfael knelt down next to Caleb and placed the tip of his skeletal finger between his brows. "Return," he said in the same quiet tone.

Caleb relaxed. Color returned to his face and he opened his eyes. They were once again black as onyx. "Guess I need more practice," he said, his voice scratchy. I couldn't help smiling at him in relief.

"Take him to the couch before the fire in my living room," Morfael said. "Help him." He turned to go, then stopped next to the eagle. "Well done, Arnaldo."

London and I helped Caleb walk back to Morfael's house while November skipped ahead and opened doors for us. Caleb tried to walk on his own, but every few steps he'd start to fall. So we put his arms around our shoulders and propped him up along the way, finally letting him collapse onto the leather sofa before the fire. His eyes closed immediately and he fell asleep.

"He has got the most ridiculous eyelashes," November said, perching on the arm of the sofa.

"Come on, 'Ember," said London, moving toward the front door.

"What?" November looked from her to me, then down at Caleb. "Oh, right. Fine."

The door shut behind them, and I knelt down by Caleb's side, watching the reassuring rise and fall of his chest.

"He'll recover after a night of sleep."

Morfael stood in the doorway, leaning on his staff. A cold breeze blew layers of black clothing against his emaciated frame until he shut the door.

"You made him force four people in a row to shift," I said, fury sparking out of me. "You endangered him."

"You think I asked too much," he said. "But he has grown in strength these last few days. If you and Arnaldo had not been so clever, he would not have succumbed to shadow."

"Don't try to blame us." I got up to face him squarely. "You're the one who pushed him too hard."

"There is no fault," he said. "Being a caller brings certain risks. Caleb knows this. And every time he pushes himself, his strength grows."

"What happens to him when he goes too far?" I said. "It's like he loses himself. He says all these things that don't make any sense."

"Don't they?" said Morfael.

That made me pause. "So everything he says is true? That would mean I'm the lost one and you're the guiltiest of all."

"Any truth Caleb may have spoken might not be the truth as you or I would see it," he said.

"Okay, enough with the cryptic pronouncements," I said. "Tell me now, does his mind get lost in Othersphere or something? What if he can't come back?"

Morfael didn't say anything, but his eyes narrowed.

"Return," I said, remembering what Morfael had said to help Caleb a few minutes earlier. "Were you calling him to return from Othersphere?" I studied his strange, gaunt countenance. It gave nothing away, but something in my head clicked into place. It was exactly the opposite. "Or were you telling something inside Caleb to return *to* Othersphere?"

His face changed. I had surprised him.

"He opens himself to . . . things from Othersphere whenever he calls out to shadow, doesn't he?" I said. "When he gets overwhelmed, he becomes a window for whatever's over there at the time, and it sees us through his eyes."

Morfael did not respond.

"Are you ready to tell me how I can go home yet?" I said, all the frustrations of the last week at last coming out. "You know so much more than you're telling. I think it's time you stop playing games and just tell the truth."

"It would be best for you to return to your cabin now," Morfael said, his voice resonating through the room. My anger slipped away, and a sudden need to be in my bunk overtook me. "Thank you for helping with Caleb."

I was outside on the way to my cabin before I realized I hadn't wanted to leave. So that was why shifters didn't like or trust callers. I'd been so caught up in my curiosity and resentment that it was easy for Morfael to get me out of his hair.

Damn him anyway! I was trying to protect my family and Caleb, and Morfael had brushed me aside. Why would he do that unless he had something to hide? All the more reason to find out what that dark sun rune meant, and anything else I could find.

I almost bumped into Arnaldo, standing outside the girls' cabin in human form.

"Sorry!" I said, stopping abruptly.

"How is he?" he said. Bundled up against the cold, he didn't look so thin and gawky. He was tall, as tall as me. If he ever filled out, he'd cut an elegant figure.

"Okay, I guess. Asleep."

"Good."

"It's not your fault," I said, realizing that worry creased his forehead. "Morfael seems to think he'll be able to learn from it, get stronger, for whatever that's worth."

"Morfael's probably pissed you figured out a way to counteract a caller's ability," he said. "Don't let him get under your skin."

I laughed. "Is it that obvious?"

He raised both brows and cocked his head as if to say, "Duh."

"All I did was ask Morfael what those things Caleb was saying meant. And instead of answering me, he used the old velvet voice and got me out the room!" I'd never talked to Arnaldo so frankly before, but I was too angry to care. "It's like I'm some puppet he can make do whatever he wants."

"Welcome to caller versus shifter," Arnaldo said. "Morfael's a good teacher and all, but it's not like you can trust him all the time. He wouldn't hurt us, I don't think. But he's more than happy to manipulate."

"Don't you ever get sick of all the suspicion?" I said. "The shifter tribes hate each other; they can't trust the callers; they're threatened with death by the Tribunal. What a crazy mess!"

"Yeah," he said, his voice becoming thoughtful. "Sometimes you can't even trust people within your own tribe."

"Some of us don't even have a tribe at all!" I said, and couldn't help laughing at my own emphatic tone. "God, listen to me. I'm ranting."

A smile flickered in his eyes. "Look, I'm here because I wanted to say thanks." At my clueless look, he continued, "For giving me that hint on how to stop Caleb from forcing me to shift. I should've thought of it myself—canceling out one frequency with another. It's so simple, it's elegant. Most kids would've kept it to themselves, you know, not wanting to give anyone else the advantage."

"Maybe I wanted to use you as my guinea pig," I said.

"No, you were being nice," he said firmly. "So I thought you should know something. Even a clueless geek like me can sense the tension between you and Caleb. But he's hung up on you. Big-time."

His eyes beneath the heavy overhang of his brow were sincere. "What makes you say that?" I asked, heart beating fast.

"He says your name in his sleep," he said, and turned to go. "Have a good night."

After he left, I don't know how long I stood there, staring off into space.

CHAPTER 19

The next day Morfael took us out into a glade in the woods
and blindfolded us. The person who found a book he'd hidden there and handed it to him would get the grade on their
history paper bumped up a notch.

The one good thing about these exercises was that they
drove every other thought from my head. I had to focus on
the task at hand so hard, I couldn't spare any brain cells on
my parents, Caleb, Morfael's deception, or the words "lost
one." Silence dropped over us as we all stilled.

Morfael had shown us a worn blue hardback and hidden it
somewhere in the clearing. I pictured the area in my head.

The book had to be inside the blackberry bushes to the
east or under one of the rocks, I decided. A flat-topped rock
was just a few yards away, so best to check it first.

I'd gotten pretty good at moving without making a sound,
but then so had everyone else. November's breathing hit my

ears before her footsteps. I stepped up the pace and made it to the rock, sliding my hands around the base to see if Morfael had left anything there.

Across the glade I heard Arnaldo and London exclaim in unison, probably as they somehow collided. There was nothing around the base of my rock. I touched something soft and pulled away with a gasp, then realized it was November's arm.

"Sorry!" I whispered.

She giggled. "This is so dumb."

It struck me how right she was.

"What if we all tried to find the way back to school instead of looking for some stupid book?" she whispered.

"Or, what if . . ." I raised my voice so that it would carry across the glade. "The book's not at this rock on the north side."

"What the hell are you doing?" hissed November.

"Morfael never said we couldn't cooperate during these exercises," I said in a normal tone. Everyone in the glade would be able to hear me. "And he hasn't stopped me so far. Has anybody checked those bushes to the east yet?"

Nobody responded.

"I'll check them," I said. "Arnaldo and London, if you're over by that big rock, be sure to check the crevices."

I didn't bother to hide the sound of my footsteps as I walked to the east side of the glade, arms outstretched.

"Actually, I'm at the big rock," said Caleb, his voice catching slightly with hesitation before growing in volume. "Nothing here."

My pulse raced when he spoke. He'd jumped right in after me, but then he was the reckless type. The others might be too cautious to follow.

A pause developed. I moved forward slowly. "What else is over there?" I said.

London cleared her throat. "Wasn't there a fallen log?"

"I'll search that next," said Caleb. His boots thumped over the dried grass.

Another pause, then:

"London and I have the two low rocks on the southwest side covered," said Arnaldo.

"I'll check the big pile of leaves over here," November called out.

My mouth widened in a smile no one could see. That was everyone but Siku. I had no idea how to draw him in.

The bushes couldn't be far now. I leaned forward, bumped my hands into something large, and recoiled. "Whoa! Who's that?"

Foliage thrashed, then Siku's voice said, low and rumbly, "I made it to the bushes first."

"Cool," I said, a rush of happiness warming me. Even Siku was in it now.

"I'll check them down here," I said, shuffling past Siku. "We can meet in the middle."

He grunted, and the bushes trembled as he searched them. I ran my hands first over the top. Then I jiggled the branches in the middle, before feeling around the base, pushing aside sticks, rocks, and crumpled leaves.

November made a gagging noise. "Nothing over here, and if I touch another worm I'm going to throw up."

"What if it's not at a landmark?" said Caleb. "It might be somewhere random."

"You mean, like the center of the glade or something?" Arnaldo's voice moved with his steps. "Maybe if we all just wander around, pushing aside leaves..."

"Sounds like fun," said November.

Crunching noises took over the clearing as we began shuffling our feet through the fallen leaves, feeling for anything that didn't belong on the ground. The leaves were very dry, and the crackling became epic, blending into what sounded like a gale force wind harassing a forest.

Something brushed my arm. As I whirled, I heard a sharp intake of breath and felt the warmth of a body near me. *Caleb*. I would have recognized his scent and the sound of his breathing anywhere. I felt his hand warm on my arm, pulling me up against him before I could protest. Something brushed the blindfold over my eyes, and the silk of his blindfold slid against my skin as his lips touched mine. My heart contracted, and I responded until my brain kicked in and I pushed against his chest.

"Of all the things I've stolen," he said, low and intimate, "I think that kiss was my favorite."

"What do you want from me?" I was still shoving against him, but not with very much strength. His arms were encircling my waist, and a delicious warmth was taking me over.

"I want just a moment with you," he murmured. "Just one." And kissed me again.

Something deep inside me opened up. As if in a dream, I wound my arms around his neck. The world melted into a single point of fire. I lost track of everything except the pressure of his arms; his soft, urgent lips; and the storm of snapping and popping as our oblivious friends romped in the dead leaves around us.

Behind us, Siku grunted out, "Ha." His large body hit the ground and made a noise as if he were rolling full length in the leaves.

I couldn't help laughing, my lips still against Caleb's. He joined in. In that moment I was completely happy.

"Found it!" shouted London. "I got the book!"

Time to take off the blindfolds. I stepped away from Caleb and reached up to remove the piece of cloth covering my eyes. But Caleb slid his hand over mine and said loudly, "Wait! As soon as we take the blindfolds off, whoever has the book has to hand it to Morfael and get the credit."

"I don't remember that being the rule," Arnaldo said, sounding befuddled.

"So let's decide who gets the credit before we take them off." Caleb pulled me close and kissed my neck.

"The game ends when the blindfolds come off, right?" I said so that all could hear. "We won this together, so let's figure this out together."

"I guess that sort of makes sense," said Arnaldo.

There was a general murmur of agreement.

"London found it," said November.

"With help from us." That was Siku's voice.

Caleb's hand slid up my neck to find my mouth, tracing my lips. I kept myself from gasping and whispered, "They'll hear us."

"I only found it because Caleb suggested we search the middle of the glade. Maybe he should get it," said London, sounding uncertain.

Caleb raised his voice as he wrapped both arms around me and lifted me off the ground. His heartbeat resounded through my body like my own pulse. "All this was Dez's idea. She should get the credit."

I wiggled as quietly as I could, kicking my legs, breathless with withheld laughter. "We all did this," I said. To my own ears, my voice sounded distracted, dizzy. "Not just me."

"One last time," Caleb whispered, and allowed my body to slide down his to the ground, his hands on my hips. Then he kissed me, strangely urgent. *One last time?* Was this goodbye?

"November's the worst at history," said Siku. "She needs it most."

"I can't learn it," said November. "So I'm doomed to repeat it."

"I vote November gets it," said London.

Caleb's lips left mine. "Me too," he said.

I felt dizzy. "Sounds good," I said.

"Okay," Arnaldo said.

"Yay! Half moon instead of crescent moon!" said November. Light footsteps marked that she was moving. "Where are you again, Wolfie?"

"Over here, Rattie," said London. "Here you go."

Caleb released me. I hastily combed my fingers through my hair and adjusted my coat.

"Got it! Blindfolds off!"

I removed the black cloth. Everyone was grinning, arms and legs covered with bits of foliage. Siku was just getting to his feet, his broad back speckled with red and brown bracken, beaming like he'd stumbled on a honeycomb. Caleb shot me a glance that made my face hot.

Morfael stood at the edge of the clearing looking like one of those elongated saints in a Mannerist painting, all pointy elbows and burning eyes. *Oh no.* He must have seen the whole thing. I blushed furiously, but no one was looking at me. November walked up to Morfael, holding the book out like it was some sort of shield.

"Here," she said.

He looked down at her, and we all stilled, waiting for his verdict. Had I ruined the test by getting everyone to collaborate?

"Very well," he said, taking the book from her. "Now back to the locker rooms for your midday shift before lunch. I believe Raynard is making pizza."

"Woo-hoo!" November swiveled and ran right at Siku. She would have bowled him over, but with that unexpected grace of his, he grabbed her by the waist and lifted her over his head. She whooped, arms outstretched like a dancer. It turned into a scream when he pretended to drop her, but he caught her a few inches from the ground, grinning. She gasped, flailing at him with her fists and giggling.

"Whoever's last to the locker rooms has to wash the dishes alone!" yelled Arnaldo, taking off into the trees toward the school. The others laughed and ran after him.

I looked for Morfael's reaction. But he was nowhere to be seen. Caleb and I were alone in the glade.

The place where he'd kissed my neck still burned like a brand. I didn't want to break the spell by talking about it.

"Guess we'll be doing the dishes," I said, trying to sound hearty and failing.

"You did it again, you know," he said.

"What?" I said, alarmed. "What did I do?"

"You broke the unspoken rules."

"I didn't mean to break any rules," I said. "It just seemed like it might go faster if we all worked together . . ."

"You were right." He smiled at me, and we turned to head back toward the school, side by side. "It was brilliant."

"Oh." I relaxed. "You're one to talk. Isn't there some rule about not grabbing one of the other players during these exercises?"

"Only if the other player objects," he said, his suppressed smile returning. "You didn't object for long."

My ears were growing warm. I didn't know what to say. "I . . ."

"You really don't know the effect you have on people, do you?" He shook his head. "The group never would've done that together if you hadn't made it happen."

"It was all of us, not just me."

"See, that's what I mean," he said. "You don't want to take the credit. You want to include everyone, make sure we all win somehow. Even kids from different shifter tribes, brought up to hate each other, are affected by it."

Again he'd rendered me speechless.

"Don't get all embarrassed," he said. "I'm just telling you what I see."

He was right there, inches away, being sweet and supportive. Just moments before we'd been locked in a passionate embrace. It would've felt so natural to take his arm or hold his hand. But now that the blindfolds were off, I remembered how he'd said he was leaving the school. That and his lies still stood like a wall between us.

"You're leaving soon, aren't you?" I said, watching him carefully.

He ducked his head and didn't answer for a moment. "I was being selfish. I just . . . I couldn't resist."

"And you still can't tell me why you have to go? Even after . . ." I gestured back toward the glade, where we'd been kissing moments before.

He shook his head, not meeting my eyes. "I wish I could."

We walked without saying anything for a few minutes. My emotions were a riot of contradictions—anger, resentment, friendship, desire. Above it all, I was now worried for him. I had no doubt that whatever he planned to do when he left was dangerous. Maybe he didn't want me to know because it would endanger me as well.

I cleared my throat and decided to settle on friendship, for now. "If this were a normal camp, I mean, a camp of humdrums . . ." He smiled as I corrected myself. "There'd be midnight raids on the girls' cabin and love triangles and lifelong friendships formed. But we're all supposed to hate each other, so it's taking a bit longer."

"Midnight raids?" He raised his eyebrows at me. "Now there's an idea."

At lunch, caught up in the giddiness left over from the book-finding exercise, November and Siku held a contest to see who could fit the most celery sticks into their mouths at once. November won. Caleb recited three dirty limericks, leaving us red-faced with laughter. Then Arnaldo stood on his chair and sang an aria from *The Marriage of Figaro* in a strong, beautiful baritone. As the last pure note faded away, we cheered and London threw bread rolls, which nearly led to an all-out food fight before Morfael squashed it with a reminder that we'd have to clean it up. That was the only time he remarked on anything, going back to cutting up his pizza into small, delicate bites.

After the afternoon's classes and dinner, London, November, and I were getting ready for bed in the girls' cabin when the front door creaked open. London shouted a warning, which turned into a laugh as the boys burst in, big grins plastered on their faces. Siku boasted how he'd give 'Ember a run at lockpicking now. Then he, Arnaldo, and Caleb wandered around the cabin, touching everything and making bad jokes about underwear and bunk beds. Eventually they settled in, and the six of us talked late into the night.

The only spot of discomfort came when Caleb sat on the floor near where I was on my lower bunk, leaning his back against the bedpost near me. I had trouble focusing on the talk because I kept looking at the back of his neck and imagining running my fingers through his hair.

London interrupted my reverie, leaning in and whispering, "Thanks."

"What for?" I whispered back. November was juggling three tennis balls as the boys applauded.

London shrugged. "I actually forgot I was a shifter today."

"Is that a good thing?"

She nodded. "My parents will never let me go to medical school. I'll be trapped in the woods in Idaho my whole life and be a carpenter like my dad."

"You'd be a good doctor," I said. "Have you tried talking to your parents?"

"Yeah. They see humdrum hunters gunning down real wolves just for being wolves and they don't get why I'd want to help heal their children. Why does everyone hate everyone else so much?"

"Wish I knew." I slid my arm around her and gave her a hug. She didn't pull away. "Things can change," I said.

"Arnie, you should be an opera singer or something." November was kicking her feet from her perch on the top bunk.

"Totally," said London.

"My voice teacher thinks so too," he said, making a slightly embarrassed face. "But my dad went ballistic when I told him that. He thinks opera's, you know, not something real men do."

"Give me a break." November rolled her eyes.

"Do it anyway," said Caleb. "Get a job, get your own place, maybe even go to college and study it. You're old enough."

"Just what I was thinking," I said, throwing London a significant glance. "Any of you could do that."

"I'd like to," Arnaldo said slowly. "But my two little brothers will still be there, and if I leave, my dad might get really angry. I don't want him to take it out on them."

"Shit," said November. "So does he, like, hit you?"

"You so don't have to answer that," London put in real fast.

Arnaldo said, his voice very quiet. "Ever since my mom got killed, he drinks more than ever, and when he's drunk, he can get really angry and crazy. I can't leave my brothers there alone."

We sat in sympathetic silence for another second until Siku grabbed a pillow and lobbed it at Arnaldo, smacking him in the face.

"Jerk," said Arnaldo, and threw it back, hard.

Seconds later pillows were flying. It turned into boys versus girls as London and I climbed up on November's bunk to join her in an assault on the boys below. They retreated to the kitchen area, grabbing some old bread and a roll of toilet paper from the bathroom to launch at us until we threw our pillows and gave them ammunition.

Eventually we all ended up in an exhausted heap on the floor, giggling. The boys left the cabin slowly and reluctantly, mocking our poor showing in the pillow fight.

* * *

We were all a bit sleepy and punchy in the morning. Morfael sent Caleb away and had the rest of us remain in animal form after our first shift that morning. Then one by one, he took us each to a different spot on the school compound, out of sight of the others.

I was last, and he led me behind the boys' cabin to a large rock. "Stay here until you hear me whistle," he said. "I have hidden the same book you searched for yesterday somewhere on the school grounds. The first of you to find it will be free from kitchen duties for a week."

As he glided away, I figured he'd deliberately made it tougher for us to cooperate in this exercise. No kitchen duty was a coveted prize no one would want to give away.

A high-pitched whistle split the air. The starting signal. I crept around the edge of the boys' cabin, sniffing for anything that smelled like leather-bound pages. Hearing nothing inside, I opened the front door using one paw and my teeth. Morfael had taught us each how to do this a few days earlier. With no thumbs, simple tasks could be challenging.

Only a sliver of light illuminated the cabin, but that was enough for me to see every detail. I quickly found a pile of books next to a bunk that smelled a lot like Caleb, but none was the right book. I rubbed my cheek over his pillow before I realized I was marking it as my territory. I smelled something familiar under the bed and pawed it out to find a duffle bag. The zipper was a challenge, but I teased it open using one claw.

Inside lay an odd collection of items, including a glass jar full of dried leaves and sticks that I recognized as coming from the lightning tree near my school in Burbank. I also found a blue marble, an empty plastic water bottle, two rocks, a saltshaker, an unused postcard of Prague, a notepad and pen, and a plush stuffed elephant. For a moment I got misty, thinking it had to be some relic from Caleb's childhood. But then I remembered that we'd fled the Tribunal compound with nothing but our clothes and Lazar's BMW. Caleb must have acquired these things in the meantime. But why?

I forced myself to put the duffle back, and my paw bumped against something else. Another familiar smell reached my nose, and I pulled my back brace out from under the bed. The last time I'd seen it, Mom was putting it in the trunk of Lazar's BMW. I'd been happy to leave it there. It looked smaller than I remembered. Seeing it brought back the pain of wearing it, the suffocation I'd felt because of it. What the hell was it doing under Caleb's bed? It was weird enough that Caleb knew about the brace. But the fact that he'd seen it, that he had it under his bed, sent a wave of shame flooding over me.

I shoved the brace back under the bed, growling to myself. Better not to think about it. *Get back to the test.* I walked around blindly, pretending to explore the rest of the cabin until the suffocating feelings went away. The bathroom held a combination of smells that made me glad I lived with girls. But the book was not in the cabin. As I left, I caught a glimpse of a lean, silvery form slipping through the trees near the girls' cabin.

London. Her nose and ears must have alerted her I was there. But while we were in animal form, the creature instincts were much stronger. And wolves did not socialize with tigers. We were competitors.

But after last night, I felt we were friends. I uttered as soft a call as I could. A second later, London's muzzle appeared through the bushes, her ears alert and upright, her eyes, so wild and blue, staring right at me.

I smacked my tail twice against the boys' cabin wall behind me, then shook my head, hoping she'd understand. She in turn pointed her snout at the girls' cabin. When she looked back at me, she also shook her head.

I exhaled a ruffled "grr" of satisfaction. So the book wasn't in the girls' cabin either.

Together we strode toward Morfael's bent house, watchful for the others. As I turned the doorknob, something crashed two rooms away. At least two of our friends were in the kitchen and, from the sound of it, still searching.

London crept in first, surveying the dark living room. Someone had pulled the rug half upside down and pushed the couch away from the wall. So they'd already searched here. I followed her in, and we inched toward the door to the library, using all our skill to move with utmost quiet.

As we entered the silent library, more rattles and a grunt signaled that Siku was one of the shifters in there. Maybe we should try to join forces.

But London had stiffened, nose trembling as her eyes scanned the bookshelves. She'd caught the scent.

It would be just like Morfael to hide the one book we wanted among hundreds of others. I moved to her side, inhaling to see if I could find that particular book. But all the dust and moldering paper invaded my senses at once. I couldn't pick out the difference.

London had a wolf's superior nose. She got up on her hind legs, front paws on a low shelf for balance, and pressed her nose against the second highest shelf.

Behind us, the hinges on the door to the kitchen groaned. I whipped my head around to see November in rat form walking on her hind feet, pushing the door open with her small pink paws. She let out a piping shriek at the sight of us.

I advanced toward her, tail lashing. She scampered sideways along the wall, letting go of the door.

It never slammed shut, because Siku burst through it. He skidded to a stop, blotting out the doorway with his enormous silhouette, and took the scene in: me standing over November, with London on her hind legs, nose at the books.

He snarled and lunged toward London. I got in the way and he barreled into me. I fell on my side, back legs trying to get a purchase against the furry bulk now pressing down on me. But he got his arms around me in a suffocating hug, his teeth near my throat. I thrashed, but he squeezed me until the air left my lungs, his grip too strong for me to wiggle out.

My own teeth were near his jugular, and my back feet could have raked his belly, possibly disemboweling him, but this was an exercise, not war. I tried to squirm again, hoping I wouldn't have to surrender. But Siku only squeezed harder. Pain lanced through my ribs, and red spots danced before my eyes. I couldn't inhale, couldn't get free. Somewhere in the distance I heard London whining.

My thoughts grew fuzzy. If only I could get smaller somehow, maybe shift to human form, shift somehow into something, anything that could evade his grasp . . .

Blackness flashed through me. Not the pillow-black of unconsciousness but the rocket-black of shifting. The pain vanished as I slipped through Siku's hold, rolling to the floor, scrabbling away from him, leaping from the floor to the top of a chair and farther up to sit on the bookshelf London had been nosing.

Wait, what? I was sitting on my haunches, front paws before me, whiskers quilling outward.

I fit on the bookshelf. I looked up to see the next shelf looming over my head. The books beside me, red and brown leather-bound, were around the height of my head.

London barked. I looked down at her and she whined, backing away. Siku let loose an ear-splitting roar. November chittered and ran back and forth along the baseboards, as if she didn't know where to go.

I looked down at my paws, which were still white, black, and orange, but now in uneven splotches, not stripes. Turning my head, I could see my back and tail, no longer banded like a tiger, but haphazardly swirled, like a tortoise shell. I had shifted into another form, all right. I was a house cat.

Siku shook his huge head as London continued to back quietly away from me, her ears tight against her skull, her tail between her legs. I meowed, not understanding. How could I be more terrifying as a small cat than as a tiger?

November pushed at the door to the back cave and disappeared behind it. London was almost out the other door when it swung open and Morfael walked in. He took in the scene, white brows lowering.

"There is nothing to fear," he said, his voice reverberating with command. "Siku, Laurentia, return to your cabins and shift."

London bolted out of the room. Siku bared his teeth at me, then lumbered through the door.

Morfael approached me, his staff tapping the floor. He looked enormously tall now that I was so much smaller, a gaunt giant in black.

"You," he said, "are precocious."

I wanted to ask what he meant by that, but could only make a trilling noise.

The living room door slammed opened to admit Caleb, a bit breathless from running. "What happened? I saw London bolt out of here, then Siku . . ." He trailed off as he caught sight of me. "What is that cat—Dez?"

I meowed.

Morfael said, "It is she."

Caleb's eyes widened and he stepped toward me. "But this is a second form, completely different from the first. It's unheard of!"

"Perhaps not completely different," said Morfael. "And perhaps not entirely unheard of."

"Well, sure, she's still a cat, but . . ." Smiling, he reached a hand out to me.

His hand looked huge, bigger than my head, and his eyes were enormous pools of darkness. He loomed over me, but the scent from him was the same, the smile the same one I'd seen on his face when he first saw me as a tiger. I stretched my neck out and rubbed my cheek against his fingers.

He scratched my chin, and a deep thrumming began in the depths of my body. I was purring. "Your fur is much softer in this form. I mean—" He cast a glance at Morfael, who remained expressionless. "The differences are astonishing."

"What the hell is wrong with her?" November said from the doorway, back in human form and clad in the sweats Raynard kept in the locker room.

"Nothing's wrong with her," said Caleb. "It's incredible."

"She's a freak," she said, crossing the room as far away from me as she could manage. "Shifters only have one form, one! I'm a rat, and that's it. I can't just decide to be a mouse or a rabbit or some other type of rodent. London's a wolf, not a dog or a fox. Dez's got two forms!"

"At least," said Morfael.

"Oh. My. God." November jerked open the living room door and stomped off.

Caleb raised his eyebrows at Morfael. "You didn't exactly reassure her."

"They need to learn the world is larger than they know, and not all of it is the enemy. Desdemona won them over before, and will again." Morfael turned to go.

"But why can Dez do this and nobody else?" Caleb asked, voicing my own thought. "Is it something to do with how the shadow was suppressed in her for so long? She's not like any other shifter I've seen."

Morfael did not turn around. "You are asking the right questions," he said, and stepped into the kitchen.

"Damn, he's annoying," said Caleb, turning back to me. "What is it? Do you want to get down?"

I stood up, back arched, tail up, and looked down at the ground, then up at him, then at the ground again.

"Okay, I'm going to pick you up and put you down. Is that all right?"

I meowed and nodded once.

"Here we go." He reached over and gently took me under the front legs and behind the back legs, then placed me on the floor. "I'll open the door."

I headed toward the door to the back cave, and he pulled it open for me. As I walked through, something buzzed. I looked up to see him touching his coat pocket, where he kept his phone.

He smiled down at me, but the corners of his eyes didn't crinkle. "The other kids are going to have a hard time with this. Shifters are terrified of anything new. Kind of a funny trait in people who change their shape. Don't let them rattle you."

I was tempted to shift into my human form right there and then, naked or not. Then I could push him to tell me who was calling him. But the thought was too shameful. I'd have time to question him later.

I meowed, and he unexpectedly reached down and stroked me from head to tail. His hand felt strong and warm. I started purring again. "You're beautiful, Dez."

He shut the door quietly behind me.

I had to shift back to human form in front of the girls' locker room because I couldn't reach the doorknob. But no one was in the back cave to see me naked. Worried about the fear I'd seen in London and November, and the rage in Siku, I rushed into the locker room to throw on some sweats before running all the way back to the cabin.

London huddled in the back corner, hugging herself. November sat on the kitchen counter, sucking on a lollipop.

I said, "I don't know what happened..."

"Get out," said London, not meeting my eyes.

My heart dropped. "What? But I..."

"Get out, get out, get out!" Her voice rose to a shriek; then she swallowed hard and squeezed her shoulders even tighter.

"Yeah, you better go," said November, her voice ice-cold. "London's gonna have a hissy if she has to sleep in the same room as you tonight."

Caleb had said they'd have trouble with this new side of me, but kicking me out of the cabin? "I'm still the same person I've always been."

"The Moon knows *what* you'll turn into next," November said. I'd never seen her eyes so flat, so dead.

"The Moon doesn't know shit," I said. "And neither do I. This is all new to me."

"Maybe Morfael will come down from the mountain and explain it," she said. "But until then, you better go."

My throat ached, but I stuffed down the desire to cry or plead with her. "Okay, I'll spend the night at Morfael's. We can talk in the morning." I stuffed a few things into my suitcase. "But I swear to you I don't know what happened."

They said nothing as I rolled the suitcase to the door. My hands were shaking. Just an hour ago we'd all been laughing together. Why kind of people just turned on you like that?

Caleb. Where was Caleb? He'd accepted me from the start, and had kept on no matter what strange thing I did. He even seemed to like that I was different. I searched for him in the kitchen, the library, and the living room in Morfael's house.

Then I heard his voice, outside. I dumped my suitcase and raced for the front door, even as I heard him say, "I can be there in half an hour."

I stopped in front of the closed door as his footsteps moved past outside. "Please wait for me. Don't leave," he said.

My heart dropped to my shoes. He had to be on the phone, talking to whomever it was. I pressed my ear to the door.

"I miss you so much." His voice was getting fainter as he

moved away, into the woods. Toward the BMW. "I promise I'll be there. This can work."

I opened the misshapen door and peeked outside in time to see the edge of his black coat disappearing into the trees. He was carrying the duffle bag I'd seen under his bed. No one else was in sight.

This was it. I'd never see him again, or find out who he was talking to. He was running off. *With some girl.*

I closed the door behind me and followed him.

All those lessons in moving silently paid off as I crept through the underbrush, keeping him just at the edge of my sight. My thoughts raced ahead of me. If he was going to the Beemer to drive away, I'd never be able to follow. No way to sneak into the trunk or cling like a superhero to the underside of the car.

The motorcycle. Siku had moved it outside so he could work on implementing his plan to make it run silently. As long as he'd left it intact, I could follow Caleb.

I heard the Beemer chirp as its lights flashed. I sped up and circled to the left, keeping low. The motorcycle sat on the other side of the car. I needed to get it revved up before Caleb got too far away.

As the Beemer backed up and began to turn around, I rushed through the check list to start the motorcycle. Older bikes were cranky and picky about how you handled them. And machines always seemed to have a special hatred for me.

Fuel shutoff to "on" position, then pull out the choke and turn the ignition. No problem.

The headlight flared, startling me. I fumbled to turn it off. My night vision would serve me well, and I didn't want Caleb spotting me.

I waited in the dark for a moment to see if Caleb had noticed it. His back was to me now, the BMW trundling along slowly down the dirt road, nearly a hundred yards away.

So set the kill switch, squeeze the clutch lever, and kick the gear shift lever, fingers and toes crossed. Balancing the bike, I kicked the side stand up and pressed the start button with my right thumb. The engine fired with a whispering *put-put*. Not sure if I should thank the Moon or some motorcycle shadow in Othersphere, I released the clutch and let it warm up for a few seconds. I didn't have the couple of minutes it needed. I reached down and released the choke, praying it wouldn't stall.

The idle slowed but still sputtered. I looked up and saw no evidence of the BMW, though my ears caught the sound of branches scraping along its sides. No time to wait for the idle to even out. I shifted and gently twisted the throttle.

I applied too much, and the bike took off. I nearly flew off the back of it. But a tight hold on the handgrips saved me, and I lifted my feet as if the ground were on fire. Wobbling wildly, I picked up speed and found where to rest my feet. I breathed deep, and the bike settled into a rut in the road.

The wind lifted my hair off my shoulders, cooling the nervous sweat down my back. The jolts from the bumps in the road made my kidneys ache, but I had to catch up. Thank goodness Caleb needed headlights to see and I didn't.

Within a few minutes I spotted the red glow of his taillights and slowed down so I didn't get too close. He turned right at the paved road and headed uphill. I followed.

As our speed increased, the wind whipped my hair relentlessly into my eyes and mouth. *My kingdom for a ponytail holder.* But only a few minutes later the frosty November mountain air chilled me down to the marrow. A worn hoodie and sweatpants didn't offer much protection. My kingdom would be better spent on a heavy coat and gloves.

Teeth clenched to stop the chattering, I endured the chill for another thirty minutes as we wound our way up and then down into a narrow valley. At least it hadn't snowed yet this year. The dense black of the soldier pines lining the road gave way to softer, more civilian oak and grass. Ahead a neon sign flashed, and I saw the warm glow of a lamp in a window. We were approaching something less than a town but more than a crossroads.

The Beemer pulled into a small parking lot next to a diner with a bright blue sign that spelled out RAE'S. Inside, the fluorescent lights cast a greenish glow over cracked red Naugahyde booths and the graying heads of men in Windbreakers seated at the bar.

I pulled over to the side of the road and kept the motor running. Caleb got out of the Beemer and headed for the diner. He'd asked whomever it was on the phone to wait for him. This must be the spot.

I threw down the kickstand and let the motor continue to idle. Beyond the diner the road was lonely, its short sidewalks empty. I didn't need to stay long, and I doubted I'd be able to sneak in and overhear a conversation without being spotted. I just wanted to see the person Caleb was meeting; then I could leave him behind forever.

Unclasping my numb fingers from the handgrips, I dismounted, stiff as a grandma. Caleb hadn't looked my way. I could see him scanning the interior of the diner as he walked past the lit windows.

I crossed the street to get closer, hands stuffed in my hoodie's pockets to try to warm them. I stopped at the corner of the diner, gazing along the front of the building at Caleb.

He didn't look back. He straightened as if seeing something important and ran a few steps. Inside, someone wearing white was running too.

Fear cut through me. White, the color of the Tribunal. I fought the urge to run. The person in white threw open the diner's glass door and moved right up to Caleb. He wrapped his arms around her and held her close, his dark head next to her golden blond one. Caleb had come to meet Amaris.

CHAPTER 20

A high, gasping inhale came out of me. I thought the ride had chilled me, but only now was I cold, cold as a corpse.

Caleb turned at the sound, too fast for me to duck out of sight. His eyes got huge as we stared at each other. "Dez..." he began.

Amaris saw me too. Her arched eyebrows drew together over her perfect little nose. "What's *she* doing here?"

Tears pooled in my eyes, threatening to spill. Caleb edged toward me, as if he wanted to come closer but was afraid. Fury battled with piercing agony inside me.

"Traitor," I said.

"No!" he said, reaching a hand toward me. "Amaris won't tell them anything. Neither will I. We're running away..."

"Together." I choked it out. The tears broke free and ran down my cheeks.

"Yes."

I couldn't hear more. I ran.

He came after me, but I was faster. The weeks of training, the aftereffects of a recent shift, all gave me speed and strength he couldn't equal. Good thing, because I didn't want to look at him one second longer. I reached the sputtering bike and threw my leg over the seat.

"Wait, Dez!" His voice was rough, desperate. "You can't . . ."

I kicked up the side stand and twisted the throttle. The motorcycle took off. I zoomed past him, then nearly toppled over as I circled back the way I'd come. But I managed to lean into the curve right and kept the wheels on the road. In the side mirror I saw Caleb stop running, then a bend in the street obscured him from sight.

The wind whipped the tears off my cheeks. My heart was gone, replaced by nothingness. Caleb had left me, just as he'd said he would. But how could it be with Amaris? She, her brother, and her father were his enemies, sworn to destroy him, me, the kids at the school, and all the otherkin on the planet. How could he have kissed me the way he did and want her?

I barely saw the road before me. My brain bounced between vivid memories of the touch of his hand, his lips, the dark desire in his gaze on me, and how tightly he had embraced Amaris. My chest ached, as if he'd embedded a knife in my heart and it lay there still.

More than anything, I wanted my mother. I wanted to be home and safe, and never to have heard of Caleb or shifters or Othersphere. But if Caleb was a traitor, or if the Tribunal caught him and made him talk . . . *I've got to tell them.* The instant the Tribunal learned about the school, they would bring all their might to destroy it.

I was so distracted that I nearly missed the tiny dirt road that led to the school. But I did a shaky one-eighty, dodging a white van as it passed by, and jolted my way back down the path. I left the motorcycle where the BMW had been and started to stumble back to the girls' cabin before remembering I wasn't welcome there anymore. Morfael. I could tell him and he'd make sure everyone got away safely.

Someone had piled sheets, a pillow, and a blanket on the couch in Morfael's living room. A fire crackled behind the grate. At least Morfael wasn't kicking me out.

He wasn't anywhere on the ground floor, so I steeled myself and crept up the spiral stairs. I came up against the door. Firelight from below insinuated itself among the shapes. They seemed bigger now, more three-dimensional. I thought I saw a knife, a lightning bolt, and a dragon, but I couldn't be sure. Only the dark sun seemed to hover longest, casting its long rays over everything else.

It took me a few seconds to get up the guts to knock. My first timid tap brought no response, so I banged on it three times with more force. "Morfael! I really need to speak with you. It's about the Tribunal. The school could be in danger."

No reply. So I made my way back down the rickety stairs and wandered into the library to stare at the phone. I had no way to call the shifter Council or my mother and Richard. Perhaps an e-mail . . .

My eyes came to rest on a small blue book on the side table near the phone. The book we'd been searching for when the trouble all began earlier that day. For the first time I noticed the embossed lettering on its spine: *Ancient Symbols and Runes.*

I picked it up. It had seemed so important to find out what the dark sun stood for. But what did it matter now? Caleb was gone. With Amaris.

I ruffled the book's pages, seeing strange squiggles and squares, crabs and daisies and grinning skulls. Then I saw it, a circular sun with black flaring rays. I read, "Rune of the Shadow Walker."

Shadow Walker. Caleb had called Morfael that after he fainted and went into a trance. There was more. "Shadow

Walkers are mythical creatures who traverse the veil between the worlds."

At first the words meant little. But I forced myself to think. Caleb had said that no one could travel between this world and Othersphere. This book even said that such creatures were mythical. Why then did Morfael have that rune carved so prominently on his door?

Those flickering shapes. I blinked and lifted my head, snapping awake as a distant pounding sounded far away. Had I fallen asleep? I was still standing by the side table in the library, book in hand, but I felt as if an eternity had passed and strange suffocating dreams had claimed me. My whole body was vibrating. Behind me, someone was humming.

I whirled, heart jumping. Morfael stood there, his strange eyes bright gold with power. He was pointing his staff at me. The dark sun rune was carved on the tip.

"What the hell are you doing?" I stepped forward, reaching for the staff without thinking. The humming stopped as Morfael drew it back.

"I am sorry," he said.

"Why?" I said sharply.

Outside, the thumping noise grew louder. Then he said, "I will do all I can. If I fail, you must do what you think best."

The *whomp whomp* noise outside grew, almost drowning out his words.

"Oh no." I pushed past Morfael and ran through the living room to open the front door. I knew what I'd see.

Dawn was lightening the eastern sky. The tops of the trees danced in a fierce wind. Waves of sound beat against us as the insect form of a large helicopter hovered over the central area between Morfael's house and the two cabins.

As I gaped up at the aircraft, its side door slid open and a person in gray dropped something. A ladder unfurled, and the figure began to descend, a long, thin object, a gun, strapped to its back. Another form in similar colors crouched behind a gun mounted on a tripod. Its point swiveled toward us.

I slammed the door shut and threw the lock. "The Tribunal," I said. "Get back."

"No," said Morfael.

Something thwacked into the door. Chips of wood flew. Bullets.

"Ximon is here." Morfael walked toward the front door, unlocked it, then turned and threw something at me. I caught it automatically and looked down. The key to the gun locker. "I'll hold them as long as I can," he said. "The wall will drop when you're ready."

"Wall?" I said. "What wall? Don't go out there!"

Morfael threw open the front door and strode out, staff held at arm's length. A terrible vibration emanated from him. Through the slanted doorway I saw someone on the ground lower a rifle and fire at him point-blank. A few inches in front of his staff, something black opened and closed in the wink of an eye, like a brief splotch of ink. The bullet was gone.

Behind that man stood another, tall and broad-shouldered, his head of thick white hair not covered by a gray hood like the others. He smiled at Morfael, his teeth even and unnaturally bright. Ximon.

"Fiend," he said, in an almost friendly tone. "Give me my son and I may spare your students."

Behind him, five more figures in gray fanned out. Two more headed for the front door of the girls' cabin. The other two fanned toward the boys' cabin, guns pointed. I recognized the blond hair and proud nose of the last one—Lazar. But if Lazar was there, what did Simon mean about Morfael giving him his son?

"If you loved him as you believe you do," said Morfael, "you would let him be what he is."

That's all I had time to see. Morfael made a small gesture back toward me and the open door.

Then it was gone. A wall of rock stood where the front of the house had been. The sound of helicopter blades vanished.

The front wall of the house had turned to stone, as if Morfael had drawn a veil of rock between me and the danger. I was now inside a cave. A cave drawn from shadow. He had given me time, and the key to the gun locker.

I ran.

Raynard stored Lazar's silver gun in a locker near the gym equipment, along with boxes of bullets and an extra magazine. I unlocked it, wrapped a towel around my hand, and grabbed the gun, the original mag and the spare, and a box of bullets.

What if they've already killed everyone? What if I'm too late?

Even through the towel, the silver made my hand itch. I wasn't the best person to use the gun, but perhaps I could get it to Arnaldo.

I ran back to the living room and made sure a round was chambered as I waited for Morfael's rock wall to fall.

What if I'm trapped here?

To stop that thought I tried to picture the landscape outside. As soon as I could, I'd move to wherever the greatest concentration of objurers was. That would be the place that needed the most help.

I stuck the spare magazine and the box of bullets in my hoodie pocket. I moved to where I figured the door would reappear if Morfael ever let me out of there. He'd sent me for the gun. That had to mean he wanted me to fight.

I made sure the gun's safety was off.

Then, without a sound, the wall was wooden again, and the thudding of the chopper's blades beat through to me.

Siku's guttural bear roar overrode the helicopter noise, followed by the rattle of bullets. Someone shouted, "He's down!"

More bullets. The eerie howl of a wolf sent goose bumps down my arm.

I unlocked the door and pulled it open.

CHAPTER 21

I stepped outside and sighted my pistol on the mounted rifle in the chopper.

I fired. The pistol kicked. Cordite stung my nose. The man behind the helicopter's gun ducked. I fired again. The bullet sparked off the gun, and the gunman threw himself backward.

I moved left, gun trained on the chopper. Only then did I take a moment to see what else was going on. Events slowed down around me. My right hand burned from the silver gun; crazy gusts of wind from the chopper whipped my hair around like a live thing. The universe narrowed down to now, and nothing else.

In front of the girls' cabin, a silver wolf tripped a man in gray with a nip and a shove. He sprawled on the ground while another objurer tried to get a bead on London without endangering his friend. A large brown rat scuttled out of the undergrowth.

By the boys' cabin, an eagle flew at the face of another man. His long wings flapped against the wash from the helicopter's blades as he clawed at the man's eyes. A grizzly bear thrashed on the ground near them, encased in silver netting as two men struggled to secure it around him. Near them, Lazar threw another net at Arnaldo. It reached out for him, but he fluttered out of the way.

Siku needed help. I swiveled to run toward him, then froze. A lean form in black lay on the ground not twenty feet away. Morfael. Blood spattered his pale neck and hands. Ximon stood over him, leaning forward, about to take the twisted staff still clutched in one gnarled hand.

Black fury narrowed my eyes and steadied my hands. I aimed the gun at Ximon. "Back off," I snapped. "Or I'll shoot."

Ximon straightened, a condescending smile baring his teeth. "Where are your fangs, Amba?"

Shock shivered through me. He was using the same word that Morfael had when we'd first met.

His voice deepened. "Drop the gun. Show me your claws." The sound of it pushed at me, and my fingers loosened on the stock of the gun. I wished they were claws so I could tear out his throat.

"No," I managed to say. My own voice stabbed through the command in his. "I won't let you trick me."

He frowned and swept his eyes over me, assessing. "What has Morfael done to you? You're able to resist me now because the shadow is gone. So this is how he hid you from me all those years."

"Hid me?" His words made no sense.

"Come with me now and I'll tell you everything you want to know," he said. "I know where your true parents are. I can show you the very essence of your self. And if you like"—he smiled again—"I can take it from you. You can be normal again. I can even take your memories of the otherkin, of these last few weeks. You'll be just like any other teenage girl. And your family can live forever safe from shifters and the Tribunal."

I felt the gun waver in my burning hand. "You're lying," I said.

"Don't you understand?" he said. "It's the easiest way for me to save the world from you."

Save the world . . . *from me?*

"Our Lord only blesses bloodshed as a last resort. Come with me, and you'll never hear the word otherkin again." He held out his hand.

There it was. The thing I wanted. Or thought I did. I kept the gun trained on him. "You'll leave my family alone?"

"I promise. If you come with me now, they will live out their days safe from all this." He swept his arm out to take in the helicopter buzzing above, Arnaldo and November battling objurers, and Siku thrashing in a silver net. "It will be as if none of this happened."

It was tempting. So tempting. Everyone here had rejected me, called me a freak. All I had to do was turn my back and soon I'd be home safe with my mother once more.

Siku flailed and uttered a guttural moan. Arnaldo flew over to pluck at the silver strands with his talons, only to be driven back by bullets. Over by the girls' cabin London dodged a tranquilizer dart and leapt at the man who fired on her. We'd all be dead soon, or taken, no matter what I did. We didn't stand a chance.

We. That was how I thought of us all, in spite of everything. We.

You must do what you think best.

Morfael had known I'd have to decide. He must have suspected Ximon would take him down. Now it was up to me.

Home, safety, and a normal life. Or death or capture with a group of people who didn't want me sleeping in the same cabin with them.

"No," I heard myself say.

Ximon's hand dropped. "Don't be a fool."

"You're a murdering son of a bitch," I said. "I'd rather die than give you what you want."

His thick white eyebrows lowered thunderously. "Very well, then."

I stepped toward him, pointing the gun as my finger tightened on the trigger. "Tell them to free Siku."

"Stupid girl," he said, touching his ear. He was wearing a headset almost too small to see. "Objurers, kill them all but the bear."

"Very well, then," I said, and fired. The gun kicked in my hand.

But the bullet did not strike him. A spark of light flared around Ximon like a shield. The bullet was gone.

"I told you to try your claws," he said, walking toward me. A low hum began deep in his throat.

I had to shift. About to drop the gun, I saw a dark-haired figure in a long black coat walk out of the woods behind Ximon. My heart lifted.

"Get away from her, Ximon," said Caleb. His face was creased with fury and exhaustion, his duffle bag over his shoulder and streaks of mud on his pants. But he'd never looked more wonderful. The jar full of leaves and twigs from the lightning tree was tucked under his arm. His right hand reached inside it.

Ximon turned, one of us now on either side of him. "There you are," he said. "My son."

I felt myself get very still, except for the hand holding the gun. It trembled. "Your son?"

Caleb's eyes shot over to mine, tension between his brows.

"He didn't tell you?" said Ximon. "Yes, Caleb is my son,

half brother to Amaris and Lazar." He turned back to Caleb. "We have your sister safe. Come with us now and I promise she'll stay that way."

Sister. Amaris was Caleb's sister. In a flash I saw it all anew. Caleb, throwing his arms around Amaris in a hug in that diner, helping her escape from a father willing to put his own son in a cage, saving her from a life of isolation ruled by fanatics. Between that moment and this, the Tribunal must have taken Amaris back, but somehow Caleb had escaped. A huge weight lifted from me even as Caleb paced closer to Ximon, power vibrating from him as his eyes flared gold.

"There's only one way she'll ever be safe," he said. "If you are dead." He drew a twig from the jar and held it out. "I call you forth!" he commanded.

The stick struck Ximon's shoulder.

And fell to the ground, rather anticlimactically. Ximon stepped back from it, his blues eyes widening. He began to intone a note of his own.

Too late. A black beam from Caleb's hand hit the stick. A blinding slash of light leapt from the ground and stabbed at the sky. I thought my heart stopped. The boom from it silenced the helicopter for a second.

Ximon cried out, illuminated in silhouette. The bolt didn't strike him directly, but the charge flung him back. I smelled ozone, and every hair on my arms stood up. Then the world went dark again, and Ximon lay in a heap on the ground. Smoke curled up from the ground where he'd stood.

Above, the helicopter bobbed like a cork. It hadn't been struck, but the pilot ascended sharply in reaction. Now that Ximon was down, I ran to Morfael, fumbling for a pulse under his pointed jaw.

Caleb strode over to Ximon. His white head lift weakly, hands grasping at the soil beneath him. So he was still conscious. Caleb stared down at his father, a grim, lean figure in black holding a jar full of lightning.

"Please, Caleb," said Ximon, his normally deep voice scratchy and frail. "I do everything only to save you. Because I love you."

"We have different ideas of love," said Caleb.

I held my breath as his fingers dropped a stick from the lightning tree back into the jar. Instead, he held out the salt-shaker in his left hand and tipped it, sprinkling salt onto his father. "Come forth," he ordered.

"Wait," said Ximon. "Please..."

But the black smoke from Caleb's hand had struck the white powder. It exploded into a thousand yellowish strands. They fanned out in a gummy net, encasing Ximon. He writhed, but the filaments held his arms clamped to his sides, his back glued to the ground beneath him.

I didn't know how to feel. Part of me wanted Ximon dead. But Ximon was Caleb's father. I could understand why he hadn't killed him.

Beneath my hand, Morfael's skin was damp but warm. A heartbeat thudded regularly. Blood was leaking from his side, but slowly. "He's alive!" I shouted to Caleb. "Get to Siku!"

Caleb hesitated. "Dez," he said. "I'm sorry I couldn't tell you..."

"You can beg my forgiveness later," I said. Urgency beat through my bloodstream. "We have to help the others now." I grabbed his arm, and we ran flat out toward the boys' cabin.

The objurers, including Lazar, had fired tranquilizing darts into Siku. He lay still inside the silver net as they dragged him into the trees.

The man under Arnaldo's onslaught screamed and fell into a fetal position on the ground. Arnaldo landed, cawing out to us with piercing urgency and prepared to take flight again.

Lazar was retreating with Siku. I pointed his own silver gun at him. But the bear's bulk got in the way, giving him and the other objurers cover. I had to lower the gun for fear of hitting Siku. Every second they gained more concealment, moving farther into the forest. Lazar was talking into his headset. *Damn.* Was he ordering reinforcements?

The helicopter descended again, rotating so that its open side allowed the gun to point at us. I fired at the gunman as he reached for the rifle. He winced backward.

"I'll cover!" I said.

Caleb nodded. "I'm on Siku."

He ran after Lazar and the men with the net, vanishing into the woods with a swirl of his coat. Arnaldo leapt into the air, wings flapping with terrific force against the crazy wind from the helicopter. A bullet zipped into the ground where he'd been. He wheeled, lost control, and tumbled through the air.

I forced back my fear and anxiety. Giving in to emotion was a luxury I couldn't afford. I fired again at the man wielding the mounted gun, but he didn't flinch this time. The gun swiveled toward me. I broke and ran behind the boys' cabin for cover. Bullets cut into the ground, kicking dirt over my feet as Arnaldo grabbed the roof of the cabin with his powerful talons and righted himself.

I looked up at Arnaldo, his cruel beak and fierce yellow eyes above me. "As long as the copter's pinning us here, we'll never get to Siku," I said. "Take it down."

Arnaldo nodded once, spread his wings, and took off, this time away from the helicopter. The choppy air from its blades caught him under the wings, and he zoomed out over the trees.

A bolt of lightning leapt into the air off in the direction of the dirt road. A brain-splitting clap of thunder followed. My heart lifted. Caleb was still out there, making life tough for the Tribunal. As soon as I could, I would shift to tiger form and join him.

The helicopter's gas tank was probably *there*, I decided, eyeing the back end. I aimed and fired. The bullet sparked off the runner. Damn. I was a terrible shot. I had to press harder on the trigger, and the pain in my hands wasn't helping.

The automatic gun on the copter rattled. Bullets smacked the ground near London, November, and the objurer as they wrestled. Blood spurted from the back of the objurer, and he lay still. So the Tribunal had stopped worrying about its own men.

London scrabbled to her feet and broke free. November scurried away, leaving a trail of blood. She'd been hit.

I fired again at what I hoped was the chopper's gas tank. The bullets penetrated something, but I couldn't be sure it was vital.

Then a large winged form spiraled down from the gray sky. Arnaldo, far above, had something huge in his talons. He positioned himself right above the center of the helicopter.

Bullets chased London and November until I lost sight of them. Then Arnaldo dropped the thing in his claws. It tumbled down. A rock, almost a boulder, plummeted toward the chopper's blades.

"Get cover!" I screamed, hoping London and November could hear me. I dove into the brush behind the boys' cabin, rolling to see the rock fall directly into the blurry circle that held the copter in the air.

A great crack interrupted the whomping storm of sound. The individual blades were outlined against the sky, warping before my eyes. Shards sliced the air. The eagle shrieked. His wing beat faltered.

Slowly, like a flying ant with broken wings, the helicopter shuddered and fell. I covered my head with my arms.

A crash like a breaking wave shook the ground. A gout of flame bellowed out, licked the boys' cabin front door, and retreated. Heat washed over me as I got to my feet and stumbled forward, coughing.

Smoking wreckage filled the space between the cabins.

Our peaceful enclave looked like a scene from *Black Hawk Down*. I looked away from the bloody mess in the cockpit and searched the sky for Arnaldo. He'd been hit. I could only hope London and November had escaped the fireball.

Arnaldo landed heavily on a tree branch ahead of me, holding one wing awkwardly. As I ran toward him, London and November crawled out of the bushes. November was limping and squeaking.

I stuffed the gun in my belt and knelt down in front of November as she rolled over. A bloody strip of flesh on her side oozed blood. "He winged you," I said. "It's not bad, but you should shift and heal it."

November raised her whiskered nose and let loose a stream of angry chirps. I thought I heard a hissing noise, then a sort of "tchu."

"Siku?"

November nodded vigorously.

"You want to go with us after Siku first." As she kept nodding, I said, "Okay. I'm about to shift. You can catch a ride on me if you want. One sec."

I moved to Arnaldo. He lifted one wing, croaking with effort. Blood streamed down his feathers from a shard of dark plastic embedded like a spear in his side under the left wing. A piece of one of the shattered rotors had stabbed into him.

"Okay, this is not good," I said. "Arnaldo, I'm going to lift you down to the ground and slide this right out, but it'll hurt like hell and you better shift right after I do it, or you could black out from the blood loss."

Arnaldo staggered a bit on the branch and nodded once. I wrapped my arms against his warm, feathered body, his powerful wings draping along my arms, his pointed beak brushing my neck.

Once he was standing more or less firmly on the ground, I gingerly placed my left hand on his side for leverage. A guttural sound of pain came from him, but he held very still. I used my towel to grab the shard in his side. "One . . . two . . ."

I yanked on two, trying to pull it at the same angle it had entered.

Arnaldo squawked. I ducked to avoid the furious flapping of wings and backed off. The shard in my hand looked whole. Blood gushed from the wound. "I think I got it all," I said. "Shift now. That's what I'm going to do."

I didn't bother removing my clothes. Minutes had passed since Caleb took off after Siku. We couldn't waste any more time. Arnaldo shifted, his long skinny body lying naked face-down on the grass, the wound in his side gone. Then the space around him warped again, and he was an eagle once more. These last few weeks of practice had made him as good at shifting as November.

"Good." I closed my eyes and dove down into the black heart of Othersphere inside me. That is, I tried. But the dark dangerous place wasn't there.

The shadow is gone, Ximon had said. *So this is how he hid you from me.*

Had Morfael done something to me in the library when I'd found him pointing his staff with the dark sun rune at me?

I opened my eyes and told myself not to panic. There wasn't time. "Something's wrong," I said. "You guys go ahead. Find Caleb. Get Siku."

November leapt onto London's back. Arnaldo cawed, his head cocked with what might have been concern. Then he spread his wings and took off.

I watched them go, then hunkered down into a fetal position and searched again for the connection to Othersphere. It had been so easy for days now. The dread still hit me before I plunged into the shift, every single time. But I'd learned to take note of it and keep going.

Now there was nowhere to go, nothing to dive into, nothing to fear. I concentrated on all the anger I felt, and there was more than enough. I was seething with fury and a desire to retaliate. Normally these emotions made shifting all the easier. Now I had nowhere to pour them. It wasn't just that a door had closed on Othersphere. A steel vault had been built around it. If I focused everything I had, I could feel it flickering there behind some barrier. But I couldn't reach it.

I stood up, as lost as I'd felt since I'd awoken in the silver cage all those weeks ago. Smoke from the helicopter rose in a thick column toward the peach sky. Bodies, some bloody, some struggling and ensnared with goo, lay everywhere. Inside me, something had changed, just when I needed to shift more than anything. Had Morfael betrayed me somehow? Whatever lay behind the change, I'd have to keep going, as a human.

Movement in the corner of my eye. I whirled, pulling the gun from my belt. Four more figures in gray stood over Ximon. The web of goo pinning him to the ground was gone. Three of them hoisted him onto a sling between them. The fourth lowered a rifle at me.

I pulled the trigger, aiming not at the gunman but at Ximon. But nothing happened. I squeezed again, shuffling toward the trees for cover. Bullets danced at my feet, but the gun in my hand would not fire.

Another lightning bolt speared the sky and thunder rolled over me. The vibration spoke of Caleb. He was alive and throwing electricity at our foes.

With my gun misfiring, I had no weapon, not even my claws, against the four Tribunal members now rescuing Ximon. I had to let them take him.

I didn't allow myself to feel disappointment. Too much still to do. Bullets bit into the leaves around me as I dove into the undergrowth of the forest and ran toward the lightning.

CHAPTER 22

I ran through the woods toward the noises, feeling the ache from the useless pistol now at my belt.

"Follow them!" It was Caleb's voice.

Through the trees I saw him as he cried out to the circling form of Arnaldo above. He was breathing hard, hair a wild tangle, coat splashed with mud, blood, and yellow gunk. But he was unharmed. I allowed myself to breathe. He had a pistol in one hand, pointed at an objurer with his hands up. London, with November still riding on her back, flanked the man, growling. Nearby lay the forms of three other objurers, one still smoking from a lightning strike, the others glued into submission.

The eagle shrieked, tilted his wings, and flew off. He remained in sight long enough that I could see he was following a set of large tire tracks rutted into the soil.

I walked into the small clearing. "What happened?"

Caleb took a step toward me, a huge, relieved smile breaking over his face. Then he refocused to keep his gun on the man before him, and said, "You okay?"

"Not hurt," I said. I didn't want to tell him I couldn't shift, not in front of an objurer. "Where's Siku?"

"They came in a truck and took Siku away before we could stop them," said Caleb.

My knees felt like jelly as I walked up to the objurer with his hands up, but I willed myself to stay upright. "Where are they taking Siku?" I didn't recognize the hard voice that came out of me.

The man was shivering, but he stared off over my head and said nothing.

"Never mind," I said. "I don't need you to tell me. But you look tired and I think you should take a nap now."

"Agreed." Caleb walked up and smacked him across the temple with the butt of his gun. The man dropped.

I pulled my own gun out of my belt. "Please take this. There's something wrong with it, and I think my hands might catch on fire."

He took the gun, eyebrows furrowed, and turned it over in his hands. Black streaks crept over the warped grip frame and now covered the safeties, hammer, and almost all of the barrel. "What happened? It's like you threw it in a furnace."

"I think my hands went in there with it," I said, holding them up. The right was bright red and covered in large blisters, as if I'd poured boiling water over it. It ached that way too. The left was sprouting hives. "I can't shift," I said. "I don't know what's wrong, but I just can't."

He squinted at me and hummed faintly, moving closer. I could see the stubble on his chin and flecks of gold in his eyes. I wanted to collapse into his arms, to sleep there for a million years. "I'm so glad you're back," I said, so that only he could hear.

"We'll talk," he said. "But the shadow is gone. At least..."

He hummed again, a little louder. London inched up to us, sniffing. November sat on her back, clutching tufts of silver fur in her small pink paws. At any other time they would've looked like the most popular video on YouTube: "Rat rides Wolf."

"The shadow's in there somewhere," Caleb said. "But it's like someone threw it down a well or something."

"I guess we can worry about that later." I used my left hand to push the hair out of my eyes. "November, you okay?"

She chirped once and nodded.

"Bullet grazed her," I said to Caleb's questioning look. "She needs to shift and we need to get back to Morfael. A bunch of objurers chased me off so they could rescue Ximon. Come on."

"You think Morfael's okay?" Caleb turned, and we ran side by side through the woods. London bolted past us with her light-footed gallop, carrying November.

"He better be," I said. "If we call an ambulance, will it be able to find us here?"

"I don't think so," he said. "Raynard should be here soon. If the authorities come, we'll end up in jail."

"Yeah, the pieces of helicopter would be especially hard to explain," I said, panting. "Arnaldo dropped a rock on it from above."

"Wow." He shot me a look.

We came to a halt in the clearing. Ximon was gone. The remains of the chopper smoldered between the cabins, the crumpled cockpit still leaking blood. A large black patch marked where the lightning had struck, and the yellow goo was gone, back to shadow.

So they'd left their dead behind but had taken those still alive. They'd left Morfael too, lying like a jumble of bones and shredded black cloth.

Caleb surveyed the blackened spot where Ximon had lain,

then walked over and kicked the side of the house. "Damn, damn, *damn!*"

"Help me with Morfael," I said. "His skin is like ice."

We got Morfael inside and laid him on the couch. I ran to the first aid locker in the cave and came back armed with disinfectant, scissors, cotton, and bandages. Morfael had taught us the basics of first aid. London had been the star in those classes.

Caleb peeled back Morfael's blood-soaked black shirt while I attempted to open the disinfectant. My burned right hand screamed every time I tried, so I had to let Caleb do it.

"You better use some on that burn," he said. "Morfael's been gut-shot."

The front door opened. I nearly jumped out of my skin until I saw it was London and November, now in human form and clad in hastily donned jeans and sweatshirts. November looked fit enough, if rather pale. The shift had healed her bullet wound.

"Is he okay?" London said, striding up to Morfael and eyeing the wound. She'd missed a smear of blood on her jaw.

"He's alive, but unconscious," I said.

"He's pretty stable considering the circumstances." London lifted Morfael's eyelids to look at his pupils, feeling for his pulse. "But the pain from abdominal wounds is horrific. Maybe that's what made him pass out. He's lost some blood, but not as much as I would've thought. Here, give me that." She snatched the bandages out of Caleb's hands.

"We should drive him to the nearest hospital now," I said.

November shook her head. "Let Raynard do that."

"Morfael's critically injured!" I looked around, but only Caleb seemed to be listening to me.

"And just how are a bunch of teenagers going to explain to a doctor that their teacher at an unregistered school got shot?" London asked.

November nodded. "The second thing shifters teach their

kids, after 'The Tribunal is your enemy,' is to avoid all inter-action with government and authority, like cops and hospi-tals. Raynard's a humdrum and an adult. He can tell the hospital that he and Morfael are roommates, that it was an accident, like the gun went off while he was cleaning it."

"But..."

"Morfael should be okay if we wait for Raynard." Lon-don finished tying up the neat bandage around Morfael's waist. Tiny splotches of blood, like Rorschach tests, blos-somed through the snowy whiteness. "The bullet went right through his side and didn't hit anything vital. I've stopped the worst bleeding. And Raynard's due any second." She looked up at me reassuringly. "Trust me."

"Okay, but if Raynard isn't here in five minutes, we take him," I said.

November jerked her thumb back to point over her shoul-der at the library. "I've got to call my parents."

"Yeah, I'll be right behind you," said London.

"What?" I stood up. November was fading back toward the library, where the phones were. "You think they'll help us with him?"

"No, stupid," said November. "They'll come get us."

London nodded. "We have to get out of here before the Tribunal comes back."

"The school is kind of out of commission for now, I guess," I said. "Do you know how to reach Siku's family?"

"No," said November.

London shook her head. "That's not our problem," she said. "My mom's going to have a stroke. We'll probably have to go into hiding."

"Hiding? Wait." I stepped toward November. "Someone has to help Siku."

"That's up to the bear-shifters," she said. "Not us."

"Why not?"

Arnaldo jerked the door open and walked in, human once

more, wearing his usual jeans and dark sweater. "They're taking Siku south and west," he said as we all turned. "I followed them till they started shooting at me."

"South and west." I caught Caleb's eye. He nodded. We knew where they were going.

Arnaldo looked down at Morfael. "How's he doing?"

"He's stable," said London.

"We need to get him to the hospital," I said.

"It's almost seven. Raynard should be here any minute." Arnaldo, too, was drifting toward the library door. "Better get Morfael out of here before my dad comes to get me. He'll blame Morfael for all this."

London wiped her hands on a kitchen towel and walked toward the library door. They were all prepared to leave. How could that be?

"But what about Siku?" I said.

November bit her lip while Arnaldo shook his head. "He's lost," said November, her voice very small. "We have to get back to our tribes. . . ."

"But we know where they're taking him," I said. "They've got a facility in the Mojave Desert. Caleb and I have been there."

"So what?" A tear escaped down November's cheek. She brushed it away with an angry flick of her hand. "So you know where he is. What good does that do?"

They were each poised to run or fly. That's what shifters did in a crisis. They retreated, rejoined their tribe, and left the wounded and captured to fend for themselves. They would go into hiding, hoping what had happened to Siku wouldn't happen to them. And Siku would remain drugged and bound in the hands of people who thought he was an agent of evil.

A sudden fierce certainty took hold of me. The isolation of tribes had to stop, or the Tribunal's plan to wipe every shifter off the earth would come to pass.

"*We* can rescue him," I said.

November let out a single, sarcastic "Ha!" London looked confused. Arnaldo was staring at me, his gaze as piercing as when he was an eagle.

Caleb came to stand beside me. "She's right," he said. "If we don't get him out of there in the next twelve hours, he'll be dead. Or worse."

"They'll kill us if we try to help him!" said November.

"He's probably dead already," London said in a small voice.

"No, think about it. They took the time to drug and capture him," Caleb said. "They prefer to take otherkin alive if they can, so they can do things, experiments."

Arnaldo uncrossed his arms. "And how do you know *that*?"

Caleb opened his mouth, but I interrupted. "Caleb and I were both captured by the Tribunal," I said. "That's how we met, in adjoining cages."

"And Dez got us out of there," Caleb said. "If you help us, we can get Siku out too."

"What kind of experiments?" said November, challenging.

"Did they do something to you?" London was looking at me. With a jolt I remembered that I was still abnormal to them, a shifter with more than one shape.

"No," said Caleb, firmly. "They didn't have time to start anything on Dez. But before they caught me, I broke into their files and read a few reports on their experiments. They believe technology is God's gift to man. They think they can find a way to force the shadow out of all the shifters, with drugs and particle accelerators and prayer. I don't know exactly what they're trying to do, but it can't be good for the otherkin. If we go in and rescue Siku, maybe we can find out more."

"Maybe even put a stop to it," I said.

"Why should we believe anything you guys say?" November's voice rose to near hysteria. London shrank back from her, already halfway through the door to the library. "You're a caller, and Dez is a freak. She doesn't really care about Siku. She just wants to use us to get rid of the threat to her family. As long as the Tribunal's around, she can't go back home. She doesn't care if we all die, as long as we help her get rid of them. I don't blame anyone for wanting their family, but no way am I going to die for it."

The muscles in my jaw tightened, and I clenched my fists.

"What is it, kitty cat?" November said, her eyes narrowing. "Did I hit a nerve?"

Then I saw it. Behind the bravado, lurking in the tilt of her eyebrows and the corners of her mouth, was fear. She'd been shot tonight, and her best friend had been kidnapped. All her life she'd been told that rat-shifters could trust only other rats. If I yelled at her, it would only confirm everything she'd grown up believing.

I closed my eyes and looked down inside myself. Instead of the big black pool of Othersphere, I saw just my heart.

I opened my eyes and said, "I know you love Siku."

November opened her mouth, but nothing came out.

I pushed on. "We all love him. But we're scared. I'm scared too. I mean, fanatical cult members with helicopters and guns are coming after us. It's insane." I took another breath and looked at the three faces ranged before me. "But if we retreat, they win. If we abandon Siku, not only do we guarantee that he'll die, we guarantee our own deaths in the long run because they'll come after us. They won't stop unless we make them stop."

Against all odds, Arnaldo was nodding. Caleb placed his hand on the small of my back, and a rush of warmth pushed back the wobbly anxiety threatening to take over my body.

"We're connected," I said. "The world keeps trying to turn us into enemies: cats versus bears versus wolves and on and on. But in spite of all the hateful things parents say, in spite of centuries of isolation, we keep coming together. One game of tag in the leaves, one night throwing pillows in the cabin, and it's like we're all the same tribe, you know?"

London inhaled a quick, sobbing breath. Arnaldo put his arm around her shoulders. She leaned into him, her eyes red, and looked up at me.

"You guys are my family now," I said. "Siku too, even though he hates my guts at the moment. Families fight, but then they make up. We have to look out for each other. That's what families do."

November's eyes were bright, her jaw tense. "They've got guns and aircraft and probably tanks and silver bombs. All we've got are fangs and claws."

"And wings," said Arnaldo.

"With his claws and wings, Arnaldo brought that helicopter down," I said. "With all the skills you guys bring to the mix, we can slip in there and get Siku free before they know we're there."

"And if they do find us there, then we fight," said Arnaldo. "Look what happened today. For all their guns and superior numbers, we beat them back. They wanted to take all of us, or to kill us. And we stopped them."

November eyed him. "You've swallowed the Kool-Aid," she said, but there was no bite to her tone. The temperature in the room was shifting. If I could just tip it a little further...

"I know it's scary..." I started to say.

"I'm not scared," November interrupted sharply.

"I am!" said London.

November let out a reluctant laugh, and the crazy-high level of tension in the room eased a bit. "Well, okay, so I'm a little scared. But it's not the danger, really. It's..." She screwed up her pointy face, trying to find the right word. "It's the weirdness of it all."

"Nobody attacks the Tribunal!" London's blue eyes blinked rapidly just thinking about it.

"That's why they'll never see us coming," said Caleb.

Arnaldo nodded emphatically. "I think they count on us staying underground. My dad's always saying the same old thing: The only way to avoid trouble is to trust no one but your own tribe. But how can you avoid trouble when it hunts you down and kidnaps your friends?"

November cleared her throat. "If, and this is strictly hypothetical, if we tried to get Siku out of their compound, how would we do it?"

I glanced at Caleb. He was smiling. "Let's talk about it," I said. "Hypothetically."

CHAPTER 23

A few minutes later, Raynard found us on the floor by Morfael's couch seated around Caleb's hastily scrawled map of the Tribunal facility. We jumped to our feet as he walked in and stood there, arms full of groceries.

"You've been busy," he said. "I love what you've done with the helicopter."

An involuntary laugh escaped me. Who knew grumpy Raynard had a bitchy sense of humor? Then his eyes traveled over the back of the couch and saw Morfael lying there. His already thin mouth flattened into a line.

As we gathered around him and babbled about what had happened, Raynard put aside the groceries, knelt down, and took Morfael's limp, emaciated hand. His head bowed slightly and he bit his lip, but he let us finish.

When we were done, he said, "I wonder if he knew he'd need first aid when he taught it to you." He lifted his head and managed a watery smile. "I'll take him to the hospital in Bishop."

"We're going to rescue Siku," I said on impulse. The others startled, but Raynard was the only one we could tell. We'd decided not to call anyone's parents. The plan was to send e-mails to our families just before we left to get Siku. We'd tell them the basics, just in case things didn't go the way we planned. "We know where the Tribunal compound is."

Raynard stood with effort, hoisting up the back of his sagging pants. He didn't look surprised, or angry. He nodded once, as if that was no more and no less than what he'd expected to hear. "I'll try to have the mess outside cleaned up by the time you get back," he said. "Now help me get him into my truck."

After Raynard and Morfael were gone, we ate a quick breakfast and loaded up the Beemer. Caleb tucked his satchel of goodies down by my feet in the front passenger seat. I saw the pink tip of the stuffed elephant's trunk sticking out of the side pocket. I asked him what it would become when he called it. He said only that it was a last resort. Before I could ask what that meant, exactly, he went on to say he had maybe two more uses left on the saltshaker that sprinkled out shadow glue. Twigs from the lightning tree were also running low.

Then he went into the boys' cabin and came out with my back brace.

"Why are you bringing that?" I asked, glad the other kids weren't there to see it. The shame attached to it hadn't gone away. The fact that Caleb had the thing filled me with conflicting feelings. He still cared about me in spite of it, but I wished he'd never seen it. "I don't need it."

"You might." He set the brace down in the trunk, his dark eyebrows pinching together as he looked down at it.

The brace lay there, like an abandoned half suit of armor.

Caleb's black eyes concentrated on it. "What do you see?" I said.

"It has a potent shadow," he said. "More so even than the leaves from the lightning tree. I couldn't see it while you were wearing it. I think whatever kept you from shifting most of your life obscured it too. But now the power just spirals off it."

The idea that the brace had some weird shadow made a strange kind of sense to me. For years it had had power over me, pushing my body around. But I wasn't sure I wanted to see its shadow form after all that time spent wrapped around me.

"I haven't had the guts to call it forth yet," Caleb was saying. "But we're heading into a situation where we'll need all the power we can get."

I ran my eyes over the curved plastic lines of the brace again, trying to see something extraordinary there. But I couldn't see past its plastic bones and the pain it had caused.

Caleb slammed the trunk shut and took my hand. "When we have a few minutes alone, I'll explain everything. About Amaris and... Ximon." He could barely say his father's name.

"Okay." I let my hand rest in his. It felt good there, right.

"Every time I think of how you put up with that brace for years, I remember how strong you are. And I marvel at you even more."

Tears sprang to my eyes but did not fall. He didn't like me in spite of the brace. The brace actually made him care for me even more.

With November in rat form, the five of us fit into the BMW. She perched on the back dash in a patch of late-afternoon sun and fell asleep.

The Internet directions had said the drive would take almost six hours, but the way Caleb drove, we'd be there in four. We stopped off in Bishop for snacks and waved symbolically at Morfael in the hospital somewhere nearby as we left.

With any luck, we'd be able to visit him, with Siku, on our way back.

We hit Barstow after dark, and Caleb insisted we eat, though I wasn't hungry. A drive-thru provided a greasy dinner. We went over the plan again in the parking lot, mumbling through hamburger buns and holding out tidbits for November to take with her tiny pink paws. She ate nearly half of my burger and most of the fries, even though she was currently one-tenth her usual size. But I didn't mind. My stomach jittered like it was full of dragonflies, and the food wasn't helping.

It was then Caleb took me aside to talk. "When Ximon's wife was pregnant with Lazar, he and my mother had an affair," Caleb said. "She was only twenty, and after she got pregnant with me, she left him and never told me who my father was. But after she died, he came to me. He brought her love letters to him to prove what he told me. I recognized the handwriting."

"And she never even hinted that he was your father while you were growing up?" I felt a surge of sympathy. I knew how it felt to grow up with a big hole in your history.

"Never," he said. "She said my father was dead, a man she'd had a passing relationship with, that I was better off not knowing him. That was it. And when she told me about the Tribunal and mentioned Ximon along with the other clerics in the Tribunal, she seemed to hate him just as much as the others."

"How did it feel to find out you still had a father?" I couldn't help wondering, for my own sake as well as Caleb's. "And that he was, you know, the enemy?"

"Confusing," he said. "Ximon found me shortly after Mom died, and I was so hurt and weirded out, I ran away. He found me again a few weeks later, and this time he brought Amaris and Lazar, and I found out I had siblings." He managed a small, ironic laugh. "It was very smart of him, because this time I listened. He told me that he...that he loved me."

"Wow." We sat in a pool of silence for a moment.

He cleared his throat. "Yeah. I'd always wondered who my dad was, and here was this seemingly nice guy with my brother and sister, telling me they wanted me to come live with them. I'd heard bad things about the Tribunal, of course, but Ximon said he wanted to change all that, to find a way to bring peace between otherkin and the Tribunal. Turns out he meant the peace of the grave. I should've known better."

"But I get it," I said. "You'd just lost your mother, and here was a new family, one that wanted you."

He slid his hand over to cover mine. "Yeah, I went to live with them in the compound. Ximon started teaching me how to force a shifter's animal form back into shadow, how to use a gun, repair an engine, memorize Bible verses, that kind of thing. He was stern and would fly off the handle if I disagreed with him, but he really seemed to want to get to know me. He said I was just like my mother, reckless and rebellious."

"He probably did want to get to know you. I mean, you are his son." I paused, then went on. "In his own twisted way, he probably does love you."

A muscle in his jaw twitched, and his eyes went hard as onyx. "Twisted is the word."

"Did you get along with Lazar then?"

His lips curled in a rueful half smile. "Lazar hated me from the start. I can't blame him. Suddenly here's this brand-new son your father's paying attention to, and he's one of the enemy. Then about three months in, Lazar let something slip about tailing an infernal shifter—that's what he said, and he probably meant you. They'd never used that kind of language around me before, and why tail a shifter unless you're hunting them? So I broke into the office."

I let out a short laugh. "Ximon should've known you couldn't be fooled for long."

"He kept thinking he could control me," he said. "The way he controls everyone else on the compound. And for a while he did."

He was looking tentative again. Admitting that was hard for him. I said, "What did you find in the office?"

"My mother's file," he said, and his voice got grim. "They keep huge files on everyone. They'll have a fat one on you in there. They'd been tracking our movements for years. They killed her. On Ximon's direct order."

"Oh, my God."

When he spoke again it was in a soft, dangerous tone that made me shiver. "She left me in a safehouse in Santa Fe to get some groceries. When she didn't come back, I went looking for her, only to see her body being loaded into an ambulance. She'd been shot. I couldn't even claim her body for fear whoever killed her would find me. But Ximon knew where I was, and he didn't want me dead. It was all there in her file, so carefully recorded: Lazar shot her with a sniper rifle from two hundred yards away. He's a hell of a good shot."

"Lazar!" My stomach clenched as I flashed on him standing in my bedroom window, firing at me with the tranquilizer gun.

"So I took one of the guns Ximon had given me for target practice and I tried to shoot Lazar," said Caleb, his voice flat. "At the last minute, Amaris got between us, and I missed him."

I held his hands tightly. "He is her brother too."

"Later she said she didn't want me to become a murderer." He looked down at my hand. "Then I tried to go after Ximon, but there were too many of his men with him. They put me in a cage in the warehouse. Then they brought in this unconscious redhead in a hospital gown and put her in the cage next to mine."

I squeezed his hand. "That's why you had that black eye."

"You saved my life when you shifted and got us out of there," he said. "I wanted to tell you everything, but I needed you to trust me. There's no way you would have ever done that if you knew Ximon was my father. I wouldn't blame you if you never trusted me again."

The only answer was to hug him. He exhaled slowly, his head buried in the crook of my neck.

"You're a good brother," I said. "To try to save Amaris from a father like that."

I pulled back from the hug, and he leaned one shoulder against the wall behind him. "Ximon set her wedding date for next week, and she got really scared and called me."

"Her wedding?"

He nodded. "His name is Enoch, and she hates him. He's Ximon's age and he's already tried to . . ." His face darkened.

"We'll get her out of there along with Siku," I said. "We have to. We'll tell the others soon. After your performance today, they'll understand."

I turned to go back and rejoin the others, but he stayed where he was, leaning against the graffiti-covered back wall of the Burger King.

"One more thing," he said. He was staring at the ground, hands in his pockets. "I did lie to you when I said that Morfael didn't test me before we entered the school."

I knew it. "You were acting so weird that day. Why lie? I told you what happened to me in the cave."

"I lied because *you* were my test." His eyes flicked up to mine, dark and full of heat.

"Me?"

He didn't look away. "You know how when you have a dream about someone, a very intimate dream, it changes how you feel about them? I mean, it's like you've been with them, if only in your mind, and it's so . . . powerful, you never look at them the same way again."

My throat was dry. "Yeah."

"After we got separated in that cave, I walked into this meadow in the moonlight. And you were there, waiting for me."

My heart beat so fast, I thought it might jump from my chest.

"You told me to come to you, and I did. You were naked and so lovely." His eyes were still on me. It had only been a hallucination, *a dream*. But the way he was looking at me, it almost felt real to me too. I was torn between an almost unbearable thrill and hot-faced shame.

"Then I heard Amaris's voice, screaming for help. I didn't want to leave you. You were so tempting, so . . ." He cleared his throat. "But I had to choose. And my sister needed my help. So I tore myself away from you and ran toward Amaris. Next thing I knew, I woke up in the boys' cabin at the school."

Caleb had dreamed about me naked?! Okay, it was just a dream but . . . *Holy shit!* I forced myself to breathe and found I couldn't look him in the eye. I'd never thought of anyone seeing me that way before. "Okay," I said, my voice shaky.

"The test, all of it, scared me senseless."

"So you *are* scared of me," I said, remembering our talk just before our first kiss.

"Not of you." He stood away from the wall and stepped toward me. "But maybe scared of my feelings for you."

I knew exactly how he felt, because I was feeling it right that second. But after all the years of fearing that even the slightest touch from a boy would scare him off, I didn't know how to deal with this, the exact opposite situation. It was terrifying.

"Now you know," he said.

I nodded. "Now I know."

"And now it's time we got going." He motioned toward the car and fell into step next to me. We walked back to the

Beemer, not touching, but side by side. Something had altered between us. The electricity that once traveled over my skin whenever he was near thrummed deeper in me now. But I didn't want to think about it too much. I pictured the brace encircling me, holding all my feelings back, shoving them down until I could figure out how to deal with them.

As soon as the others saw us moving toward the car, they piled in. We filled up the Beemer's tank and headed into the desert. As I gazed out at the monotonous landscape, I realized how fortunate we were that Caleb had lived on the Tribunal compound. Even though I'd been there a couple of weeks ago, I never could have found it again. But Caleb, his dark eyes keen on the road, had no problem finding the tiny dirt track that curved off the highway.

The familiar talcum smell of desert dust hit my nose. Cold air bit into my cheeks, but I was glad to have the windows down. Riding down the road with the wind in my hair was the next best thing to galloping down it in tiger form. The thought that I might never be able to do that again gnawed at the back of my mind. I missed my tiger self. At first I'd been so terrified of it, I just wanted it to go away. Now I missed my scary parts. Plus jumping, climbing, and tracking prey were almost as much fun as kissing a cute boy when you were both blindfolded.

I glanced over at Caleb's profile, finely etched in the glow of the dashboard lights. He looked over at me, and the smile that made my heart twist played around his mouth. The elegant fingers of his right hand lifted off the steering wheel to take hold of mine.

"I like going into battle with you," he said, in that low nonwhisper meant only for my ears.

At the horizon, a shining sliver of the rising moon sent shafts of vibrating light across the landscape. To my sharp night eyes, it outlined every needle on every cactus, every grain of sand.

Caleb switched off the headlights, and I got in the driver's seat. My night vision would serve us better. Arnaldo and London shifted into animal form. I opened up the moonroof, and Arnaldo perched there, his razor-sharp talons gripping the edge as we trundled down the road again. London put her front paws on the windowsill and stuck half of her lean, muscular body out of the car, lifting her nose to catch the different scents in the air.

A halo of light hit my eyes before I saw the buildings in the compound. Caleb directed me off the dirt road, and we bounced slowly over the desert. I dodged the larger rocks and clumps of cacti, keeping an eye out for the smoother dirt of the landing strip Caleb said lay east of the compound.

Arnaldo gave a soft caw, then leapt off the top of the car and flew low in front of us, his wingspan wider than the car.

"He's seen something," Caleb said, as Arnaldo curved to the west. I followed. In eagle form, Arnaldo could spot the date stamped on a penny from three hundred yards.

Then I saw it, the outline of a crouched "T" on a suspiciously smooth patch of ground. The T turned out to be the wings of a small plane with a propeller on the nose, tilted back on its tail at the end of a short dirt runway. It was a relief when the tires finally hit the level airstrip and the car stopped jostling.

A few hundred yards away, spread out under the stars, lay the rectangular buildings of the Tribunal compound. I half expected to see the side door of the warehouse swing open and distant versions of me and Caleb run out, hounded by bullets. But everything lay quiet.

The office abutted the warehouse on its north side, but about one-third its size. It too had a door that opened on the parking lot, as well as a side door to the north, which gave onto a small pathway. On the other side of the path, just a few feet away, sat the building which the Tribunal called the laboratory. Caleb had been inside it only once, when he'd hurt his hand, and even then he'd seen only the first two rooms. So he knew that it served as a sort of first aid station. Beyond that, we could only guess.

Follow the pathway west, Caleb had told us, and you'd find the house where he had lived with Ximon and his siblings, along with other homes for the objurers. We speculated that a few of the people we'd fought that morning would be sleeping in those buildings. I could just see the outline of those faraway structures, where not long ago Caleb had gotten to know what was left of his family.

"Stop here," said Caleb. I let the car roll to a stop at the edge of the runway, its nose aimed at the compound. Arnaldo circled around and landed once more on the Beemer's roof. It rocked slightly as he shifted his weight.

"It's been over eight hours since the battle at school," I said. "So everyone should have at least one more shift in them. Keep that in mind in case you get injured and need to heal. November, you ready?"

November squeaked, then climbed, upside down, along the seam where the car's roof joined the side to poke her head up through the open moonroof. Arnaldo gingerly lifted one razor-tipped foot as she scuttled underneath him. He grasped her firmly around her plump middle, careful not to poke her. She lifted her head and chirped up at him. I couldn't help thinking she was saying that if he dropped her, she'd kill him. He looked down and cawed three descending notes that sounded like a laugh.

"The cameras are aimed at the ground, so you probably won't be spotted," said Caleb, turning in his seat so he could stare up through the roof at them. "But just in case they've changed that, be quick."

Arnaldo fixed one fierce eye on Caleb and squawked once, fluttering his wings to keep his balance.

I reached up and stroked November on the top of her head. "You're a badass rodent," I said.

She chirped fiercely, as if to say, "You know it."

I met Arnaldo's eye, bright as the moon above his cruel yellow beak. London pushed her pointed snout past the backs of the front seats and gave a yip, her icy blue eyes also glinting up at them. "See you soon, Arnaldo," I said.

He bounded into the sky, the wind from his wings pushing my hair back. I pulled myself up through the moonroof to watch them go. Caleb opened his door and got out to do the same. To my night eyes, the moonlight turned Arnaldo's brown feathers into a silvered black, except for his shining snowy head and tail. His wings cut shapes out of the spattered stars slowly paling next to the rising moon.

It didn't take the eagle long to cross the hundreds of yards to the sleeping compound. "He's nearing the roof of the warehouse," I said, tracking his now-tiny form against the sky. "He's dipping down. . . ."

I lost sight of him against the silhouette of the building. We all waited in silence; then I caught a faint movement. Arnaldo, airborne again. "He must've dropped November off."

"It'll take her a few minutes to find a way inside," Caleb said. "And then a few more minutes to figure out how to disable the generator. We've just got to be patient." His voice was more on edge than I'd ever heard, like he was trying to persuade himself as much as me and London. He walked to the back of the car and opened the trunk. "Time to get started."

My heart thumped faster as I got out of the car and joined him at the trunk. London followed. We looked down at the brace, lying there like a broken alabaster statue against the black interior. "This is going to be a tough one," Caleb said. "I think I should call this forth now, so I have a minute or two to recover before we head into the compound."

I nodded. London cocked her head at me. I swallowed hard. "That's my back brace," I said. "Caleb says it's got a powerful shadow that we might need."

Her doglike eyebrows lifted at me; then she backed up a step, giving us room. I felt a little better. It was hard to have her see the brace, but she had, and maybe it wasn't such a big deal.

"Okay, here goes," said Caleb, rubbing his hands together. He found a deep note and hummed it, staring down at the brace. I couldn't look at it for a second, because it felt so peculiar to be here, doing this. The note grew colder and somehow nebulous, as if made of air and ice rather than sound. I rubbed my arms, feeling the chill, and watched rings of gold form around the black depths of his eyes.

Caleb pointed at it. "I call on you," he droned. "Come forth from shadow!" A black ray shot from his pointing finger and struck the brace. It winked in and out, as if an invisible hand wanted to pull it behind a curtain I could not see. Then it was gone.

Lying in its place lay a wide black belt with a buckle made of tortoiseshell. A pointed scabbard made of thick woven leather was slung on it. I blinked, trying to make sense of what I saw. Caleb picked it up with care and slid away the stiff leather scabbard to reveal a long, wicked knife, blacker than any black I'd ever seen. Even the moonlight streaming down on it didn't reflect in the surface of its blade. Its edges were amorphous instead of sharp, as if made of darkest smoke, and the hilt was smooth-grained wood, carved into the shape of some mythic beast with wings, whiskers, pointed ears, and a snarling snout. A sudden longing to hold it gripped me, as if it had belonged to me once, long ago.

It had been the brace, and the brace had been made especially to fit my body. Had this dagger been made for me too?

"This is yours," said Caleb, echoing my thoughts. He slid the knife back into the scabbard and unbuckled the belt. A few feet away, I saw London's nose twitching, her eyes fixed on it.

The belt was made of some sort of silk, glossy and smooth

to the touch. I looped it around my back and slid the end through the buckle. In one move, it was fastened, draped around my waist. I waited to feel the weight of it, for it to somehow echo the clamped-down pinch of the brace. But the wide silk rested lightly, lying exactly where, under my clothes, the purple bruises from the brace still stood.

Something dark and happy flooded through me. I closed my fingers around the carved hilt and my burned hand cooled, as if plunged into ice. It felt marvelous. Then I drew the knife forth, staring in wonder at the murky edge of the blade.

"Try it on something," said Caleb. He looked a bit pale, but his eyes, still glowing gold, were lit with excitement. "Here." He reached into the trunk and pulled out the tennis racquet of Lazar's that had been lying there since we'd stolen the Beemer. He held the racquet by the handle and extended it toward me. I touched the opaque tip of the knife against the racquet's rim. The lightweight metal parted instantly beneath the blade, offering no resistance.

"Wow," I said, then turned and tried the blade on the lip of the BMW's trunk. Again, the knife cut through it with only the barest pressure from my hand.

"Hmm." Caleb frowned in thought. "Try this." He held up the bottom edge of his coat. "It's wool."

"If it can cut through metal, it can cut through wool," I said.

"Then why is the scabbard made of leather? And the handle's made of wood. Just try it."

I didn't understand where he was going with this, but I slid the blade over the bottom half inch of his coat. It didn't cut so much as a thread. I pressed harder, but the cloth stood against it as if made of diamond rather than sheep hair.

"Just as I thought. Watch." Caleb reached out and tapped the hazy blade with his pinky. I gasped, drawing the knife back, fearing a bloody cut, or even a severed finger. But Caleb held up his hand, smiling. His finger was unhurt.

"It won't cut anything alive, or that which was once alive," he said. "But I bet you it could cut through the strongest plastic, the toughest Kevlar, or any rock or metal on earth." His eyes met mine, now fully black once more, satisfied and thrilled.

"It feels good in my hand," I said. "The Shadow Blade."

"The Shadow Blade." He nodded. "I don't know how long it will stay in this form, but I think we might be ready for the Tribunal at last."

I sheathed the blade, and we went back to the car. I tried not to drum my fingers on the roof as I stood craning my neck. Occasionally I saw Arnaldo again, circling far above. Nothing else in the compound moved.

Inside that warehouse, Siku lay prisoner in a silver cage. Any minute now, November would be inside, heading for the generator. If she succeeded, our next signal would be the lights going out. Then we'd be able to do something other than wait while our friends were in danger.

London stuck her head out of the window, paws on the sill, thrust her head back, and uttered a soft, high-pitched howl of impatience. Or perhaps she was praying to the moon, hovering a handspan above the horizon. Goose bumps rose across my arms at the haunting sound. I gripped the pommel of the Shadow Blade and felt a hunger to draw it forth.

The compound plunged into darkness.

My heart lurched into my throat as I thumped down into the driver's seat. I looked over at Caleb, and our eyes locked. A reckless half smile touched his lips, and an answering rush of excitement flooded through me.

"Let's go," he said.

I shoved the car into gear and gunned it for the parking lot.

CHAPTER 24

The BMW bounced like a covered wagon across the unpaved desert as I pushed the speedometer past fifty. Using my less-burned left hand, I swerved to avoid a pile of rocks, then hauled the wheel around again. Ahead in the Tribunal compound, a man in white walked out of the office, looking around the darkened buildings. A woman in white stepped out of the laboratory and yelled something to him. They walked toward each other, gesturing, as we closed in.

A hundred yards from the parking lot. Fifty. Both people turned toward us. The sound of the engine must have reached them. They didn't look alarmed yet. They had no idea who was in the car.

Twenty yards, ten . . .

Bang! Something exploded nearby.

We all ducked. The car tilted abruptly to the right. We'd blown a tire. London skittered sideways in the backseat, slamming against the right side panel. We hit the parking lot, scraping along on the rim of the right front wheel. I stomped on the brake and we veered to the left, skidding around nearly one hundred eighty degrees, and came to a halt.

Voices shouted. Caleb was out of the car before I blinked. London leapt through her window in a graceful arc and vanished into the darkness.

I stayed low and crawled over to Caleb's side of the car, toward his open door. We'd agreed I'd stay back at first, since I had only a knife and was unable to shift and heal myself if bullets flew. Just the act of bending over inside that car flashed me back to the first time I'd struggled over those seats, impeded by the brace. This time I wasn't running away.

"Who are you?" a man yelled.

Their footsteps approached. Caleb crunched over the packed dirt toward them. I poked my head out of the open passenger side door.

Caleb was walking away from me, his black coat flapping. A man and woman in white jeans and button-down shirts stood facing him. The woman had her hand on a pistol at her belt. The man held a rifle.

Caleb reached one hand into the duffle bag he'd slung over his shoulder. "We've come for Siku, the bear-shifter," Caleb said in a commanding tone that left no room for disagreement. "Hand him over to us now, and we won't harm you."

"It's Caleb!" the man shouted, aiming his rifle at Caleb's head. Of course they knew him. "Sound the alarm!"

Caleb let loose a ringing laugh. "I think you'll find the alarms don't work without electricity."

The woman was looking around in apprehension. "Something else jumped out of the car," she said. "Something with four legs."

"Just get Ximon and Enoch," the man said, still sighting on Caleb. "Now!"

Caleb took out the empty plastic water bottle I'd noticed

the other day in his duffle bag. The man with the rifle, now less than ten feet away, frowned, confused, as Caleb began to unscrew the blue cap. The woman turned toward the laboratory building. Was that where Ximon was? Or Enoch? But before she could take a single running step, London bounded out of the darkness and slammed into her.

The woman shrieked and went sprawling. The man with the rifle startled, and exactly then Caleb removed the top of the water bottle, pointed the open end at the man, and intoned a low, buzzing noise.

Under the moon, the bottle turned black. The man jerked the end of his gun toward Caleb as a droning stream of tiny objects shot out of the bottle. The man swatted one hand in front of his face, then twitched and dropped his rifle with a horrified cry as a churning cloud of insects swallowed him. I winced and felt a pang of pity. Through the swirling haze of insects I could just see his white outline, jerking and slapping. Even if he were the most trained objurer, he was going to have trouble concentrating long enough to send the creatures back into shadow.

The woman was still on the ground, whimpering as she crawled backward on her hands and heels. London, fur tipped silver in the moonlight, growled menacingly at her. We'd talked about trying to hurt as few people as possible, so London hadn't yet torn the woman's throat out. But it was anyone's guess how long she'd hold off.

I got out of the car, circling around the swarm. Inside the haze the guttural cries were growing fainter.

"Much sneakier to use bugs instead of lightning," I said, coming to Caleb's side.

"I only have two more leaves from the lightning tree," said Caleb, pulling out the saltshaker. "And I have to save one to set the fuel on fire."

"Let's goo her up." Then I remembered that the Beemer was shot and we needed a way out of here. "No, wait!" I put a hand on his arm. Caleb frowned at me, questioning, but drew the shaker back.

The woman tried to shy away from me as I reached down to her, but London gave a vicious growl and shoved her snarling face into the woman's. She collapsed on the ground, flat, her face pale and sweating. I patted her down, aiming for her pockets and came up with a fistful of keys. "We need a new car," I said.

"Good thinking," Caleb said, then held the saltshaker out over the objurer as London backed off. He gave the woman a hard smile. "I'm doing this because I have to. Not because you always treated me like trash."

London cocked her head toward him, as if wondering what that meant. He sprinkled salt over the objurer as I backed up toward the warehouse, watching. He'd lived with these people, the same people who had murdered his mother. He hummed, calling to shadow as the salt erupted into a gluey yellow mess. The woman wouldn't be moving for a while.

Voices cut through the darkness from beyond the nearest buildings. The people in the residences behind the warehouse would soon be here to find out what had happened to the generator. Caleb looked in that direction, catching the sound a moment after me. We needed to move fast.

London stood by the door into the warehouse. Her ears pricked forward, and then something inside crashed. A man cried out.

The door was locked. Killing the generator hadn't disabled the deadbolt. As glass splintered inside, Caleb tried a key from the batch we'd stolen from Lazar. But none of them fit. They had changed the locks. So I fumbled in my jeans pocket for November's lockpicks. Caleb swiped them from me, inserted one into the lower part of the keyhole, then jiggled the other at the top. Two heartbeats later, the lock clicked open.

"I knew you were good, but . . ." I shook my head at him.

He flashed me a grin and threw the door open. "There's a long list of things I'm good at," he said. "And I've had you in mind for numbers six through twelve for a while now."

I didn't have time to react as London charged in. Then I got in the doorway first, blocking Caleb. "I see better in the dark, remember?"

He bowed, and I stepped inside, my pupils opening to take in the cavernous space. To the right lay a familiar squat, shiny cage. My skin crawled at the sight, and even at this distance, the pain all that silver had inflicted on me echoed through my body. Now a bulky prostrate male with dark brown skin in a too-short hospital gown filled the cage. His long, straight black hair spilled out between the bars. Siku, still unconscious.

Along the far wall lay a table, an overturned camping chair, and a man in white, lying on the floor. He wriggled and grunted like a kid with poison ivy who couldn't reach the itchy spot. A foot-long bump moved under his white shirt, slithering down toward his belt. November. One of his bleeding hands looked useless, but the other was plucking at the lump under his shirt. Then a streak of gray lunged, and London sank her teeth into his arm.

He screamed. London shook his arm, and his whole body flailed helplessly.

"London's got it covered," I said to Caleb. "The cage is over here." He relocked the door behind us as my hand slipped into his to pull him over to Siku's prison. Even getting within a few feet of the silver made my skin itch.

"Now I see it," said Caleb as he got right up to the bars of the cage and hunkered down near Siku's head. "Looks like the silver's keeping him unconscious." He cast a glance back at me. His mouth tightened as he registered my pain. "Don't come any closer."

I backed up a step. By the overturned chair, something thumped. London let go of the man's bleeding arm. His head slumped to the side, eyes closed, a bloody bump on the side where it had struck the wall. November's head poked up through the neck of the guy's shirt, nose twitching.

"She's the rat from hell!" I said. "Can you guys guard the door? They'll be coming in any second."

London trotted to the door, ears up, as November climbed up my legs to stand on my shoulder. London yipped. Someone was approaching.

"Did the guard here have any weapons?" I asked November, turning toward the unconscious man on the floor.

She cheeped and ran down the line of my body as if it were a racetrack, then bounded over to a long, lean silhouette propped against the wall. I strode over and recognized it—a tranquilizer gun, loaded with several darts coated with tranquilizer that would quickly send anyone, otherkin or not, to sleep. I picked it up, grateful that the gun itself was not made of silver. Grabbing the table by the back wall, I pulled it over the floor, then turned it on its side. The shiny metal surface stood between us and the door. I crouched down behind it, ninety percent of my body covered, and rested the barrel of the tranquilizer gun across the top.

"Okay, we all cover for Caleb, keeping them back until he gets Siku out," I said. "Only one of them can get through the door at a time. They'll have seen the two objurers we disabled outside, so they'll be ready for us. Don't give them a chance to fire."

London barked agreement and pressed herself against the wall next to the door as keys scraped in the lock outside and voices spoke urgently to each other.

Caleb grabbed the tranquilizer gun from me. "The lockpicks are taking too long. Use the Shadow Blade."

Of course. I knelt down by the door to Siku's cage as Caleb took my place, covering the door with the tranquilizer gun. Trembling from the silver, I drew the blade. My skin calmed, as if doused in cool water. With the blade in my hand, I felt as if no metal, not even silver, could hurt me.

The door trembled as a key rattled in the lock. London crouched, ready to leap. November was climbing up the doorframe and made it to the top just as the door flew open. The muzzle of a rifle flashed as London leapt for the throat of the man wielding it. Bullets sprayed across the floor to my right before he fell under two hundred pounds of wolf.

The man behind him stepped in, aiming at London, but November dropped down onto his head, rat claws extended. He yelled out and swiped at her, giving Caleb a chance to fire at the person behind him, a woman with another automatic weapon. His dart hit her in the neck. She winced, staggered, then fell. Caleb sighted down the barrel at the man trying to keep a rat from crawling down his pants and shot a dart into his leg. He gurgled and slumped. The door was now full of prostrate bodies in white. No one else stood in the doorway. Yet.

I lowered the blade's foggy edge onto the block of metal that housed the lock on Siku's cage. The faint hum I always heard coming from silver turned into a hiss. The knife cut through it like pudding and came out the other side darker than before. Its edge, normally blurry, had sharpened, as if pleased to have taken such a large bite.

"Awesome." Caleb handed the air gun to me, opened the cage door, and dragged Siku out of the low-ceilinged enclosure. I didn't want to sheathe the blade. I wanted to cut that cage to pieces so that no one, shifter or otherwise, could ever be held captive there again. But there wasn't time. I slid the blade back into its scabbard and felt somehow that as long as it was in my hand or at my side, it would remain a knife and not become the brace. Or maybe that was wishful thinking. I made myself leave the blade alone and checked the air gun. Three shots of tranquilizer left.

Caleb laid Siku on the cement floor, away from the silver

of the cage. Siku stirred and coughed. Caleb pulled out a big blue marble from his duffle bag and hummed a wavy tune. Water trickled out of it, and he held it over Siku's mouth. The big guy's eyes opened and he swallowed eagerly.

Over by the door, November was chirping like a canary. She scampered to Siku and crawled up his shoulder to sit on his chest, rubbing her whiskers on his chin.

Siku raised one hand to cradle her round body against him. "Hello, chitterbox," he said.

I grinned down at them. "How are you feeling?"

Siku sat up, grunting and holding November so she didn't slip. "Better," he said. He lifted his eyes to mine, then to Caleb, not smiling. "Thank you for coming for me."

Caleb put the blue marble in his bag. "We still have to get you and Amaris out of here."

"Amaris?" Siku lumbered to his feet.

It was time to tell them everything, now that Siku understood we would never abandon him. "Caleb's half sister is being kept here against her will."

Siku pursed his lips and considered Caleb. "Okay, then."

London gave a vicious bark that sharpened into a painful whine. Over by the door, someone was humming.

"I command you, return to shadow," sang a familiar male voice, strong and certain. Lazar stood in the doorway, his blond head haloed in the moonlight, pointing at London. She tried to leap at him, but her legs shuddered and collapsed as the outline of her form shifted, and human once more, she fell flat on her face right in front of him.

Lazar placed the muzzle of his pistol against her head. "Move and she's dead."

CHAPTER 25

Caleb stepped forward. Lazar's finger tightened on the trigger, and London winced as he ground the point of the gun into the back of her head. She lay in the doorway naked and facedown, her hands gripping the floor with white knuckles. "I'd love to kill one of your friends right in front of you, *brother*," Lazar said.

Caleb checked himself, and we all stood frozen in a strange tableau. Only November, perched on Siku's shoulder, let loose a stream of ferocious shrieks.

"Didn't he tell you?" Lazar smiled with blue-white, even teeth so like his father's. "He's my half brother. He lived with us. But he couldn't hack it as an objurer and turned traitor."

I could see the resemblance to Caleb now. He had the same tall, broad-shouldered frame and handsome, high-cheekboned face, with a voice like steel encased in velvet, bright blond day to Caleb's night.

"Caleb." It was Siku who spoke. "I hope you don't mind if I tear your half brother to pieces."

"Save some for me," said Caleb, his eyes burning. "I can send the pieces to our dear father."

"So you don't care if she dies." Lazar straightened, his pistol still aimed at London. "Did you feel the same way when you left your mother to die alone?"

Caleb lurched forward, an ominous, low note vibrating in his chest. I put my hand on his arm. "Not yet." I could feel the effort it took him to stop moving.

Behind Lazar, another man came running up. "Sir! Your father requests you bring any survivors to the lab."

"Good," said Lazar. He motioned to London. "Cover up this demon's shame and get her up. As long as we've got her, they'll do as we say."

"Yes, sir!" The objurer took off his jacket, threw it over London, wrapped his arms around her, and hauled her to her feet.

Her dull black hair half covered her face. Next to the ivory-colored coat enveloping her, her lean legs stood out pinkish white. But her glacial blue eyes were as fierce as ever. The objurer seemed to know he was holding a wild animal, leaning his head as far back as he could from her face, his mouth a grim line.

Lazar made sure his pistol never wavered from her head. "Now," he said, backing up a step, with the objurer following his every move. "Follow us, otherkin."

We moved forward. Siku rumbled something under his breath and advanced with November on his shoulder, followed by Caleb.

Lazar smiled, backing up outside so that we could follow. He would have been dazzlingly handsome if he hadn't been such a self-satisfied ass. "How happy my father will be to see you all. We appreciate you walking right into our hands."

As we stepped into the cold night air, a sweeping shadow

fell across Lazar's face, blocking the moonlight. He glanced up, and a fury of wings and talons fell upon him. Arnaldo descended, one wing thwacking the man holding London across the face as his claws grabbed at Lazar's head and shoulders, drawing jagged lines of blood. Lazar cried out and threw his hands up to protect his face. The gun no longer pointed at London.

That's all it took. In a blur of gray fur, London shifted. The white coat slipped to the ground. The man who had been holding her stepped back, pulling his gun from its holster in one smooth move. But she was on him. The gun flew from his hand as she pushed him to the ground and sank her jaws into his throat.

Near me, Siku roared, spreading his arms wide, and shifted into a grizzly bear the size of a truck. November scrambled to the floor as he shook out his thick brown coat of fur, dropped to all fours, and charged. Envy flashed through me. Would I ever be able to shift again?

Lazar screamed as he fell under the bear's attack. Arnaldo winged up and away. Caleb moved ahead to protect me in case there was anyone else outside. I saw the woman he had bound with saltshaker glue, now goo-free and aiming a rifle at Siku. Lazar must have shoved the sticky stuff back into shadow and freed her. The man who'd been afflicted with insects was lying very still not far from her. There was no sign of the swarm. It, too, must have returned to Othersphere.

"Put the gun down or the bear kills Lazar!" Caleb shouted.

"Siku!" I hissed at the bear as he worried Lazar's arm. Guttural sounds of pain leaked from Lazar, his white shirt streaked with blood. "Siku, don't kill him! We can use him against Ximon."

Siku placed one huge paw on Lazar's chest and lifted his head, blood on his snout, growling deep. Next to him, London had made quick work of the man who had held her.

"Put the gun down!" Caleb ordered the female objurer again. Siku pressed his curved black claws against Lazar's neck. The woman hesitated, then lowered the gun. I thought better of trying to shoot her myself and handed the gun to Caleb. He aimed and fired. She crumpled. Two darts left.

Arnaldo landed on the warehouse roof to overlook us as we all took a deep breath. Lazar lay gasping under Siku.

"Nice timing there, Arnaldo," I said. He cackled. Nearby, November clambered up Siku as if he were a hairy mountain, standing on his shoulder again, her beady eyes glaring down at Lazar.

Caleb gave me back the air gun, then ran to the unconscious woman, grabbed her rifle, and came back, pointing it down at Lazar. "Let him up," he said.

Siku backed off, and Lazar sucked in air, as if the bear's weight had kept him from breathing much.

"Abominations!" Lazar spat blood. He bled from several gashes in his scalp and one long scrape down the cheek from Arnaldo's talons. His arm, where Siku's teeth had bitten down, was punctured, oozing, and hanging wrong, as if the bone was broken. He sat up, took another deep breath, then tottered to his feet. Pain wrote lines on his face, but he made it and stood, swaying. He was a murdering bastard, but he had guts. With his high cheekbones, broad shoulders, and tousled blond hair, he looked like a bloody, vengeful angel. Only his eyes gave away the poison inside.

"Where's Amaris?" I asked.

He uttered a one-note laugh. "Did you wish to congratulate her? Enoch took her to wife tonight. The ceremony concluded not long before you arrived."

"What?" Caleb looked around wildly. "Liar."

Lazar shrugged painfully. "Father thought the ceremony could mark the beginning of her reindoctrination into the light. A way to detoxify her after so much contact with her half brother the demon."

"Thanks to your father, she's starting to realize who the real demons are," I said. "Now where is she?"

One corner of Lazar's mouth curved up in a smug smile. "I've lost too much blood to remember." His voice deepened, softened. "You're too lost to care. You all are. Too far away from your parents, too far in over your head, too certain to lose your friends, your families, and your lives."

Despair washed over me. My limbs felt heavy. Siku hung his head and November's whiskers trembled. A small whine escaped London. She wasn't snarling at Lazar anymore. Why snarl? Nothing we said or did mattered anymore.

Caleb shoved his gun into Lazar's face. "Stop that or I'll stop it for you." The sharp, light tone in his voice cut through the thick mantle of desolation surrounding me. I snapped back to myself, as did everyone else.

Thank the Moon for Caleb.

"Do you remember what I did to you the last time you tried your little voice trick on me?" I said, wishing I had claws to brandish. "One more word out of you, and it'll be the last time you speak."

He sneered, looking suddenly very young, like a boy who thought acting like a man meant behaving superior all the time. That must be what Ximon had taught him. Pity for him touched the edges of my wrath. With a father like that, he'd never stood a chance.

"In front," Caleb said to Lazar. "Walk toward the lab. Amaris won't be healing you this time, *bro.*"

Lazar's jaw muscles tightened, but he said nothing. He paced toward the lab, Caleb right behind him, with me, Siku, November, and London trailing and Arnaldo overhead. I eyed the body of the man lying on the gravel nearby. We'd dealt with him and four other objurers so far. "How many do you think are left?" I said quietly into Caleb's ear.

"Maybe five," he replied. "Ximon, Enoch, Amaris, and probably two more."

"There are six of us," I said.

"Don't underestimate Ximon," Caleb said. "He's equal to ten more."

"The real question is," I said, allowing my voice to become loud enough for Lazar to hear. "Does he really care about the son he raised? Will he give up all his ambitions to save Lazar?"

"My father does not surrender," Lazar said through gritted teeth.

Caleb cuffed him lightly across the back of the head. "Quiet."

The moon shone bright upon us. I thought I could feel its light touch my skin, like a cool hand telling me to keep my head, to stay sharp. The greatest challenges still lay ahead.

"The first room as you enter is a sort of reception area," Caleb said as we neared the door to the lab. The cameras above it lay dormant without power. "The door to the right leads to a doctor's office, so don't bother with that. I haven't been through the other door, but it's larger and has an electronic lock. So that's where we go. Without power we can't open the lock, so Siku, you may need to bash it down."

Siku grunted, sounding the same as he did in human form.

"It might be a good idea if November scouted ahead and made sure no one else surprises us," I said, thinking how her small form could easily be missed in a melee. I looked over at her, crouched now on top of Siku's broad head as he lumbered along on all fours. "That okay with you, 'Ember?"

She squeaked once and nodded.

"Arnaldo, stay back until we see how much room there is inside," I went on, glancing up at him as he circled overhead. The eagle's long wings might have difficulty beating through doorways or crowded laboratories. "I like having you as kind of our secret weapon. People don't look up much, do they?"

He croaked at us, then landed on the roof of the lab. We

halted in front of that building's door. I could hear the pain in every breath Lazar took. His good hand held his broken arm gingerly at the elbow.

I said, "If you see a girl who looks like Lazar in there, don't hurt her. Get her out of the building. And try to keep Ximon alive. I have questions for him."

"The fuel barrels are right there." Caleb tilted his head to the right. Siku swung his big head to look. Sure enough, a dozen large oil drums lay stacked to the side of the lab building. "Once everyone's out, I'll light them up."

"Ready?" I hoisted my air gun. Siku grunted, November cheeped, London gave me a nod, and Arnaldo squawked.

"Ready, General Desdemona," said Caleb, grinning at me. A few locks of dark hair had fallen over his forehead, and his black eyes glinted with those hints of gold, sharp and ready in the moonlight. Every channel in my body was open, every nerve alight. We just might pull this off.

"Look how far we've come," I said. "Let's finish it." Around me, I felt muscles tense. "Open the door, Lazar."

Caleb pushed him forward, and Lazar put his hand on the doorknob. I angled my gun to fire through the door as it cracked open. Moonlight revealed a small room with a reception desk, three waiting chairs, a door to the right, and a door straight ahead. Nothing moved inside.

Siku went in first and ran straight at the door. At the last second, he ducked his head and slammed into it with his shoulder. The walls trembled, and the door buckled but did not open. Siku shuffled backward, huffing his breath in and out indignantly, as if the door had dissed him. Then he smashed into it again at top speed.

It flew open, banging into the wall behind. Siku's momentum rolled him forward through the doorway. Caleb hustled Lazar over, pistol at the back of his head, and I caught a glimpse of November's tiny, pod-shaped body scurrying past Siku into the darkness.

A hallway stretched about twenty-five feet down, with a door on each side. November darted down it, paused, sniffing, then pointed one pink paw at the door on the right and squeaked.

"Ximon's in there," I said.

Caleb pushed Lazar into the hallway as Siku got to his feet. "Siku, the door on the right."

As Siku moved up to obey, I drew the Shadow Blade and walked to the door on the left. "Here, 'Ember. Do reconnaissance." I slid the dusky blade between the door and the wall, feeling the wood resist it on either side. But as I cut down near the lock, it bit through the metal there. No lockpicks necessary. I pulled it open just wide enough for November to slip through. I had time only to get the impression of a large, utterly dark room, filled with tables and empty cages.

Then Siku huffed and bashed the other door with one huge paw. It sprang open. I sheathed the blade and hoisted my gun. London trotted in to stand beside me, her teeth bared.

Light radiated from the room. As my eyes adjusted I saw a small battery-operated lamp next to a hospital bed surrounded by people. London shoved me sideways, and a bullet whined past my ear.

"Thanks," I said breathlessly, spotting the man in white who had fired. I raised my air gun and fired at him. The first dart went wide, of course, but I stepped closer, aiming for his chest, and finally buried a dart in his thigh. A lucky shot, at last. He fell.

At the same time, Caleb jammed his pistol into Lazar's temple and shouted, "Guns down or he's dead!"

Everyone froze. A white-haired man lay in the hospital bed. Ximon. His still-firm skin looked pasty under the tan, and an IV hung by his side, the tube disappearing into the crook of his elbow.

On the far side of the bed stood Amaris in a high-necked white gown, dark circles under her eyes, her skin blotchy with fatigue. Her wide brown eyes darted from one of us to the other, mouth half open in surprise. Beside her, one arm around her shoulders, stood a short, pot-bellied man with dull brown hair graying at the temples. His other arm pointed a silver pistol at us, his thin upper lip curled in anger. Amaris was leaning as far away from him as she could, and no wonder. He had to be Enoch, her husband.

The other person was another objurer toting a rifle. He had it trained on me, but he hesitated as Caleb jammed his own gun farther into Lazar's ear. "Not feeling well, Ximon?"

Ximon raised his head. "It's kind of you to visit, son." Despite his pallor, his eyes glittered with shrewdness and feverish energy.

"It's your fault, turncoat," said Enoch in a nasal voice, his arm tightening around Amaris. "The lightning damaged his heart. Even your beautiful sister can't heal him."

"What a shame," I said. "Let go of her."

"She couldn't heal me because her heart wasn't in it," said Ximon. A muscle in his cheek quivered. Amaris shot him a horrified look. But then Ximon's eyebrows flattened over his narrowed eyes, calculating. "God has abandoned her, and He punishes me for failing to keep her unstained. Now you've come."

"Perhaps it's a sign," said Caleb. "A sign for you to give up. Let her go, Enoch."

"No!" Enoch's arm tightened around Amaris's shoulders, his jowls shaking.

Amaris opened her mouth, as if to say something, but her father said, "Enoch, point your gun at Amaris's head."

Enoch stared at Ximon in shock, but his gun hand obeyed as if it had a mind of its own. He pressed the muzzle of his gun against Amaris's cheek, and she became very still. Caleb's shoulders stiffened.

"It seems I have something you want," Ximon said, the corners of his eyes crinkling in a smile.

"You wouldn't kill your daughter," said Caleb.

Ximon shook his head slightly, as if disappointed in him. "If she dies in this cause, she may make it to Heaven. If she goes with you, she'll be damned forever." His eyes slid over to me. "And I have something you want too, Amba. The location of your real parents."

"I..." My throat went dry. Goose pimples crept up my arms, and every plan in my head, every stratagem, fled. *He knows where my parents are.* I forced myself to pull away from the deep allure in that sentence. Ximon could not be trusted. "I wouldn't believe anything you told me."

He sat up with a huff of effort, reached behind Amaris, and held up a black file folder. "Given how well you fought back at that so-called school of yours, I thought it might be a good idea to read your file again. We analyzed you from every angle and learned more than you could ever dream. But I chose not to include some crucial information. In fact, I am the only one in this world who knows the truth about your parents. They are both still alive."

I felt hollowed out, like a sphere of blown glass that would shatter at a touch. If he hadn't used the word "Amba," I might've been able to ignore him. But Morfael had used the same term. Answers resided in Ximon's head and in that file. If we killed him, I might never know the whole story. I stared at the file as he leaned over and placed it back on the table behind Amaris, out of sight.

Ximon's voice deepened. "Kill me and you'll never know it. Kill Lazar and Amaris will die. But you don't really want to kill anyone, do you? *Put down your guns.*"

My head buzzed, and my arms lowered the rifle. It felt like the right thing to do. I needed to know the truth about my heritage. And killing was wrong. Right?

The objurer in front of the bed released his rifle. Enoch's gun dropped onto the hospital bed. And Caleb's fingers opened. His rifle clattered to the floor.

A bird shrieked. I looked up, dazed, to see Arnaldo flying down the hallway toward us, his wingtips brushing the walls. London growled, and I knew something had gone wrong. But what? One moment I'd been holding a gun and so had Caleb, and all parties were in a standoff. Now no one was armed, and Ximon was showing all his teeth in a smile.

"I forbid you entry to this world, shadowkind." Ximon's voice was strong and sonorous. Beside me, the outline of London's wolf shape trembled, as did Siku's bear.

Arnaldo tilted his wings, curved into Ximon's room, and opened his beak in a great cry. At the same moment, Ximon extended both hands toward us all and commanded, "Return to Othersphere!"

London stumbled on her two legs, human legs, and fell to her hands and knees, gasping. Siku shook the long, straight black hair falling down his broad, naked back and roared, but it was a human roar of frustration and fury.

But the great eagle remained. Arnaldo gave another ear-piercing call, as if daring Ximon to try it again. Then, talons extended, wings back, he fell upon the white-haired man.

Both Enoch and Amaris cried out. Foolishly, Enoch tried to get between the eagle and his leader. One of Arnaldo's huge wings smacked him in the face. Blood poured from his nose. So he lunged for the gun he'd dropped on the bed.

But Amaris reached it first. Her small hand gripped the stock firmly, and she swiveled around to try to point the gun at Enoch, but he tackled her. Amaris screamed. They fell behind the bed, out of sight. A moment later, Enoch's gun skidded under the bed, along the floor, and out into the hallway.

Everything seemed to happen at once. Caleb yanked Lazar by his good arm, trying to move closer to Amaris. Lazar pushed his shoulder into Caleb hard. They sprawled in a heap.

London, all naked skinny arms and legs, whirled to the door November had gone through and dodged inside. She couldn't shift again today, and without a weapon she was better off out of the line of fire.

Enoch rose from behind the bed, blood still streaming from his nostrils and down his chin. "Damn you, traitorous bitch!" he shouted at Amaris, and kicked her as she lay on the floor.

I grabbed for my air gun, but it clicked, empty. The unknown objurer was doing the same with his rifle. He sighted on me and fired. I dove for the floor, but something thumped into my upper arm, knocking me sideways. I put a hand on my arm, and the hand came away covered in blood. I stared at it, the truth not registering. I'd been shot.

Siku stood to his full height and shifted. The objurer swung his rifle toward him, so I threw myself at the man's knees, my arm ablaze. He shouted in surprise and fell forward, on top of me. His weight jolted my wounded arm and pressed the Shadow Blade painfully against my waist, right where my bruises from the brace lay.

Amaris still lay on the floor, her mouth full of blood, as Enoch's boot swung to kick her again. She deflected most of the blow with her arm, then tried to hold onto his leg. He rained curses down on her.

The objurer rolled off of me, trying to get his gun in a position to fire from where he lay. I jerked the Shadow Blade from its scabbard and slashed across the barrel. I felt only the slightest resistance as the blade sliced through the metal. The objurer was left gaping at the two pieces of rifle in his hands.

Back in the hallway, Lazar reached into his pocket and jabbed something into Caleb's shoulder. A syringe. "Let's see how it works on callers," he said.

Caleb tried to grab Lazar as he shoved him away and stood up, but his movements were slow, his eyes unfocused. "Damn you," he said, through gritted teeth, and managed to pull the syringe out of his arm. Half its contents remained.

Lazar didn't take time to gloat, but turned and vaulted

over his father's bed. "Enoch. Deal with the bear!" he barked. Enoch stiffened, as if brought to attention, and swiveled from Amaris to grab something off the table where my file lay. Another syringe. Next to it lay three more and some other medical instruments.

I didn't have time to see anything else as the objurer swiped at me with the severed barrel of his rifle. I deflected it, then grabbed it and tore it from his grasp. My hand burned from the silver, but I slammed it into his temple. He reeled but didn't fall back, so I hit him again. He collapsed.

I sat up, ignoring the jolt of pain in my arm, and threw the rifle barrel at Enoch as he climbed over the bed. It flew wide as Lazar helped the frail Ximon to stand. Ximon ripped the IV from his arm and closed his fingers around my file. Lazar grabbed one of the remaining syringes, then hauled Amaris to her feet.

I lurched toward them, but Lazar, standing behind Amaris, looped his good arm around her neck and placed the tip of the syringe against Amaris's throat. "The dosage is made for large shifters," he said. "If I inject all of it, it will kill her."

Amaris's neck convulsed as she swallowed. Syringe poised to stab Siku, Enoch stood, transfixed at the sight of his bride in danger. Siku's paw, lifted to swipe the syringe out of Enoch's hand, was frozen in midair. His shiny dark eyes shifted from Amaris to the syringe and back. If he attacked Enoch, Lazar might kill her. I could see that Siku was torn. Amaris was no one to him, and a member of the Tribunal. But still Siku held himself back.

Caleb had managed to stand, clinging to the doorframe. He was shaking his head. "Leave her," he said, his lips barely able to form the words. "Leave her and we won't pursue you."

"As if I could trust you," Lazar said. Behind him, Ximon was backing up, holding the battery-powered lantern and my file. The shadows lurched around us like crazed monsters as the lamp swung. The room was larger than I'd thought, with two rows of four empty beds stretching away from us and a door set into the far wall. Lazar muscled Amaris back as Ximon unlocked the far door and opened it to the night.

Caleb tried to step forward but had to stop, keeping hold of the door to stay upright. I pushed past Ximon's bed and picked up the two remaining syringes. The objurers who had invaded my house all those weeks ago had carried an antidote to the tranquilizer; maybe there was one here as well.

Sure enough, one of them looked just like the syringe Lazar had plunged into Caleb. But the other had one-tenth the liquid in it and was labeled "Anti-tranq."

I leapt over the bed back to Caleb and stabbed the needle through his sleeve into his arm.

He inhaled, lifting his head, then nearly fell. I placed one of his arms around my shoulders to support him. I could feel the deep tremor in his body as he struggled back to full consciousness.

Standing in the doorway, Ximon held my file up so that the moonlight shone upon it. "You will never know the truth about yourself, Amba," he said, his teeth white in the light from the lantern.

I said, "Would your God approve of you threatening your own daughter? Let her go."

He surveyed me. "Now I see what truly motivates you. You're filled with compassion. That is as it should be. You will lead your friends to death and see the destruction you bring to the world, and it will shatter that tender heart of yours. I'll be there to see it break."

He stepped through the door. I moved forward, bringing Caleb with me. "You could come with us too, Lazar," I said. "You don't have to follow your father. You can be your own man, a better man."

Lazar frowned, as if not quite understanding. He was breathing in short, painful pants, fighting the pain in his arm after the scuffle. Even though he still held a syringe to Amaris's throat, he looked like a small boy, a bit lost and in need of care.

Ximon laughed. "You see, son? Compassion. It will be her undoing. She does not understand your strength. You have more than proved yourself worthy to be my son and heir this day."

Lazar took a deep breath and focused, his father's words bolstering him. "Your words are meaningless to me, demon." He eyes shifted to Caleb, who was awake enough now to stand on his own. Fury and helplessness were written in every line of his body.

"Good-bye, Caleb. I'll be sure to make Amaris aware of the pain she has caused us every single day. And that she has you to thank for it." He pressed the needle tip into Amaris's skin. A spot of blood appeared on her neck. He hadn't injected anything into her yet, but the threat was clear.

As we watched, Lazar gave one last little wave with the syringe. Then Ximon helped him pull Amaris through the far doorway and they disappeared from sight.

CHAPTER 26

Siku roared and slapped Enoch in the face with one enormous paw. The man dropped like a wet sack, unconscious.

"Hey!" London grabbed my arm, snapping me out of a horrified daze. She had thrown on a white lab coat and looked like a naughty goth scientist with her bare legs and feet peeking out. "Time to burn this place down."

"Okay," I said, although my head felt like it might float off my body. "Let's go."

Caleb was holding my hand. "Your arm's bleeding," he said.

"It won't kill me," I said. "Get out there. Get her back."

His eyes flicked up to me, very dark and uncertain. "I don't want..." He stopped himself.

"What is it?" I searched his face.

He ran one hand up my good arm and slid the other around the back of my neck, under my hair, pulling me closer. My breathing quickened as the warmth of his body encircled me. "I don't want us to separate, but I have to go."

"I know," I said. "It's okay." The skin of his throat was sunbrowned and smooth. One corner of his shirt collar curled up.

"It might not be." His voice carried an edge of fear. I opened my mouth to ask him what was wrong, but then he said, "Whatever happens, know that I love you."

His eyes were black pools and they were swallowing me up. My heart expanded to fill my entire body. He bent his head and kissed me, his arms tightening and crushing me into him. I slid my hand under his coat and kissed him back.

Then he released me. I couldn't speak. Caleb smiled, a sweet, slow smile I'd never seen from him before, tinged somehow with regret. Then he ran off down the hall. I stared after his fluttering black coat, my brain swirling and frozen at the same time.

"What . . ." I didn't even know who I was talking to. He had said them, the words I hadn't let myself think he'd ever say. But he'd looked so melancholy. Somehow I felt it was more than losing Amaris just now. Something worse.

"Come on, lover girl." London grabbed a roll of gauze and wound it around the hole in my upper arm. The pressure made me dizzy, but I couldn't afford to lose any more blood, and I couldn't shift to heal myself. It didn't seem to matter anyway.

Caleb said he loved me.

And what had I done? I'd gaped like the world's biggest idiot. I hadn't said it back.

My arm jolted with pain as London ripped the gauze across with her teeth then tied it off neatly.

"Thanks," I said.

"I heard him too," she said. "He really said it. But let's get rid of this evil place now, okay?"

"Okay," I said. We were still midbattle, and people needed me.

Outside, the chilly breeze and the moonlight felt like a benediction. Not far away, Siku had pawed a couple of the fuel barrels away from the others and was rolling them across the gravel of the parking lot.

And at the far edge of the lot, Caleb was running into the darkness. He had something in his right hand that I couldn't see from this distance. Beyond him, racing toward the airstrip, was a large black sedan. Lazar had to be at the wheel, with Ximon alongside and Amaris his prisoner.

"No lightning around to set the fire without Caleb," London said, unlocking the van with the keys I'd taken from the objurer earlier. Arnaldo had settled on top of it, shaking out his wings.

November was chittering by my feet, bouncing up and down on her tiny back legs.

"They'll have something in the lab to light the Bunsen burners. I'll go," I said. November grabbed the hem of my jeans, tugging. "I'll be right back. 'Ember, why don't you shift so we don't have to play charades."

"No, she's right," said London. "You're injured. I'll go get one of those lighter thingies." She jogged back toward the lab in her bare feet.

November scampered a few yards toward something dark lying on the ground. But I couldn't help looking after Caleb again. He was still visible to me, running full tilt toward the black sedan, which was nearing the silhouette of the single engine plane on the small runway. So that was Lazar's escape plan, to fly out.

A piping call from November called me back to her. She was running in circles on something square and black lying on the ground. A file folder. "My file!" In a second I was there, tugging it from under her. "Thanks!"

I could easily read the white label on the folder in the

streaming light of the full moon. It said, "First Quarter Projections."

"What?" I opened the folder up and found rows of figures, headings like "Shifters Captured," "Objurers Recruited," and "Revenue." "This isn't my file," I said like an idiot, not quite sure what was going on. "Maybe Ximon had more than one file and he dropped this one?"

November shook her whiskers at me as London ran full tilt out of the lab, holding a long lighter used for fireplaces and barbecues. "All set, Siku," she shouted. "Let it rip!"

Siku stabbed his claws into the top of the first barrel of fuel, piercing it. Then with all his enormous strength, he lifted it with his front paws, stood to his full height, and hurled it up onto the roof of the laboratory. Gas poured from the holes, spreading outward in a noxious puddle all over the building.

"Woooo!" London whooped in excitement, fired up the lighter, and lifted her arm, holding it aloft. Arnaldo swooped down from above and snatched it expertly from her hand, keeping the flaming end away from his feathers. He flew over the roof and dropped it.

Instantly the fuel ignited, licking along the spine of the roof and down to the eaves. Arnaldo beat his wings and sailed back over the parking lot, calling out in triumph. London threw her hands up in the air in elation. "You'll never use these buildings to hurt anyone again, you bastards!"

Siku, grunting and huffing, grabbed the other barrel and hurled it at the office building adjacent to the lab. Dripping gas, it caught on fire as it passed through the flames. It landed on the office roof, and the entire barrel exploded at once.

London hooted again and twirled around, arms up in a joyful dance as Arnaldo spiraled around her and Siku bounced on his front paws. I stared at the flames, the pain in my arm throbbing with my pulse.

"Ximon never had your file," November said, putting her hands on her naked hips. I hadn't even noticed her shift.

"What?" I focused on her. The light from the growing fire danced over her smooth skin. "How do you know?"

"I heard him say it to Lazar just a minute ago. I ran out here and saw him and Ximon forcing Caleb's sister into that car. He said, 'Stupid girl thinks I carry her file around with me! She's too trusting. We can use that to destroy her.' Then he dropped that file on the ground and got in the car. It was the only file he was carrying."

As her words hit my brain, I knew where my file was. I looked from November to the flames swirling over the roof of the office building. It was about to be turned into ash. My history, my biological family, everything the Tribunal knew about me was in there. My past was about to be cremated.

I began walking toward the office. The flames were spreading from the roof downward, about to take over the front wall. The roof would collapse any moment now, but if I was quick . . .

I bumped into November, still naked. She stood squarely in my path. "Don't be a moron," she said. "You've been shot, you're weak, and you can't shift. You'll die if you go in there."

"No . . ." I started to say, stepping to go around her.

"Dez." She grabbed my wrist. "I'm worried about Caleb."

That got my attention. "What?"

"When he saw Lazar and Ximon put his sister into that car and drive off, his face got this look on it I'd never seen before. Like he'd seen the end of the world. Then he grabbed that stupid stuffed elephant out of his duffle bag and he said 'Better to be dead than in their hands.' Then he turned to me and said, 'Tell Dez I'm sorry.' And he ran after them."

Horror shot up my spine. So that's why he'd looked so uncertain, why he'd felt the need to say those three words to me. I turned around and squinted into the darkness, trying to see him. My file was about to burn, and Caleb was on the verge of doing something very stupid. He'd said that stuffed elephant was a last resort, and now he was carrying it as he raced to stop his father and brother from taking his sister away forever. Whatever he was about to call forth might kill them all. He was too far away from me now for me to stop him. I had only my feeble human legs to run on, and a bleeding arm that weakened me further every minute.

"Arnaldo!" I called out, waving my good arm to his circling form slicing through the air.

He swooped down and landed on the roof of the van. "Stay near Caleb. He won't risk his own life if it means risking yours."

Arnaldo turned his head to stare out over the flat desert landscape at Caleb's distant figure. He cawed, nodding once. The van bounced as he pushed off from it and flew toward the airstrip.

November began jogging toward the Beemer with the flat tire. "I'll get our clothes and stuff out of the trunk, then maybe we can pick Caleb up in the van." London ran to help her. Siku rumbled happily as he watched the flames rise higher.

I stood there, helpless and frozen. We'd saved Siku, but I was about to lose any chance of knowing who my family was, and even worse, possibly lose Caleb as well. I still had a bullet in my arm and was getting dizzier every second.

Stupid human body. It had failed me again, just as it had all those years ago when they'd diagnosed the scoliosis and put me in the brace. The feelings of humiliation and vulnerability I'd felt then crowded in on me now. I was smothered by my own weakness, suffocated in the shame of being *that* girl. I was the too-tall weirdo encased in plastic, the girl with only one friend who never got dates. I had brought danger to Mom and Richard that had cost them their home. Then, just when I thought I'd found a haven, I'd had to fight to keep the

Shifter Council from having me killed. As of last night I was the shifter who couldn't shift. Above and behind it all, I was the baby left to die in a ring of dead trees in Siberia. Unwanted, unloved. No connections, no past, no family.

I didn't want to be that girl.

The heat from the burning lab pressed against my skin. The fire leapt from the roof of the office to the warehouse next door. Soon the silver cage inside it would be blackened, perhaps melted down, never to be used again. I tried to feel happy about that, but I couldn't.

A wave of pain from my bullet wound doubled me over. The hilt of the Shadow Blade at my belt jabbed into my side. *Just like the brace.*

I had buried my hatred for the brace so deep because I couldn't bear to think of myself as a girl who wore one. It was too bizarre, too humiliating. Better to bury it, pretend it wasn't there. Pretend I wasn't there inside it.

But it was because of the brace I'd first turned into a tiger. I'd finally acknowledged not just my rage but that I was a girl who felt rage, and a whole lot of other things. I was *that* girl, like it or not.

Something sparked inside me. It was more than anger. It was greater than my shame and my fear of all the things I was.

The dark, hot place inside me that led to shadow. I'd thought it was gone forever, but I felt it now, roiling at my core. The heat from the fire seemed to pour into it, to feed it. I tiptoed to the edge, looking down into the yawning void. For the first time, I felt no dread. That mysterious place, that maelstrom that drew forth the tiger, that was me. I'd been so afraid that I'd cut myself off from . . . myself. I'd had no idea what would happen if that girl was ever unleashed.

But I knew now. Being that girl wasn't so bad, after all. Not with Mom and Caleb and the otherkin on my side. Not with the tiger and all her power lurking beneath my skin.

To find the great cat again, I didn't have to be angry. I had to dive in and embrace.

I could feel myself smiling. Then I plunged over the edge.

White energy shot up through my spine and down every nerve of my body. I fell forward onto all fours, the thick pads on my paws immune to the bite of the gravel, my tail lashing, the pain in my arm gone as if it had never been. The bullet in my arm dropped to the ground, and I flexed the lean muscles of my shoulders and haunches. My whiskers fanned out to catch the currents of the air whipped by the flames before me. The fire lit up the whole front wall of the office, cracking the door, popping the glass out of the window, shooting a dozen feet into the air. In a blink my eyes adjusted to the flaring light, seeing exactly where the fire was and was not. The sizzling sound came still only from the external walls and the roof. I could hear that inside there was space enough, at least for the next few seconds.

I roared and ran straight at the window. Gathering the great muscles in my hind legs, I leapt, front feet out, back feet tucked, head down. I smashed through the remaining glass. The scent of burning fur singed my nose, and I felt a shaft of heat sting my side; then I splayed out my paws and landed inside.

Flame licked the ceiling above me and ran down the walls. An office chair was melting before my eyes. The heat pushed against my fur, but that extra layer between my skin and the flames made it bearable for a few seconds. I squinted and curled my whiskers back against my face. Smoke poured into the empty space around me like a liquid torrent. It seared the inside of my nose and coated my lungs.

Through the miasma I examined the filing cabinets. It wasn't hard to find the one marked Shifters, A–K. I caught one claw under the handle and pulled. Locked. No time for finesse. My paw pads were getting raw and sparks flew down from the ceiling to singe my fur.

I shoved the entire cabinet against the wall with my shoulder, as easily as I could shut a door in human form. The cabinet crashed onto its side. I hooked two claws through the handle and yanked with all my strength.

The drawer shot out of the cabinet. I coughed, eyes smarting with every blink. A large wooden beam, black and wrapped in flame, plummeted from the ceiling and landed on my tail.

I yowled, wrenching it from under the blazing timber. Agony echoed down every vertebra in my spine. I kept my breath shallow and ignored the pain, as I'd ignored the brace. I'd worn that torture device twenty-three hours a day for almost three years. I could stand this.

I scanned the exposed folders and saw a few that began with G. Garcia, Enrique. Gardner, Jill. I had to trust that mine was in there somewhere. I took the entire section from G to K in my mouth, my incisors sinking into the cardboard folders at either end.

Several smaller shafts of wood showered down around me in a spark of orange fireworks. I couldn't see the window; the smoke was too thick. Even the front wall, though it had to be fully ablaze, was obscured. I had to find the opening I'd made and leap back out soon or I'd be dead. Above me the ceiling cracked loudly and groaned. It'd be falling all around me any second.

I shut my eyes and let my whiskers expand, turning my ears to catch any change in the almost uniform roar of the flames. They sounded now almost like the sea.

The sea. How nice it would be to go for a swim. I stumbled and shook my head to clear it. The lack of oxygen was getting to me. I had to focus. But images of cool water and the crash of waves kept intruding. My head drooped under the weight of the files I carried. Why not just put them down and plunge into the ocean?

Caleb. He was still out there, about to take his revenge, possibly at the cost of his own life. I couldn't let that happen.

Forget the stupid ocean. If I didn't get the hell out of here now I'd never see Caleb again. Caleb, who loved me.

The faintest shift in the air current struck my whiskers. At the same time I caught a tiny alteration in the sound of the flames. They weren't as thick over there, where the air came from. I turned my nose in that direction and tried to see, but it was no use. I'd have to jump without knowing what I was jumping into. I'd have to trust myself.

No time like this instant. I jumped, using every last ounce of my failing strength, my muscles crying for oxygen. My right shoulder brushed something boiling hot, then I was out. I stumbled and rolled as I landed, but I kept hold of the folders in my mouth. I only dropped them when I'd made it to the center of the parking lot, a safe distance from the fire. Then I took in great lungfuls of sweet, cool air.

Something poked at my throbbing tail. I yowled and whirled to see Siku, a hulking brown mountain silhouetted against the flames, nosing my tail, concern creasing his furry brow. London and November stood on either side of him, clad in their spare clothing, tiny and frail next to his bulk.

"Holy shit, Dez," said November. "You look like that beat-up cat Pepe LePew's always chasing because he thinks she's a skunk."

I snorted and coughed, my version of a laugh.

"You okay?" London walked up and looked into my eyes. "You've inhaled a lot of smoke. Better shift."

I shook my head and turned to look out over the desert, toward the airstrip. A lean figure in black flung something at a huge winged bird. The bird swooped away, and a blaze of lightning cracked upward from the earth, shaking the sky with thunder. So Caleb had tired of Arnaldo interfering with his plans.

A hundred yards beyond them, the black sedan had pulled up to the airplane. An eternity had seemed to pass while I was inside the burning building, but it must have been only seconds.

Arnaldo arced away from Caleb, unhurt, and clearly unwilling to get any closer now that he'd been threatened. I got to my feet. Caleb still had to get to the airplane. Tigers were built more for stealth and strength than speed. But I was faster than a human, and I was going to get to Caleb before he did anything dumb.

I looked back at Siku, London, and November. Siku lifted his nose in acknowledgment. London was going through the files at my feet, reading their labels in the light of the blaze. She jerked one out of the pile and waved it at me. "Yours, okay? Now go."

Presiding overhead, the moon ran its rays like a cool, soothing hand down my burned flanks and singed whiskers. Maybe it was my imagination, but I felt a renewed strength. My mother would have said it was the moon goddess. The old me would've said it was strictly psychological. The new me just gloried in the feel of it.

Gathering every ounce of power inside me, I sprang forward.

My strides ate up the ground. Caleb hadn't looked back since Arnaldo winged away from him. So he didn't know I was coming. Right now that was for the best.

I leapt over a low cactus without breaking stride, my claws helping me find purchase in the unstable desert sand. Every grain lay outlined before me in the moonlight. My paws made soft crunching noises as they hit the ground for a split second and then lifted away. A snake, asleep under a rock, slithered off with a sandpaper glide as I rocketed past. I'd catch up to Caleb in moments.

Up ahead, Lazar was removing the wooden blocks around the wheels of the small plane as Ximon shoved Amaris into its hunched doorway.

"Leave her!" Caleb's voice cut through the stillness. "Leave her or you won't live to regret it!" He was running flat out toward them, his right hand clutching the small stuffed elephant.

Lazar turned to look at his brother for a moment, his face creased with pain. Then he turned, climbed up into the plane, and shut the door. Caleb was only twenty yards away, and I only thirty more behind him. I heard a click from the plane, and the engine puttered to life. The propeller began to turn.

"No!" Caleb put on a burst of speed, but the plane slowly taxied away from him.

He extended his arm, desperately reaching for the door handle. Through the window in the airplane's door I saw Ximon's face, creased in a nasty, dazzling grin. Then it disappeared as two hands grabbed him from behind and shoved. Inside the plane, Amaris lunged toward the door and struggled to get it open. Ximon grabbed at her as the plane circled away from us, and I lost sight of them.

The door opened, and I slowed, uncertain what was happening. I could see a small feminine hand on the door, and a narrow girl's foot in a white sneaker dangling. Inside, Ximon shouted "Faster!" But as the plane picked up speed, Amaris fell through the doorway, rolling awkwardly and crying out in pain.

Ximon grabbed for her, but too late. The plane's speed quickly left her behind. Ximon stuck his head out of the open door, white hair flapping in the breeze from the propeller, his clear blue eyes wide in shock. Amaris, her hands and knees scraped and bleeding, struggled to her feet.

Caleb came to a pounding halt as Amaris got to her feet and ran to him. "No!" he shouted. "Get out of here, Amaris. Run!" The plane was facing down the runway now. Ximon shut the door and the aircraft picked up speed, about to leave the ground.

Amaris stopped, uncertain. Caleb gave her a shove back toward the burning buildings of the compound, holding the elephant aloft. "I have to do this," he said. "Now go! It's not safe."

She backed away fast, her eyes wide with horror. "Don't, Caleb, no!"

He still hadn't heard me approach. I was a breath from pouncing upon him.

"I call on you, come forth from shadow!" Caleb's voice was deeper than I'd ever heard, more commanding, elegant, and vicious. It sent vibrations shuddering down my skin, and I knew whatever he was calling forth was greater and deadlier than I. The lifeless stuffed animal in his hand seemed to stir.

I didn't hesitate. No way was I going to let him risk his life with whatever-it-was. He might think revenge was worth it, but I knew better. And, selfishly, in the back of my head, I didn't want him to kill Ximon, who maybe held a few secrets from my past inside his head. I sprang toward Caleb's upraised arm and swatted. The elephant flew from his grip as he recoiled.

I landed, then bounded again, grabbing the elephant in my mouth as it rolled along the ground. It writhed in my grip, much larger than it had been moments before. Something like a horn or a tooth stabbed the inside of my mouth, a scaly wing flapped frantically, and one long, black arm reached up, clawing with too-long fingers at my eyes. The elephant was becoming whatever its shadow form was in Othersphere. I had only seconds before the transformation was complete.

"Dez, no!" Caleb's eyes were still flecked with gold, but he looked pale, tired, slightly stunned as he often did after exercising his power for too long. He held his hand out to me. "Put it down; let me stop them."

As an answer, I sank my claws into the squirming thing

growing in my jaws, and tore it to pieces. For a moment, I felt flesh and bone give way. Then it was nothing but white bits of stuffing, puffing into the wind and covering my tongue.

"What have you done?" The command flooded Caleb's voice, shuddering around me like a great wind. Then he shook his head, as if fighting something off. "No," he said with a kind of desperation, though I wasn't sure what he meant. "No, not like this."

"Yes." His voice echoed again, only this time it wasn't his voice, but something harsh and grating. He drew himself to his full height, but he looked even taller and leaner now. I blinked at him. Were those reptilian *scales* covering his skin?

He shook his head and closed his eyes, and when he opened them they were strangely tilted and pure gold, the pupil gone. He smiled, lips thinning, teeth sharpened to dangerous points. His hands were black, the nails like yellow dagger points. He was no longer Caleb, but rather some avenging demon in human form, a dark specter ready to exact any price to get what he wanted.

Fear made my tail lash. I'd seen Caleb struggle internally before, when he got tired and overreached himself with calling. Morfael had as much as admitted that it opened Caleb up to being overtaken by things in Othersphere. But it had never changed how he looked, never altered his voice so drastically. Now it seemed he was being possessed by the very thing he was calling. I'd shredded the elephant, so it was coming into the world through Caleb instead.

Amaris looked at the altered face of her brother, screamed, and tried to run. But she stepped on the hem of her long gown and went down in a heap. She whirled so as not to have her back to the creature.

"What . . . *who* are you?" she asked.

The demon looked down at its fingers and scales, and the mouth that used to be Caleb's smiled at her. "I'm the one who watches, who conquers. For years I observed him. I knew that one day the temptation to call upon me would become too great."

I spat out the remains of the stuffed toy and gathered all my remaining strength. I wanted to leap upon the demon, to fight. But how could I do that and not hurt Caleb?

The Caleb creature regarded me with scorn and reached out one hand. "Return." His voice pulsed through me. "Return to shadow from whence you came. . . ."

The words poured into me, trying to propel my tiger form back to Othersphere. I roared back with all my might, ears back. The vibrations from my throat interrupted his. I felt my own voice, like a shield around me, holding his back.

The thing that was no longer Caleb smiled a horrible, warped grin like a death's head. "Now he regrets defying you and calling me," it said. "Now that he is weary and it is too late. He wishes he could return to you, but he cannot. Go back to where you belong, little beast." He pointed a blackened hand at me again. Waves of power rippled over my fur. "I will swallow this moon and all its blood. Go, and leave this world to me."

I jumped at him to push at his chest with one paw, claws sheathed, trying to jolt Caleb back to this world. He stumbled back two steps, but did not fall. This creature was stronger than Caleb, stronger than I was.

Caleb had to be somewhere in there, between this world and shadow. I had to bring him back somehow, find a way to make him fight. But tigers couldn't talk. The answer was obvious. I hesitated only a moment, weighing my old fears against my love for Caleb; then I closed my eyes and stopped my growling.

"Go back," said the Caleb thing. "Return to your feeble human form, I command you!"

And I did as he commanded. I allowed him to sweep my tiger form back into shadow. Then I stood there, nothing but a naked teenage girl with windblown hair and a full-body

blush. Still wrapped around my waist was the belt and scabbard holding the Shadow Blade, as if I had never shifted. The
bruises that had been at my waist for years thanks to the
brace were gone.

The Caleb creature was staring at me, spiked eyebrows
frowning over golden eyes.

"I love you, Caleb," I said.

It drew back, puzzlement twisting its almost familiar fea-
tures.

I waited a moment. The thing still stared. "Caleb! Would
you please hurry up and kick this thing's ass? I'm freezing!"

Something like a full-body hiccup shuddered through the
creature's frame. Its dragonlike eyes widened in surprise,
then narrowed in fury. "No," it said in its hissing, guttural
voice. "I will not go—" Its voice cut off, choking. The sharpened, demonic outline wavered, flickered. And like a slate
wiped clean, it was no longer the creature but Caleb standing
before me, tall but not too tall, lean but not skeletal, devil-
ishly handsome but not demonically so.

"Dez?" It was Caleb's voice. His eyes traveled over me,
and I shivered but not from the cold. I stayed, bare feet
clutching the sandy ground, anything to keep from ducking
away.

He stepped to me and I was in his arms. His whole body
trembled, but somehow he got his coat off and wrapped it
around me before he collapsed. I laid him down carefully on
the desert floor. The gold was fading from his eyes as he
stared up at the moon. Then his eyes closed. All I could hear
was the sound of my own breathing and Amaris, crying quietly, crumpled in a ball of white next to a stunted Joshua tree.

The engine of Lazar's airplane clattered, and I turned to
see it rise from the ground. It seemed to hover for an instant,
then shot up into the firmament, eclipsing the moon as it
turned south and west.

I leaned down and placed one ear on Caleb's chest, wanting only to hear proof he was still here, still the Caleb that I knew. His heartbeat was hasty but not dangerous, his breath coming in jagged gasps. His skin looked gray and clammy.

I lay down next to him, hoping the warmth from my body would help him somehow. He smelled of air and storm clouds.

He blinked and turned to me. I wanted only to tell him how much I loved him, how I would do whatever it took to keep him safe and happy in this world or any other. But the emotions crowded my throat and I couldn't speak.

His eyes took me in. Then he wrapped his arms around me and buried his face in the crook of my neck. "Thank you," he said. "Thank you."

CHAPTER 27

Caleb had seen me naked.

Of all the crazy stuff that had happened, that was the thought that kept beating through my brain as I limped across the desert with him and Amaris. It shouldn't have been that big of a deal. Shifters found themselves naked all the time after they shed their animal form. But I'd never been kissed before I met him, never even considered showing any part of my body to a boy. I'd been in the brace for years, armored against all contact, safe and alone. Now that armor was gone, and I'd bared everything. I got hot all over as I thought about it. Part of me wanted to ask him what he was thinking. Part of me wanted to run away so I'd never have to look him in the eye again. And a very small part of me, a new part, wanted to tell him it was his turn next.

We were all a mess. I stumbled forward in bare feet, wearing nothing but Caleb's coat. Caleb drooped with exhaustion. Amaris, walking on the other side of Caleb, was bruised and scraped after falling from a moving plane and being held hostage by her father and brother. On top of that she'd been forced to reject the people who'd raised her and thrown her lot in with a group she'd always heard were minions of Satan. Caleb's near possession by a powerful, demonic force from shadow probably hadn't been very reassuring. I was proud of her for fighting back and jumping out of that plane, but I wasn't sure she'd give a damn for praise out of a shifter's mouth. Every now and then she cast a fearful little glance at me, as if expecting me to pounce.

Ahead, the flames roared around the buildings and reached for the sky. The entire Tribunal compound was burning to the ground. Its leaders had fled; its files and equipment were ash. Maybe, just maybe, we'd put a stop to their work in this part of the world. At least for a little while.

Caleb held my hand as we walked, our shoulders touching. I tripped, trying to avoid a cactus, and Caleb caught me. "Here, put my shoes on," he said, slipping off one of his boots.

Amaris looked down at my battered and bleeding feet. "Do you have some clothes in the car? I can run ahead and get them." Her voice wasn't as melodious as Caleb's, but I could hear the resemblance now that I knew they were related.

"That'd be great, thanks." I tried to smile up at her.

She managed a weak smile back and jogged on ahead. Caleb helped me find a more comfortable spot to sit, which ended up being half on his lap, leaning back against him, his arms wrapped around me, my head on his shoulder. I closed my eyes as I realized that everything was all right now.

"What did it mean?" I asked. "That demon thing. It said it watched you...."

Caleb's arms tightened around me. "I was ten years old, shopping with my mother in this department store in Sweden, when I saw that stuffed elephant. I knew it was something powerful, something dangerous, but I had no idea it was watching me."

"Let me guess," I said. "You stole it."

He let out a rueful laugh. "Yep. I stole it, and I hid it from my mother, because I knew she'd make me give it back, or destroy it. But I thought we might need it one day. We were always on the run from the Tribunal, you know. I wasn't sure exactly what would happen if I called forth that particular shadow. But I figured it was better than getting killed by Ximon and his crew." I felt him shake his head. "Now I'm not sure which is worse."

"Please don't ever do anything like that again," I said. "I thought I'd lost you."

His mouth was against my hair. "You meant what you said, didn't you?"

I pulled away enough to be able to look him in the eye. His face was creased with concern. "Of course I did. You saw me out there, you saw . . ."

"Everything." A roguish smile curled his lips. "My dream came true. I thought I was gone forever. But I fought the devil himself on the chance I might get to see all of you again."

I flushed and buried my face in his shoulder again, jitters running up and down my ribs. "Then how could you think I didn't mean it?"

"Well, you're kind of noble and stubbornly heroic, and you ran all the way out there to save us. You're not the type to give up, on anyone. So there was a chance you said it not because you actually meant it, but because you knew I'd rip the veil between the worlds with my bare hands to get back to you once I heard that."

"I meant it," I said. "I love you." It was easy to say now, with my clothes on, his arms around me, his breath on my ear.

He reached up to tilt my head back and kissed me, like a man lost in the desert drinking from a well.

"Maybe she doesn't need shoes." November's voice cut through the roar in my ears. "Maybe she'll float home on pink clouds pushed by the breath of angels."

Caleb and I began to laugh and turned to see November walking up next to Amaris. Amaris looked a little lost, but she put my spare set of shoes and other clothing down by my feet as November tossed a large bottle of water at Caleb.

London, Siku, and Arnaldo, all in human form and clad in their spare clothes, walked up behind them, silhouetted in the sunset-like red haze of the Tribunal fire.

Caleb took a long swig of water from the bottle and helped me to my feet as I slipped on my sneakers. "I take it you all have met my sister, Amaris," he said, and walked over to her as she stood a little apart from the others, arms crossed over her chest.

"She shoved Ximon out of the way and jumped from a moving plane to get away from them," I said. "Pretty badass, actually."

"But you let them get away," said Siku, his expression not changing.

"I—" Caleb started to speak.

"I stopped Caleb from using the nuclear option," I said, wanting to take the blame for that, because it was my fault. I wasn't sorry about it though. "Not one of our lives is worth theirs."

"And we did basically take out their whole western American operation," said Arnaldo.

"I think maybe we did okay." London was smiling.

"You surprised everyone," said Amaris, startling us. "The shifters have never banded together to fight like this. My father was . . . impressed."

"He'll be even more impressed when we find him and kill him," said Siku. "No offense."

Amaris bit her lip and shook her head, rubbing her scraped hands together. Caleb looked down at them and the bloody rips in the elbows of her gown. "Can you heal yourself, you think?"

"Maybe," she said. "After I eat and rest a bit. I haven't been able to—not since you used the lightning on Father."

"Psychological block," said November. "You'll get over it. Dez did, didn't you, Dez?"

"I guess so," I said.

Arnaldo wiped his hand on his pants and stepped forward, extending it toward Amaris. "I'm Arnaldo," he said. "Nice to meet you."

"The, um..." She gave his hand a quick, limp shake. "The eagle, right?"

"Right." He grinned at her, then stepped back.

She swallowed and stood up straighter as the others moved toward her slowly, shaking hands with an odd formality. I ended it by walking over and giving her a hug. She didn't react at first, taken aback. Then she put her arms around my shoulders and gave me a tentative squeeze.

"Welcome to the insanity," I said.

"Let's get to Barstow," said November. "I'm starving!" She turned and jogged back toward the van. As we followed her, Caleb slipped one arm around Amaris's shoulders and the other wrapped snug about my waist.

We heaped into the van, Caleb driving, me riding shotgun with my black file folder on my lap. I'd taken off the Shadow Blade and put it in the back. Thirty seconds after I took it off, it turned into my brace again. Maybe my feeling earlier was correct—as long as I wore the Blade, it stayed a blade. But once I let it go, the brace returned. It looked strange now, small and not embarrassing at all.

Amaris huddled in the back of the van with the others. Behind us, the flames were dying down, but two fire engines passed us, lights flashing, as we headed into town.

Phone service came back in Barstow, and after the shifter

kids called their angry but relieved parents, I used November's phone to e-mail my mom.

"All safe," I wrote, typing as fast as I could as we circled the drive-thru again. "Tribunal facility taken offline, so I think we can go home. At least for now. Should be back at Bishop Hospital to see Morfael in a few hours. Tell me where to find you when you can. Miss you. Love you." With the tension draining from me, I felt a stab of loneliness at the thought of my parents. How far had they fled? Now that Caleb was safe, the thing I wanted most was to see my mother.

Caleb parked, and we passed the food back to everyone. The van quieted with the sounds of chewing and slurping.

"You were still wearing the Shadow Blade when you shifted to human form," Caleb said, dipping a bundle of fries in ketchup. "Yes, indeed. I noticed *everything*." He waggled his eyebrows at me, and I blushed. "But I didn't see it on you in tiger form."

"Yeah, I know. Weird," I said. "I figured it fell off me when I became a tiger, but there it was when I turned human again."

"It's accommodating your shadow form," he said. "As if it was made for you."

"Maybe it was," I said. "It just feels . . . right when I hold it. And the back brace was made especially for me after they found the curve in my spine."

"So somehow the brace was made for you and tied to a knife that was made for you too?" he said. "Something else we need to ask Morfael about."

"Check it out." Arnaldo had made his way up from the back of the van to kneel between us. He held out a tranquilizer gun taken from the Tribunal. Its stock was warped as if from a fire, with black streaks snaking up the barrel.

"Did you take that out of the fire?" I said.

"No. I picked it up on my way out of the lab because I noticed these." He ran a finger along the dark lines. "It's the one you used, Dez. It still works, but barely."

I took it from him, recognizing it now. "Just like the silver gun that broke down after I used it during the raid on the school."

"Looks like you have a destructive effect on any sort of metal mechanism," he said. "It's like the shadow is seeping out of you and distorting them."

"Why me?" I said. "Why doesn't this happen to you or the others?"

"Maybe it's the Blade affecting other things you hold?" said Caleb.

"The silver gun got warped before she ever had the Blade. There's got to be another explanation." Arnaldo shrugged and went to the back of the van.

I leafed through the file and its detailed listing of my daily activities, starting with the first time I climbed the lightning tree. "There's nothing in here about who my parents are, or where. All that's in Ximon's head, I guess."

I looked out the window as the cactus and sand, clear under the moon, sped past. "I feel like you and I are always driving into or out of a battle zone," I said.

He nodded. "We'd better get used to it."

Everyone but Amaris got out of the van in the hospital parking lot in Bishop. She had fallen asleep. A faint snoring sound came from her mouth. Caleb stared down at her, lips twitching.

"Sleep tight," said November as she shut the back doors to the van as quietly as she could.

"She snores," said Siku, looking at me. "You better get earplugs. That kind of thing runs in the family."

I opened my mouth, glancing at Caleb, whose eyes got wide in disbelief. Had Siku made a joke? I was too dumbfounded to reply.

We found Morfael wide awake and waiting for us, his eyes alight with the old fire in spite of the tubes in his arm and the thick bandages around his body. Raynard snorted awake from his chair as we poured into the room, surrounding the bed.

"One at a time," Morfael said, as we all began babbling at him about what had happened at the compound. "Raynard, would you shut the door, please?"

Raynard shut the door to make sure no one overheard, and we took turns telling the story of the Raid on the Tribunal. Or the Rescue of Siku, as November called it. I noticed she was standing awfully close to him.

Morfael listened carefully but without expression. "You seem to have learned a lot in my school without my having to teach it to you."

We grinned at each other. That was about as close to a compliment as you could get from Morfael.

"Fat lot of good it does," said November. "My dad's going to kill me when I get home."

"I guess we all should make plans to go home," said Arnaldo. "No way our parents will let us stay at the school now that the Tribunal knows where it is."

"But what about the rest of the school year?" London pushed her hair behind her ear and looked a little defensive as we all stared at her in surprise. "Hey, it's better than home. Plus there's six months left before we graduate."

"A new location will be established soon," said Morfael. "Perhaps Caleb and his sister can help us."

Caleb stood up straighter, a smile breaking over his face. "We'd be happy to."

"We'll need you scouting for a perfect place right away.

Everyone else should go home until they find it," said Morfael.

"Maybe Dez could come with us and help too," Caleb said, casting a hopeful glance at me.

"Desdemona needs to return home, for now," said Morfael. And I knew he was right, though it hurt to think about being away from Caleb. "After your endeavors this night, she and her family will be safe there for a few months at least, until the Tribunal gets back on its feet in this area."

"And maybe by then we'll figure out how to get rid of them all for good," I said, sounding more hopeful than I felt. It had been a long night.

Nobody hugged Morfael as we left. He wasn't the type. I figured I'd ask him about the Shadow Blade and other things once he was feeling better.

As we shuffled down the hallway, I saw a small, familiar female figure shoving aside a nurse as she hustled toward me. A bearded man behind her stopped to apologize to the nurse. "Desdemona!" she shouted, waving.

"Mom!"

A second later, she and Richard and I were enveloped in a three-way hug.

"But what are you guys doing here?" I said when I could breathe.

"Well, you e-mailed us that you were going to see Morfael in the Bishop Hospital, and since we weren't that far away . . ."

"Where have you been?" I was smiling all over.

Mom made a face. "Fresno. We knew you were somewhere in the mountains, and I wanted to be nearby if possible. Not the most exciting town in winter, I must say. But who cares!" She beamed at me. "We're together again. Now you need to introduce us to everyone. Caleb I recognize, of course. Hi, Caleb."

Caleb walked over and took her hand, then gave Richard a handshake. I introduced them to London, Arnaldo, Siku, and November. Mom's eyes got very large and bright as she took them all in.

"Wait now," she said, stopping dead as we began to walk down the hall again. "I have to meet Morfael. Would you all mind waiting for us? It won't be a moment."

They all nodded and said sure. I motioned for Caleb to follow us as Mom took my elbow and walked me into Morfael's room. Raynard stood up, eyebrows rising.

"This is Raynard, Mom. He helps out around the school."

Mom shook Raynard's hand, but her eyes drifted to the bed. She finally got a good look at Morfael lying there, all bones and skin.

Her brow knitted. "I . . . I know you, don't I?" She released Raynard's hand and drifted to the side of the bed. "You look so familiar."

Morfael said nothing, but the corners of his mouth deepened in what might have been a smile.

"You've met Morfael?" I asked. That couldn't be.

Mom squinted, as if something had been triggered. "You were in Russia. That's where I saw you. At the orphanage where I found Desdemona."

"What?" I felt like my brain was going to explode. "You met him in Moscow?"

Still Morfael was silent, though his smile grew wider. He waited as Mom's memories coalesced.

"It was you who told me where to find Dez." She grabbed his skinny hand, her eyes alight. "I was waiting to meet with the director of the orphanage, but you came in and said to follow you. You took me to a room and Dez was there, in her crib, waiting for me." Tears welled in Mom's eyes. "Later on, I met the real director and you were nowhere to be found. But I knew Desdemona had to be mine."

Morfael, finally, nodded. "I knew you were the one."

Mom let loose a sob and leaned to rest her forehead

against his hand. Morfael's face softened as he looked down at her.

"Okay," I said, fighting off the chills that threatened to take over my body. "Time to start telling me what's going on before I lose it."

"About sixteen years ago, I was in Tunguska, Siberia, trying to see if there were any tiger-shifters left in the world, and I found you."

"You found me?" I tried to take in the information calmly, though my brain was rioting.

His pale eyes looked into mine, as if liking what they saw there. "I found you first, and later I made it so the reindeer herder would hear your cries and take you to safety. I ensured that the right woman found you after you were transferred to the orphanage in Moscow."

"Oh, my God," I said. Caleb walked up and took my hand as I tried to process everything.

Mom took a hankie from Richard to blow her nose. "Thank you," she said to Morfael. "Those words are inadequate, but they're all I have."

"No, thank you for being exactly the parent Desdemona needed," he said, then looked at me. "I suspected you might be the last tiger-shifter in this world. And as such the Tribunal would be after you. So I used everything I knew to suppress the signs of shadow in you. When the time was right, I knew you would overcome the barriers I had set."

"So that's why you didn't start shifting until such a late age," Caleb said. "Morfael was trying to protect you."

"I—I have a question," said my mother, half raising her hand as if she were in school. "Why didn't you place her with other shifters—that's the correct term, am I right? They at least could have helped her understand who she was. Why pick me? Not that I'm not grateful, of course!"

"The shifter tribes are too insular and filled with fear of outsiders to ever take in a child born to someone they did not know," Morfael said. "Even so, for the first year after I found Desdemona, I tried to track down the tiger-shifters of Siberia, to see if they would raise her. But I found no trace of them anywhere. The Northeast Asian division of the Tribunal appears to have wiped them out. Eventually I concluded I would have to find a nonshifter to care for her until she was of age to make her own way in the world. As soon as I saw you, I knew you would not try to force her to be something she was not."

"The Shadow Blade and the brace," I said. "That was you."

"In a way," he said. "When I found you, I also found the Blade and scabbard hidden among your blankets. They were strongly linked to you via shadow in a way I still don't understand. I kept them to prevent the orphanage from taking them, and I also kept an eye on you, thinking I would give them back to you. Then one day the Blade vanished. Somehow it linked itself to the brace."

"Maybe because the brace sort of became a part of me too," I said. "I wore it so much, and the belt fits right where the bruises from the brace used to be."

"The Blade won't cut living things, only metal and plastic," said Caleb. "And when Dez touches metal technology like guns for too long, they stop working. Do you think those two things are related?"

"Probably," said Morfael. "Silver and other worked metals are antagonistic to shadow. I suspect they do not exist in Othersphere. For some reason, your shadow nature opposes technology, and may have the power to destroy it."

"But it also makes the tomatoes grow like crazy under your windowsill," Mom said.

"But then why haven't cars and computers been blowing up around me for years?" I said. "It's only started happening since . . ." Then I realized.

"Since you first shifted," Morfael finished for me. "By suppressing the shadow in you as a child, I made it easier for you to function in this world in many ways."

Things were coming together. Some of them in a good way, and some of them not. I looked at Morfael. "You suppressed the shadow in me twice," I said, anger flaring. "The first time I can understand—I was just a baby. But you did it again yesterday."

"It was necessary," he said. "You had not yet fully come to understand who and what you are. By cutting you off from it again, I hoped you would fight to find your way back."

He met my gaze squarely, and in a way he was right. I'd found some kind of peace with everything out there in the desert. But my resentment didn't soften. "You've played puppet master in my life long enough," I said.

"Desdemona!" said my mother, squeezing my arm.

I ignored her. "Don't get me wrong—I'm grateful for all you've done. But your secret interference stops now, all right?"

His smile irritated me, as if even now I was following a path he'd laid out. "I see that you have indeed found your way back," he said. "You have nothing further to worry about from me."

It wasn't exactly a promise to stop interfering, but I had a feeling it was the best I was going to get from him right now. And he had saved my life in the Siberian woods all those years ago, and brought me to a family where I'd found love and respect.

"I'm glad you're feeling better," I said. "I'm looking forward to rejoining the school once you've found its new home."

We left after that. The sun had risen, and the other kids were anxious to get on the road so they could see their families.

"Thanks for helping us save Amaris," I said to Siku when we were all out in the parking lot. Mom and Richard were bringing their car around to get me, and I was putting off having to say good-bye to Caleb as long as I could. He was checking on Amaris.

"I guess maybe some nonshifters are okay," he said, and I found myself being crushed briefly in a bear hug.

November stood on the bumper of the van to give me a good-bye hug, her head almost level with mine that way. "Try not to take over your humdrum high school while you're waiting to come back to ours, okay?" she said as London also gave me a swift embrace.

"Whatever you do, don't listen to November," said London, pushing a strand of hair behind her ear, her eyes sliding over to see November's reaction. "That's the first rule for getting through life."

"Yeah, by all means listen to the death-obsessed moper for advice," November shot back, crawling into the van.

London followed her in, retorting something I didn't hear because Arnaldo was standing in front of me. "Thanks," he said, and handed me the black folder that contained my file, then leaned in and kissed my cheek. "See you soon."

Richard's car pulled up. I turned to see Amaris climbing into the passenger seat of the van with Caleb holding the door for her. But he was looking at me.

His long black coat fluttered in the breeze as we walked toward each other slowly, knowing that the sooner we came together, the sooner we would part.

"I'll call as often as I can," he said. "I have a feeling Morfael's going to keep us busy."

I swallowed, trying not to feel lost. "It's just till you find a new place for the school, right?"

"And we get the buildings up." He slid one warm hand around my shoulders, the other at my waist, pulling me closer.

"Try not to be too reckless," I said, my arms encircling his neck.

"You're one to talk," he said. "Try not to shift back to human in front of any other guys while I'm gone." As my face flushed, he put his lips to my ear and said, in that low nonwhisper of his, "I want you to do that only for me."

We kissed then, and I lost track of things. The world seemed to spin and catch fire, and I might have fallen, if Caleb's arms hadn't been around me.

Eventually my mother called my name, and he pushed himself away from me, shoving his hands into his coat pockets. "It's not a bad drive to Burbank," he said in a strangled tone.

Something heavy ached inside my chest. "You know where I'll be," I said.

He nodded. "Just down the street from the lightning tree."

BEYOND
THE
STORY

READER CHAT QUESTIONS

**Warning: Spoilers! Read this only after
you've finished reading *Otherkin*.**

1. The first time Dez shifts into a tiger, what are the emotion she is feeling and why? How do these emotions relate to the first word in the book?

2. The second time Dez shifts, she's feeling similar emotions, but they have a very different cause. Why do you think it's these emotions that cause her to shift? Have you been through anything that triggered similar emotions in you?

3. What does a tiger symbolize to you? How does that tie into what Dez is going through with her back brace and her feelings about her body?

4. At the start of the story, Dez allows the back brace to define her in several ways. Why is that? How and why has this changed by the end of the book?

5. Dez knows she is adopted, but for most of her life, she hasn't wanted to discuss it with her mother. Why would she feel that way? How is that possibly connected to the emotions that cause her to shift?

6. Why does Morfael make Dez and Caleb undergo a kind of test before they join his school?

7. Why do the different tribes of shifters dislike each other? How is this reflected in the relationships between the shifter kids at Morfael's school? Is there any parallel between that and what goes on in your school?

8. Dez's mother writes to her: "Don't be afraid of yourself." What does she mean by that? Is there any part of yourself that you're afraid of? If so, how do you deal with it?

9. During the blindfold test, what does Dez do that helps bond the kids from different tribes into real friendship?

10. Why do the other kids have such a problem with Dez after she shifts into a house cat? Why are they so quick to try to leave the school and a wounded Morfael after the Tribunal attacks?

11. At one point in the story, Morfael prevents Dez from being able to shift into a tiger. Why does he do this? How does Dez overcome the block?

12. Why does Ximon claim he does everything "out of love"? How does this conflict or coincide with your own ideas about love?

13. Dez brings Caleb back to this world with a somewhat embarrassing action. How does it reflect her changing feelings about her body? Why do the bruises around her waist disappear after that?

Turn the page for a sneak peek at

OTHERMOON

by Nina Berry.

Available in February 2013

CHAPTER 1

The night before we moved away, I couldn't sleep. Not bothering to turn on the light, I sat up in bed at three a.m. and put my earbuds in to blast the audiobook for *The Tempest*. Rain beat down on the jacaranda tree in our front yard. I resolutely gazed out at it to avoid seeing the walls of my room, which had been stripped of all my posters and photos, leaving nothing but uneven holes and sticky tape residue.

The man reading Shakespeare's play had a crisp English accent, but his voice didn't have the depth of Caleb's. No one did. No one human anyway.

Caleb. Thinking his name sent a stab of longing up from my heart to tighten my throat. We'd talked till midnight, but I hadn't laid eyes on him in weeks.

> *Our revels now are ended. These our actors,*
> *As I foretold you, were all spirits, and*
> *Are melted into air, into thin air . . .*

Something glinted in the corner of my eye. I caught sight of a gray van slipping into the rain-soaked fog down the street.

We'd stolen a van like that, a white one, from the Tribunal, my otherkin friends and I, after we burned their compound to the ground. But the Tribunal had other sites, other acolytes.

Crreeeeeee...

I tapped the headphones. Electronics and metal gadgets tended to break down around me. That last noise was more like a creaky floorboard in a horror movie or the rusty door to my medicine cabinet than Shakespeare. The iPod snapped on again.

> *We are such stuff*
> *As dreams are made on...*

A shape glided through the downpour outside. The gray van was back, but now the headlights were off. The downy hairs on the back of my neck stood up as it came to a stop across the street.

Creeeee...

That didn't come from the headphones. I popped them out of my ears and rolled silently to my feet, senses alight with fear. For a moment the only illumination came from my iPod, the only sound the interrupted lines of Shakespeare still coming faintly from the headphones.

Then, down the hall, light as a feather falling on grass, came a footstep. And another.

Someone had been in my bathroom at three a.m., opening and closing my medicine cabinet, and was now heading toward the living room.

It couldn't be my mother or Richard. I knew every variation of their footsteps, and neither one had any reason to search my nearly empty medicine cabinet.

I used all my training to move quietly to my bedroom door

and turned the knob. I didn't want to wake my parents. Perhaps there was an innocent reason for the sounds. If not, I could deal with the Tribunal. And if I couldn't, better it be me who was taken or killed.

The hallway was dark and empty. I stilled and heard the footfalls again in the living room, moving faster now. Half running down the hall, I kept my body out of sight as I peered around the doorframe.

To my night-sensitive eyes, the living room lay before me clear as day, unfamiliar territory now that packing boxes and bubble-wrapped furniture dominated. The front door creaked open, and a hooded figure was silhouetted for a moment against the dim greenish streetlight before it stepped outside. Gray hood, gray camouflage, the slender waist and broad shoulders of a man. Someone from the Tribunal. An objurer whose only purpose in life was to rid the world of my kind. But why would they leave without trying to kidnap or kill . . . ?

"Desdemona?" Mom's sleepy voice came first, then the creak of her bedroom door opening. She had always had a motherly sense for when I was restless at night.

That was all it took. The gray figure took off, slamming the door shut behind him.

"Stay here, Mom!" I shouted, and ran. In a heartbeat I had the door open and leapt down the front steps, blinking against the rain. The hard, heavy drops were icy cold and drenched me instantly.

The figure sprinted straight for the van, rounding the jacaranda tree. I was fast, inhumanly fast in short spurts, but he had too big a head start. Then his foot bumped hard against one of the tree's roots, his legs shot backward, and he sprawled facedown onto the grass.

"Thanks, tree," I said, lunging for him.

He rolled out of reach, brown eyes behind his muddied ski mask very wide, and scrambled to his feet. I knew those eyes.

The sound of his breath coming hard and fast brought back a memory of a tall blond boy, his arm broken, his once angelic face sneering to hide just how lost he was. It was Caleb's half brother, and his betrayer.

"Lazar," I said.

He pulled off the soggy ski mask as I moved to get between him and the van. Beneath it his wavy blond hair was already dark with rain, curling against his forehead. Droplets raced down his temples and aquiline nose, collecting on his lips as they tightened in a familiar way. The gray trousers clung to his lean hips and thighs, and the wet gray shirt outlined the taut definition in his shoulders and chest. His breath misted briefly in the rain as it came fast and even. A muscle in his jaw clenched as he stared at me, and for a moment he looked so much like Caleb that my heart skipped a beat.

Then he spoke, and his voice, harsher, more guarded than Caleb's, broke the spell. "Desdemona. Let me go." It was a warning, not a plea.

I glanced over my shoulder. Behind me, steam rose from the van's exhaust pipe, but no one had yet emerged. Maybe they hadn't seen us in the darkness and the deluge. But that didn't explain why Lazar hadn't summoned them on the communicator every objurer wore on every mission.

His slightly tip-tilted eyes, with their thick, rain-spiked lashes, were the same size and shape as Caleb's, but with rich brown irises rather than black. His gaze flicked up and down my body.

Water ran down my face, plastering my T-shirt to my skin, and I realized I was only wearing that and my underwear, my usual bedtime apparel. My cheeks grew so hot under his stare that I was suddenly grateful for the icy rain. A month ago that would've been enough to send me running for safety. Now I ignored the blush and stood my ground. *Who cares? Let him look. And if I have to shift, it means fewer clothes to shred.*

"What were you doing in my house?" I demanded.

He lifted his eyes to my face, a tiny smile playing around his mouth. I realized I'd never seen him genuinely amused before. It lit up his dark eyes and carved dimples into his cheeks, highlighting his high cheekbones and strong chin. "I'd love to stand here all night discussing my activities with a beautiful half-naked girl," he said. "But I don't think my father would approve."

His tone made me want to smack that look off his pretty face. *Focus, Dez.* Lazar's voice, like Caleb's, was a powerful instrument, able to persuade, anger, or paralyze in just a few words.

"Still Daddy's little boy," I said, and was glad to see his smirk drop away. "It doesn't look like you took anything, but maybe you planted something. Is there a bomb in my house, Lazar?"

He considered me, eyes narrowing. Then, almost imperceptibly, he shook his head.

I frowned. The gesture seemed oddly sincere. But it couldn't be. Was he trying to throw me off, delay me?

"If we wanted you dead," he said, "you would be."

"Your father tried a couple of times and failed," I said. "How is Ximon, Lazar? Does he beat you now that your sister isn't available?"

"Amaris." His voice softened when he said his sister's name. Something in his face changed.

A weird stab of pity hit my gut. Lazar's estrangement from his sister had been sudden and violent. Amaris had chosen to come with us, her supposed enemies, rather than live under her father's thumb and marry a man she hated. Lazar had wavered for a heartbeat, but ultimately he'd chosen to leave her with us and escape with Ximon. When I imagined what it would be like being raised by such a monster, all I could feel was sympathy.

"She's doing well," I said, wanting to reassure him, but

wondering if that was a good idea even as I did so. "She says she misses you. Though I can't imagine why."

His face hardened. "Let me go. Don't make me call the others."

"Go ahead." I bared my teeth, fingers curling like claws. "Call them, and I'll kill you all."

"Desdemona?" My mother stood on the porch, arms crossed to keep her robe closed. "Are you okay?"

I startled, turning my head toward her. Lazar seized the moment and ran down the middle of Kenneth Avenue, away from me, leaving the Tribunal's van behind.

"I'm fine, Mom!" I shouted. "Get Richard out of the house!"

The van's tires made wet sucking noises as they began to roll, following Lazar. So they weren't here to hurt Mom and Richard, which meant I could tear after Lazar. I bolted down the sidewalk, outpacing the skidding van, and kept my ears peeled to make sure it didn't head back toward my parents.

Ahead of me, Lazar raced flat out, cutting left into the park. Behind me, the van was gaining. No time to waste. I'd never shifted while running full speed before. But I needed to find out what Lazar had been up to in my bathroom, and I'd never catch him this way.

I kept sprinting as I sent my mind down into the darkness that always roiled at my core, blacker than a night sky without stars.

I asked. A blazing answer of power poured forth, shooting up my spine, along every limb. Then my feet were feet no longer, but great striped paws. My clothes ripped and fell away as I gathered my back legs to leap forward twenty feet per stride. It felt so good to stretch and run. The rain bounced off my coat, no longer a nuisance. Darkness was my time to hunt, and every sound, every scent, every current of air bent to my will. I laid my tufted ears back, shook my whiskers, and roared.

Lazar pelted across the grass even faster at the sound. But my great galloping bounds ate up the ground between us. He ran past my favorite tree, the lightning tree, and I heard another engine rev. My ears flicked forward. The gray van was still behind us, keeping to the road, but ahead, alongside the park, another van waited, engines on, but headlights off.

Damn it. The Tribunal was thorough.

Just three more leaps, and I'd have him between my paws once more. The side door of the van up ahead slid open, and a figure in gray aimed a rifle at me and fired.

I zigged left, putting the lightning tree between me and the gun. Something thunked into the trunk, and I smelled the silver-laced tranquilizer the Tribunal used on shifters. So they weren't trying to kill me. Yet.

No time to wonder why. Lazar was steps from the van. I gathered all the power in my back legs, and jumped.

Lazar ducked into the van as I left the ground, while the man with the rifle followed my arc with his gun and fired. But I was going faster, farther than he reckoned, and the dart zoomed harmlessly beneath me.

I went farther than even I had reckoned. I'd asked my body for all it had without thinking enough about accuracy, and instead of launching myself into the van, I arced completely over it to land on the other side. In my astonishment, I stumbled slightly as I hit pavement, then rolled, coming to my feet.

I looked up to see Lazar staring at me through the rain-smeared window of the van, eyes wide in amazement. Then the tires spun hard, and the vehicle took off. I lashed my tail and sent them off with a roar that made the raindrops fly.

The van vanished into the mist. Still energized with anger, I turned and ran at the lightning tree, jumping onto its rough, familiar trunk, digging in my claws to climb higher. The tree was closely linked to Othersphere, vibrating with shadow, and it drew me like the scent of blood. Better the neighbors saw a naked girl than a tiger in the treetops. But I didn't want to shift back to my human form just yet.

Being a tiger felt so right, so perfect, especially near the lightning tree. A current of power seemed to flow from deep within it up through my paws. I was atop the world now, invincible, at one with all, yet more myself than ever.

As I watched Lazar's van screech toward the freeway, I felt as if I could leap onto it even now and tear its roof off with one swipe.

"Desdemona!" I turned to see our sedan headed toward me, Richard at the wheel, my mom in the passenger seat, her head out the window, yelling.

So much for Tiger Queen rules the world. I climbed down, then dropped to the ground as Mom got out of the car, clutching a thick terry cloth robe, and ran on her tip toes across the squelchy grass to me.

"Are you all right?" She patted my neck as I butted my head into her waist, automatically marking her as mine. "What the hell were they doing? Richard couldn't find anything different about the house. They didn't take anything we could see, and left nothing behind."

She draped the robe over my long back. It was drenched already, as was she, but when I shifted back to my human form, at least I had something to cover me up.

"It was Lazar," I said, pushing long damp strands of hair from my face.

"Caleb's brother?" She blinked back water drops, one hand massaging her stomach, looking faintly sick.

I nodded. "I have no idea why he was here. And he seemed kind of . . . I don't know. Different."

Mom's eyelids fluttered more rapidly. She looked pale, even considering the greenish light of the street lamp. "Are you okay?" I asked.

"I . . . something's wrong," she managed to say, staggering

a few steps to lean against the lightning tree. Then she clutched her stomach with both hands and doubled over.

"Mom? Did they do something to you? Richard!" I screamed at the car.

Mom gasped. "I feel this way in dreams, sometimes . . ." Then, as if the texture would sustain her, she ran her hands up the bumpy bark of the tree, tilting her head back to stare up into its branches, her eyes glassy.

Then she curled her fingers into the tree, and I saw long, shiny claws cut into the wood. Thunder boomed deafeningly as lightning flared just a few feet away, knocking me flat on my back. A smell of ozone cut the air.

But my mother still stood by the tree, looking somehow taller than usual. Her hair, which should have been brown and limp with rain, looked long and red as another bolt of lightning shot up between her feet, illuminating yellow-green eyes that were usually hazel.

"Mom?" I said, suddenly not sure who stood before me.

"The storm." It came out of her like a growl. Her voice, normally sweet and slightly high-pitched, now sounded like she'd spent her life drinking whiskey and smoking cigarettes. She swiveled her head to me with an odd, unnatural suddenness, like a marionette. "I came to the midst of the eternal storm that I might speak to you."

"Who . . . ?" Over by the car, Richard was getting out of the car. He'd be here any second. "What's going on?"

"I can only speak to you briefly here and now." Lightning stabbed up at the sky all around her, raising the hairs on my arms, and haloed her head like a crown. Thunder shook the ground.

Richard came to a pounding halt beside me, one arm up to shield his eyes from the terrible brightness. "My God, my God, Caroline!"

"Even I, who rule here, may not long endure this tempest," she said, in that dusky voice that cut through the crackling and rumbling. "But you must learn who you are."

My mouth went dry. "Who are you?" It came out as a whisper, a gasp.

A bolt of lightning bigger than the tree itself thrust up from the ground where she stood. The deafening boom knocked Richard to his knees.

Mom screamed in agony, draining every ounce of blood from my heart. Then she cried out something as more lightning danced around her, but I couldn't hear through the explosions. I caught just a word here or there, like the voice on my malfunctioning iPod. "Never . . . belong . . . Amba!"

Then the lightning was gone, and the thunder and the claws, leaving nothing but my tiny, wet mother leaning against an old oak tree in her bathrobe. She crumpled into the mud and lay still.